Sheila O'Flanagan is the au... ...
novels, including *If You Were Me*, *Things We Never Say*,
Better Together, *All For You* and *Stand By Me*.

Sheila has always loved telling stories, and after working
in banking and finance for a number of years, she decided
it was time to fulfil a dream and give writing her own
book a go. So she sat down, stuck 'Chapter One' at the
top of a page, and got started. Sheila is now the author of
more than sixteen bestselling titles. She lives in Dublin
with her husband.

Sheila O'Flanagan. So much more than stories.

'Romantic and charming, this is a real must-read' *Closer*

'A big, touching book sure to delight O'Flanagan fans'
Daily Mail

'A spectacular read' *Heat*

'A lovely book that will keep you guessing right up until
the end' *Bella*

'Her lightness of touch and gentle characterisations have
produced another fine read' *Sunday Express*

By Sheila O'Flanagan

Suddenly Single
Far From Over
My Favourite Goodbye
He's Got To Go
Isobel's Wedding
Caroline's Sister
Too Good To Be True
Dreaming Of A Stranger
Destinations
Anyone But Him
How Will I Know?
Connections
Yours, Faithfully
Bad Behaviour
Someone Special
The Perfect Man
Stand By Me
A Season To Remember
All For You
Better Together
Things We Never Say
If You Were Me
My Mother's Secret

Sheila O'Flanagan

My Mother's Secret

headline
review

First published in Great Britain in 2015
by HEADLINE REVIEW
An imprint of HEADLINE PUBLISHING GROUP

First published in paperback in 2016
by HEADLINE REVIEW
An imprint of HEADLINE PUBLISHING GROUP

9

Cataloguing in Publication Data is available from the British Library

ISBN 978 1 4722 3385 1 (A-format)
ISBN 978 1 4722 1070 8 (B-format)

Typeset in ITC Galliard by
Palimpsest Book Production Ltd, Falkirk, Stirlingshire

Printed and bound in Great Britain by Clays Ltd, St Ives plc

MIX
Paper from
responsible sources
FSC® C104740

Headline's policy is to use papers that are natural, renewable and
recyclable products and made from wood grown in well-managed forests
and other controlled sources. The logging and manufacturing processes
are expected to conform to the environmental regulations of the
country of origin.

HEADLINE PUBLISHING GROUP
An Hachette UK Company
Carmelite House
50 Victoria Embankment
London EC4Y 0DZ

www.headline.co.uk
www.hachette.co.uk

To my husband and my family, always
looking after my back

Acknowledgements

As always, many thanks to:

Carole Blake, who looks after business

Marion Donaldson, who looks after the creative stuff

Jane Selley, who looks for the mistakes

Team Hachette/Headline, who get the finished book to the shops

The booksellers and librarians, who get it to the readers

My translators, who do such a great job at making the story come alive in other languages

And, most especially, all of you, who read my books in so many different countries, and who are fantastic about letting me know your favourite characters, locations and books. You make it all worthwhile! I love hearing from you, and you can keep in touch with me through my website, Twitter, Facebook and Pinterest. I do hope you enjoy *My Mother's Secret*.

The Party

The Party

Chapter 1

A tiny bead of perspiration rolled along Steffie's eyebrow, gathering momentum as it slid down her cheek before landing with a plop on the enormous cardboard box she was carrying. She used the top of her shoulder to wipe her face as she walked gingerly towards her ancient blue Citroën C3, and sighed with relief as she finally placed the box on the passenger seat. As far as she was concerned, the thirty-second journey from the bakery to her car couldn't have been more nerve-racking if she'd been carrying a box of gelignite. And the consequences of dropping it would have been equally explosive.

She pushed a damp wisp of cinnamon-gold hair from her forehead, and shuddered as she imagined Roisin's reaction to the loss of their parents' anniversary cake. A missing cake would have been a major disruption to the Master Plan, and Roisin didn't allow her plans to be disrupted by anyone or anything. Secure in the knowledge that for once she hadn't fallen short of her older sister's high expectations, Steffie eased into the driver's seat and rolled down the car windows. Then she turned the fan up as high as possible in an effort to combat the unexpected end-of-summer heatwave. During the last fortnight the media had happily replaced gloomy reports on the wettest

1

August on record with daily guides to staying cool, as fore-casters pointed out that Dublin, Ireland was currently as warm as Dublin, Ohio, and hotter than Madrid, Paris or Rome. Which would be wonderful, Steffie thought, as a weak stream of tepid air finally began to flow from the vents in front of her, if Irish houses had air conditioning and outdoor swimming pools instead of central heating and double-glazing.

A swimming pool in the garden of Aranbeg, her parents' home in Wexford, would have been something to look forward to this afternoon. But even if they could have afforded it, Pascal and Jenny weren't the sort of people who'd install something that would be used approximately one summer in five. Steffie, and the rest of the day's guests, would simply have to cool off with lots of chilled drinks at the fortieth wedding anniversary party instead.

She exhaled slowly as she thought of the surprise they were about to spring on their parents, who were in blissful igno-rance of the fact that they'd be arriving home to a party later. She still wasn't entirely convinced that surprising them was a good idea, but Roisin had been adamant and Steffie knew from long experience that when her sister's mind was made up, changing it was pretty much a lost cause. All the same, she muttered darkly to herself, the next time she rings me with one of her covert plans in which she gives all the instruc-tions and I'm left with the donkey work, I'll do what I keep promising myself and say that I'm too busy to get involved. I'll remind her that I keep proper working hours even if my office is Davey's old bedroom. I'll take a stand and be strong, firm and businesslike and I won't allow her to railroad me into anything because she's twelve years older than me and she thinks that entitles her to boss me around.

She luxuriated for a few minutes in the fantasy of telling Roisin to sod off and then allowed herself a wry smile. It was never going to happen because Steffie knew that in the face of the force of nature that was Roisin in full organisational mode, there was nothing she could say to stop her. Besides, it isn't only me she bosses around, she acknowledged. She's the same with everyone and we all accept it because Roisin is a born leader, methodical and organised, and the rest of us, maybe with the exception of Dad, are too lazy to bother. Which makes it all the more surprising, she muttered to herself as the Citroën surprised her by getting up enough speed to pass a plodding Fiesta, that I'm the one with my own business and Roisin is a full-time mother. Even as the thought crossed her mind, she conceded that the reality of their situations was quite different from appearances. Roisin had been a high-flyer in the insurance company where she worked, only deciding that she needed to devote more time to her family after the birth of Dougie, her third child. And describing herself, as she did, as a full-time mother was disingenuous. Roisin still did occasional contract work for various insurers, while being an active member of the parents' council at the local school, and currently running a summer sports camp for under-tens. Every second of her day was managed and accounted for and she frequently remarked that she was busier now than she'd ever been. Steffie, on the other hand, had set up Butterfly Creative in her brother's old bedroom because she hadn't been able to find a job as a graphic artist anywhere else, and justified the time she frittered away on social media sites as important networking opportunities to get her brand noticed.

She liked to think that working for herself suited her free-spirited nature, but she was uncomfortably aware that her current status as the owner of a company where she was the sole employee had more to do with her lack of corporate solidarity than her entrepreneurial skills. Her previous job, with a design studio on the far side of the city, had come to an abrupt end after she'd refused to work on a campaign where they wanted to use images of semi-naked women to promote a line of jewellery.

Both her parents had been totally supportive of her stance (although she'd had to apologise profusely to her dad, who'd lent her the money to buy the Citroën and whom she couldn't immediately repay), but Roisin hadn't been able to hide her exasperation with her younger sister when she heard the news.

'Are you out of your mind?' she asked, before launching into a diatribe about there not being room for principles when you needed a job. 'You've got to roll with the punches, Steffie.'

'You can't possibly mean that,' retorted Steffie when Roisin finally paused for breath. 'Not when those punches are blatantly sexist. If you can't have principles about your work, then what's the point?'

Roisin said it was all about being pragmatic and realising what was important.

'My principles are very important to me,' said Steffie.

'Oh, grow up. You're in the real world now,' said Roisin. 'You're like all those girls who scream harassment every time a co-worker passes a remark about how they look. You're letting yourself be offended.'

'It depends on the remark, don't you think?' said Steffie. 'But in any event, nobody has ever passed one about how I look.'

4

'Seriously?' Roisin was so astonished she forgot to keep haranguing her.

Her astonishment was due to the fact that Steffie was the sort of person people tended to notice. She was tall and willowy, her open face framed by a tumble of burnished curls. Roisin made no secret of the fact that she felt the looks genes had been unfairly distributed between them, because she herself had inherited their father's darker colouring and stockier frame, which meant she was locked in a constant battle to keep her figure in the kind of shape that Steffie didn't even have to think about. That battle was the only one she'd never quite succeeded in winning, despite her enthusiastic embracing of various diets and workouts, and it infuriated her. Steffie would tell her that willowy implied you could sort of glide into rooms looking cool and sophisticated whereas she was all arms and legs and falling over herself. On the other hand, when Roisin walked into a room everyone knew she was there thanks to the force of her personality, not because she'd tripped over her own two feet.

'But I'd like to tower,' said Roisin. 'It'd give me a greater presence.'

'You wouldn't really,' Steffie told her. 'It's not always comfortable. Besides, you don't need a greater presence. Everyone does what you tell them anyway.'

'That's because I'm always right,' said Roisin. 'And I'm right about this work thing too. You need to grow up, Steffie. Get out there, work hard and prove yourself.'

Which by setting up her own company she thought she had, even if the decision had been forced on her by a continuing failure to find a full-time job following the jewellery debacle. She wondered if she'd been blacklisted from the graphic artist community – if there was such a thing – because she'd never gone through such a job drought before. In the end she'd got her break by designing some flyers for a friend who owned a café on the nearby industrial estate. The flyers were noticed by a marketing manager at one of the estate's manufacturing companies and they'd asked her to be involved in a packaging design for them.

When she got the business she was elated, even though she knew in all likelihood it was because she'd quoted such a ridiculously low price for the job that they couldn't turn it down. Her parents were happy to see her busy, and even happier when she got more work from other companies in the area. They suggested that instead of having the laptop in a corner of the living room, she use Davey's bedroom as a work zone. After he'd moved out a number of years earlier they'd kept it as a guest room, but as they hardly ever had guests it didn't matter if she took it over. So she bought some office furniture from IKEA (which Pascal assembled for her), registered her business and hoped she hadn't made a terrible mistake.

It hadn't been a mistake, but it continued to be a rocky road. She'd built up a small number of regular clients and she occasionally landed more complicated and interesting projects. Nevertheless, her income was erratic and she wouldn't have been able to keep going if it wasn't for the fact that she was living practically rent-free in the house.

Shortly after Command Central, as Roisin called it, was moved to Davey's bedroom, their father took an early retirement package from his job at the Revenue Commissioners, and he and Jenny moved to Aranbeg, the Wexford house where they'd spent every summer for the past thirty-five years, leaving Steffie to live in the Dublin house alone.

'It's your corporate headquarters now,' her father had joked the day they loaded up the car. 'We're only in the way.'

'I hope you don't think I'm forcing you out.' She looked at them anxiously.

'Oh, for heaven's sake, Steffie, it's a joke.' Pascal, a good two inches shorter than her, had to reach up to squeeze her shoulders. 'I hope you'll be very successful.'

'So successful that you'll be moving into bigger and better premises in no time,' added Jenny.

That had been a year ago. So far there was no danger of her needing to look for anywhere bigger. But she lived in hope. Not because she didn't like the fact that her daily commute was a matter of walking from one room to another, or because she could work in her PJs if she felt so inclined, though she tended not to, feeling more creative when she was properly dressed, but because she wanted to believe that she could support herself and not have to rely on the generosity and good nature of her parents to keep her going.

She fiddled with the Citroën's air vents again. Thinking about her work always made her hot and bothered, as if the whole party thing hadn't got her hot and bothered already. When Roisin had phoned to say that they should surprise Jenny and Pascal with a celebration of their forty years of marriage and invite all their family and friends to Aranbeg, Steffie hadn't voiced her own opinion, which was that she hated surprise parties and she wasn't sure they'd be their mum and dad's cup of tea either, because Roisin was already well into her stride and telling her what had to be done. Nor did Steffie say that she was too busy to do all the things that Roisin had already designated as her responsibility. Roisin wouldn't have believed her, because Roisin didn't really think that

Butterfly Creative was a proper job at all. And even though she really was occupied with a proposal that could turn out to be her most profitable contract yet, Steffie was simply unable to resist the unstoppable force that was her sister in full flow.

'We'll do it the Saturday before their actual anniversary to properly surprise them. Aranbeg is the ideal place too. So many of us used to gather there when we were younger. It must be years since it was full of people, and Mum loved it so much like that,' Roisin informed her.

That was true. During their childhood years, aunts, uncles and cousins from both sides of the family regularly descended on Aranbeg, turning it into a buzzing hub of social activity. These days Steffie only saw her cousins at family gatherings, where she always felt as though she'd let Jenny and Pascal down by not being as successful as everyone else.

'Obviously there are logistical issues to think about given that Mum and Dad are actually living there now,' continued Roisin. 'However, I have a plan to get them out while you sort things. They'll stay overnight with me and you can nip down and get it all organised. I'm too busy with the summer camp to do it. But you can take time out whenever you like. One of the big perks of working from home.'

Which was true, Steffie agreed, but what Roisin didn't seem to grasp was that if she took time out during the day to do everything her sister wanted, she'd have to make it up later. Whenever she allowed herself to get distracted from her work by looking at cute kittens on YouTube, or playing games on Facebook, she reminded herself that it was her own time she was wasting. It didn't stop her but it did mean that she often ended up working in the middle of the night. It would be the same with party planing. Roisin simply didn't get it. She never would. And she wasn't taking any excuses from Steffie this time either. Steffie had listened as Roisin listed her instructions, which included buying balloons and other decorations for the house, designing the invitations and keeping on top of the guest list. The invitations should be child's play to her, Roisin pointed out, they wouldn't take any time at all. And as far as the guest list was concerned, it was easy for Steffie to co-ordinate that if she was sending off the invitations. As for the decorations – well, she was the creative one, wasn't she, so Roisin would leave it all up to her, but she'd send her a link to a wonderful website that did the most amazing stuff. It was a US site, she pointed out, and Steffie probably wouldn't be able to order in time for the party, but it would give her ideas. Not that you need them, of course, Roisin added. You're the designer, you probably know loads of great sites. And you can probably get a discount too. Steffie's head was reeling when Roisin finally stopped giving orders, and instead of telling her sister that she'd certainly design the invitations but she didn't have time to do everything else, she meekly asked if Roisin had thought about plates and cutlery.

'Of course I have,' Roisin replied. 'I got the most fabulous disposable plates with the cutest little hearts on them from a shop in Blanchardstown. Totally appropriate. Mum will love them. And I've got disposable cutlery too, decent stuff, not horrible bendy plastic.'

'Sounds good,' was all Steffie said. So now, as she hurtled towards Aranbeg with the precious cargo of the cake (chocolate sponge with a ruby-red frosting, for which Roisin herself had taken total responsibility), she had to admit that it was entirely her own fault that she'd been landed with the role of invitation designer, guest-list co-ordinator and home decorator. All she hoped was that it would all have been worthwhile. Despite her personal misgivings about the surprise element of the party, she had to accept that everyone who'd been invited thought it was a brilliant idea and they were all looking forward to it immensely. Roisin had told her to count on a twenty per cent refusal rate, but hardly anyone had turned down the invitation, which meant that they'd be dealing with close to seventy people turning up at Aranbeg to surprise her mother and father.

She supposed the phenomenal acceptance rate had a lot to do with Jenny and Pascal's popularity, and because Aranbeg was actually a fantastic venue for a summer party. Set in a secluded location close to the small village of Castlemoran, it was far enough from Dublin city to be rural and yet near enough to Wexford town not to feel completely isolated. Most of the non-local guests had managed to book rooms in nearby bed and breakfast accommodation and some had opted to stay an extra day to make a weekend trip of it. Fortunately they'd booked before the heatwave had broken out and everyone in the capital had decided to try to take a break near the sea, because there wasn't a room to be had anywhere near the coast now. The traffic was heavy on the main road and Steffie knew that it would take her longer than usual to reach Aranbeg. She hoped that all the guests would take the traffic situation into account. It would be a total nightmare if Jenny and Pascal arrived before the people who were going to surprise them. Roisin would have a fit. And that was something that would make everyone very hot and bothered indeed.

Chapter 2

It was nearly two sweltering hours later when she turned up the winding country road that led to her parents' house. The car's air-conditioning system had totally given up the ghost halfway through the journey, and even having both windows open hadn't cooled her down. The atmosphere had been so sticky and the humidity so high that Steffie had felt like she was breathing through a damp cloth. However, the alternative to the hot and humid weather was the rain and thunder that had been forecast for the following day. Much as Steffie longed for the freshness it would ultimately bring, she didn't want the surprise element of the party to be that everyone ended up huddled in the house while a storm raged outside.

As she pulled up outside the wrought-iron gates of Aranbeg, she had a sudden panic that they might be locked. Locked gates wasn't a scenario that Roisin had considered when she was going through the plans. God, thought Steffie, if I have to ring her and say that Mum and Dad's surprise will be a massive crowd standing outside the gates to the house, she'll go flipping ballistic.

But when she got out of the car and tried the latch, the gates swung open easily. She heaved a sigh of relief and drove up the short driveway before parking her car at the side of the house so that it was out of sight. Then she hurried back to the gates and closed them again. The guests had been asked to park in the grounds of the GAA club a little further up the road. The president of the club played golf with Pascal and was coming to the party himself, so there'd been no problem in getting him to agree to the parking situation. That was the thing about small towns, thought Steffie. Everyone knew everyone else. It was why she could never actually live here, no matter how beautiful it was. But she understood completely why her parents had made the move as soon as her dad had retired.

She glanced at her watch. She had almost three hours before the first of the guests arrived. Roisin had planned that their parents would turn up about an hour after that. The late afternoon start time was to facilitate the surprise element and so that they could enjoy being outdoors. Using the garden had been an aspiration when Roisin had first outlined her plan. It had seemed an inspired choice earlier in the week. Steffie looked up at the sky. It was still bright blue with a slight scattering of billowy clouds and no sign of a storm on the horizon. It was a perfect day for a garden party.

She twisted her hair into a knot high on her head and allowed the whisper of breeze to cool her neck. Everything would be fine, she told herself as she put the key in the lock. Roisin would be proved right as always. Their parents would be delighted. And the slightly uncomfortable feeling that she herself was nursing was entirely down to the heat of the day and the feeling of thunder in the air, and not because she had any psychic abilities to discern trouble ahead.

*　　*　　*

Jenny and Pascal Sheehan had bought Aranbeg shortly after their second child, Davey, was born. It had been a run-down stone house set in an overgrown garden when they first saw it, but both of them had instantly fallen in love with it. Over the years Pascal – who was an excellent and exacting handyman – had renovated and improved it, turning it into a fine home with a large reception room, extended kitchen and four bedrooms. The initial purchase had been a big gamble with the proceeds of money they'd won on a prize bond. Both Jenny and Pascal had agreed that the sensible thing to do would be to pay off the mortgage they had on their Dublin home, but Pascal's family had originally come from Wexford and he'd always hankered to have a place there too. There had been times when they regretted not having taken the more conservative option, but both of them loved decamping to Aranbeg every summer, even though Pascal could only join Jenny and the children at the weekends. They went there at other times of the year too; sometimes as a family, sometimes as a couple for a night alone, and from time to time Pascal went on his own to plaster a wall or sand the stairs or regrout tiles. Aranbeg became more than a holiday home for the Sheehans; it became a second home and the place where both Jenny and Pascal preferred to be. Pascal's retirement gave them that opportunity.

Even though the children were grown up and hardly ever stayed there any more, Aranbeg was a family home to Pascal and Jenny in a way their house in Dublin never had been. They'd put more of themselves into the country house than they ever had in the city. The floors were polished hardwood, there were elegant drapes at the windows, and the decor was simple and understated but reflected Jenny's artistic personality. Sketches of Roisin, Davey and Steffie done

13

by Jenny herself adorned the walls and provided a clue to their growth into adulthood. Steffie's own favourites were the ones her mother had done of each of them, aged about four, standing under one of the apple trees in Aranbeg's garden. Roisin looked fierce and determined, a lock of dark hair falling over her forehead; Davey was sketched arms akimbo, wearing football gear that was way too big for him; and Steffie's own drawing showed her leaning against the now much wider tree trunk, a faraway expression in her eyes. Steffie always thought that those sketches captured them exactly, and told you all there was to know about the Sheehan siblings.

She brushed past the sketches, carrying the cake (as gingerly as before) and then the party decorations from the car. She'd just poured herself a long glass of water when Roisin rang to see how things were coming along.

'I only got here a few minutes ago,' Steffie told her. 'So nothing's coming along yet.'

'Did you get the cake?'

'Of course. And I phoned the deli on the way down. They're going to deliver the food shortly. How are Mum and Dad?'

'Urgh!' Roisin grunted. 'It's been really difficult to stop them from haring off to Aranbeg. If the weather wasn't so tropical they'd have probably been happy to spend more time with the kids, but as it is I know they're chomping at the bit to get away.'

'Traffic was heavy enough,' advised Steffie. 'I thought I'd be here half an hour ago, so you'd better leave a little earlier than you planned.'

'It's always crap on sunny days,' Roisin said. 'I still think you should've driven down last night, such a waste not to have used the time to decorate and stuff when Mum and Dad were here. You could have—'

'I was busy,' Steffie interrupted her. 'I had a meeting with a client.'

'It hardly took up the whole evening, did it?' said Roisin, who didn't wait for a reply but changed the subject by asking her if she'd heard anything from Davey.

'He texted to say that he was on the plane.' Steffie decided not to argue with her sister. 'I can't wait to meet the girlfriend.'

'She looks pretty stunning on Facebook all right,' said Roisin. 'Maybe she's not as gorgeous in real life.'

'Or maybe she's better.' Steffie laughed. She was never able to stay annoyed for long. 'Can you believe it, though? Our Davey. With someone like her.'

'He's a thirty-seven-year-old man, for heaven's sake.' Roisin sounded impatient. 'He should be married with kids by now.'

'Well, I do agree that thirty-seven is old enough to settle down,' agreed Steffie. 'Obviously. It's just that Davey . . . well, you know what he's like.'

'An eternal child,' said Roisin. 'I hope she has the patience for him.'

'I guess we'll have the chance to check it out.'

'I didn't arrange this party so you can run another one of Davey's girlfriends out of town,' Roisin said.

'For the love of God!' Steffie cried. 'I never ran anyone out of town. All I did was mention that I'd seen Emily Mahon with Laurence Gibson. I never for a second suspected she was actually two-timing Davey with him.'

'Scarred him for life,' said Roisin. 'That's why he's commitment-phobic now.'

'It was *years* ago,' protested Steffie.

'Hmm. And how about you? Have you got a date for today?'

Roisin's words were more of a challenge than a question but Steffie kept her voice light as she replied that Steve might show up but she wasn't sure. 'Steve. Steve. Is he a new guy?' asked Roisin.

'Not exactly new. I've known him a while.'

'And you practically have the same name! Steve 'n' Steffie – how cute. And how promising.'

Steffie knew it was a lot less promising than Roisin thought. Steve was a programmer with one of her client companies and she'd met him a few months earlier. He was laid-back to the point of being practically horizontal, they had fun together and he was good in bed. Not that her sole criterion for a boyfriend should be his expertise between the sheets, she would tell herself, but when he was notoriously bad at punctuality and calling her, it was nice to have those deficiencies offset in other ways.

'At the moment we're taking it easy,' she said. 'No strings.'

'Oh, for heaven's sake!' exclaimed Roisin. 'At this point in your life you need to be making decisions about men. Not having no-strings friends-with-benefits relationships. There are times I think I'm the one person in this family who's done the grown-up thing. Honest to God, you and Davey are like kids the way you carry on.'

'I wasn't aware that getting married was the only measure of adulthood,' retorted Steffie, stung by the friends-with-benefits accusation, which was a tad too close to the truth for her liking.

16

'At the moment I'm bearing all the filial responsibilities,' Roisin said. 'I'm the one who's provided Mum and Dad with grandchildren . . . I could do with you and Davey taking up the slack. Thing is, if he stays in Denmark with Camilla, Mum and Dad won't get to see them that often either and all the pressure stays on me.'

'So you want me to marry Steve and get pregnant to help you out?' Steffie could imagine what his reaction to that would be.

'Yes,' said Roisin.

'If and when I decide to marry someone to provide our parents with extra grandchildren, I'll let you know,' Steffie said drily.

'You can't be the baby for ever,' Roisin said. 'You're twenty-seven and you run your own business, as you keep pointing out. That makes you a grown-up.'

'Running my own business doesn't leave me a lot of time for getting married,' said Steffie.

'Of course it does. You have to prioritise, like me with putting my family first and taking contracts if and when they suit me.'

'Been there and done that,' Steffie reminded her. 'I've had enough of contracts and sharing jobs and working for other people to last me a lifetime. Butterfly Creative might be small and it might not make me a millionaire, but at least I'm managing to hold it all together. I want to enjoy that for a while.' Although enjoy wasn't really the right word when you were barely keeping your head above water, she thought. Still, it was challenging. And maybe one day it would all come spectacularly right.

'Hmm.' Roisin wasn't convinced.

'Anyway, I'm not thinking about marriage now,' said Steffie. 'I've plenty of time for that.'

'I wanted to marry Paul the moment I met him,' Roisin told her.

'Things were different back then,' said Steffie. 'Lives were less complicated.'

'Back then. Less complicated. You cheeky thing!' Roisin sounded affronted. 'It wasn't the dark ages, you know.'

'It was the nineties,' Steffie told her. 'There was nothing else to do except get married and have babies.'

'You're lucky we're not in the same room right now or I'd deck you,' said Roisin.

'Ah, I'm only teasing you, Ro,' Steffie said. 'You struck gold with Paul and you have a lovely family. I envy you.'

'You do?' asked Roisin.

'Absolutely,' Steffie replied, although the idea of being married with three children was overwhelming. 'I've got to go. I think I hear the food arriving.'

'Thank God for that,' said her sister. 'I'll see you later.'

'Right.'

Steffie hung up. She hadn't heard the sound of anyone arriving, but as she walked through the house to her car, she realised that she'd inadvertently told the truth. A blue van with Patty's Pantry on the side had just driven up outside.

'Right,' she murmured to herself as she opened the front door. 'Let's get this show on the road.'

18

Chapter 3

As always, Roisin felt slightly exasperated after talking to her younger sister. Steffie, despite her pretence at being a business-woman, didn't live in the real world. She was merely playing at having a company, trying to make herself feel important after making herself virtually unemployable by refusing to work on that jewellery campaign. Roisin was quite sure that whenever a prospective employer checked Steffie out, he or she would hear about the incident and decide that she was too much trouble. Roisin had tried to point that out to her but Steffie refused to listen. She'd had it too easy, that was the problem. Being the unexpected arrival, ten years after Davey, she'd been utterly indulged by their parents, who'd adopted a far more relaxed approach to her upbringing than they ever had to their two older children. Roisin knew that she and Davey had paved the way for Steffie and made things easier for her, but Steffie never acknowledged that. Nor did she give Roisin credit for having looked after her when she was younger. She simply didn't remember all the times Roisin had pushed her around the housing estate in her pram, or fed her or played with her when she would much rather have been doing something else. Steffie wasn't one bit grateful, that was the problem.

Roisin sighed as she went into the kitchen and looked out the back window into the garden. Her mother was sitting on the canopied swing chair that Roisin and Paul had bought at the beginning of the summer and which was coming into its own in the heatwave. Jenny was reading the newspaper while Daisy, Roisin's thirteen-year-old daughter, sat on the grass nearby, carefully varnishing her nails. Roisin was normally fairly strict about allowing her elder daughter to wear any kind of make-up, even though Daisy insisted that she had to experiment with different looks if she was going to fulfil her dream of becoming a top model. Roisin occasionally worried that her daughter might actually achieve this insane desire, because Daisy, like Steffie, was tall and coltish and very slender. She had a beguiling quality in photographs, in which her heart-shaped face and wide sea-blue eyes managed to appear both innocent and knowing at the same time. Fortunately, from Roisin's point of view, there were thousands of gorgeous, quirky-looking girls wanting to be models, so the chances of Daisy being plucked from a sea of hopefuls was, she reassured herself, fairly slim. And with a little luck Daisy would eventually change her mind and get a proper job. Nevertheless, Roisin was careful never to make disparaging remarks to her about having to starve yourself to death to maintain your teenage figure in your twenties in order to stay at the top of the modelling industry. The last thing she wanted was for Daisy to suddenly start having negative body issues and haunting anorexia sites. So she said nothing, hoped for the best and only allowed her worries to surface in the middle of the night.

It was funny how your worries about your children changed with every passing year, she thought. When they were small and she was working outside the home her concerns were all about decent childcare. Later, the main anxiety she had about Daisy was making sure that she had friends. Her daughter had been so dreamy and disconnected from the world around her that Roisin feared she'd always be an outsider. But her childish dreaminess had vanished almost overnight, and these days she was about as popular as it was possible for a girl to be. Which was an extra worry too. Being super-popular was nearly as bad as being the outcast. As far as her other children, nine-year-old Poppy and six-year-old Dougie, were concerned, right now it was all about keeping them happy and ensuring that they weren't fighting with each other or with their friends. And in Dougie's case it was important that he got picked for the under-seven football team too.

That was where he was today, along with his dad and grandfather, at a friendly against an opposing team from a neighbouring estate. Roisin had no compunction about using moral blackmail to persuade her father that Dougie's day would be made by him turning up at the game. Pascal had been a keen footballer when he was younger and Dougie looked up to him as the fount of all footballing wisdom. Poppy was equally mad about sport and equally keen to offer advice from the sideline, so it made sense to send them all off together.

So many people to look after, thought Roisin. So many things to juggle. And that was something that Steffie, who had it easy with only herself to think about, would never understand. Left to her own devices, she wouldn't even have remembered Jenny and Pascal's wedding anniversary, and even if she had, she wouldn't have done anything about it.

She definitely wouldn't have bothered to organise the kind of party their parents deserved. Roisin had heard the hesitation in her sister's voice when she'd called and asked her to be involved in a little of the planning. She'd known that Steffie wasn't all that keen. But she'd shamed her into being part of it, and later today, when Jenny and Pascal were suitably surprised and pleased, Roisin would bet her bottom dollar that Steffie would happily accept any plaudits that came her way without admitting that nothing would have happened if it wasn't for Roisin.

To be fair, Roisin conceded, when she'd finally come on board Steffie had done everything that she'd asked of her. Roisin knew she'd ultimately left her sister with a lot to do, but she'd kept the hardest part for herself, which was getting their parents out of Aranbeg on the pretext of babysitting, so that they would be in Dublin and under her control on the day of the party itself. Of course either one of them was always willing to babysit; the difficult job had been getting both of them to turn up the previous night. The football match had been a good diversion today, and she'd given Paul, her husband, strict instructions not to rush home. On their way out she'd whispered to Poppy to ask if they could stop off at McDonald's after the match, a treat that was very rarely allowed. So she was hopeful that it would easily be mid afternoon before her parents set off.

The plan was that Paul, Roisin and the children would leave as soon as possible afterwards and – given that Pascal stuck to a self-imposed 80 kph speed limit – overtake them somewhere on the N11, getting to Aranbeg before them. As she also had to get herself ready, and then organise both Paul and the children, Roisin was looking at a logistical nightmare, but over the years she'd become an expert at sorting out logistical nightmares.

She made some tea and brought a cup to her mother.

'Thank you, darling.' Jenny accepted it gratefully. 'I was gasping.'

'It's too hot today.' Daisy sounded cranky. 'It's melting my nail varnish.'

'Don't be silly,' Roisin said.

'It is,' protested Daisy. 'It's going all gloopy on me and I want it to be perfect for—'

'You can do it in the kitchen so,' Roisin interrupted before she blurted out something about the party, 'but don't get it all over my table.'

'Mum! I'm not Dougie.' Daisy looked affronted as she gathered up her bits and pieces and stalked off to the house, her tanned legs shown off to their very best advantage by the skimpy denim shorts she was wearing.

'They grow up young these days, don't they,' mused Jenny.

'And how.' Roisin nodded. 'I don't think you would've allowed me wear shorts like those at thirteen.'

'Probably not,' agreed Jenny.

'Not that you can keep them from doing anything now,' Roisin said. 'They give you a pitying look, mutter about calling ChildLine and go right ahead.'

'I'm sure Daisy will be fine,' said Jenny.

'I hope so.' Roisin frowned. 'You don't want to turn them into sex objects and yet they're bombarded with pictures about how they should look – those awful celebrity magazines are the worst.'

'Agreed. Though if I looked as good as Daisy, I'd be wearing minidresses and micro shorts every day,' said Jenny.

'Mum!'

'It's true,' Jenny said. 'The amount of time you have when all your bits are perky and unwrinkled is a lot less than you think. Best to flaunt it while you can.'

'I don't want Daisy flaunting it,' protested Roisin. 'She's still a kid, for heaven's sake!'

'Well, no, I understand that,' agreed Jenny. 'It's just that young girls really can look so pretty, can't they?'

'She's obsessed enough about how she looks,' Roisin said. 'Please don't encourage her.'

'Actually it was probably always that way,' observed Jenny. 'How she looks is the obsession of almost every teenage girl. Unfortunately, there are so many more products these days to feed it.' She smiled. 'My obsession when I was younger was hair colour. My natural colour was mousy and I wanted something more dramatic. Your gran thought colouring your hair was only for harlots. She expressly forbade me to get it done. I did, of course, and she went mental.'

Roisin laughed. 'Not really?'

'Oh yes. Kay was very strict.' Jenny's expression was grim for a moment.

'Not with me,' Roisin said. 'I remember she used to allow me to use her perfume.'

'Eau de cologne,' remembered Jenny. 'It was called 4711. It was very popular back then.'

'I haven't smelled it in ages,' said Roisin, 'but if I did, I'd think of Granny straight away.' She looked pensive. 'It would be lovely to be able to see her and talk to her again,' she said. 'As a grown-up.'

'I remember thinking that about my grandmother too.' Jenny nodded. 'We're clearly very alike.'

'You always say I'm like Dad.'

'In appearance you are,' agreed Jenny. 'Dark hair, dark eyes. You and Davey both.'

'And Steffie is more like you,' said Roisin.

Jenny nodded.

'Although you when you were younger and more of a hippy,' added Roisin. 'Now you're sort of cool and elegant.'

Jenny chuckled. 'I'm not cool. I'm turning into a puddle here. Daisy was right, it's getting very hot. And sultry. We could do with that thunderstorm to clear the air.'

Roisin made a non-committal sound. The last thing she wanted was a thunderstorm.

'Will they be back from the match soon?' asked Jenny. 'It would be nice for your dad and me to get to Wexford earlier rather than later.'

'Any minute,' lied Roisin, knowing that they were almost certainly in McDonald's right now.

'Ah well, we'll be back in plenty of time for our dinner,' said Jenny.

Roisin knew that her parents had made a reservation at Cody's, an upmarket restaurant in the village near Aranbeg, which she assumed was their attempt at celebrating forty years together. She'd already cancelled it.

'You'll be back in plenty of time, don't worry,' she told her mother.

'I've got fidgety in my old age,' confessed Jenny. 'I usen't to worry about time or punctuality at all, but now I'm obsessive.'

'Not a bit of it,' Roisin told her. 'What are you planning to wear tonight?'

'Just a little black dress,' replied Jenny.

'Ah, the little black dress.' Roisin smiled. 'So useful. How many do you have?'

'Only the one,' Jenny said. 'But it's super-comfortable and I can accessorise it up or down.'

'Up tonight, I guess.'

'My diamonds,' Jenny confided. 'I don't get much opportunity to wear them.'

Roisin made a mental note to ring Steffie as soon as Pascal and Jenny were on the road. She'd get her sister to have the dress and the diamonds ready for Jenny to change into, so that her mother would feel properly glam at her party. As for Pascal, well, he wasn't someone who ever dressed up. Not even for classy restaurants. But perhaps he'd find something more suitable to wear when he got home.

While Jenny glanced through the newspaper again, Roisin checked her phone to see if Davey's flight had landed. According to the app, it had just touched down. She sent him a text saying that she was looking forward to seeing him and reminding him to park in the grounds of the GAA club, in case he'd forgotten.

Organising everyone, she thought again. Whether they appreciated it or not.

Chapter 4

The flight from Copenhagen had arrived ten minutes early but the cabin crew made an announcement about a problem with the air bridge that would delay them for a short while. The majority of the passengers, already standing in the narrow aisles with their cabin baggage, grumbled impatiently, but Camilla, who was still sitting in her seat, simply shrugged.

'We're always so bloody inefficient,' complained Davey as he switched on his mobile phone. 'It's embarrassing.'

'These things can happen anywhere,' Camilla pointed out.

'Always here.'

'Don't be silly. I'm not judging your entire country on a broken air bridge. Same as I didn't judge it on you.' She grinned and he couldn't help smiling in return.

'I judge yours entirely on you,' he told her. 'Cool, chic and competent.'

'True,' said Camilla.

Davey's phone beeped with Roisin's incoming message and he grunted. Didn't she think he read his emails? She'd sent him a detailed missive the day before in which the instruction to park at the GAA club had been highlighted in bold. He was about to send a terse reply when there was a sudden flurry at the front of the plane and the door finally opened.

'See,' Camilla said. 'A delay of five minutes. Which means we are exactly on time.'

'They were probably thrown into a complete panic because of us being early in the first place.' Davey abandoned the text to Roisin and shoved his phone in his pocket. 'OK, let's go.'

They disembarked the aircraft, cleared immigration and went directly to the car hire desk. Davey had rented a VW Golf for their drive to Wexford. Fortunately for his efforts to impress upon Camilla that modern Ireland was a smoothly efficient and businesslike country, the rental agency was completely competent, and less than twenty minutes later they were driving out of the car park.

'I can't believe it's so warm.' Davey took his sunglasses out of his jacket pocket and put them on. 'It's not normally like this.'

'Climate change,' said Camilla.

'Everyone in Ireland would like climate change to mean hotter summers,' Davey told her. 'But maybe not as humid as this; it's like Singapore, for heaven's sake!'

'Not quite,' Camilla told him. 'In Singapore, the temperature—'

'It was a figure of speech!' cried Davey. 'I do know it's not the same here, honestly. Still hot and sticky, though.'

Camilla raised an eyebrow.

'Sorry,' he said. 'I'm a bit tense.'

She relaxed back into the seat and looked around her with interest. It was her first visit to Ireland and she was surprised at how much it seemed to matter to Davey that she approved of it. Ever since he'd received the invitation to his parents' anniversary party, he'd been praising and deprecating his homeland in equal measure.

'We're very outgoing,' he'd said on numerous occasions. 'More chatty, more open. But we're hopeless at stuff too. Sort of hopeful that things'll work out rather than making sure they do. Though it usually ends up OK.'

She'd smiled.

'It's not the same as Denmark.'

She couldn't count the number of times he'd said that. As though Denmark was a shining beacon of all that was right and smart and – most of all – efficient in the world and Ireland was some kind of shambolic maelstrom where things got done by luck rather than intent. Yet so far Camilla had seen nothing but competency and good humour, and Davey's clear complex about his homeland intrigued her.

Camilla Rasmussen had known Davey Sheehan for about six months and she cared for him very much. She didn't permit herself to use emotive words like love, which conveyed feelings that she wasn't yet prepared to acknowledge as far as Davey was concerned; but he was an attractive companion, she enjoyed his company, and he was fun. They had a shared interest in renewable energy (she worked for a sustainable energy organisation, while his company produced turbines for wind farms); they both enjoyed playing chess and were addicted to online puzzle games. If she were looking for a long-term relationship, she told herself, if she were even thinking of marriage, then Davey Sheehan would be high on the list. She was surprised he hadn't been married before. At thirty-seven, most men she knew had been around the block at least once. But Davey had neither married nor lived with anyone, which was both an advantage and a disadvantage. She'd ironed out most of the disadvantages, such as his initial inability to remember there was another person in the house which meant him having to learn to compromise on TV programmes, music and decor; his habit of forgetting that they owned both a washing machine and a dishwasher; his meltdowns when something was moved from where he'd put it, especially when he'd put it in the wrong place. And, more importantly, his lack of knowledge about what actually constituted a home-cooked meal – Davey wasn't a reconstructed man in the kitchen, and if it couldn't be heated in a microwave, he didn't eat it. Well, hadn't eaten it; it was different now.

However, the advantages of living with someone who hadn't had another woman's likes and dislikes imprinted on his consciousness were obvious. He didn't have anyone to compare her to, unless you counted his mother, which Camilla didn't, since Jenny Sheehan hadn't been, from what she could gather, a domestic goddess of any consequence. Davey was almost grateful, Camilla thought, to have a woman around the house who, although a hundred per cent committed to her career, also knew about healthy eating and comfortable living and, of course, was good in bed. Camilla smiled to herself. She knew that she was very good in bed and that Davey was reaping the benefit of her experience. It was nice, as the woman, to feel that you were the one with the more varied past; it was also nice that Davey didn't feel the need to quiz her about it. Of course sex with Davey wasn't all about her own talents; he was a generous and adaptable lover, and far more concerned about her pleasure than her previous boyfriends had been, which was a refreshing change. But she was definitely the one with more skills in the bedroom.

Nevertheless, from Camilla's perspective, Davey Sheehan was a good bet and she was certainly happy to be sharing a spacious loft apartment in Østerbro with him. She thought it was sweet that he still wanted to impress her. And she knew that he wanted her to like his family, and for them to like her too. She leaned her head on his shoulder for a moment. He took one hand from the steering wheel and squeezed her knee before she sat upright again.

Davey returned his hand to the steering wheel and glanced at his girlfriend. Sometimes he really did pinch himself to see that he wasn't dreaming, because it seemed inconceivable to him that he, Davey Sheehan, without any great redeeming features to his name, had somehow managed to land a beauty like Camilla Rasmussen. From the moment he'd first seen her at a conference on alternative energy sources, he'd been attracted by her unshakeable poise, her effortless good looks and her easy conversation. When she'd accepted his invitation to dinner, he'd been astonished. And it was still a mystery to him why she'd agreed to move in with him. Yes, he admitted to himself, he was successful in his job. Yes, in comparison perhaps to some of the earnest people that populated the industry, he was easy-going – Camilla said that she liked that about him. But still. His hair was thinner than it had been ten years earlier and flecked with grey. His abs weren't exactly a six-pack. (They hadn't been in his twenties either, but back then he could have fantasised.) And while he knew he'd upped his game over the past few months, he would never be as ruthlessly groomed as Ivar Nygaard – of the black jumpers, black trousers and silver-rimmed designer glasses – who worked in the same company as Camilla and with whom she'd had a year-long relationship that had ended shortly before he, Davey, had met her at the conference.

He was afraid of being her rebound man. He was afraid that she'd temporarily fallen for him because he was so different from Ivar. He was afraid he'd lose her and he didn't want to. He loved her. He wanted to marry her. He'd already bought the engagement ring.

He patted the inside pocket of his jacket. It was actually too warm to be still wearing a jacket, but he hadn't wanted to take it off in case the box containing the beautiful diamond in its distinctive setting fell out. Davey had bought it a few weeks earlier in a moment of confidence and enthusiasm, thinking that making a romantic proposal to his girlfriend would be a grand gesture. But he'd chickened out. Camilla wasn't a grand gesture person. And what if he asked her and she said no?

It was all very well for girls, he thought as he turned the air-con up a notch, they had all these books and movies telling them that they were worth it, and that they deserved the best. They could get into a state about hoping that a guy would propose to them, but they didn't actually have to do it, did they? They didn't have to open themselves up, put it all on the line and then wait for a yes or no. Girls had all the power. They just didn't realise it.

Davey had brought the ring with him because he'd thought that seeing his parents so happy together after forty years, Camilla might be ready for a proposal. And he hoped there'd be a suitably romantic opportunity to ask her. They had, in a very forthright and Nordic sort of way, discussed marriage before. Camilla had said that it was a right but not a duty, and Davey, trying some forthrightness himself, asked what exactly that meant her position was regarding it, and she'd replied that she was certainly entitled to get married to someone if and when she felt the time was right, but she wasn't obliged to, now or ever. Which had left him wondering where he stood in the entire scheme of things. And yet he loved her and he believed that she loved him, despite his inadequacies. So it was just a question of asking her at the right time. He hoped.

He wanted to marry her. He wanted to have a family with her. He wanted to be as lucky as his mum and dad and he wanted his own kids to be as lucky as him.

He hoped it wasn't too much to ask.

'Tell me about your parents,' she asked after they'd been on the road for nearly an hour and the playlist from her phone had finished. 'Forty years together is some achievement.'

'I know,' he said. 'I wonder how many people make that any more?'

'Hardly anyone, I'd've thought. So what is it about your mum and dad that make them so special?'

'They work well together,' said Davey after a pause. 'They complement each other. Mum's always been a bit dreamy and artistic and Dad is the one who gets things done.'

'You said your mum is a painter. Is she well known in Ireland?'

'Oh, she's not all that serious about it,' Davey clarified. 'It's more of a hobby than a job.'

'It's a gift,' Camilla pointed out.

'Yes, it is. But it's not like a career or anything. Although . . .' His voice trailed off as he trawled through his memories. 'She went away for an exhibition or a course or something

33

when I was younger. I can't really remember it too well. She was away for what seemed like weeks. Probably only a few days though.'

'And did she sell paintings at this exhibition?'

'I've no idea.' He shot a shamefaced glance at his girlfriend. 'I guess I was never interested enough to ask. That's awful, isn't it?'

Camilla shook her head. 'You were a child. You had your own concerns.'

'Yes, but when I was older I could've taken more interest. Oh well, I can ask her about it today.'

'Your parents will like this surprise?' asked Camilla.

'I sure as hell hope so,' said Davey. 'My sister Steffie is convinced Mum will hate it. But when Roisin puts her mind to something, we all have to agree.'

Camilla knew a little about the two Sheehan girls, having asked Davey about his family on a number of occasions. But like all the men she knew, he was sparing with his information. Not because of any deep desire to be mysterious, but simply because as far as he was concerned, none of it mattered very much.

'I always got on better with Steffie,' he told her now. 'Maybe because she was the baby of the family and we were in the house together for a long time. Also, she's always up for a laugh. Roisin takes everything very seriously and she expects everyone to do what she wants all the time.'

'Perhaps it's the Roisin sister I will get on with best, in that case.' Camilla shot him a mischievous look. 'Because you tell me that I'm too serious sometimes, don't you? And that I order you around.'

'Oh God, do I?' He glanced at her in dismay. 'You're not

in the least like Ro. You're serious in a completely different way. And you're not bossy. You're . . . um . . . you're a perfectionist.'

'And that may be a good thing,' she said in amusement.

'Indeed it is.' He nodded.

'So,' she said, in her forthright way, 'some more about your parents, please. I would like all the information possible before we arrive.'

Davey sighed. They were his mum and dad. They were in their sixties. They'd lived an average life. They still loved each other. There wasn't anything else to tell her, even though Camilla clearly felt there should be. Maybe she'll think I'm as boring as them, he thought, as he fiddled with the air-con again. Maybe it was a bad idea to bring her along with me after all.

Chapter 5

Steffie was hot and dusty, and she'd broken two nails trying to tack up the Happy Ruby Anniversary party banners. As she'd specifically varnished her nails bright red to go with the anniversary theme, she'd had to go in search of an old bottle to do a repair job after she'd filed the jagged edges. The colour she'd eventually found at the back of a drawer in her old bedroom didn't exactly match, but it was the best she could come up with. After having spent more time than she wanted on beauty repairs, she blew up a selection of red balloons, wiped the glassware and then arranged the glasses neatly on the table she'd dragged, along with as many chairs as she could, on to the covered veranda. The veranda stretched across the entire back of the house and was accessed by folding doors from both the kitchen and living room. It looked over the gently sloping garden towards a small stream, and in Steffie's opinion was the best part of Aranbeg. It reminded her of some of the lovely American houses she'd seen during her gap year, with their huge wooden decks furnished with cushioned chairs and ceiling fans.

It would be nice to have a ceiling fan today, she thought longingly. There wasn't a breath of a breeze. She kicked off her shoes, then strolled the length of the garden until she reached the stream that marked the rear boundary of the property. She'd spent many happy hours as a girl paddling in the stream, which was a tributary of the river Iske, a few kilometres away. Her dad had brought her fishing on the Iske once, and although she'd felt squeamish when she'd seen fish wriggling on the riverbank, she'd been intrigued by the fishermen who'd waded into the middle of the water to cast their lines. The following day she'd donned her bright yellow wellington boots, borrowed her mother's green apron for an authentic fisherman look, found one of Davey's old fishing nets on its bamboo pole and walked into the middle of the stream to fish herself. Even though the water wasn't very deep, it was enough to come up over the boots. When she'd sloshed her way back to the house with sodden boots carrying a jar full of muddy water containing a tiny tiddler, Jenny had gone berserk.

Steffie smiled to herself as she remembered the ticking-off she'd got from both her parents, for going down to the stream without permission and for ruining her boots. It hadn't dampened her spirits, although she'd eventually given up on fishing when she failed miserably to catch anything else.

Now she paddled happily in the clear water, balancing carefully on the stony riverbed so that she didn't end up soaked again. She was beginning to feel cool and relaxed when the buzz of her mobile phone startled her. She made a face when she saw Roisin's name on the screen.

'What's up?' she asked.

Roisin told her about the black dress and the diamonds and Steffie said that their mother was perfectly capable of getting her own dress out of the wardrobe.

'I don't want her to have to fuss,' said Roisin.

'She won't,' Steffie told her. 'You're the fusser, not her.'

'I'm a planner, not a fusser,' said Roisin. 'Has the food arrived?'

'Yes, and I've got everything ready. Except for the plates and cutlery, of course.'

'I'm on the way with them now.'

'Already? What happened? You're all going to be way too early.'

'It's only me who's on the way,' clarified Roisin. 'I'm calling from the car. Mum's still at the house with Daisy. She was peppering about leaving and I made up an excuse about me having to go out.'

'I thought you'd packed Dad off to a footie match. Mum couldn't leave without him anyway.'

'Yes, but I was afraid I'd give it away by making ever more ridiculous excuses about why they were taking so long. I should have planned it this way from the start. I get to help you and Paul will come down with the kids later.'

'It's nice of you to help,' said Steffie. 'But everything's done.'

'I'm sure it is.'

Steffie recognised the tone in Roisin's voice. It had her 'you might have done something but not to my exacting standards' quality.

'OK, well I'll see you later,' said Steffie.

'Yes, right. Get out of the way!' The last remark was clearly addressed to a driver not living up to Roisin's standards either.

Steffie put her phone back in its leather sleeve, stepped out of the stream and went to see what preparations she could improve on.

* * *

In the Dublin house, the bathroom was adequate but small. However the Aranbeg bathroom was huge and easily accommodated the antique roll-top bath that Jenny had bought at a market and restored, as well as a very modern separate rainfall shower. Steffie had already taken a shower that morning but she'd been saving a soak in the bath as a pre-party treat. With Roisin already on the way and nothing more she could possibly do, she decided she'd treat herself right now. She turned on the taps so that it filled with tepid water – it was too warm today to contemplate her usual skin-blistering water temperature – and then added some pink bath salts from the container on the ledge. The bathroom was immediately filled with the scent of roses, and Steffie slid her pretty cotton dress from her shoulders, removed her underwear and got in.

The bath brought back memories too. When she was younger, and a good deal shorter, she used to lie full length in it, her long hair spread out in the water around her. She would pretend to be a drowning princess, waiting for her prince to come and rescue her. She didn't have a clear idea of what her prince looked like, but he always gazed into her eyes and told her that she was safe with him. Years later, when a friend asked to help illustrate a self-published children's book about a princess who fell into a lake, she drew the picture as she imagined she'd looked herself, a pale face framed by a fan of curly hair.

Now, however, she was far too tall to be able to lie down in the bath, so she filled it as full as she could before dipping her toe into the water. Maybe Roisin was right about this party after all, she thought as she sat down and closed her eyes. Aranbeg was full of memories and was a major part of her parents' lives. Perhaps it was only fitting to celebrate those lives together in a place that meant so much to them. Although she still thought the surprise element was a bad idea.

However, with everything ready and in place, there was no point in worrying about it any more. Instead she allowed her thoughts to return to her recent bid for a design contract, the one she hoped would move Butterfly Creative up a notch and earn her some really decent money. She'd sent her proposal in two days before the actual deadline, initially feeling smug that for once in her life she was ahead of the game, but later panicking in case she might have had more inspiration by waiting until the last minute. Either way, she'd expected to hear the outcome before now. Landing the contract would be an enormous boost to her confidence. It would make her believe, for the first time since she'd set up the company, that she really had done the right thing. Failing to get it, on the other hand, would reinforce all the feelings of general inadequacy she had when it came to being a hard-nosed, successful businesswoman. Well, she conceded, she'd never be hard-nosed. It wasn't in her nature. But successful, even semi-successful, would be nice.

She added some water to the bath and told herself that nobody was going to call on a Saturday and that there was no point in wishing she'd tweaked the design a bit more or submitted her proposals in another way. She'd done the best work she could. It was out of her hands now. So she tried to put it out of her mind, and had drifted into lazy oblivion when her mobile rang again. She snapped her eyes open and looked around the bathroom. The phone was on a small wooden stool, just out of reach.

'Oh crap,' she muttered, not wanting to miss it in case it was the company calling after all. She leaned half in and half out of the bath so that she could reach the mobile with her fingertips, but the moment she had it in her hand it stopped ringing. She looked at her missed calls and her heartbeat slowed down as she hit dial.

'Hi, Steve,' she said when the phone was answered. 'I was in the bath.'

'And I'm liking that image,' said the voice at the other end of the line.

'Shut up.' She chuckled. 'I was hot and sweaty and I was using the bath to cool down.'

'I'm not at all sure you should've told me that.'

'Probably not,' she agreed. 'So, what's the story? Will you be able to get here?'

'I'm sorry,' he said. 'I'm working on the mobile site and I really can't get away right now.'

'It's Saturday!' she cried. 'You're entitled to some down time.'

'And you know yourself that the day of the week means nothing to GoTronics,' he said.

She had to admit he was right. The company's MD was one of the toughest men she'd ever had to deal with. He demanded total dedication from his staff – and when she was working on anything for them, he demanded it from her too.

'I'm sorry,' Steve said again. 'I know you wanted some moral support today, but to be honest, Steff, I'm not sure it's really my sort of thing.'

She'd half expected this to happen. From the moment she'd told him about the party, Steve had given off negative vibes about coming along. Maybe it was her own fault for having complained to him so much about all the work she was doing for it in the first place. And for giving him some frankly freaky descriptions of her relatives. And for painting Roisin in such an unflattering, bossy light. She'd exaggerated because she was irritated by how put upon she felt. But she'd probably made it sound like the party from hell.

'No problem,' she said. 'I'm sure you'd have been bored out of your brains anyway.'

'Very likely,' he agreed. 'I'm not the best in social situations.'

At least, not social situations that weren't all about chilling out with friends and a few cool beers. She sighed. Those were the sort of social situations she preferred too. It was just that sometimes you had to step up to the plate and leave your comfort zone.

'Don't worry,' she told him. 'All I wanted was for you to keep people off my back. Single girls' love lives are always a hot topic of conversation at weddings, engagements and anniversaries. Being a single man is fine – it's like you've escaped a fate worse than death – but being a single woman is a total admission of failure. You'd swear we were still in the last century.'

Steve laughed. 'That's why I like you, Steffie,' he said. 'You tell it like it is. Call me when you get back to Dublin. We'll get together and have a bit of fun in our own private social situation.'

'Sounds good.'

'Great. See you soon.'

'See you,' she said and ended the call.

She replaced the phone on the stool. Then she slid down into the cool bathwater again.

She wasn't really surprised that Steve had got cold feet at the idea of all the Sheehans en masse. And not only Sheehans, she thought. There would be Mullens and Marshalls and Carmichaels too, all of whom had at various times stayed at Aranbeg. Nobody with even the slightest family link to Jenny and Pascal had been omitted from the guest list. Maybe it was for the best that Steve had bailed out. You didn't bring people you weren't fairly serious about to family occasions, and it was perfectly clear to her that even if she'd had notions about being serious with Steve, he currently didn't feel the same way about her.

Her best friend Brianna often told her that she went out with the wrong sort of men deliberately, that she always chose the ones who weren't looking for commitment, and that Steve was a prime example of this. Whenever Brianna voiced her opinion, Steffie would retort that it was impossible to know at the start how committed anyone was going to be. And yet . . . She sighed. Was she simply fooling herself? Was Brianna right, and she was afraid to find someone to be totally serious about just in case, like Steve, he wasn't equally serious in return?

She slid further down into the bath. A girl could go mad guessing and second-guessing her own motivation, she thought as she captured some foam with her hands and sculpted rose-scented pyramids on her breasts. Maybe the reason I don't want to get too serious is that I'm going to get that design contract and am therefore on the cusp of being the kind of ball-breaking woman who puts her career ahead of anything else in her life. And then dies alone and is eaten by her cats! She giggled to herself. Serious career women didn't make conical bras from the foam in their baths, for heaven's sake. She was an idiot. And she shouldn't get annoyed, as she always did, about the remarks that would undoubtedly be made about her single state today. It was apparently an obligation at family events for every married member to ask the single women if they were thinking about giving up their freedom any day soon. Besides, she wouldn't be the only one without a partner in tow. Her cousins Colette and Alivia, slightly older than her, were both single too. In fairness, Colette had actually been engaged three times but she'd broken it off long before actual wedding plans were made. In Alivia's case, her career as a presenter on a popular afternoon TV show was on the up-and-up and she didn't have time for serious relationships. The show had recently been commissioned for another series and Alivia was the anchor, so Steffie couldn't see anyone telling her that she'd be better of being married with kids.

It's only the women on Mum's side who stay single, Steffie mused as she closed her eyes again. On Dad's side, they're all married. But perhaps I was right when I told Roisin there was nothing else to do in the nineties. All the married women are hitting forty. All the single ladies are in their late twenties or early thirties. We're a different generation. We have a different outlook. And that's a good thing.

A distant chime startled her and she sat up abruptly, sending a tidal wave over the side of the bath. She swore under her breath and for a brief moment wondered if it was Steve after all. Maybe he'd phoned her from his car on the way down to the house and had told her he wouldn't be there so that she'd be pleasantly surprised when he did turn up. Highly unlikely, she admitted to herself as she got out of the bath and grabbed two towels, one for herself and one for the wet floor. It wasn't his style. As she hastily wrapped the towel around her, it caught the edge of the stool and knocked her mobile to the floor, where it slid across the white tiles and slammed into the wall. Her heart sank as she picked it up. But although the screen was cracked for the third time in as many months, the phone itself was still working. She gave both it and herself a hasty wipe with the towel before pulling her dress on to her still damp body and then hurrying down the stairs in her bare feet, re-securing her hair with clips as she ran.

'All right, all right,' she yelled as the bell rang again. 'Give me a second.'

At first she could hardly make out the man on the doorstep in front of her, shielded as he was by a simply gigantic bouquet of flowers arranged in a bronze vase. But then he lowered them and she could see that beneath a shock of ink-black hair, and day-old stubble, his indigo-blue eyes were sharp and piercing and looking at her with recognition.

'Hi,' he said. 'Sorry if I disturbed you. It's Steffie, isn't it?'

'Um, yes.'

'You don't remember me, do you?'

Steffie hated when people did this. Nobody in the world could be expected to remember everyone they'd ever met. And she met a lot of people these days. Although, given the still precarious nature of her business, she could always do with meeting more.

'I'm sorry.' Better to 'fess up now than try to pretend. 'I'm not sure . . .'

'Liam. Liam Kinsella,' he said.

It took a moment and then she remembered.

'Liam Kinsella? Michelle's brother?'

The Kinsellas lived in Castlemoran and she and Michelle had played with each other as children during the long summer holidays. But they'd lost contact when they'd left school and Steffie hadn't heard from the other girl in years.

'You've changed,' she said, barely managing to keep the shock out of her voice. When she'd known him, Liam had been a barrel of a boy. Overweight, with train-track braces on his teeth and a perpetual hangdog expression, he hadn't given any indication of turning into the undeniably attractive man standing on her doorstep.

'So have you.' His eyes flickered up and down her body and she suddenly realised that her cotton dress was sticking to her. And that she hadn't bothered with any underwear.

'Yes, well,' she said as she tugged at the dress and hoped that it wasn't too revealing. 'What can I do for you?' As far as she remembered, he hadn't been invited to the party. Neither had Michelle. Although Mr and Mrs Kinsella were on the guest list, and had accepted.

'Mum asked me to bring these around,' he said, indicating the floral display in his arms. 'She wanted to get it here early so that you could place it somewhere suitable.'

'That's really nice of her,' said Steffie. 'It's gorgeous. And very extravagant.'

'Mum owns the florist's,' Liam reminded her.

'Oh. Yes. So she does.' Steffie had forgotten that too. The truth was, she'd left her life at Aranbeg and all the people in it behind her a long time ago. 'I'll put it on the veranda,' she suggested. 'It's where most of the party will be happening.'

'Do you want me to carry it for you?' asked Liam.

'If you wouldn't mind.' It wasn't that she was weak or

feeble or anything, but the arrangement looked heavy and Steffie didn't fancy dropping it on the floor that she'd swept and washed half an hour previously. She led the way to the veranda, where Liam commented on how festive the celebratory banners and balloons made it, before placing the floral arrangement on a small table that he thought was prominent enough to satisfy his mother.

'It really is nice of your mum to send it,' said Steffie.

'She's good with flowers,' agreed Liam.

Steffie vaguely remembered occasionally calling to the florist's to meet Michelle. She'd liked the scent of the cut flowers and the artistic way that Liam's mum had arranged them.

'Do you work with her?' asked Steffie.

Liam grinned. 'Not me. I'm a chef.'

Recalling the fact that she'd rarely seen him without some kind of food when he was younger, Steffie wasn't altogether surprised. Although clearly he cooked more than he ate these days.

'In Cody's,' added Liam. 'It's my restaurant.'

'You own a restaurant?' And perhaps that shouldn't have been a surprise either.

'The best in town,' he assured her. 'If you're staying for a while, you should come and eat there. I guarantee you'll like it.'

'Unfortunately I'm going back to Dublin first thing,' Steffie told him.

'That's a shame. We do a superb Sunday lunch at Cody's.'

'Sadly, I have to pass,' she replied. 'Another time, maybe.'

'I look forward to welcoming you.' He smiled at her. 'What are you doing with yourself these days, Steffie?'

'I'm a graphic designer,' she said. 'I have my own company.' She added the last with a touch of pride.

'Good for you,' said Liam. 'I always thought you'd end up in something arty. I remember you trailing around the place with notebooks and pencils, drawing stuff. Just like your mum.'

'Oh.' Steffie was taken aback. She hadn't thought he would've noticed her at all. Older brothers generally didn't have time for their younger sisters' friends. 'Well, I suppose you've found your right choice of career too.' Even as the words were out of her mouth she felt her cheeks flame, and regretted her lack of sensitivity.

'I always loved my food,' he said, unperturbed. 'Now I love cooking it for other people. So do please drop in if you change your mind and stay longer. Or indeed any time you come down.'

'Thank you. I will.'

'Meantime it looks as though you're all set up for a great party,' Liam said.

'I think we've gone a bit overboard on the red.' Steffie wrinkled her nose as she looked around her. 'But it's their ruby wedding so we've kind of embraced the theme.'

'They'll love it,' he assured her.

'Hope so.' She hesitated. 'We didn't invite you or Michelle, did we?'

Liam shook his head. 'But I wouldn't have expected you to.'

'All the same . . . if either of you want to drop by, you're very welcome.' She shrugged. 'It's a case of the more the merrier.'

'I'm working tonight, and Michelle is away on holidays, but thank you anyway,' said Liam.

She nodded. 'Of course. Saturday night must be your busiest.'

'Thankfully,' said Liam. 'I'll be off. I hope you have a wonderful time and that the weather holds.'

'Fingers crossed,' said Steffie. 'Thanks again for bringing the flowers, and tell your mum we'll see her later.'

'Will do.' Liam gave her a cheerful smile and turned back towards his car at the front of the house. 'Lovely seeing you again, Steffie. You look fantastic.'

When he was gone, Steffie went back upstairs to the bathroom. She picked up her cracked phone and checked the weather forecast. The icon had changed from a smiley sun to white clouds, although the temperature was still high. So was the humidity.

She closed the app, then looked at herself in the full-length mirror and squeaked in horror. Thanks to her damp skin, the dress was practically see-through. Liam Kinsella had probably been laughing at her, if not leering at her, the whole time. She went into her room, peeled it over her head and put on the light robe hanging from the door instead. Then she opened her overnight bag and took out the summer dress, white with a purple floral print, that she'd chosen to wear to the party. She was fastening the tiny mother-of-pearl buttons when she heard the sound of the front door opening.

She waited, immobile, until she heard Roisin call her name. Then she stepped on to the landing and peered over the banister.

'That was quick,' she said. 'You must've driven like a maniac.'

'Not a bit,' said Roisin. 'I was in Bunclody when I rang you.'

49

'Oh.'

'Anyway, Paul texted a while back. He managed to delay them some more because Dougie insisted Dad help him shower.'

'Good old Dougie,' said Steffie.

'They won their match,' Roisin said in satisfaction. 'And I bet Dad enjoyed it anyway.'

'Are Mum and Dad on their way now?'

'I guess so. There were getting ready to leave when Paul texted me.'

'You still think he'll manage to get here ahead of them?' Steffie sounded doubtful.

'Everything was ready. I laid out Poppy's dress and Dougie's shirt and shorts earlier. Daisy, of course, has had her own outfit selected since last week, and despite the fact that she takes an age to get ready, she's been primping herself all day. So they don't have to do much and at least this way I get time to do my own make-up.'

'Mum wasn't suspicious when you left with a case?' asked Steffie.

'I put most of my stuff in my biggest handbag,' said Roisin. 'Anyway, let's have a look at what you've done so far.'

Still fastening the buttons of her dress, Steffie came downstairs again and both sisters walked to the veranda.

'Not bad,' said Roisin as she rearranged the balloons. 'When did you get the flowers? They're nice. A bit OTT, but nice.'

Steffie told her about Liam's delivery of them.

'That was good of Mrs Kinsella.' Roisin moved the arrangement to a different part of the veranda and looked at it critically. 'Better there,' she said. 'D'you think we should've invited Liam and Michelle?'

'I asked him if he'd like to drop by later,' said Steffie. 'But he's working and Michelle's away. He owns a restaurant, by the way. Cody's. He's the chef.'

'Really?' Roisin looked surprised. 'Mum never told me that. Hopefully he doesn't mind that I cancelled their reservation.'

'What reservation?'

'They were supposed to be eating there tonight. That's why I asked you to put out Mum's black dress. It was what she'd planned to wear.'

'No! Maybe she would've preferred a flashy meal out to a party.'

'Don't be silly,' said Roisin. 'Nobody would prefer dinner in a restaurant to a party.'

Steffie said nothing.

'Where are the lanterns?' asked Roisin.

'Oh, sorry, I left them in the car,' replied Steffie. 'I'll get them now.'

'I got some citronella torches too,' added Roisin. 'To keep the midges away. Get them as well, will you?' She handed her car keys to her sister.

Steffie left Roisin rearranging the veranda while she ferried in the torches as well as the half-dozen glass lanterns plus candles that she'd picked up from Roisin earlier in the week. Roisin had got them on one of Lidl's discount promotions, saying that it was too good a deal to pass up and that even though Jenny and Pascal already had some lanterns themselves, a party situation needed more.

Roisin always thought of the extra touches, Steffie acknowledged as she placed them on the veranda, and then noticed that her sister had scattered red and gold foil hearts on the table. She's good at this sort of stuff. And I shouldn't doubt her. It's going to be a great party. She'll make sure that it is.

Chapter 6

Steffie and Roisin were drinking pre-party glasses of wine on the veranda when the first of the guests showed up. Roisin went to answer the door because she half expected that it would be Paul and the children, but the arrivals were her mother's younger sister Sarah and her eldest son Carl, who was accompanied by a striking young woman that neither Roisin nor Steffie had ever seen before. Carl's companion was wearing a very short, very low-cut yellow sundress and matching yellow high-heeled sandals. Her champagne-blond hair was arranged in a deliberately messy updo, secured by diamanté clips and topped by a pair of sunglasses with heart-shaped frames. Her wide blue eyes were accentuated by even bluer metallic eyeshadow, while her lashes were sweeping and black. Her lips were cherry red. Carl introduced her to them as Summer.

'Summer, as in the season?' asked Roisin after she'd greeted her aunt with a kiss and a hug, then given her cousin a peck on the cheek. He hadn't emailed his acceptance until the last minute, adding that Bernice, his girlfriend of eight years, wouldn't be with him owing to the fact that they were currently 'on a break' but giving no indication that he was 'on a break' with someone else. And that the someone else bore no resemblance to his former girlfriend, who outwardly at least was as staid as Summer was startling.

Summer herself giggled at Roisin's question and confirmed that she was indeed named after the season, although she'd originally been called Sarah.

'Like Carl's mum,' she added, giggling again. 'So just as well I changed it for career purposes.'

'And that career is?' Steffie was finding it hard to believe that this girl was Bernice's replacement. It was as though Carl had deliberately sought out the polar opposite of the woman he'd lived with for nearly a decade.

'I'm a model,' said Summer, a reply that made Roisin immediately determined to keep her well away from Daisy. 'Thanks for inviting me,' she added. 'I'm really looking forward to the party.'

Roisin didn't say that the invitation had gone to Carl and Bernice, and that it hadn't made any mention of substitute girlfriends. Steffie, seeing that her aunt's eyes were hard and flinty, guessed that Sarah hadn't known there'd be a substitute either. When she'd last spoken to her a month or so earlier, Sarah had been mentally planning Carl and Bernice's wedding.

'What would you like to drink?' she asked her now.

'Gin and tonic,' replied Sarah. 'Make it a double.'

'And you?' Steffie looked at Summer.

'A mojito would be nice.'

'I don't actually know how to make mojitos,' Steffie confessed. 'I know it's rum and mint leaves, but . . .'

'If you have the ingredients, I can do it myself.' Summer beamed at her. 'I'm good at mojitos. And daiquiris. Cocktails generally.'

'Um, OK then, as you're the expert . . .' Steffie led the way into the kitchen, the other girl following her.

Meanwhile Roisin looked quizzically at her aunt and cousin.

'I said he shouldn't bring her,' Sarah told her. 'I said it was very bad manners.'

'Oh, chill out, Mum,' said Carl. 'It's a party.'

'It's fine, Aunt Sarah,' said Roisin, although inside she agreed totally with her aunt. In her view Carl shouldn't have brought anyone other than Bernice. And certainly not this . . . well . . . the girl might call herself a model, but given the way that she was bursting out of that dress, the word 'glamour' should clearly have been put in front of it. There was no way Summer would be gracing the catwalk, not with those boobs. Page 3 was another story altogether. However, Roisin didn't want to start off the party by arguing with the first guests, so she simply turned to Carl and asked him what he was going to have to drink.

'I'd love a beer,' said Carl.

'We have a cooler over here.'

She led him to the other end of the veranda, where she took a can of beer from the large tub of ice in the shadiest corner and handed it to him.

'Don't go all judgemental on me, Ro,' he said as he pulled the tab.

'Judgemental? Me?'

He laughed. 'Come on. It's written all over your face. You're looking at Summer and you're thinking that she's a total ditz and you're horrified to have her here.'

'I'm thinking that it would've been nice to know in advance she was coming,' Roisin told him.

'Sorry about that. I didn't know myself until yesterday.'

'Carl!'

'I asked her and she said yes.'

'How long have you known her?'

'Not long. But I'm having a good time with her. She's fun to be with.'

'And Bernice wasn't?'

Carl's eyes darkened. 'Fun and Bernice don't even belong in the same sentence.'

'I know it's none of my business—'

'You're right, Roisin, it's not,' said Carl.

'It's just that you and Bernice were together a long time. And we all loved her.'

'I think the more pertinent question there is whether she and I loved each other.'

Roisin was momentarily abashed, then she looked him straight in the eye. 'You're supposed to be on a break,' she reminded him. 'That implies that you still love each other but that you're working through some issues. I'm not entirely convinced that working through them with Miss Bubblegum there is the way forward.'

'Fortunately it's not up to you,' said Carl. 'And Summer's a lovely girl, so don't start dissing her in front of me.'

'OK, OK,' she said. 'How old is she?'

'Twenty-two,' said Carl.

'Are you sure you're not having a mid-life crisis?'

'If I am, I'm loving it,' said Carl and walked back to the centre of the veranda, where Davey and Camilla had just arrived.

Steffie was still in the kitchen watching Summer mix her mojito when she heard a squeal of delight from Roisin and the sound of her brother's voice. She hurried outside and flung herself at Davey, laughing as he gave her a massive bear hug. As he introduced them to Camilla, Steffie and Roisin exchanged awed glances. She was as sophisticated as Summer was brash and as reserved as the other girl was outgoing. And although she also had blond hair in an updo, hers was sleek and smooth – and, Steffie thought, fighting back the uncharitable thought, the colour was natural. Camilla wore a figure-hugging print dress and elegant strappy sandals. She was even more staggeringly beautiful than her Facebook photos.

'It's lovely to meet you.' Roisin was immediately regretting that she'd decided to wear a pair of flat sandals herself. She'd chosen them because she thought they'd be good for a day when she'd be mostly on her feet, and they were very pretty, with blue and white sequins and a large silver buckle, but they meant that Camilla was towering over her. In fact all of the women were. She was used to it with Steffie, but now Summer had returned to the veranda, mojito in hand, and was standing on the other side of her, making her feel like the short straw in a pack. Dammit, she thought. When I was a full-time working woman I didn't dress for comfort. As soon as I get back to Dublin, I'm going shopping. Although, she conceded, it was a long time since she'd shopped for style rather than comfort.

Steffie wasn't quite as intimidated as her sister, because even in kitten heels she was taller than Summer and able to look Camilla in the eye. But she could see that Camilla's dress and jewellery were quietly expensive and not the cheap and cheerful stuff that she was wearing herself. (She hadn't figured out if Summer's sundress was designer or not. Either way, there wasn't much of it to assess.) She shook hands with

Camilla and asked her what she'd like to drink, and when Camilla said that Summer's mojito looked nice, she turned to Carl's girlfriend and asked her if she'd mind taking over bar duties again.

'Love to.' Summer caught the startled Camilla by the hand and pulled her towards the kitchen so that she could watch her drink being made.

'There's beer in the cooler,' Carl told his cousin. 'I reckon that's more your tipple than a cocktail.'

'Lead me to it.' Davey ambled towards the far end of the veranda, followed by Steffie.

'Heavens, Davey,' she murmured as he grabbed a can. 'You're punching above your weight with that girl.'

'You cheeky thing.' He made an amused face at her. 'She's lucky to have me.'

'Well, of course,' Steffie agreed with a smile. 'But you've got to admit she's a stunner.'

This time Davey laughed. 'She's more than that. She's a vice president of the company she works for, is paid way more than me and is ferociously intelligent.'

'As well as being a babe? Then you're definitely punching above your weight.' Steffie laughed too.

'Actually,' said Davey quietly, 'I agree with you. I have to keep pinching myself to make sure I'm not dreaming. She's great, she really is.'

'You sound sort of serious there,' said Steffie.

'Could be.'

She opened her eyes wide. 'Something more permanent on the cards?'

'I'm thinking that way.'

'Oh my God!'

57

'Don't say anything!' Davey glanced to where Roisin, Carl and Sarah were standing. 'It's not . . . I haven't . . .'

'My lips are sealed,' she promised him. 'But it's very exciting, Davey.'

They both looked towards Summer and Camilla, who'd walked outside again with their drinks.

'Before we rejoin the others,' Davey said, 'whose idea was it to hire the cocktail waitress?'

The doorbell was beginning to ring more regularly as the garden filled up with friends and relatives. Summer's mojito was proving very popular and she continued to make them good-naturedly for anyone who asked.

'We'll run out of mint soon,' Roisin muttered to Steffie.

'Not before we run out of rum,' Steffie replied.

'I should have thought of cocktails.' Roisin looked annoyed. 'But I assumed everyone would be on beer or wine.'

'Hopefully the sparkling rosé will distract them,' said Steffie. 'Or Summer might get fed up mixing them.'

'Oh look! Lucinda and Alivia are here.' Roisin was distracted by the arrival of her mother's youngest sister and her daughter.

'About time,' said Steffie as she waved at them, and then added an 'oops' when she realised that Lucinda was wearing an almost identical floral dress to Sarah.

'Oops indeed,' said Alivia as she kissed Steffie in greeting. The two girls had always been friendly, although most of their contact was through social media these days, as Alivia and her mother lived in Galway. 'Mum thinks she's the youngest, hippest of the three of them. She's not going to be impressed at being in the same dress as Aunt Sarah.'

'How in God's name did they manage that?' Roisin muttered under her breath. 'They live two hundred kilometres apart, for heaven's sake.' She was becoming increasingly irritated by things she could do nothing about. Her own flat sandals. The arrival of Summer. The popularity of the mojitos. And now her aunts' fashion faux pas. Unforeseen events when she'd tried so hard to anticipate everything about the day. Hopefully, she thought, everything else is under control. And indeed there was nothing else to surprise or annoy her as the remainder of the guests turned up, including Mr and Mrs Kinsella (who checked to see that her flower arrangement was looking fresh and vibrant) and finally Roisin's own family. Paul said he'd passed Jenny and Pascal on the road and he reckoned they were about twenty minutes behind them.

'OK, everyone!' cried Roisin. 'They'll be here soon.' She told Daisy and Poppy to stand at the front window and watch out for their grandparents. They were to let her know the instant they turned into the driveway so that everyone would be ready to surprise them. The other younger children insisted on joining them, so that in the end, there was a small crowd on the lookout.

'What about the boyfriend you're taking it easy with?' Roisin turned to Steffie. 'Is he coming?'

'Oh, he called earlier,' Steffie replied. 'He's working and can't make it.'

'Hmm,' said Roisin.

Steffie glanced at her, but her sister's face was neutral. She walked into the kitchen, but Carl and Summer were in there together, foreheads touching, and she beat a hasty retreat, thinking dark thoughts about her sister, her boyfriend and her cousin in equal measure.

Then Daisy cried out that Grandad and Granny's car was at the gate. There was a flurry of movement as everyone tried to take up position out of sight on the veranda and Roisin told them all to be very quiet and not make a sound.

'All very well for you to say,' said Charlie, Pascal's brother. 'I had beans for dinner.'

'Charlie!' His sister-in-law, Moya, glared at him.

'It's a joke,' the older man grumbled.

'Please be quiet,' begged Roisin. 'We don't want to spoil anything.'

Everyone held their breath. Then they heard the key in the front door and got ready to surprise the anniversary couple.

Chapter 7

Jenny's thoughts on her way from Dublin to Wexford were almost entirely about her children and what sort of mother she'd been to them. She frequently asked herself that question and just as frequently feared that she'd been wanting in a lot of respects. And yet, she thought, she'd raised them to be independent people, able to cope with life on their own. Even Steffie was managing to keep her head above water with that company of hers despite being the child most like Jenny herself – dreamy and not entirely practical. Admittedly she and Pascal had helped her out in ways they hadn't had to with Roisin or Davey, but it had been worth it to see their younger daughter finally finding her place. Davey, her easy-going son, seemed to have found his place too, although she wished it wasn't in another country. But he was happy with his latest girlfriend. Davey didn't do love and girlfriends very well, so despite the fact that – like all Irish mothers – she would have liked him to settle down at home with someone suitable, she was pleased he'd found someone he was happy with, at least for now. Roisin, of course, had never really been a worry because practically from the moment she'd been born she had been quietly determined about what she wanted from life. And so far, she'd got it.

Which meant, Jenny thought, she'd done a reasonably good job. And that would surely have to stand her in good stead when she ended up talking to them about things she'd rather not have to talk to them about. When she eventually told them about the mistakes she'd made when she was as young as – and younger than – they were now. It wasn't as if they weren't aware of some of them. Roisin knew that she'd been an unplanned pregnancy when Jenny was only twenty-one. Jenny had told her that she had made them into a family, and she occasionally thought that Roisin's habit of organising everyone and everything stemmed from the fact that she'd been the cause of her parents staying together in the first place. Or maybe it was simply because she had a bossy eldest child!

She knew that Roisin would have views on everything she needed to talk to them about too. She'd been putting it off, telling Pascal that it would be best to get them all together. Pascal had raised his eyebrows at that and Jenny knew the argument wasn't exactly a good one. There had been plenty of time to talk to the three of them together years ago. But they were both to blame for not saying anything before now. There was a comfort in the status quo, in not dragging up things from the past. Except that everyone had a right to know.

Or did they? It was a valid question. These days everyone thought they should know everything about everybody. And with Facebook and Twitter and all sorts of other social media sites, they also seemed to feel obliged to tell everybody everything. That wasn't how Jenny had been brought up. Her parents, Kay and Terry, had believed in keeping your private life private and never washing your dirty laundry in public. There was none of this 'talking things through' that was so popular nowadays. You did something, you kept it to yourself. That was the way back then. It might not always have been right, Jenny conceded, but it still had a lot to recommend it.

That was then. This was now. Times had changed. And the trouble with that, Jenny thought, was that things you hadn't talked about became secrets. And secrets took on a life of their own. Which meant that when they finally came into the light, people could misjudge your motives for keeping them in the first place.

She sighed.

'Everything OK?' Pascal glanced at her.

'Don't mind me,' she said. 'Just thinking.'

'Hard work?' He smiled and so did she, but she couldn't help the nagging worry that she hadn't done as good a job as she'd hoped as a mother. And when she eventually got around to talking to them and explaining . . . She shook her head. Maybe she'd leave them a bundles of neuroses that would come back to haunt her in the future. She hoped not. She'd done her best. She'd learned from her mistakes. Although it hadn't stopped her making them.

'By the way,' said Pascal when they arrived at the house and he slid the key into the lock. 'I meant to mention it earlier.'

'What?'

'That I love you.'

At his words, her worries faded into insignificance. 'I love you too.'

He didn't open the door but instead pulled her close to him and kissed her.

'Why, Mr Sheehan!' She giggled. 'Is that a gun in your pocket?'

'Let's go inside and check it out,' he said.

When Jenny thought about it afterwards, the one positive thing she took out of it all was that at least they didn't race up the stairs to the bedroom and tear the clothes off each other. There had been a time when they might have, but they were both hot and thirsty after the drive and so they headed for the kitchen instead. That was when Jenny realised the patio doors leading to the veranda were open. And when Pascal noticed the big banner saying 'Happy Ruby Anniversary'. And when all of their invited guests shouted 'Surprise!' as Roisin appeared at the doorway.

'Mum, Dad!' she cried. 'Welcome home. Happy anniversary!'

Poppy, who was in charge of the music mix, hit play on the iPod and Frank Sinatra singing 'It Had to Be You' filled the room.

Jenny and Pascal were in shock as Roisin took them by the hand and dragged them to the veranda.

'My God,' said Jenny when she saw how many people were there. And then, when Davey came forward and hugged her, she felt tears prickle at her eyes. Even Davey, she thought. That's nice. Isn't it?

'Well done, Pascal!' His older brother Charlie thumped him gently on the back. 'Fair play to yeh! Forty years with the same woman. Couldn't manage it meself, although maybe if it had been the beautiful Jenny I might have!'

Charlie had been divorced from Peggy for the past fifteen years. He turned up at every family occasion although most of the women in the family wished he wouldn't – he had a habit of patting them on the behind and calling them 'darling' or 'sweetheart', which drove them mad.

'Congrats, Mum.' Steffie edged out of Charlie's reach.

'Yay, Grandma. Yay, Grandpa!' Daisy pushed her way forward to hug them.

'Jenny. Pascal. It's such an honour to be here.' Breege Behan, who was chairwoman of the local community centre, added her words. 'Such a wonderful occasion. Many congratulations. You're an example to us all.'

Jenny's head and heart were pounding as she smiled blankly at her.

'Forty years,' said Roisin. 'It's so lovely to know that people can stay together. Breege is right, you're an example to all of us – but I guess most especially to me and Paul. We're hoping that we can match you sometime in the future.' She glanced at Paul, who was busy uncorking the bottles of sparkling rosé wine that had been on special in Tesco the week before. Meanwhile Poppy and Daisy were handing glasses to all the guests.

'A toast,' said Paul when all of them had been filled. 'To Jenny and Pascal. Marriage sometimes gets a bad press, but they've shown us how good it can be.'

'Jenny and Pascal!' cried the guests.

'Speech,' said Davey.

'Um, well . . .' Jenny looked at Pascal, a slightly hunted expression in her blue eyes.

'This is a surprise,' he said. 'Well, of course it is, it was meant to be! So thank you for being so thorough about it.'

There was a murmur of laughter.

'I don't know what to say,' continued Pascal. 'Other than that the first thirty-nine years are the hardest.'

Everyone laughed. Jenny's hand tightened around the stem of her glass.

'So happy for you,' murmured Sarah. 'So happy it all worked out for you. That you've managed it when so many of us didn't.'

'Thanks. Thanks.' Jenny was too shocked to care that Sarah seemed to be getting a dig in at her. She looked around at all of them, uncertain if she was supposed to say anything herself and feeling that she should, that perhaps this was the exact right time. But suddenly everyone was laughing and talking and knocking back the sparkling rosé, and she realised that her own throat was dry and that she couldn't speak at all. She swallowed a large mouthful of wine.

'I know you were meant to be going to Cody's tonight,' Roisin told her. 'But we've rebooked it for next week.'

'Oh. OK.' Jenny nodded.

'And if you'd like to nip up and change, you'll find your dress and jewellery laid out.'

'Oh,' said Jenny again. 'Thank you, darling.'

'No problem.' Roisin kissed her. 'Was it really a surprise?'

'Totally.'

'Good.' Roisin looked pleased. 'You deserve it.'

No I don't, thought Jenny. It's lovely to think that you believe I do, but . . . She tried to gather her thoughts. Pascal deserves it, she said to herself. He deserves to be acknowledged. As for me . . . She released her breath slowly. It didn't matter, she told herself. It was a shock because she hadn't expected it; hadn't even dreamed that they'd do anything like this. But she wasn't going to get into a flap about it.

She'd never been someone who flapped. She always believed everything worked out for the best, and usually, in the end, it did. But she wished they hadn't done it. She really did.

She looked in Pascal's direction. Her husband was laughing with his brothers, his champagne glass already empty. He glanced up and caught her eye. And winked at her.

He's a good man, she thought. I'm lucky to have him in my life. Luckier than anyone here will ever know.

Chapter 8

The words that were used to describe Jenny Marshall in her school reports were usually 'daydreamer' and 'flighty'. According to her teachers, she could be a really good student if she put her mind to it. Unfortunately, most of them said, she preferred doodling in the margins of her copybooks to dealing with the assignments she'd been given. The one class in which she excelled was art, where her paintings were energetic and colourful. Her other skill was calligraphy. Whenever posters were being done for the classroom, it was Jenny who would be entrusted with whatever script went with them, and she always did a great job. It was a pity, her form mistress said, that she didn't apply herself with as much enthusiasm to subjects like maths and history. Her parents weren't too perturbed about her reports. After all, they reckoned, Jenny was a pretty girl and they were certain she'd get married and have a family of her own. Education, Kay said, was important. But only up to a point.

In her third year in secondary school, Jenny had to do a project on a European capital city. Back then, without the internet and Google, gathering information meant a hard slog of trawling through the library, buying magazines and – because she'd chosen Rome as her city – writing to the Italian embassy and the tourist board for information. At first she'd been less than enthusiastic, but by the time she'd completed her project, she'd fallen in love with Rome and its history, and had stuck a poster of the Colosseum that had been sent as part of the tourist board's information pack on her bedroom wall. She loved looking at the vibrant blue sky and the ancient stone construction as she pictured herself walking around it. The tourist board had also included a picture of a crowded square with attractive women and handsome men drinking coffee at tables beneath parasols. Every time she looked at it, Jenny wanted to be with them. In fact, she wanted to *be* them. Life in Italy looked a damn sight more colourful and exciting than life in Ireland, which from Jenny's perspective seemed unbearably drab by comparison.

Shortly afterwards, to celebrate Ireland's accession to the European Economic Community, her school organised a trip to Rome. It was a sign, she told herself. A sign that she would go there and meet Italian people and make new friends and live a different life, even if it was only for a few days. She brought the information sheet home to show her parents and told them that she'd love to go. That she'd get a Saturday job and pay them back. After all, she reminded them, the trip was educational, and she'd received her first ever A grade for her project. She stood in front of them with her fingers crossed as they read through it, but when they got to the end and saw that the five-day stay cost a whopping £75, Jenny knew there was no chance.

'We can't afford it,' Kay said as she folded the information sheet in half. 'We can't spend that much money on you and

69

not your sisters and you'll never get a job that will pay us back.'

'I might,' protested Jenny. 'Mrs Murtagh in the newsagent's is looking for part-time staff.'

'We can't afford it and that's that.' Terry picked up the newspaper he'd put down to glance at the information sheet.

Jenny had known all along that they'd say no, although she'd longed for them to surprise her by saying yes. She'd hoped that telling them she'd try to find a job would swing it. But Terry and Kay weren't going to change their minds. They didn't care how educational the trip might be, although they didn't see any educational value in it at all. There was no reason for her to go to Rome, Kay said. There was nothing there for her.

'When you're working and earning your own money you can go wherever you like,' Terry told her over the top of the paper when she said there were plenty of reasons to go to Rome, that it was a major cultural city. 'Although why anyone would want to go to a foreign place like that where you can't drink the water or eat the food, I don't know.'

'The Italians drink the water and eat the food,' Jenny murmured, but Terry had already turned his attention back to the paper. And Jenny made up her mind that as soon as she was in a position to travel abroad, Rome would be the first place she visited.

When she left school and got a job in the Civil Service, she began to put a little money away every week for her travel fund, although it grew so slowly she couldn't help wondering if she'd be a pensioner before she ever left the country. Kay insisted that she hand over a large chunk of her wages to help with household expenses every week, which put a big dent in her ability to save. Jenny didn't begrudge her parents the money, but she sometimes wondered if it would be cheaper to live in a flat with one of the other girls in the office. People would think she was weird, though. It was the country girls who lived in flats. No Dubliner wasted money on rent when they could be at home, even if they were contributing to living expenses. But those country girls always seemed to have more money than her!

Then she met Pascal Sheehan. He also worked in the Department of Agriculture and she'd seen him walking around the office before, but their paths didn't cross until they got into conversation at a booze-up to celebrate a raft of internal promotions and transfers. It's mad, she said later that evening when she'd blown that week's travel fund on an unaccustomed amount of cheap white wine, that the first time I get to talk to you is when you're moving to Revenue.

'Maybe that's a good thing,' he whispered into her ear. 'After all, it's hard to go out with someone who works in the same office as you.'

'Are you asking me out?'

'Would you like me to?'

'Yes,' she said.

He was easy to get on with. She liked being with him. She didn't mind that he was more organised and methodical than her. He didn't mind that she was impulsive and untidy, or that from time to time she retreated into her own world. Although they approached life differently, they both liked the same things. But getting married hadn't been part of the plan. Not when she was still putting money aside for her travel fund.

Now, sitting in her bedroom and fixing her diamond earrings in place, Jenny wondered how it was that the events of forty-odd years ago should be so clear in her mind when there were times she couldn't even remember what had happened yesterday. Gazing into the mirror, she looked for the person she had been in the reflection of the person she had become.

Leaving aside the older face, drier skin and fine lines (as well as some more obvious wrinkles that not even the most expensive serums had been able to shift), the biggest difference was how groomed she appeared. Of course everyone looked groomed now, thanks to hair-smoothing treatments and skin-perfecting creams and a plethora of products that nobody had heard of in the 1970s. She smiled as she remembered wrestling with her unruly hair before going out with Pascal, desperately trying to tame the wayward curls into something more stylish but inevitably, without a GHD or dry oil to help, failing every time.

She looked at her hair now. Somehow, over the years, it had seemed to tame itself. Maybe it was the result of her regular colouring sessions at the hair salon, supplemented by her weekly blow-dry. Maybe it was the expensive keratin-enriched shampoo she used. For whatever reason, her blond bob was easy to maintain and appropriate for her age. Still, she thought, she'd had an extravagant mane of untamed curls in her youth. Sometimes she missed them.

She picked up her mobile phone. She'd made a late appointment for a blow-dry at Marie's Klip Joint in the village before going to the restaurant this evening, so she had to text to cancel. Something Roisin hadn't thought of, mused Jenny as she sent the message. She really wished her daughter had asked her about this party. She knew Roisin had wanted to surprise her, but she didn't like being surprised. And certainly not like this. Not for this.

The black dress was carefully laid out on the bed. Jenny put it back in the wardrobe. A little black dress was fine for eating out in the poshest restaurant for miles, but totally wrong for a garden party. She looked through her options, finally selecting a white summer dress with a red rose design. It had a fifties retro look with its narrow bodice and wide skirt, and when Jenny had first seen it, she'd been reminded of a day when her own mother, wearing a similar dress, had taken her to the park.

'You look lovely.' Pascal walked into the room and kissed her on the nape of the neck.

'Thanks,' said Jenny. 'How are they all downstairs?'

'Having a great time,' said Pascal. 'The girls have managed to get a big crowd together.'

Jenny nodded.

'You OK?' he asked.

'I wish they hadn't done it.' Jenny stood up. In her bare feet she reached Pascal's shoulder, and now she leaned her head against his chest. 'Perhaps we should have guessed when Roisin asked about the babysitting.'

'How could we?'

'I should've listened to you before now,' Jenny said. 'I should've told her we wanted them to come here because we had important stuff to tell them and—'

'They'd clearly planned this for ages.' Pascal interrupted her. 'It wouldn't have made any difference. Besides, it's right to celebrate.'

Jenny said nothing.

'They're all here to have fun,' murmured Pascal. 'And we have to have fun with them.'

'It's just . . .' Jenny sighed. 'I suppose I feel like a fraud.'

'Forty years,' said Pascal. 'Nothing fraudulent about that.'

She laughed softly.

'I always loved you, you know,' Pascal said. 'From the moment you walked into the department in that skin-tight tartan dress.'

'And my red platform boots,' she remembered. 'I thought I looked so cool.'

'You didn't get the red boots till later,' he said. 'I'm remembering your very first day. You were wearing black boots then. I saw you but I was afraid to speak to you.'

She lifted her head. 'No way.'

'Yes way.' He smiled. 'I thought you were the prettiest girl in the office by a country mile.'

'But you didn't speak to me until the day you were being transferred!' she exclaimed.

'Shy,' he said.

This time her laugh was louder. 'Never.'

'Absolutely,' he assured her. 'I wanted to ask you out but I was afraid you'd turn me down. So the longer I went without asking, the more I could hope that you'd say yes.'

'You never told me that before.'

'I like to keep a touch of mystery.' He smiled.

'You're mad, you know that, don't you?'

'Everyone has to be a little mad,' he said.

She rested her head on his chest again.

'Come on, Jen,' he said. 'It's a day to celebrate.'

'I . . .'

'Everybody's waiting for us,' he said.

Jenny sniffed and nodded. She wiped her eyes, thankful that she hadn't yet applied mascara. Then she touched up her make-up, slid her feet into her favourite high heels and followed Pascal downstairs.

Most of the guests were either on the veranda or wandering around the garden. Jenny watched them for a moment, puzzling over the only person she didn't recognise, the girl in the canary-yellow dress who was standing close to Carl. Then Steffie came over to her.

'Oh Mum, you look fantastic!' she exclaimed. 'I haven't seen you wear that before.'

'Don't get much opportunity,' said Jenny. 'And the black dress would've been too heavy for today. If I was forty years younger, I could've rocked bright yellow too. Who on earth is that girl ? And where's Bernice?'

As Steffie explained the situation, Jenny continued to observe Carl's date. Charlie had come up to the group she was in and was trying to position himself beside her, but Summer moved adroitly so that Carl was between them again. Jenny smiled.

'She's well able to handle Charlie,' Steffie remarked. 'Well able to handle Carl too, I reckon. I don't know what's got into him, though. He and Bernice were perfect for each other.'

'Things go wrong, even in perfect relationships,' said Jenny.

'But not for you and Dad.'

'It wasn't always perfect. Nothing is.'

'Well of course not. But you're the most rock-solid couple I know. Plus you're my parents. Which is pretty damn perfect from where I'm standing.' Steffie beamed at her.

Jenny's smile in return was slightly strained.

'Are you OK with all this?' Steffie had noticed the

reservation in Jenny's eyes and understood it. She'd been right about surprises not being Jenny's thing, and despite the fact that her mother was making the best of it, and was undoubtedly enjoying it to a certain extent, she still believed that Jenny would have preferred a quieter celebration.

'It's a very thoughtful gesture,' her mother replied. 'Thank you for organising it.'

'It was Roisin mostly.'

This time Jenny's smile was broader. 'I'm sure it was.'

'Mum! There you are at last.' Davey waved at her and came over, pulling Camilla by the hand. He embraced Jenny and congratulated her on sticking with his dad for so long, and then, before she had a chance to say anything else, he introduced Camilla.

'Lovely to meet you,' said Jenny. She thought about hugging the tall Danish girl, but Camilla didn't seem to want to be hugged; she simply extended her hand, which Jenny shook.

'It's good to meet you too,' said Camilla. 'I didn't realise Davey had such a big family.'

'Not everyone here is family,' Jenny said. 'There are plenty of friends too.'

'But lots of them are your relations,' said Camilla. 'It's nice.'

'Yes, it is. Is this your first time in Ireland?'

Camilla nodded. 'I like it.'

'Because we're having such a scorcher,' said Davey. 'It makes everything look so green and so gorgeous. The garden has never looked better, Mum.'

'Thanks to your dad,' said Jenny. 'I'm afraid I'm still hopeless at practical things.'

'Are you busy with your painting?' asked Camilla. 'Davey

76

told me you are an artist. I would love to see some of your work.'

'He can show you,' said Jenny. 'It's scattered around the house. But it's not that good.'

'He said you had an exhibition.'

Jenny looked startled. 'Not really. I had a spot around Merrion Square for a while.'

'Artists hang their paintings on the railings around the park on Sundays,' Davey explained. 'They sell them.'

'Yes, but when he was younger, yes?' said Camilla. 'He told me you had an exhibition overseas.'

'Oh my goodness, I can't believe you remembered that, Davey.' Jenny looked at him in surprise. 'It wasn't an exhibition. I went on a painting course.' She glanced across the lawn. 'Can you excuse me for a moment, Camilla. My sister is waving at me. I'll talk to you again later, possibly after you've seen my daubs. And Davey, I'm so very glad you came.'

She left them standing together and walked into the garden. The high heels of her shoes kept sinking into the grass, and so, after a few steps, she removed them and swung them from the tips of her fingers.

'Congratulations,' said Sarah. 'Terrific party. Sorry Lucinda and I didn't manage to co-ordinate our looks.' She made a face as she caught sight of the youngest of the three sisters, who was talking to Summer and Roisin.

'These things happen,' said Jenny. 'You both look lovely anyway.'

'Hmm. I would've preferred us to look different. Who wears it better? No, don't answer that. Unfair question. And none of us can hold a candle to the younger generation.'

'That's true.'

77

'What's she like?' Sarah was staring at Summer. 'And what was he thinking?'

'God knows,' said Jenny.

'It's a massive mistake.'

'We all make them.'

'But Carl, for heaven's sake! I was a little disappointed when he and Bernice moved in together without getting married, despite the fact that lots of couples do that now. I just expected that one day . . . And she talked about it occasionally. So I thought they were going to do it eventually. I never imagined . . . and this girl. Look at her!'

Summer had moved from the group and was now sitting on one of the garden benches, her long golden limbs stretched out in front of her.

'She's very pretty,' said Jenny.

'Oh come on, Jen! She's cheap and tarty.'

'Sarah! That's an awful thing to say. She's a bit brash, maybe, but . . .'

'OK, OK.' Sarah grimaced. 'It's not her fault she chose to wear a few strips of material and hooker shoes today.'

Jenny shook her head. 'You're pissed off with Carl and taking it out on her.'

'You could be right,' conceded Sarah. 'Thing is, I thought I only had one child left to worry about.'

'Is Colette here?' asked Jenny.

'At least you know who I mean.'

'You're always worrying about Colette,' Jenny reminded her.

'Wouldn't you?' demanded Sarah. 'Three fiancés! Three! And not a sniff of her actually ever getting near the altar.'

'Better she doesn't get there than it all goes wrong afterwards.'

'I'd say that if I thought she broke up with them for valid reasons,' said Sarah. 'But she can never say why. Only that it didn't feel right.'

'It's a good enough reason.'

'She has a feckin' collection of engagement rings but no damn husband.'

'Maybe she's better off without one,' suggested Jenny.

'That's hardly a line you can take. Not after forty years of perfection.' Sarah couldn't quite keep a smidgeon of envy from her voice.

'Nothing's perfect,' Jenny said for the second time that afternoon. 'Pascal and I have had to work at things, the same as everyone else.'

'You must be very proud all the same,' said Sarah. 'Of your kids. Of your marriage. Of your forty years.'

'It's worked out for me.'

'Last woman standing,' said Sarah.

'Huh?'

'You. Here am I, divorced. And poor Lucinda never managed to find someone who'd take her and Alivia on. Was it luck or judgement that got you this far, Jenny?'

'I . . . I'm not sure.'

'I remember when you came home,' said Sarah. 'All tanned and glowing and looking fabulous. With a wedding ring on your finger.'

'I remember that too.'

'Mum was devastated.'

'She got over it.'

'When Roisin was born,' Sarah nodded. 'And you became the golden girl again.'

'Oh, stop with that golden girl nonsense,' said Jenny. 'It's

79

all in your head, you know.'

'No it's not,' said Sarah. 'You always were the best in her eyes. And she's probably looking down on us all now and thinking you still are.'

Jenny winced. She'd won a gold star for one of her art projects, and for the rest of the day her mother had called her Golden Girl. Sarah had never forgotten it. Because she'd taken it as a slight, a signal that Jenny was the favourite daughter. Which wasn't true at all. If Kay had had a favourite, Jenny thought, it was Lucinda. She'd always gone easier on Lucinda than anyone else.

'I've been lucky,' she told Sarah. 'Things have worked out for me.'

'And yet they so very nearly didn't.'

That was true, thought Jenny. But Sarah didn't know the half of it.

Chapter 9

When Jenny and Pascal touched down at Rome's Fiumicino airport at the start of their Italian holiday, she almost fainted with excitement. After all of her years of dreaming, she'd finally made it to the Eternal City. Pascal, whom she'd told of her dream, had arranged the trip through a travel agent to surprise her. She'd been completely shocked, especially as they'd only been going out a couple of months and hadn't even spent a weekend away together, let alone a fortnight. Her parents had been horrified. The idea of their unmarried daughter going away with a man who wasn't her husband was something they weren't in the slightest bit happy about.

'I hope you have separate rooms,' Kay told her.

Jenny didn't bother to answer. She was twenty years old and there was nothing Kay could do this time, either to stop her or to prevent her from having the time of her life.

She could feel the heat in the air as soon as the aircraft door opened. Mixed with the smell of jet fuel was another smell too – the smell of a hot country. She'd never experienced anything like it before. On the coach from the airport to their hotel, she fanned herself vigorously with the brochures she'd kept from her school project all those years before.

Pascal had laughed at her when she showed them to him. He said that times had changed since they'd been printed and that the city would surely be a lot more modern now. Jenny didn't care. She was glad to be there even though the heat was making her feel seriously dizzy.

Their hotel was small and inexpensive. It was located on a side street a twenty-five-minute walk from the centre of the city, but it was scrupulously clean and the woman behind the polished-wood reception desk was friendly and welcoming. She told them that they were in a room on the fifth floor and indicated an old-fashioned lift with wooden doors and iron safety grilles that rattled its way up and down.

The room was small but neat, and thankfully had air conditioning and a full-length window leading to a tiny iron balcony. Jenny gasped with delight as she stepped outside and took in the vivid blue sky over the jumble of terracotta roofs of the surrounding buildings, the colourful potted plants hanging from the railings of other balconies, and the constant chatter of people in the street below. It was when she leaned over the railing to look down on the street below that dizziness overwhelmed her and Pascal had to grab her by the arm as she stumbled back into the room and sat down on the bed.

She'd recovered enough by the evening to enjoy the walk to St Peter's Square and was astonished at the sheer number of priests and nuns who thronged the nearby streets.

'I suppose it's like being at Global Headquarters for them,' remarked Pascal, which made her laugh.

After a visit to the Basilica (and the purchase of some rosary beads for her mother), Jenny fulfilled her long-held dream by having coffee in a pavement café. It was a tiny place, well away from the main tourist areas and therefore not as ruinously expensive as some of the others they'd seen. The coffee was nothing like she'd tasted before: strong, dark and aromatic, with a slightly nutty flavour. She drank it tentatively before telling Pascal that it was the best she'd ever had, and that she wanted to buy a cafetière to bring home.

He laughed and told her that she was turning Italian, and she smiled and said that she felt different here. Adventurous. Carefree. Glamorous even! She perched her sunglasses on top of her head as she spoke.

'You're certainly that,' said Pascal as he reached across the table and gently touched her face. 'And more than glamorous. You're fabulous in every way, Jenny. And I love you.'

He'd said it before, but hearing the words now made her heart swell with happiness. And with love for him too. It was easy to be in love in Rome. And it was easy to be in love with Pascal Sheehan, who might not have been as handsome as the young men who swaggered along the streets with their fashionable haircuts and even more fashionable clothes, but who made her feel cherished and secure and special. He made her feel more fabulous than ever when they went back to their inexpensive hotel and made love with the windows open and the sounds of the street as a backdrop to their passion.

The next morning she woke early and was sick in the bath. Pascal, who'd drunk an unidentified liqueur in the tiny hotel bar the night before that had effectively knocked him out almost immediately, slept through it. After she'd cleaned the bath and showered properly, she went back into the bedroom, where he was still sleeping soundly. She left him a note saying that she'd gone to breakfast, although the idea of food made her stomach churn again. Later, after he'd got up and found her sipping a glass of water in the shadiest spot on the terrace, they went exploring the city. Although the Roman ruins and architecture were wonderful, Jenny, who'd completely recovered, was more enthralled by the street life. She was entranced by the fruit and vegetable market they passed, where everything was colourful and noisy and where people squeezed the oranges and lemons and argued about the size of the peppers. (She'd never seen a red pepper before. She thought it was the most fantastic vegetable in the world.) She was enchanted by the narrow streets with cafés on every corner. She loved the musical language and she enjoyed saying *ciao* and *grazie* to people. She told Pascal that she wanted to paint it all and she said that she wished she'd gone to college and studied art instead of getting her Civil Service job.

'I was good at it in school,' she said. 'But it was never considered an option.'

'You can take night classes,' he said. 'Nothing to stop you.'

And he put his arms around her and kissed her on the mouth, much to the joy of the people on the street, who wolf-whistled and clapped their approval and made her feel like a movie star.

The next morning she woke early again. This time Pascal heard her vomiting. He was concerned about her, saying that perhaps they'd overdone it in the sultry August heat and that they'd take it easy for the rest of the day. But she said she felt much better and insisted that they take their planned trip to the Villa Borghese gardens. When she wolfed down an enormous plate of spaghetti for dinner that evening, Pascal told her that she was obviously fine and that he was glad her bug had been fleeting.

However, when he heard her throwing up the following morning, he went into the bathroom and held her hair from her face while she was sick.

'Sorry,' she said afterwards.

'For what?' he asked. 'For being pregnant and not telling me?'

She looked at him in dismay.

'For heaven's sake, Jenny,' he said. 'Morning sickness? Even I know about morning sickness.'

'I'm being sick in the morning,' she said. 'It doesn't mean it's morning sickness. It could be the food.'

'When did you start being sick?' he asked.

'Just before we came away,' she answered. 'I thought it was excitement.'

He frowned.

'Have you . . . you know . . . are you late?'

Jenny said nothing.

'Well? Are you?'

'I can't be pregnant,' she said. 'I really can't. I'm too young. It's too big a deal. And besides—'

'Besides, you told me you were on the Pill,' he interrupted her.

'I am,' she said. 'That's why I think maybe it's something else.'

She didn't tell Pascal that she was hopeless at taking the little tablet every day. That sometimes she forgot. She hadn't truly believed it would make a difference.

'Have you had a test?'

She shook her head.

'You need to see a doctor and do a test.'

'It'll ruin our holiday if we . . . if I . . .'

85

'There are more important things than holidays,' said Pascal.

'Not for me,' she told him. 'This was my dream and you made it come true. The longer I don't know if I'm pregnant or not, the longer I can hold on to it.'

He stared at her. She was so lovely, her untamed hair tumbling around her shoulders, her eyes bright with emotion. So lovely and so naive and so damn silly. And if she was pregnant, she was pregnant with his child. He couldn't abandon her. He wouldn't. Besides, he was in love with her. He'd told her so.

'I love you, Jen,' he said. 'If you're pregnant, we can sort it out.'

'We can?'

He took her in his arms and kissed her.

The next morning, despite waking just as early, she wasn't sick. She said that it must have been a bug after all. She told him he was fussing over nothing and that she wasn't going to a doctor. But Pascal was insistent. As a compromise, they went to a pharmacy where, after a long conversation in broken English mixed with a couple of Italian words from Pascal, the pharmacist sold them a home pregnancy test.

'I didn't think we'd be able to get one you could do yourself,' said Pascal as she disappeared into the bathroom of the hotel room with it.

'And I knew I didn't need to go to the doctor,' she called through the closed door as she took it out of the packet. But when she saw the result, she started to cry.

'Hello, you two!' Lucinda walked across the grass to join her sisters. 'Nice dress, Sarah.'

Sarah gave her a wry smile. 'I spent ages looking for something. And I end up with an outfit that looks better on you.'

'Nonsense,' said Lucinda.

'At least you got the one with the cap sleeves. I would've preferred that myself but they didn't have it in the shop in Galway. I don't know if that's a good thing or a bad thing. Possibly good, because I would've bought it and then we'd be absolutely identical. But bad because I could've done with those sleeves to hide my feckin' bingo wings. I should've brought a cardigan or something.'

'Your arms are fine,' said Lucinda, although mentally she was feeling slightly smug that hers were definitely more toned than her older sister's.

'Thanks,' said Sarah. 'But you don't have to be nice. You definitely look a million times better in that dress than me.'

'It suits both of you,' said Jenny.

'You're wasting your time trying to smooth the troubled waters,' said Sarah. 'Two women turning up at a party in the same dress is a total disaster.'

'However, it's not your disaster.' Lucinda grinned. 'And we'll get over it. C'mon, Jen, we should be celebrating your big day. You must be delighted.'

'It was certainly a surprise,' said Jenny.

'Jen hates surprises,' remarked Sarah.

Lucinda laughed. 'But this is a nice one. How could anyone not like a nice surprise?'

'I would've liked the opportunity to get my hair done,' confessed Jenny.

'It's fine, what are you on about?' Lucinda made a face. 'You look fab, you always do. That's what forty years with a good man will do for you.'

'Not that either of us would know,' remarked Sarah.

Jenny heard the edge to Sarah's voice. She knew that her sister had always resented the way she and Pascal had come home from Italy and sprung the entire Roman wedding and baby thing on them. But it had been the only way to do it. Nevertheless, her relationship with Sarah had never been the same afterwards. It probably hadn't been the same with Lucinda either, but at least she didn't seem to harbour a grudge in the same way that Sarah did.

We're all adults, she reminded herself. Neither of them are my responsibility. And yet she couldn't help feeling as though they still were. And that she'd let them down. She took another slug of rosé. And wondered if she was going to be completely off her head before the day was over.

Steffie could feel heat rising from the wooden veranda. It reminded her of the time she was small and her parents had brought her to a beach with a pier. She couldn't remember the beach but she did remember the warmth of the wood and the slightly tarry smell of it as she sat dangling her legs over the side. Her mother had warned her to be careful and she'd complained that they were always telling her to be careful of things and that she wasn't a baby any more. She couldn't have been more than four or five then. Neither Roisin nor Davey had been with them that day and she'd looked forward to having her parents' undivided attention. It was a pity so much of it had been of the 'watch what you're doing' variety. Afterwards, though, her dad had bought ice-cream cornets and they'd walked along the seafront with them, dipping the chocolate flake into the whipped cream and licking it. She smiled to herself. Summer memories were always good. Warm summer memories even better.

Camilla Rasmussen walked over to her.

'This is very nice,' she said. 'Very nice for your parents, and for Davey to come home.'

'He can come home any time he wants,' said Steffie. 'It's not that far, is it?'

'No, but when you are in a different country, you live to the rhythm of that country,' Camilla said. 'You are caught up in your life there and you don't think of anywhere else.'

Steffie leaned against the wooden rail that surrounded the veranda. 'I travelled abroad for my gap year, but I guess that was different to actually living abroad,' she said.

'I lived in Malaysia for a year,' said Camilla. 'It was good, but I was glad to return to Denmark.'

'You wouldn't think of living in Ireland?'

'Perhaps,' said Camilla. 'If the right opportunity presented itself.'

'And would you and Davey being together be the right opportunity?'

Jeepers, thought Steffie as the words left her mouth, I'm as bad as the aunts trying to find out if one of us wants to get married. I'd better cut back on the fizz before I say something I'll really regret. But Camilla didn't seem to be offended by the question. She smiled and said it was possible but that she didn't know what the future held.

'He's a good guy, my brother,' said Steffie.

'Yes.'

'A touch drifty, maybe,' Steffie continued. 'More like me than Roisin.'

'Drifty?'

'Roisin is the organised one in our family,' Steffie explained. 'Me and Davey allow our lives to flow along and fall in with whatever happens.'

Camilla nodded. 'But Davey is changing, I think.'

'Do you?'

'He is good at his job and is doing well in his career.'

'And with you?' asked Steffie. 'Is he doing well with you?'

Camilla nodded. 'I think, at least for the moment, we are good together,' she replied.

It was hardly a ringing endorsement, thought Steffie as she left Camilla to fill her glass with something non-alcoholic. And not exactly encouraging for Davey's prospects.

Paul was rummaging in the drinks cupboard to see if Jenny and Pascal had another bottle of rum when Summer came into the kitchen carrying some empty glasses.

'It's my fault,' she said when he told her there was none left. 'I shouldn't have asked for a mojito in the first place.'

'You weren't to know.' Paul couldn't be angry with her when she looked so apologetic. 'And from what I hear, they were a great success.'

'Yes, but I think that your wife is pissed off at me,' confessed Summer. 'She wanted everyone to be drinking wine.'

'There is rather a lot of it,' he said. 'There's a lot of sparkling rosé too.'

'We could make Bellinis with that,' suggested Summer. 'What else is in that cupboard?'

'Tequila,' said Paul. 'Vodka. And brandy.'

'You don't want to make anything with brandy. Not in the middle of the afternoon,' Summer said. 'Is there any Cointreau? We could do margaritas. Well, if there's more lime juice, that is.' She looked enquiringly at him. 'Or perhaps I should butt out?'

'Cocktails are fun and the mojitos were great,' said Paul. 'We should've thought of it ourselves.' He took a bottle of Cointreau from the cupboard. 'How d'you make a margarita?'

'Easy peasy,' said Summer. She rinsed a glass and then sliced one of the limes that Roisin had brought to add to the jugs of water for the guests who asked for it. 'This is the version we do in the bar,' she said as she mixed it and then handed it to him. 'I can make it stronger.'

'It's pretty good the way it is,' said Paul when he tasted it.

'I could do with a proper cocktail shaker,' Summer said.

'I bet Jenny and Pascal have one somewhere.' Paul started rummaging in the cupboard again.

'What are you doing?'

Neither of them had noticed Roisin walking into the room.

'Ow!' Paul yelped as he banged his head on the cupboard door. He turned slowly, rubbing his temple. 'Hi, sweetheart. I was looking for a cocktail shaker.'

'For heaven's sake! There's to be no more cocktails.' Roisin looked angrily at him. 'This isn't an episode of *Mad Men*. It's a garden party. With wine and beer. Nobody is supposed to be having hard liquor.'

Summer laughed.

'Excuse me?' Roisin glared at her. 'You find something funny?'

'Hard liquor,' said Summer. 'I've never heard someone call a margarita hard liquor before.'

'It doesn't matter what I call it,' said Roisin. 'Cocktail hour is over. It's wine, beer or water from now on.'

'OK. OK,' said Paul. 'Sorry.'

'Well I'll take this with me before the ban comes into force.' Summer picked up the margarita and disappeared through the doors to the garden.

Roisin continued to glare, this time at Paul.

'What?' he asked defensively.

'She gatecrashed this party and you're encouraging her to get the guests totally legless!' cried Roisin. 'For God's sake, Paul. What d'you think you're at?'

'She didn't gatecrash. Carl brought her. And they're not that strong, those cocktails.'

'Are you mad?' demanded Roisin. 'Aunt Moya is half cut already. Bobby and Tom are guzzling them like there's no tomorrow. Alivia is posing in the garden with hers.'

'So what?' Paul smiled at her. 'It's a party. Lighten up.'

'I'm in charge,' Roisin said. 'And I'm telling you that I don't want the guests on the floor before we've cut the cake and made proper speeches and everything. You did remember to bring the gift, didn't you?'

Roisin planned to give her parents a crystal bowl with an inscription after they cut the cake.

'Of course I did,' said Paul.

'Well then,' said Roisin. 'I want you to be sober enough to hand it over at the right time.'

'I've only had a couple,' protested Paul.

Roisin said nothing.

'OK, OK. I'll switch to water for a while.'

Roisin sighed as she rubbed the back of her neck. 'I'm sorry,' she said. 'I didn't mean to get stroppy. But I've worked hard to make this a nice day and I don't want it ruined by the actions of that . . . well, whatever she is.'

'She's just a kid,' said Paul. 'She's harmless.'

'Oh sweetheart, if you think that . . .' Roisin shook her head slowly and left the room.

Colette Mullens arrived late to the party. She hadn't wanted to come in the first place. She had no interest in family gatherings, and although she liked her aunt and uncle, she didn't think that her being there would make the slightest difference to them. But her mother, Sarah, had nagged and nagged at her, telling her that Roisin and Steffie had gone to a lot of trouble to get as many people as possible to celebrate with their parents, and that Colette should remember that Jenny and Pascal had had her entire family stay with them one summer and that she should show her gratitude by turning up.

Colette remembered the summer – a particularly wet and miserable one, when she was about twelve, which had confined them to the house a lot of the time and probably driven Jenny mad. It had been the year that her parents had split up. But instead of talking to them about it like normal people, Sarah had packed Carl, Colette and their two younger brothers off to Aranbeg so that she and James could . . . well, what? Colette wondered. She'd never figured that out. She didn't know if her father had left the day after they'd gone or if he'd stayed at home for a while afterwards. She didn't know if her parents had tried to work at their marriage without the stress of four children around the place. All she knew was that her mum rang every night and ordered them to have a good time. Colette didn't know how she was supposed to have a good time when she was stuck in the middle of nowhere with her three brothers, plus Steffie, who was the baby of the family, and Roisin, by then too wrapped up in her own life to notice her. Despite the fact that Aunt Jenny tried to cheer her up with visits to the cinema and offers to teach her to paint, Colette spent most of the summer in her bedroom reading Sweet Valley High books, pouring her heart out into her diary and wishing she lived in California.

It was a long time since she'd seen Roisin or Steffie. Or Davey. Davey had been the only one of Jenny and Pascal's children who'd bothered with her while she was at Aranbeg, mainly because he'd got a motor scooter and was always looking to take people places. So every time she wanted to go to Wexford to buy another book, Davey offered to take her. She'd felt quite grown up putting on her helmet and climbing on the back of the scooter behind him. And she'd enjoyed whizzing along the country lanes, her arms tightly around his waist.

Of course Davey was living abroad now, like so many people. Roisin, as the oldest of them, tended to ignore her completely. And Steffie – well, she always felt a little uncomfortable with Steffie, because she'd pushed her cousin out of an apple tree that summer and Steffie had broken her arm. They'd both got into terrible trouble over it. Although they kept in occasional contact through social media, Colette wasn't sure that Steffie had truly forgiven her.

As it was over an hour since the party had been due to start, and her aunt and uncle had undoubtedly been surprised by now, Colette didn't bother parking her Hyundai Santa Fe in the GAA grounds as requested on the invitation, but simply drove up to the house and left it outside the front door. She checked her appearance in the rear-view mirror. Her hair, raven black with a gold streak at the front, was held in a high quiff by industrial quantities of spray. Her eyeshadow was smoky and dramatic and her lips (her best feature, she thought, soft and pouty) were glossy and red. She leaned down and changed from her flat driving shoes into a pair of sparkly gold slingbacks before opening the car door and hopping on to the driveway. She was tugging her yellow and black striped dress into place when another car, driven far too fast, slid to a halt on the gravel beside her. The driver emerged and Colette opened her mouth, ready to complain about the dangers of speeding. But she didn't. She looked at the driver in surprise.

'Hello, Bernice,' she said.

Chapter 10

Steffie had abandoned the veranda to sit in the shade of an apple tree. She adjusted the purple comb that was holding up her hair, and wriggled her toes in the slightly too long grass as she sipped the glass of cranberry juice she'd opted for in the place of more fizzy rosé. Leaning back against the tree trunk, she saw Roisin stalk out of the house and stand on the veranda overlooking the garden. She hoped she wasn't looking for her to do anything. She was feeling nicely chilled from the rosé and not inclined to move from the shade. She wished that Roisin knew how to chill out too, but it was one skill she doubted her sister would ever possess.

If Steve had come to the party, they'd be having a laugh together now at Roisin's unstoppable energy. Having a laugh was Steve's speciality. He didn't take life or himself too seriously. Which made it all the more irritating that he'd decided to be serious about work today. Or maybe it was just that coming to the party would have implied he was serious about her.

We're not a serious couple, she reminded herself. We don't want to be. But she couldn't help thinking that right now she'd love to have someone in her life who'd turn up at a family event even if he didn't want to, simply because he cared.

Her eyes flickered around the garden and rested on Jenny, who was in her bare feet, talking to one of the neighbours. She wondered if her mother had ever felt anxious about her relationship with Pascal, if there had been times when she'd felt that the balance of power between them was all wrong. There must have been bad days, Steffie acknowledged, but whatever they might have been, they overcame them. I bet she never kept checking her phone and wondering if Dad was going to call. Not that there were mobile phones back then, of course. But I bet Dad always called whenever he said he would.

They were lucky to have found each other, she thought, but it's more than luck that's kept them together for so long.

She found it hard to imagine herself living with someone for such a long time. She certainly couldn't imagine spending forty years of her life with Steve. In fact, right now, she couldn't even imagine spending another forty minutes with him. And what was the point of being with him at all, she wondered, if they were always going to be friends-with-benefits? Where was it leading?

Maybe I should follow Roisin's advice and start looking for The One, she thought as she idly pulled the white petals from a daisy. Or maybe I should forget about men altogether and concentrate on my work instead. So that one day I'll have a proper office in a proper office building. I might even have an assistant. And a receptionist! She thought of Liam Kinsella and how he had moved on from the overweight teenager into someone who had his very own restaurant. Not only that, she conceded, but those saturnine good looks, totally unexpected from the teenager he'd been, wouldn't have gone amiss on a celebrity chef. She should tell Alivia about him. Her cousin could even interview him on her show and put Cody's on the map.

'I was just thinking about you,' she said as Alivia herself flopped on to the grass beside her.

'You were?' Alivia ran her fingers through her dark hair and fixed her huge brown eyes on Steffie.

'Don't do that,' said Steffie.

'What?'

'Put on your caring presenter look. The one you use when you're doing one of your human interest sob stories.'

Alivia laughed. 'It gets results.'

'It creeps me out,' said Steffie.

'Not really?' Alivia frowned. 'It's meant to be empathic.'

'Yeah, but I know you,' Steffie said. 'I know it's a TV thing.'

'You wagon!' Alivia made a face at her before dissolving into laughter. 'I *am* empathic. Everyone says so.'

'Of course you are.'

'Really,' she said. 'I do honestly care about the guests. Not all of them, of course. Some are there for publicity and to flog whatever their latest thing is, but lots are good people. I want them to feel OK about being on the show and I want to highlight whatever their problem is.'

'Well whatever you do, it's working,' said Steffie. 'Your face has been all over the papers the last couple of weeks.'

'Because the new season is starting,' Alivia said. 'I'm looking forward to it. Actually,' she leaned closer, 'I was thinking it would be really cool to do a piece about couples who've been together for a long time. I know forty years is pretty good, but I bet there are a fair few golden wedding anniversaries and more out there too.'

Steffie nodded her agreement.

'But I could wangle your parents on as well,' said Alivia. 'Ask them the secret of their success.'

'Gosh, that'd be fun.' Steffie immediately forgot about Liam Kinsella and celebrity chefs. 'Although Mum doesn't really like a fuss, so she might not be too keen.'

'She's enjoying the fuss today,' Alivia said.

'Maybe,' said Steffie. 'Or maybe she's making the best of it. Well, more than that, you're right: with it being a fait accompli, she's getting into it a bit more. But it's not something she'd ever have thought of herself.'

'I definitely think I'll try to put that show together,' said Alivia. 'I bet I could persuade her to agree on the basis that it would be a serious programme about love and marriage. We could get a newly engaged couple on as well, see how long they think they'll last.'

'I'd imagine they'd be hoping for ever.' Steffie grinned. 'I don't think anyone gets engaged thinking their marriage is only going to last a couple of years.'

'You're not thinking about it yourself by any chance, are you?' asked Alivia. 'It'd be supercool to have you and your mum and dad all on the same show.'

'Not a chance,' said Steffie. 'I think I've just dumped my boyfriend.'

'Steffie!' Alivia looked around as though she might see the rejected man walking away.

'I was thinking about where I am with him and stuff and . . . well . . . all of a sudden it didn't seem as great as it had before.'

'Oh dear.'

'I asked him to come today and he ducked out of it. Not that I can totally blame him. Family things can be a nightmare for an outsider.'

'Though not for Carl's new girlfriend.' Alivia grinned as she looked across the garden. Summer was standing beside Carl, her arm around his waist.

'She's something else, isn't she?' Steffie grinned. 'And what's he like with her? I mean, Liv, I know he's not some middle-aged aul' fella with a young wan on his arm, but really and truly, she's nothing more than eye candy, is she? And I can't help thinking he should have more sense. Poor Bernice, too. She's a pet, and she thinks they're on a break, not that he's having his ego massaged by Lolita.'

'More than his ego, I bet,' said Alivia.

The two of them laughed.

'Thing is,' Alivia continued, 'if he's not going to marry Bernice, he might as well have a bit of fun.'

'And I agree with him, mostly. But thinking about Mum and Dad and their forty years together has put me into a different frame of mind.'

'So you're looking to get hitched?'

Steffie laughed. 'No. Not yet. It's made me think the complete opposite. That I should steer clear of men altogether and concentrate on developing my career. Although that'll piss Roisin off big time.'

'Why?'

'She thinks I should get married and have kids so that she's not the only one providing grandchildren for Mum and Dad.'

Alivia smiled. 'That's so Roisin, isn't it?'

'She means well, I guess.'

'Yeah, we all say that about people who do things that drive us nuts. Like my mum.'

'What's your mum doing that's driving you nuts?'

'She's on at me to move back in with her,' said Alivia. 'I'm renting an amazing apartment in Galway but she thinks it's a waste of money and I'd be better off at home. I know it's because she hates not being able to keep tabs on me every minute of every day.'

Steffie nodded sympathetically.

'It's partly because I tracked down my dad,' added Alivia. 'She sees it as a massive betrayal.'

Alivia's father had disappeared as soon as he'd heard that Lucinda was pregnant.

'But I needed to know,' said Alivia. 'And it's not like I've abandoned her for him or anything. I see him a couple of times a year, that's all. I think it's the fact that he got married and had a family of his own that bothers her as much as anything. That he married someone and had kids and it wasn't her.'

'It was thirty years ago,' Steffie said. 'Surely she's got over it by now!'

'You'd think,' agreed Alivia. 'But you know my mum. Never forgets.'

'Whereas mine would forget her own head if it wasn't screwed on,' remarked Steffie.

'Mum will be fine eventually,' said Alivia. 'But her overwhelming interest in my life is driving me mad right now. Especially as . . .' she lowered her voice, 'I have a new man in it.'

'Ooh, sounds exciting? Is it serious?'

'It's early days.' Alivia's eyes twinkled. 'But it could be. It's Dermot Falconer.'

'From *Inisfree*? The Irish-language soap?'

'The very man.'

'But he's married!' cried Steffie.

'Not for much longer,' Alivia said.

Steffie looked enquiringly at her.

'He's getting a divorce.'

'I don't want to appear less than enthusiastic for you,' said Steffie, 'but weren't he and his wife together at that music award thingy a few weeks ago?'

'It's PR,' said Alivia.

'Really? They seemed very loved-up to me.'

'He's an actor!' protested Alivia. 'He's meant to be able to look loved-up with her.'

'Sophie Fisher, isn't it?' said Steffie. 'The newsreader?'

'Yes.'

'Are they still living together?'

Alivia shook her head. 'He has a place in Galway, she's in Dublin. So not surprising it's all fallen apart.'

'I can't believe it's not in the gossip mags. I can't believe *you're* not!'

'We're keeping it totally under wraps,' said Alivia. 'Until he gets the divorce.'

'And when will that happen?'

'He's working on it,' said Alivia.

'Sure?'

'For God's sake, Steff, stop being so feckin' negative!'

'I'm not, I'm not!' she cried. 'It's just – I guess I thought they were a solid couple.'

'Nobody's a solid couple these days,' said Alivia. 'Except

102

Aunt Jenny and Uncle Pascal, obviously. It's not possible any more.'

'Oh, I hope you're wrong about that,' Steffie said. 'I'd like to think that one day . . . maybe . . .'

'I never took you for a soppy romantic,' teased Alivia.

'It's not romantic to want to find someone you'll stay with for ever,' said Steffie. 'It's practical. After all, it's expensive to extricate yourself, as Dermot will undoubtedly find out.'

'That's true.' Alivia took out her phone and began to tap out a text. 'They both have their own lives and their own careers, but she still wants money. That kind of does women and women's rights a disservice, doesn't it?'

Steffie nodded. 'I hope it all works out,' she said.

'It will.' Alivia was confident. 'And the sooner the better. I'd've loved to bring him here today, but he was doing a charity thing later this afternoon. He couldn't dump sick kids for me.' She smiled as her phone buzzed with a return text and began typing furiously again.

'You'd certainly have set tongues wagging if you'd rocked up with him on your arm. Nobody knows about him and Sophie getting divorced.'

'The tongues are busy enough wagging about Carl and Bernice,' remarked Alivia as she sent her text. 'Davey and Camilla, too. Isn't she gorgeous? I reckon he's hit the jackpot with her.'

'He thinks so too.'

Alivia grinned. 'Well, he'd want to keep an eye on her so. I've seen Uncle Charlie give her a few lascivious glances.'

'Alivia!'

'Oh, it's a hotbed here today,' said Alivia happily. 'Loads of stuff to keep us amused. But I'm sorry you've broken up with your absent boyfriend, Steff. You deserve someone nice in your life.' Her phone buzzed again and she frowned as she read the message.

'What I deserve and what I end up with are two completely different things,' said Steffie. 'Anyhow, I've my business to think about. That's far more important.'

'You don't mean that.' Alivia started to type again.

'I don't see you putting your love life ahead of your career,' Steffie said.

'Why do you think me and Dermot are keeping things under wraps? Being linked with him right now wouldn't do me any favours. But you don't have to worry about being in the spotlight. You can jump on whoever you like.'

'I need to get over my broken heart first.'

'Has the guy who doesn't even know he's been dumped yet broken your heart?' Alivia reread her text before sending it.

Steffie considered it for a moment. 'Not as much as I thought,' she admitted eventually. 'In fact, I'm sort of happy about it.'

'It takes me ages to get over a break-up,' said Alivia. 'I sit at home and watch weepies so that I have an excuse to cry.'

Steffie laughed.

'Whereas you're Miss Cool Cookie,' added Alivia.

'Not today.' Steffie drained her glass. 'I'm melting. I have to get more of this. Can I bring one back for you?'

'It's OK, I'll get some myself,' said Alivia. 'And I'd better do some mingling. That's what these occasions are all about. Talking to people who tell you what you were like as a five year old and treat you as though you still were. Oh well.

104

Once more unto the breach.' She stood up, put her phone in her bag, and walked into the crowd.

'Where's Carl?' asked Colette. 'Hasn't he come with you?'

'You didn't hear?' Bernice exhaled sharply. 'We're on a break.'

'What! Nobody tells me anything. But that's not entirely surprising. It's not like I talk to them that often. But Bernice, I think Carl is here with Mum.'

'I guess so.'

'And you've come too.'

'I was invited.'

'You were?'

'Of course I was. Before Carl and I . . . The invitation was to both of us. So I came.'

'Are you certain that's a good idea?' asked Colette.

'Just because we weren't married doesn't mean I haven't been part of this family for eight years. I think I've a right to celebrate with Pascal and Jenny.' She reached into the car and took out a bottle of Bollinger, tied with a giant ribbon. 'Besides, we're only on a break. We're still a couple. I'm not going to hide away.'

'Fair enough. And if you're here to show him what he's missing, you're doing an outstanding job,' said Colette. 'You look stunning.'

'Thank you.' Bernice smoothed back her flaming-red hair, which she'd styled into a mane of big curls. She didn't normally do curls, but she'd wanted to look different today. Not only so that Carl would see her and realise that he'd been wrong to say the things he had, but also to show confidence. Because inside, she really wasn't feeling it.

'Mind you, I wouldn't have wasted all that glamour on a family party,' added Colette. 'If I was in your situation, I would've jumped at the chance to stay away.'

Bernice smiled slightly.

'However, now that you're here, I guess we could enter the fray together.'

'All for one,' said Bernice, and linked Colette's arm.

Having greeted everyone at the surprise party she'd never wanted, Jenny had retreated to her bedroom for a few moments of calm. But finally on her own again, she realised that she wasn't feeling as calm as her outward appearance suggested.

In fact she was in turmoil. The last thing in the world she wanted this weekend was for family and friends to be gathered in Aranbeg congratulating her and Pascal on forty years of married bliss. Why on earth had Roisin decided it was a good idea when she already knew that Jenny hated surprises? Why was it that people who liked making a big deal of things, like Roisin, couldn't see that not everybody else shared their views? Why did her eldest child always think she knew better? Why was she such a meddler? Why couldn't she leave well enough alone?

Damn Roisin, she muttered. Damn her relentless optimism and wanting everyone to have a good time. But even as the thoughts formed in her head, she was reminding herself that Roisin was a loving and caring daughter and that she was lucky to have her.

But still, she thought, as she reapplied her lipstick with a shaking hand. She's left me in a very awkward position.

Chapter 11

You'd think that someone would notice she was doing it all on her own, thought Roisin, as she added more bottles of wine to the fridge and more ice to the cool box where the beer was being stored. But no, Steffie had spent the last half-hour lounging around under a tree chatting to Alivia, while Davey was busy showing off his glamorous girlfriend to the neighbours. Neither of them had bothered to check on her although they must have known that there'd be things to do. Always me, Roisin muttered to herself. Always having to take charge. Even when I left it to Steffie to set up the table and the veranda, she made a complete mess of it. Why don't they see what I see? Why do they think that a job half done is good enough? That's why Steffie's career is in the doldrums, she thought. And why Davey still hasn't made a commitment to a decent woman. She wasn't entirely convinced that Camilla was the woman for him either, despite the fact that he was parading her around the place. Roisin thought she recognised a kindred spirit in the Danish girl. Someone who liked order and organisation, who liked everything to be in its place. Someone dependable. Which made her totally hopeless for Davey.

Roisin stood at the doorway and stared down the garden. Alivia had abandoned Steffie for Bobby, a cousin on their father's side, and his partner, Tom. She was flirting happily and harmlessly with both of them and they were laughing at her moves. Honestly, thought Roisin, you'd imagine they'd be a bit more grown up. She left the house and strode down the garden to where Steffie was sitting staring into space.

'I need you to help organise the food,' she told her sister. 'I want the guests to eat before they have too much to drink. Also, I'm going to ask Dad to make another speech, because now that he's had some time to get over the surprise, he'll want to say something a bit more meaningful. And Paul will say a few words too before giving them the crystal bowl.'

'We don't need too many speeches,' said Steffie as she stood up and brushed grass from her dress. 'It gets boring.'

'People want to say things,' said Roisin. 'It's right that we give them the opportunity.'

'Maybe they don't. Maybe they just want to have fun.'

'Don't be— What the hell . . .' Her voice rose and Steffie followed her surprised look across the garden. Colette and Bernice were crossing the lawn.

'Oh-oh,' she said. 'Cat among the pigeons alert.'

'God almighty! What's she going to do when she sees the bimbo Carl has brought with him?'

'Kill him?' suggested Steffie. 'And I'm saying that quite seriously.'

'Stay here and keep an eye on things.' Roisin marched across the lawn to intercept the two new arrivals.

'Hi, Roisin,' said Colette. 'Sorry I'm late.'

'Glad you finally got here.' Roisin gave her cousin a quick

hug. 'We were wondering where you were. Bernice . . . we didn't expect to see you at all.'

'You invited me,' said Bernice.

'I know. Along with Carl. But under the circumstances . . .'

'I came to wish your mum and dad well,' said Bernice. 'They've always been very nice to me.'

'And they'll be delighted you wanted to share the day with them,' said Roisin. 'All the same . . .'

'We're on a break,' said Bernice. 'That doesn't mean that I can't be in the same place as him.'

'I know,' said Roisin. 'But the thing is, Bernice . . .' She looked around the garden. She couldn't see Carl, but Summer had joined Alivia, Tom and Bobby.

'What?' demanded Bernice. 'Am I being airbrushed out because Carl and I never got married?'

'It's not that at all,' said Roisin. 'It's . . . well . . . Carl brought someone else with him.'

Bernice paled beneath her make-up. 'He what?'

'It's clear he brought her along as a stand-in for you,' Roisin said. 'But you can see it's a little awkward.'

'Her?' Bernice's eyes widened as she followed Roisin's gaze. 'That chit of a thing?'

Colette gave her a quick hug. 'You don't have to worry, Bernice. That's rebound stuff if ever I saw it.'

'He's not meant to be rebounding,' said Bernice. 'He's meant to be on a break. Like me.'

'Men are hopeless at that,' Colette said. 'All my exes were off with other women before the tan line on my engagement finger had faded. You'd have thought they'd want to be off the hook for a while, but they don't really like it.'

'I'll fecking kill him,' said Bernice.

'I can't let you do that,' said Roisin. 'It would ruin the party.'

'OK, I won't kill him.' Bernice's eyes narrowed. 'I'll maim him for life instead.'

'Would you please do me a favour, just for today, and ignore him,' said Roisin. 'I'm sorry, Bernice. She certainly wasn't invited and I'm raging at him for bringing her, but . . .'

'Out of respect for your parents,' said Bernice. 'Not because I don't want to take a meat cleaver to him.'

'Thanks.'

'You're welcome.'

'That's sorted, then.' Roisin wasn't completely convinced that Bernice and Carl weren't going to create a scene, but she couldn't do much more about it. 'Paul is dishing out drinks on the veranda, so that's the place to go for some refreshment. We'll be serving food shortly.'

'I'll get a drink,' said Bernice. 'Coming, Colette?'

'Yes. Could do with one myself.' Colette smiled briefly at Roisin, then followed Bernice to the veranda.

'Has she got a knife in her bag?' asked Steffie when Roisin returned.

'It wouldn't surprise me!' said Roisin. 'What on earth is going through her head? If I was having a row with Paul, I sure as hell wouldn't turn up to his parents' party, even if I did want to kill him.'

'Actually you would,' said Steffie. 'Although in your case, you'd pretend that everything was fine.'

'You might have a point,' agreed Roisin. 'But that's because we're married.'

'Maybe she feels they might as well have been married,' said Steffie.

'In that case she should've dragged him up the aisle. Or given him up as a lost cause. All this faffing around is pointless. She needs to fix things, either by staying or going.'

'Not everyone sees things in black and white like you,' said Steffie. 'By the look of her, she's either trying to woo him back or show him what he's missing.'

'It's a massive makeover all right.' Roisin decided to ignore Steffie's comment about her seeing everything as black and white. She didn't. She was a realist. 'She's lost a ton of weight, too,' she added. 'Clearly having a break is foolproof in the diet department.'

'Not for me,' said Steffie. 'I usually eat my way out of misery.'

'You'd never guess,' said Roisin.

'I never get miserable enough.' She laughed before her expression changed as a low rumble in the sky above distracted both of them. 'Oh crap. That sounded like thunder, didn't it?'

Roisin glanced upwards. The sky was now a hazy blue, with banks of thick clouds on the horizon.

'It doesn't look thundery,' she said. 'And it's not forecast until tomorrow.'

'I checked it on my phone a little earlier,' Steffie told her. 'It had changed to a lightning symbol for this afternoon. Although it could've been the crack on the screen from where I dropped it.'

'Idiot,' said Roisin. 'We'd better get a move on, though. Just in case.'

* * *

The bedroom door opened, startling Jenny, who smudged her lipstick, leaving a red slash across the corner of her mouth. She reached for a tissue and wiped it away as Pascal walked into the room.

'You all right?' he asked.

'Of course.'

'I was wondering where you'd got to.'

'Not far, obviously,' she said.

He sat on the bed behind her.

'Sure everything's OK?'

She sighed, and turned to face him.

'I would be if I felt that all this was OK too,' she said, extending her arms to include the house and, Pascal assumed, the people in it.

'It doesn't matter, you know,' he said. 'It's irrelevant.'

'Roisin has gone to so much trouble,' said Jenny. 'Steffie and Davey too. It seems wrong to . . . to pretend, basically.'

'We're not pretending,' said Pascal.

'Excuse me?' Her eyes widened.

'Forty years isn't a pretence.'

'I have to tell them.' She stood up. 'I have to tell them everything.'

'Jenny!' Pascal stood up too. 'Not today. Tomorrow, maybe.'

'It's always tomorrow,' said Jenny. 'And that's my fault.'

'In later years that might have been true,' conceded Pascal. 'But earlier it was mine. Look, Jen, today is all about having a good time and celebrating. And there's no reason we can't celebrate. None whatsoever.'

'But what exactly is the celebration?' she asked.

112

'We are.' He put his arms around her and pulled her close to him. 'We are, Jenny Marshall. We're celebrating forty years of us.'

He kissed her.

She kissed him back.

He was right.

He was always right.

Steffie and Roisin had just taken the last plate of carved ham from the fridge when Jenny walked into the room. She was holding a glass of the sparkling rosé, although she didn't appear to have drunk any of it.

'Are you enjoying your party, Mum?' asked Steffie when she saw her mother at the doorway.

'I'm about to enjoy the bubbly that your dad poured for me,' said Jenny.

Roisin beamed at her. 'You deserve it.'

'Do I?' asked Jenny.

'Of course. You're celebrating.'

Jenny swallowed a mouthful of rosé.

'Are you all right, Mum?' There was a hint of concern in Steffie's voice. She thought that Jenny sounded brittle and anxious.

'Of course,' said her mother. 'I'm still in shock, that's all.'

'Good,' said Roisin. 'We wanted to shock you. In a nice way, of course.'

'You're very thoughtful,' Jenny said. 'Both of you.'

'And me.' Davey walked in the door. 'I'm hearing nice things being said about the Sheehan siblings and I want my due respect.'

Roisin laughed. 'Respect for turning up?' she asked.

'And why not?' Davey gave her a playful punch on her arm and Roisin yelped.

'You have horribly bony fingers, Davey Sheehan,' she said. 'You always did have. That hurt.'

'Cry baby,' Dave teased.

Jenny smiled at them. She knew they were joking around for her benefit, but it was nice to see all the same. It didn't matter that her children were adults now. Whenever they were together she saw them as she'd aways seen them. Her babies. She released a slow breath.

'So we'll tell everyone to come and eat, then cut your cake afterwards,' said Steffie.

'Cake?' Jenny blanched.

'Of course there's cake!' cried Roisin. 'It'll be just like your wedding. Or maybe not, because you didn't get to do the whole cake thing in Rome, did you. Or the speeches or anything. So it's nice to do it now, don't you think?'

Jenny was prevented from replying by a roll of thunder, which was clearly audible even over the music from the iPod in the speaker.

'Please let it not rain,' begged Roisin out loud. 'It isn't supposed to rain today.'

'Even if it does, it'll be dry on the veranda,' said Steffie. 'And it's not cold or anything.'

'This is a garden party, not a veranda party,' wailed Roisin.

'That thunder was miles away,' Davey assured her. 'It mightn't make it here at all.'

Jenny glanced towards the increasingly cloudy sky.

'You should be good at weather forecasting, given that you're into all that climate control stuff,' Roisin said to Davey. 'What do you think?'

'Um, there's a big difference between making wind turbines and weather forecasting,' he told her.

'Same ballpark,' said Roisin.

'Not.'

'I thought that's how you met the gorgeous Camilla,' Roisin said. 'Weather stuff.'

'At a conference,' said Davey.

'And you love her madly,' said Steffie.

Jenny was enjoying their banter but didn't speak herself.

'We're good,' Davey said, even though Steffie knew it was more than that.

'Good?' Roisin snorted. 'What does that mean, Davey Sheehan?'

'Taking it easy.' He hadn't minded saying something to Steffie, but he didn't want Roisin to know about the engagement ring in his pocket. She'd only start trying to stage-manage his proposal. 'No pressure.'

'You too?' Roisin shook her head. 'You and Steffie are quite a pair. There's some excuse for her – she's still in her twenties – but you're nearly forty. Practically middle-aged. The time for taking it easy has passed you by.'

Steffie chuckled at Davey's offended expression.

'It's true. Tell them, Mum.' Roisin put her hands on her hips. 'These days everyone thinks they have all the time in the world to do what they want. But it's not that straightforward. Women leave it late to have their children and then find out they can't get pregnant. Men can't keep up with their kids because they're the wrong side of forty.'

'Roisin has a point,' said Jenny. 'You think you can have it all, when you want it, but you can't. Life isn't like that, no matter what the self-help books and the advertising companies want you to believe.' She set her empty glass on the table, surprised that she'd finished the rosé without noticing.

'I don't believe I can have it all,' said Steffie. 'But I have what I want right now.' If you discount the fact that I'm going to break up with Steve and I haven't heard anything about my design bid yet, she added to herself.

'So do I,' said Davey. He went to pat the box in the pocket of his jacket and then remembered that he'd finally taken it off and hung it in the hallway. Which possibly wasn't the brightest thing to have done, he supposed. But he'd been sweltering and the time wasn't right to propose to Camilla yet. That would be later, when everyone was chilled after a pleasant day. Which it had been so far.

'Does it seem like forty years?' Steffie asked her mother.

Jenny shook her head. 'My entire life seems to have passed in the blink of an eye,' she said.

'Exactly my point.' Roisin looked pleased with herself.

'I bet it was amazing getting married in Rome,' Steffie said. 'You looked so happy and so pretty in your dress. It was really cute and simple.'

'Simple was all I could afford,' said Jenny.

'I prefer the pic of you on your honeymoon in Sorrento,' Roisin remarked. 'The one on the boat. You look very glamorous in that one.'

Jenny had been feeling glamorous. And forgetting how things really were. But then, she told herself, I'm good at that, I do it all the time.

'It's a pity they're all so fuzzy,' observed Steffie.

'Your iPhone takes better photos than the camera we had back then,' Jenny said.

116

And just as well Steve Jobs had only started tinkering in his garage in the seventies, she thought, as she refilled her glass. If there had been iPhones and internet and streaming and everything in 1975, things would have been very, very different.

After Rome, Sorrento had been glorious. The sea breeze was a welcome relief from the stifling heat of the city and Jenny had felt fresh and energised again. Pascal asked her every morning if she felt OK and she told him that she was fine and that it mustn't have been proper morning sickness, because if it had been surely it would've lasted much longer. In fact, she said, she was sure it really had been nothing more than a bug. The test could have been wrong. After all, she didn't feel pregnant. She didn't feel anything.

Jenny wasn't all that clued about pregnancy. Her mother had given her a booklet about it when she first started having periods, and there had been two lessons on The Female Body in her convent school, but neither had gone into any great detail about what was in store. The lessons had been given by Sister Genevieve, the youngest and prettiest of the nuns, but she'd blushed bright red every time she'd said the word vagina, and the class of girls had blushed along with her.

Pascal suggested that she take another test. It was harder to find a home kit in Sorrento than it had been in Rome, but when she did and she took the test, it confirmed her pregnancy. Which was just as well, she thought, given all the trouble they'd gone to in Rome a few days earlier.

Every morning she looked at her stomach, trying to assess how much it had grown. She thought she had a slight bump, but she was still significantly slimmer than most of the other people on holiday. So she was perfectly happy to lie on a sunbed by the pool of the Villa Maritimo in her skimpy bikini and devour the Harold Robbins book she'd bought at the airport. She'd never read a blockbuster before and she was enthralled by the glamour and sex on the pages in front of her. If she'd read it before sleeping with Pascal for the first time, she thought, she'd have been much more adventurous in bed. Although she supposed in the end she'd been adventurous enough.

It wasn't all lying around – with her Celtic complexion Jenny couldn't take too much sun, even under the biggest umbrella the Villa Maritimo could provide, and Pascal was happy to explore the town and surrounding area. They also took the ferry to Capri, where they visited the Certosa di San Giacomo and the Grotta Azzura before finding a pavement café where they ate ice cream and drank espressos. (Both of them developed a lifelong addiction to Italian coffee after their stay.) They only had a few photos left on their film roll, and they were keeping them for a visit to Pompeii, but on the return journey Pascal took one of her as she channelled her inner Sophia Loren and Gina Lollobrigida by standing at the handrail of the ferry, a large sunhat on her head and equally large sunglasses on her face.

In the evenings they ate in the least expensive of the restaurants near their hotel, but it was still a big thrill to sit at a table in the night air and be waited on. That was another new experience for Jenny. Eating out in Dublin usually meant going to some kind of burger bar, because most of the other restaurants were out of her price range. Italy was a different life and she wanted to make the most of it. Because after her baby was born, she knew that things would change for ever.

She said this to Pascal, who agreed that there would be changes but who also reminded her that he was ready for those changes. He promised her that he'd be a good father to their child. He told her that she meant more to him than anyone in the world, and on their last night in Sorrento he didn't wave away the flower sellers who went from table to table in the restaurants trying to get people to buy overpriced roses, but bought one for her and told her to keep it for ever.

Jenny wasn't a sentimental person. She didn't believe in keepsakes. But she'd kept the rose.

Chapter 12

'Sweet Mother of God,' muttered Carl. 'I don't effing believe it.'

'What don't you believe?' Summer leaned her head on his shoulder.

'Bernice,' said Carl. 'Over there.'

'Your ex?' She straightened up, her eyes wide. 'Your ex has shown up?'

'I don't know why. She wasn't invited.'

'Neither was I.' Summer grinned and kissed him.

'Don't,' said Carl. 'Not while . . . not . . .'

'You don't want her to know that you're with me now?' Summer looked archly at him.

'It's not that,' said Carl. 'I need to keep an eye on her. See what she's up to.'

He knew that Bernice had seen him. She had to have. She was walking in his direction. But then just as he thought she was going to come up to him, she turned away and started talking to Alivia. He released his breath slowly.

'D'you think she's here to create a scene?' asked Summer.

'I don't know.'

'Well if she wants a fight . . .'

'God almighty, Summer, you're not going to fight with her.' Carl was horrified.

Summer giggled. 'Of course not. What d'you think I am? Anyway, what would I have to fight about? She's the ex. Mind you,' she added, her voice hardening a little, 'she's very attractive.'

'She doesn't normally look like that,' said Carl. 'I've never seen that hairstyle on her before.'

'Hmm.' Summer frowned. 'Maybe she's here to make a play for you. Maybe I'll have to fight her after all.'

'A play for me?'

'You don't have to sound so pleased with yourself,' said Summer. 'Just because she might want to get you back doesn't mean you're totally God's gift.'

Carl beamed at her. 'I love the way you say what you think.'

'It's the only way,' Summer told him. 'I hate people who make things complicated. Why say one thing and mean something else. Life's too short.'

'Indeed it is.' He put his arms around her slender waist and pulled her towards him. Then he kissed her on the mouth.

He didn't care if Bernice saw them or not.

As soon as Steffie and Roisin started loading paper plates with food, the guests began to drift towards the house, and it wasn't long before there was a queue of people waiting for the cold meats and salads. Jenny had wanted to help but the two girls shooed her out of the kitchen with a couple of plates piled high and told her to find Pascal and feed him.

'I'm glad I don't work in a canteen,' Steffie told Roisin when they'd eventually finished serving. 'This is exhausting.'

'I know. We should've got someone in to do it for us,' said Roisin. 'I don't feel I'm having much of a good time myself. I'm too stressed about food and drink and whether people are enjoying themselves.'

'And if some kind of fight is going to break out between Bernice and Carl,' added Steffie. 'Or Bernice and Summer. Or Bernice and Summer and—'

'OK, OK, I get the point.' Roisin groaned. 'Why does there always have to be some kind of potential disaster at every damn party this family has?'

'That's why I don't like them,' said Steffie. 'Alcohol mixed with people who normally can't stand each other is an explosive combination.'

'Are you saying today was a bad idea?' Roisin's voice was dangerously even.

'No,' lied Steffie. 'But you never know what crazy things people will do to mess up the day. And when you're the one in charge of the party, you feel responsible.'

'I know, I know. I'm always the one who's responsible for everything,' said Roisin. 'I won't let anything bad happen.'

'You're not entirely resp—' began Steffie and then broke off as Daisy walked into the kitchen and Roisin gasped in dismay at her daughter's outfit.

'Daisy Carmichael, what in the name of all that's holy is that you're wearing?' she demanded.

'My top and shorts,' said Daisy.

Roisin looked at the cropped top, which left an expanse of bare flesh from beneath Daisy's chest to the top of her low-cut denim shorts.

'You weren't wearing it when you left the house.'

'I was,' said Daisy.

'I wouldn't have let you out looking like that,' said Roisin.

'I had my other T-shirt over it,' said Daisy. 'But it's so hot I took it off.'

'You can put it right back on again,' said Roisin.

'Mum!'

'That's not a good look,' said Roisin.

'It's what everyone's wearing this summer,' protested Daisy. 'And it's not like I'm out on the streets. It's all family and friends here.'

'She has a point,' Steffie said and received a grateful smile from her niece but a daggered glare from Roisin.

'Anyway, all the men are either too old or too young to appreciate me.' Daisy took a plate and marched out of the kitchen.

Steffie couldn't help laughing

'Just wait,' said Roisin grimly. 'Wait till you have your own.'

'I think you've made a very good case against it there,' said Steffie.

'Would you seriously not have kids?'

Now that everyone had taken their food outside, Roisin helped herself to the remnants of the ham and then poured white wine into a fresh glass.

'I told you, they're not on my radar yet.'

'Don't come crying to me when you have to have IVF because you're too old to conceive.'

'For crying out loud, Roisin. Get a grip. I'm twenty-seven, not fifty-seven.'

'We had loads of cousins when we were small. It was great. My kids should have them too.'

'It'll be a bit late for them by the time I get around to it.' Steffie looked at her in amusement. 'Maybe Davey and Camilla are a better bet.'

'Maybe they are,' said Roisin and added more wine to her glass so that it was almost overflowing.

Bernice had told herself over and over again that she didn't have an ulterior motive in coming to Jenny and Pascal's party, although there were a number she could have chosen from if she'd sat down and thought about it for long enough. Perhaps the most important was that she wanted Carl to see her looking good. Not because she wanted to show him what he was missing, but because she wanted him to know that no matter what they decided, she was able to look after herself.

She hadn't expected him to be with somebody else. When she saw him kiss that girl, Summer, in front of her, she'd wanted to punch him in the head. She knew he'd only kissed her like that because she could see them. It was pathetic. Or at least it would have been if it hadn't had the effect he'd undoubtedly wanted. Not the part about her wanting to punch him in the head, but the very real surge of jealousy she'd felt at the sight of another woman acting that way with a man who until recently had been hers. She'd been shaking with anger and humiliation as she'd turned away and she'd thought then of taking the neatly folded oblong of paper out of her handbag and shoving it at him. But she hadn't. She'd stood and talked to Alivia as though everything was perfectly normal, as though none of it mattered.

But Alivia had known it mattered and had told her that Carl was making a holy show of himself and that it was all about him putting on an act and that Bernice wasn't to worry about it at all. Bernice thought Alivia was probably right. But it didn't make it any easier. She wished now she hadn't come. She supposed everyone else wished she hadn't come either. Which was unfair. She was the one who'd made sure that, as a couple, she and Carl had kept in touch with the family: Carl's two brothers who'd emigrated and lived in the States; Colette, even though she was mad as a brush; the cousins, because they'd always been a close family. She'd been the one to buy the Christmas cards and the birthday cards and congratulate people on various achievements and he'd got the kudos too because his name was on everything. And yet she was the outsider now, while Summer (who in God's name was called Summer!) was the girlfriend and somehow had more right to be there than her.

She helped herself to a glass of sparkling water even though she desperately wanted to grab a bottle of wine and drink the lot. But she had to drive home later and it would cap a really horrible day if she was too drunk to get behind the wheel. In any event, she didn't want her actions to be influenced by alcohol.

She didn't want to do something she'd regret.

Jenny didn't want to do anything she'd regret either. But she knew she couldn't let the day go by without saying something. The question was, how much did she want to say? And who did she want to say it to? She pressed her fingers to her forehead as she heard another rumble of thunder in the distance. Like Roisin, she hoped the weather would hold. But she couldn't help feeling as though a storm was breaking around her already.

Chapter 13

There had been a storm on their last day in Italy. The morning was warm and sultry and by the afternoon the heavy air seemed to be physically pressing down on them. Jenny and Pascal had gone to their room in the Villa Maritimo and were lying side by side on the bed when an enormous fork of lightning split the sky and lit up the room. The following crash of thunder was so intense that the entire building seemed to shake.

Jenny sat upright on the bed and looked out of the narrow window as another lightning bolt snaked its way from the sky to the sea.

'Oh my God,' she said. 'I've never seen anything like that before.'

She was used to the more familiar sheet lightning of Dublin, where the sky was momentarily bright but it was hard to locate any specific source for the light. What she was seeing now, as the lightning continued to rip the sky, was like something out of a horror movie.

Pascal got up and stood on the balcony.

'Is it safe?' asked Jenny.

'In what way?' He glanced around.

'That railing is made of metal.'

Pascal laughed. 'The lightning is a few miles away,' he said. 'I think I'm OK.'

'Good,' said Jenny. 'I don't want to think my child would grow up without a father.'

'That's not going to happen. C'mere.' Pascal held out his hand and she slid off the bed and stood beside him.

'I'm afraid of storms,' she admitted.

'Why?'

'When we were small, Dad used to say that a storm was God being angry with us. That he was throwing furniture around the place. I always imagined a wardrobe or something falling from the sky and hitting me on the head.'

Pascal laughed again. 'But you're grown up now. You don't think that any more.'

'No, but at the back of my mind . . .' She shrugged in embarrassment. 'I know it's daft. But let's face it, I'm pregnant and what we did here, what we did in Rome – it's a sin, it has to be.'

'Don't be silly, Jen,' said Pascal. 'And regardless, you're hardly likely to be hit by a celestial wardrobe. What sort of clothes did you imagine God had in there? Shirts and ties?'

'Oh, I know it's nonsense,' she told him. 'I do realise that. It's just . . . when you're brought up to be afraid of God, you can't help feeling a bit worried even if you think He should understand.'

'We'll be fine,' said Pascal. 'We're going home tomorrow as Mr and Mrs Sheehan. What's to worry about?'

Jenny looked at him, a doubtful expression on her face.

'There's nothing to worry about at all,' he said. 'I promise.'

He kissed her on the lips. Then he led her back to the bed, where they made love to the soundtrack of the rolling thunder followed by a relentless downpour of rain.

Jenny was remembering it now as she walked into the house. She recalled the strength of Pascal's arms around her and the weight of his body on hers. She'd been a little afraid then, for the baby. She knew it was OK to make love when you were pregnant, but she was very aware of the fact that there was another person growing inside her and she didn't want to disturb the baby in any way. She was almost overcome by the responsibility, thinking that she wasn't adequately prepared for it, worried that she'd make a terrible mess of it. But Pascal had been a calm and soothing influence the whole time. He'd told her she'd be fine. That she'd be a fantastic mother. And that he'd do his best to be an equally fantastic father. Their child would be the luckiest boy or girl in Ireland.

Seeing Roisin in the kitchen, clearing the debris from the table into a black refuse sack, Jenny could hardly believe how terrified she'd once been both of her and for her. It was hard to believe too that Roisin's conception had been the catalyst for the route her life had taken. That because of Roisin, she and Pascal had become a family when the truth was, she'd had other plans. She stood and watched her daughter until Roisin looked up and asked if she was going to stand there watching, or if she was going to lend a hand.

'I thought it was my party,' said Jenny. 'I thought I wasn't allowed to lend a hand.'

'Just this once,' said Roisin. 'You can hold the refuse sack while I put the last of these bits into it.'

Jenny did as she was asked. She's turned out fine, she thought, as Roisin added the final bit of rubbish to the sack. She's where she wants to be. If only my other two children were as settled, I'd be happy. She laughed at herself. Being settled had never been a priority for her; it had happened without her thinking about it. She shouldn't wish it on her children. And yet, she thought, there was a comfort in having accepted your place in the world, a tranquillity in knowing that you were content with how things had turned out. It was a tranquillity she'd allowed herself over the last few years even though, she reminded herself now, she hadn't yet earned it.

'It's getting awfully dark.' Roisin's words jolted her back to the kitchen. 'I think the storm might reach us after all. Bugger.'

'That would be a pity,' said Jenny. 'It's been such a sunny day so far.'

Nevertheless, many of the guests were drifting to the veranda in case it rained.

'It's as well I got those extra lanterns; light them, Davey, will you?' Roisin looked at her brother as he walked into the kitchen.

Davey nodded, and the glow of the lights brought most of the guests to the veranda. It was welcoming and cosy, but there were too many people to comfortably fit and so some of them moved into the house.

'As everyone is here, this might be a good time to cut the cake,' Roisin suggested to Jenny.

'Do we really have to do that?'

'Of course you do.' Roisin looked horrified. 'It's traditional.

And Paul has a speech.' She didn't say anything about the crystal bowl. That was meant to be another surprise.

'Sweetheart, it's been a lovely party, but cutting a cake isn't necessarily—'

'It's the most important part of the day,' Roisin interrupted her.

'I'd rather you simply cut it and handed it around,' said Jenny.

'Oh Mum, don't be silly. You have to do it properly. We want to be able to cheer about you and Dad and the longest marriage in the whole family. Maybe even in Wexford if you think about it.'

Jenny didn't say anything.

'So that's sorted,' said Roisin. 'I'll get everyone up here for the big event.'

Jenny stood in the kitchen and watched her daughter march through the garden. Roisin meant well, but Jenny wished she didn't always have a plan. That she'd listen to other people sometimes.

She opened the door to the fridge and saw the celebratory chocolate cake with the ruby-red frosting.

She felt sick.

Roisin was struggling to round up the guests who'd chosen to remain in the garden while the thunder and lightning, now virtually overhead, crashed and flashed around them. These included her own children, and as she saw Poppy climbing one of the apple trees, she hurried towards her.

'Get down this instant,' she ordered. 'It's dangerous.'

'I'm a good climber,' protested Poppy. 'I won't fall.'

130

'I'm not thinking of you falling,' said Roisin. 'I'm thinking of you being hit by lightning.'

'I won't be hit by lightning,' protested Poppy as she climbed higher.

'Ooh, Mum, would that kill her?' Dougie's voice was full of ghoulish anticipation.

'Yes, it probably would. You too, Dougie. Into the house and away from the trees. Poppy, get down this instant.'

Poppy was protesting vehemently when more lightning split the sky. There was a loud bang, followed by an equally loud crack and the smell of burning. For a moment Roisin thought that the apple tree – despite her actual belief that it was pretty safe – really had been hit. But it was still standing, although Poppy, with an almighty shriek, had fallen from the branch and landed with a thud at her feet.

There was a moment's silence in which Roisin felt her heart skip multiple beats, and then Poppy started to cry. Roisin heaved a sigh of relief as she bent down to her daughter. At least when they were crying they were conscious.

'My head hurts,' moaned Poppy. 'And my arm. And my leg.'

'Don't move,' said Roisin. 'Stay still.'

As she spoke, there was another shriek, this time from Dougie, as flames erupted from the massive chestnut tree in the field adjoining the house.

'Oh my God!' Roisin couldn't believe what was happening. 'Fire! Fire!'

The male guests raced down the garden, followed by all of the children, ignoring Roisin's entreaties to stay where they were, as well as some of the women who'd realised that Poppy was hurt.

'Was she hit? Is she burnt?' cried Paul, who'd been around the front of the house so that he could puff another cigar in peace but who'd instinctively known that the shrieks from the garden were from one of his children.

'No, but she fell. I'll look after Poppy. You do something about the fire. We need to stop it before it takes hold.'

'Do you have a fire extinguisher in the kitchen?' Paul turned to Pascal, who'd made it from the house to the end of the garden with a speed that belied his years.

'We have one of those fire blankets,' Pascal replied. 'I'm not sure how much good that'll do, but I'll go check.'

'I'll go,' said Carl. 'You stay here, Pascal.'

'Do you want to try to sit up now, sweetheart?' Roisin asked Poppy, who whimpered and said that everything hurt.

'Let me.' Bernice made her way through the cluster of people, whose attention was divided between Poppy and the burning chestnut tree. Roisin looked at her in relief. She'd completely forgotten that Bernice was a nurse.

'Let's have a look at you, honey,' said Bernice.

'Fire!' yelled Dougie. 'More fire.'

'Oh shit!' cried Roisin as the flames from the chestnut tree fanned towards the garden. 'Everyone who doesn't need to be here, get back to the house. Bernice, we have to move Poppy.'

'In a minute.' Bernice's voice was calm and reassuring.

At that moment Davey returned carrying a large bucket full of water, Carl following behind with the fire blanket. Davey threw the water at the chestnut tree. The fire sizzled for a moment and the smoke turned black, but there were still some yellow flames licking the base of the tree.

Carl had begun to edge closer with the fire blanket when

the rain started. It fell from the sky in a heavy downpour, soaking everything and effectively putting out the fire for them.

'Well thank God for that,' said Tom, who'd already called the fire brigade and now began to dial again to cancel the emergency.

'Talk about luck,' said Paul. 'It would've been a challenge to put it out ourselves.'

'We dodged a bullet there,' agreed Pascal as he turned towards his daughter and granddaughter. 'How's Poppy?'

'I think she's OK,' replied Bernice as she pushed her wet hair out of her eyes. 'Nothing broken as far as I can see, although she's got a few bruises and I think she's damaged her wrist a little. I don't think there's internal bleeding or anything as serious as that, but she should really go to hospital to be checked out.'

'Should I call an ambulance?' asked Roisin.

'An ambulance.' Poppy sounded both thrilled and slightly scared.

'I don't think—' began Bernice when Paul interrupted to say that it'd be much quicker if he drove his daughter to the hospital himself.

'Don't be daft, you've been drinking. I don't want you ending up in a ditch with her.' Roisin gave him an irritated glance.

'I'll bring her,' said Davey.

'What is it with you guys?' demanded Roisin. 'You've been drinking too. I'm not letting her in a car with anyone who's had alcohol.'

'I'm sure I'd be OK,' said Pascal. 'I've only had a glass of the fizzy stuff and a pint.'

'I'll do the driving.' Bernice spoke firmly. 'I've been drinking sparkling water and it's probably a good idea for me to be with her in any case. Plus my car is in the driveway so we wouldn't waste time collecting it from the GAA car park.'

'Oh Bernice, would you? That'd be great.' Roisin looked at her in relief. 'I'll grab my bag and come with you.'

Paul scooped his daughter into his arms and walked back to the house. By now, everyone who'd been in the garden, including Poppy, was soaked and bedraggled as the rain continued its relentless downpour.

'Oh, you poor pet!' cried Jenny as Paul walked into the house with her. 'Are you all right?'

'I'm going to hospital.' There was a touch of pride in Poppy's voice. 'Bernice is going to bring me. It's in case I'm bleeding internally.'

'Poppy!' Jenny looked anxiously at Pascal and then Bernice.

'I think she's fine,' said Bernice. 'But we'll let A and E have the last word.'

'Thank you so much,' said Jenny.

'You're welcome.'

'Accident and Emergency?' Breege Behan grimaced. 'You could be there all night.'

'Hopefully not,' said Roisin.

'You need to dry off before you go anywhere,' Jenny said. 'I'll get towels for everyone who's wet through. And if any of you need a change of clothes, we can muster up something from the wardrobes.'

'We'll go now,' said Roisin. 'I'll take a towel with me.'

'Are you sure?' Jenny looked at her daughter and at Bernice.

'Yes.' Roisin nodded.

134

'Come on then,' said Bernice as she led the way to her Volkswagen. Roisin got into the back seat with Poppy and Bernice set off.

'I'll put the kettle on,' said Steffie when they were out of sight.

'A few hot whiskeys might be a good idea,' suggested Davey.

'Now you're talking,' said Paul.

'I'll help you.' Summer smiled at him while Jenny handed around towels and told the guests who'd been in the garden that she'd find them something to change into. The men insisted that they were fine and didn't need to change at all, but as most of the women were soaked to the skin and shivering, she insisted they needed dry clothes.

'I have jogging bottoms and fleeces upstairs,' she told them. 'You can come and try them on.'

'There are some T-shirts in my wardrobe too,' added Steffie.

Jenny led the way upstairs, the sodden guests following her. Is it wrong, she thought, to be relieved that the cake cutting and speeches have been disrupted? And is it wrong to hope that they'll have been forgotten by the time Roisin, Bernice and Poppy return?

Chapter 14

The sound of thunder and the flashes of lightning had begun to lessen, but the rain was even heavier as Paul, Davey and Summer offered a choice of tea, coffee or hot whiskey to anyone who wanted a warm drink. Those who hadn't been outside when the rain started were beginning to look a little out of place among the T-shirts, fleeces and sweat pants that had been substituted for dresses and heels.

'In a million years I didn't foresee this.' Steffie, who'd been in the house and so hadn't needed to change, turned to Alivia. Her cousin hadn't changed either but had dried her fuchsia-pink dress with Jenny's hairdryer. She'd also dried her hair and repaired her make-up and was looking as good as she had when she'd first arrived.

'The best-laid plans and all that,' agreed Alivia. 'I hope Poppy's OK.'

'She'll be fine,' said Steffie. 'After all, I fell out of that tree too and I'm still here.'

'You ended up with a broken arm,' Jenny interjected.

'It wasn't my fault,' said Colette, who'd been standing nearby.

Steffie stared at her. 'I never said it was.'

'Yes you did. You didn't speak to me for ages afterwards.'

'Oh!' Steffie remembered now. 'We were both pushing and shoving, weren't we? We were struggling over something.'

'My diary,' said Colette. 'You'd robbed it.'

'So I had,' recalled Steffie. 'Gosh, that was horrible of me. Sorry, Colette.'

'Steffie Sheehan! I didn't know that.' Jenny gave her a stern look. 'You should never rob other people's diaries.'

'I know,' said Steffie. 'But back then – well, she used to spend hours and hours scribbling in it. I wanted to know what she was writing.'

'It was none of your business,' Colette said.

'I know that too,' said Steffie. 'We were kids when it happened. I'm sorry.'

'Did you read it, Steff?' Alivia was amused at the passion in Colette's voice.

Colette gave her cousin a concerned look. 'Did you?' she asked.

'If I did – and I don't think I got around to it – I don't remember what was in it.'

'Oh look, young girls write all sorts of nonsense in their diaries,' said Jenny. 'Mine was full of tortured soul stuff.'

'You had a diary, Jen?' Sarah, who'd drifted across to join them, looked interested. 'I wish I'd known that when we were smaller.'

'Why? Would you have tried to read it?' asked Jenny.

'I certainly would,' Sarah said. 'It might have given me an insight into why you were so . . .'

'So what?' Jenny stared at her.

137

'Oh, nothing.' Sarah shook her head. 'You were different to me, that's all.'

Steffie could hear the tension in her aunt's voice. It had never occurred to her before – at least not in a conscious way – that her mother and her sisters could have had the same uneasy relationship that she felt she had with Roisin. But she could hear it now.

'I don't have a diary,' Summer said. 'But I have a blog and loads of followers. On Twitter and Facebook too, obvs.'

'That's what you should've had, Colette.' Steffie winked at her. 'Then it wouldn't have mattered.'

'A diary is private,' said Colette. 'You had no right to look at it. That's why I pushed you and you fell out of the tree.'

'In which case perhaps I deserved the broken arm,' said Steffie.

Alivia smiled. 'But you still don't remember any salacious details from the diary?'

'I must have bumped my head too,' said Steffie. 'Amnesia.'

Colette stared at her. She wasn't entirely sure she believed her. She felt herself grow hot with embarrassment. As she did every time she remembered her damn diary.

'We should get Mum and Dad to cut the cake now.' Davey caught Steffie by the arm. 'We need something to distract this lot.' He encompassed the guests with his look.

'You're right about a distraction, but we can't possibly do it until the others get back,' she said. 'Roisin would never forgive us. Apparently she has some kind of presentation to do as well.'

'Presentation? From whom? Her and Paul, or the three of us?'

'I dunno,' replied Steffie. 'But we can't do cake cutting without her. She'd have a fit, you know she would.'

'Why do we let her run our lives?' demanded Davey.

'We don't know how to stop her,' said Steffie.

'I can't believe she didn't plan for a storm, a lightning strike and someone having an accident,' Davey remarked.

'Even Roisin can't think of everything.' Steffie sipped the coffee that Paul had given her. 'Mind you, there have been a few distractions today. Like Carl and Summer. And Bernice.'

'Carl's convinced she came to have it out with him but that she was stopped in her tracks when she saw Summer.'

'That girl would stop anyone in their tracks!' said Steffie. 'Did he tell you what the break is all about?'

'Nope. But he's pretty sore about it.'

'So's she. This day is getting a bit tense,' she added. 'Carl, Bernice and Summer are loose cannons. Plus I thought Colette was going to explode over that diary.'

'*Did* you read it?' asked Davey.

'A few pages,' admitted Steffie. 'But it was all soppy stuff about her unrequited love for someone who . . .' Her voice trailed off.

'Who what?' asked Davey.

She shook her head. 'Nothing, nothing. An idea struck me, that's all. I'd better steer clear of her for a while. Keep the drama to a minimum.'

'I bet the neighbours are loving it,' said Davey. 'It'll keep them in gossip for years.'

'Poor Mum and Dad. You know she doesn't really like surprises and the gossip factor is off the scale! The anniversary party where the house nearly burned down, the guests were soaked in a downpour, a kid fell out of a tree and a Jeremy Kyle situation is ongoing.'

'Sounds like almost every party I've ever been at,' Davey said.

'Even in Denmark?' asked Steffie.

'I've never been to a family party in Denmark,' he admitted.

'Ah, they're probably much the same,' said Steffie. 'I bet Camilla is thinking that she could just as well be at home.'

He grimaced. 'I doubt that's what she's thinking.'

'If she marries you, she'll have to get used to it.'

'I haven't asked her yet.'

And, thought Davey, I may not ask her now. Not today, anyway. Not the way I meant to. All the same, I wish things would go the way I wanted. For once in my life.

Bernice couldn't remember the last time she'd driven in such awful weather. Visibility was deteriorating by the second and the rain was heavier on the return journey than it had been on their emergency dash to the hospital. Despite the fact that the windscreen wipers were on full, she could hardly see in front of her. She dropped her speed to less than 40 kph to minimise the chances of ending up in a ditch. And how would Carl feel about that? she wondered as she wiped the steamy windscreen with the back of her hand. Horrified that they'd had a crash, or relieved that it wasn't Summer in the car? She felt tears sting her eyes and she exhaled sharply. She was a professional nurse transporting a patient home from hospital. She would *not* allow her thoughts to wander towards Carl Mullens.

'I'm cold,' said Poppy from the back of the car.

'So am I,' said Roisin.

'It's because your clothes are still damp,' Bernice told

140

them. She turned the heater on, although the truth was that despite the rain, the air temperature hadn't really fallen very much and all it was doing was making things stuffy.

'This wasn't in the game plan for today,' Roisin said, as Bernice dropped her speed even further.

'There's a lot that wasn't in today's game plan,' said Bernice.

'I'm glad you came,' said Roisin. 'Even though . . . well, you know.'

'I have my uses,' said Bernice.

'And I have a sling.' Poppy sounded satisfied. 'People will have to be nice to me because I have a serious injury.'

'Not that serious,' said Roisin. 'You were very lucky. In future when I tell you to get down from something, you do it straight away. OK?'

'OK.' Poppy heaved an enormous sigh that made both Bernice and Roisin smile.

They continued to drive on in silence, Bernice concentrating hard on keeping the car as far away from the verge as she could, while being aware that another car could round a bend at any time. But they didn't encounter any traffic and she felt a surge of relief as she turned on to the narrow road that led to Aranbeg.

'Oh crap!' She stopped the car.

'What?' asked Roisin.

'The road has flooded,' said Bernice. 'Don't tell me that piddling little stream has burst its banks.'

'It can't have.' Roisin rolled down the rear passenger window and looked out. A torrent of muddy water was racing across the width of the road. It was impossible to tell how deep it was. 'Though it certainly looks like it.'

'Are we stuck?' asked Poppy.

'Of course not,' said Roisin. She leaned towards Bernice. 'It's probably not that deep,' she said.

'You're kidding, right?'

'You said it yourself, Ber. It's a piddling little stream.'

'It's more than that right now,' said Bernice. 'Look at that massive puddle!'

'I'd say it's a pothole,' said Roisin.

'Whatever, I don't think we can negotiate it.'

'Of course we can,' said Roisin. 'Put the hammer down and keep going.'

'What if we get stuck in the middle?' Poppy looked anxious 'We could drown.'

'We won't drown in six inches of water,' said Roisin.

'Although we could get stuck,' said Bernice. 'And then we'd have to abandon the car and wade home.'

Poppy began to cry. 'I don't want to get wet.'

'You won't.' Roisin shot an irritated look at Bernice. 'We'll be fine.'

'I don't want to damage the car,' she said.

'You've got insurance.'

'That's not the point.'

Roisin gathered her thoughts. Bernice had legitimate concerns about driving through what was definitely more than a mere puddle, but there was no way Roisin wanted to abandon the car and walk more than a kilometre up the road with her injured daughter in this sort of weather, not unless it was the only option. And not even then, she thought. She was going to have to make Bernice do it.

'Go for it,' she said as persuasively as she could. 'You've been amazing so far today; don't let us down now.'

'I'm not letting you down just because I won't drive through a raging torrent!' cried Bernice.

'You can do it,' said Roisin. 'I know you can. You're one of the most capable people I know.'

'Capable maybe. Stupid not.' Although, Bernice thought suddenly, Carl might have different views about that.

'If we have to leave the car, we have to leave the car,' said Roisin. 'But it would be more stupid not to give it a go first.'

Bernice tapped her fingers on the steering wheel and said nothing.

'I didn't mean to imply that you're stupid!' cried Roisin. 'I want us to get home, that's all.'

'In one piece would be nice,' said Bernice.

'Bernice?' Poppy's voice quivered. 'I want to go home too.'

Bernice took a deep breath and put the car into gear.

'Give it some welly!' cried Roisin as she revved the engine.

'I'm not sure that's the most appropriate word,' said Bernice. Then she depressed the accelerator as far as it would go and released the brake.

A wave of muddy water swept over the bonnet of the car as it leaped forward, sloshing against the windscreen and cascading over the roof. There was a crunching sound and the car listed to one side as the front right-hand wheel hit some kind of obstacle.

Poppy screamed. So did Bernice.

'Keep going!' yelled Roisin.

They could all feel the car wavering. But Bernice didn't let up. With a sudden spurt they were over the obstacle, out of the puddle and on to the relatively safe road on the other side.

'Well done,' said Roisin.

'Yay!' cried Poppy. 'You're so cool, Bernice.'

Bernice wiped the sweat from her brow and tucked the damp locks of her hair behind her ears. She drove on at a more sedate pace, allowing her heartbeat to return to normal as Poppy and Roisin continued to compliment her on getting them through the flooded road.

And that's what real women, not Barbie dolls, can do, she thought as she turned in to Aranbeg. It was a pity Carl hadn't been with them to see it.

Jenny had been watching for their arrival, and as they pulled up outside the house, she opened the front door and hustled them out of the rain. She gave Roisin an anxious look, which faded to relief when her daughter reassured her that Poppy was fine. Jenny hugged Poppy and told her she was a very lucky girl.

'I know.' Poppy wriggled free. 'I have a sling. How brill is that!'

'Most of it is bumps and bruises,' Roisin told Paul when she joined him in the living room. 'The sling is to protect her shoulder, she hasn't broken anything.'

'You're a brave little soldier,' said her father.

'A brave little soldier who'll do what her parents tell her in future,' said Roisin.

'Thanks for looking after me,' Poppy said to Bernice. 'And for driving us through the water.'

'Through the water?' asked Paul.

'There was a huge flood at the end of the road,' explained Poppy. 'We went through it with a whoosh like a submarine. The road is filling up with water too.'

144

'What!' More than one of the guests spoke at the same time.

'We thought the stream might have burst its banks, unlikely though that seems,' said Roisin.

'Surely we'd notice that from the house?' said Paul. 'The water would be coming up the garden by now. Most likely it's some localised flash flooding. That rain is fairly bucketing down.'

'Is the road impassable?' asked Jim Kinsella.

'Not yet,' said Bernice. 'But if it keeps raining like this . . .'

'Maybe we should go.' Seamus looked at his wife and then at Jenny. 'Before the car park floods and we can't get out.'

There was a general murmur of concern at the idea that they might not be able to move their cars, and more people began to talk about leaving.

'Wait until Mum and Dad cut the cake,' begged Roisin. 'And give me five minutes to change first.'

'You and Bernice and Poppy definitely need to change out of those wet things,' agreed Jenny. 'But let's not bother about the cake. I quite understand that people want to go.'

'Of course we'll wait for the cake,' said Carl. 'We can't miss that.'

'Please don't feel you have to,' said Jenny.

'I've been waiting ages for this cake,' said Davey. 'So the sooner the better.'

'We'll stay till after you cut it,' Lillian Kinsella said. 'Then we'll head off too. Our house is in a hollow and I don't fancy getting stuck on the way.'

'I won't be a minute changing,' said Roisin. 'Come on, Poppy.'

Steffie told Bernice that there were some dry clothes on her bed if she wanted to change into them.

'I guess this dress is ruined.' Bernice looked sadly at the L.K.Bennett number she'd bought specially for the day, which was grass-stained and mud-splattered. 'And as for my hair . . .' She glanced at her reflection in a wall mirror and saw that her curls were bedraggled. 'I'm a mess.'

'But all in a good cause,' said Jenny. 'Thank you so much, Bernice. You've been wonderful.'

'Yes indeed,' added Paul. 'I wanted to drive her myself, you know I did, and I bet I would've been fine. But in the end perhaps it was just as well it was you.'

'You're welcome,' said Bernice.

'C'mon,' said Steffie. 'Let's get you something dry to put on. And I'll lend you my hairdryer.'

'Thanks,' said Bernice.

She could feel Carl's eyes on her as she walked out of the room. She wondered what he was thinking.

Eventually everybody was gathered in the kitchen to see Pascal and Jenny cut their anniversary cake. Pascal's arm was around Jenny's waist and she was holding the big knife in her right hand. She was just about to slice into the cake when Roisin told her to wait, that Paul hadn't made his speech yet.

'Before he gives it, I'd like to say something,' said Davey.

'You would?' Roisin's eyes narrowed. She didn't want Davey stealing Paul's thunder by giving an extra speech.

Steffie glanced at her brother and his girlfriend and wondered if this was the moment he was about to ask her to marry him.

'It's not much,' Davey reassured Roisin. 'A few words,

that's all.' He started to talk about his parents, about how inspirational their love for each other had been and the security that had brought the three of them growing up. He glanced at Camilla from time to time as he spoke, hoping that his words would impress on her how much she too meant to him. When he'd finished, Jenny thanked him and got ready to cut the cake again.

'Oh, me!' cried Seamus. 'I'd like to say something too.'

For crying out loud, thought Roisin. People will be fed up with speeches before Paul gets his chance. Why don't they keep their mouths shut and let him do the talking?

Jenny's fingers tightened around the knife as her brother-in-law told them of the time he'd called to see her and Pascal at the flat they'd first moved into on Haddington Road, and how struck he'd been by how much they loved each other. Even though, he added to general embarrassment, the marriage itself might have been somewhat rushed.

Then Steffie chimed in with how important it was to her to know that her parents had loved and cherished each other for such a long period of time. It went to show, she said, that true love always won out in the end. And even if her parents had been somewhat rushed into their marriage, it hadn't mattered because they'd made such a tremendous success of it.

It seemed as though all thoughts of going home early had been forgotten as more and more people gave their own reasons why Jenny and Pascal had been an inspiration to them, and after every speech there was tumultuous applause.

'People just live together now,' Paul said when he finally got the opportunity to speak. 'But Jenny and Pascal have proved that there's something enduring about marriage. Something special that binds them together. Maybe they were lucky because they were married in Rome. Maybe they received an extra blessing that's helped them through the hard times. All I can say is I've looked up to Pascal ever since meeting Roisin and I hope that we can follow in their footsteps.'

Jenny knew that her hand was trembling because she felt Pascal put his own hand over it to steady it.

'Marriage matters.' Paul – knowing that he, Roisin and the children were staying at Aranbeg for the night and so consequently having had more to drink than he normally would – continued to talk, despite the fact that the other guests were beginning to get restless and Jenny's smile was becoming fixed on her face. 'People say it doesn't, but it does. Everyone should be married,' he said as he waved his glass of whiskey in the air. 'Everyone should be as lucky as Jenny and Pascal. Forty years. Forty bloody years. They're amazing and they're an example to all of us. And because of that, we'd like to present you with this . . .' He looked to Roisin, who'd taken the bowl from its hiding place in the cupboard and now handed it to her parents.

'Oh my goodness.' Jenny put the knife on the table and looked at the glass bowl with its *40 Years* inscription on the front. 'This is so beautiful, but you shouldn't have. Really you shouldn't.'

'Of course we should,' said Roisin. 'Now cut the cake!'

There was a roar of approval from the assembled guests. Pascal picked up the knife and held it out to Jenny. She hesitated before taking it from him. She was breathing quickly and she could feel her heart thudding against her chest. All that praise, she thought. Everyone looking up to them. Envying them. Proud of them. Wanting to be them. They were right in one respect. She and Pascal had made it work. But she couldn't let them think it was because they'd been married in Rome. She really and truly couldn't. It was time to come clean.

She placed the knife on the table again.

'I'm sorry,' she said. 'I really—'

'Jen, sweetheart,' Pascal whispered. 'Not now.'

'Oh Pascal, I have to . . . I mean – I can't not . . . Everyone's gone to so much trouble and . . .'

'Mum?' Steffie looked at her apprehensively. 'What's the matter?'

'Nothing's the matter. Not really. Everyone is right. We've been very lucky.'

A relieved smile spread among the guests.

'But you've got it wrong too,' she said. 'It's all about love but not all about marriage.'

Beside her, Pascal took a deep breath.

'We've put it off for so long and I can't let everybody think . . . We're not exactly the role models you imagine.' She turned to look at him and then at everyone else. 'The thing is, yes, we've been together for forty years, and to be honest, most of that is because Pascal is the best man any woman could have in her life. No question. His love for me has been steadfast and true and I really don't deserve him.'

There was a round of applause and Steffie said that Jenny absolutely did deserve her father, just as Pascal deserved Jenny.

'But,' said Jenny, as though her daughter hadn't spoken, 'we have to be honest with you all. We should have been before.'

'Honest about what?' asked Roisin.

'Honest about . . . well . . .' Jenny paused.

The guests looked expectantly at her.

'Well, the thing is,' she said, 'Pascal and I – we're not actually married at all.'

The Storm

Chapter 15

When the pregnancy test proved positive, the first thing Pascal did was ask Jenny to marry him. She immediately forgot all of the other dreams she'd had, of travelling the world, of moving to Rome, of becoming a painter. She'd known then that all she wanted was to be married to Pascal and have his baby and be a good wife and mother. She couldn't imagine another man in the world who would've reacted as brilliantly as he'd done to the news. She'd kissed him hard on the lips and said that she'd be honoured to be Mrs Sheehan. And she meant it.

Because the first thing she'd thought of when she saw the blue line on the test was that her parents would kill her when they found out. Times might have moved on since Kay and Terry had started going out together, but they certainly hadn't embraced a more permissive outlook on life. She'd had an immense row with them over coming to Rome with Pascal in the first place – Kay had warned her that under no circumstances was she to share a bed with him. Jenny wondered if her mum was really in the dark about the fact that she'd slept with Pascal already. It was the 1970s after all, what did she expect? But still . . . arriving home as a pregnant unmarried woman was a horrific prospect. Returning as an engaged pregnant woman would surely temper their fury.

'I've a better idea,' said Pascal.

She looked at him questioningly. Her boyfriend – now her fiancé – had been brilliant so far, but there was no way they could pretend that she wasn't pregnant.

'Of course not, you idiot,' he said when she asked him if that was what he had in mind. 'I meant that we could get married before we go home. Kill two birds with one stone so to speak.'

'Married? Where?'

'Here in Rome,' he said. 'It would be a sort of appropriate thing to do, wouldn't it?'

It would be more than appropriate, she thought. It would be perfect. If she went home a married woman, nobody could say a word. Other than to congratulate her.

'Is it possible?' she asked.

'Why not?' Pascal grinned. 'It's the wedding capital of the world! C'mon. Let's see what can be done. Always provided . . .' he looked at her with a sudden flash of doubt, 'always provided that you really do want to get married.'

'Of course I do.' Jenny threw her arms around him.

Jenny Sheehan. It sounded good. It sounded safe. It sounded like the right thing to do.

But of course it wasn't possible to get married in Rome at short notice. Couples needed all sorts of things – letters of release from their parish priests, birth and baptismal certificates and other legal papers that neither Pascal nor Jenny had with them and that they certainly wouldn't have been able to have sent to them in the time they had left, even if they knew how to go about getting them in the first place.

'I don't see why it has to be so complicated,' she said crossly as they sat on a stone seat opposite the Trevi Fountain. 'You'd think the Church would *want* people to get married.'

Pascal agreed. They'd spent the morning realising that there was simply no hope of getting married in Rome – or anywhere else in Italy for that matter – within a few days. They'd seen newly married couples having their photos taken at the Forum or the Spanish Steps or other iconic places, but they knew they wouldn't be one of them.

'Maybe I'll tell my mother we're married anyhow. After all, how would she know otherwise?' Jenny said the words more as a joke than anything else but Pascal's eyes narrowed as she spoke.

'It's not an impossible idea,' he said slowly. 'After all, people come here and how would you know if they're actually married or not? You could go home with a piece of paper that says you are and no one would be any the wiser.'

Jenny laughed. 'They'd guess.'

'How?' asked Pascal.

She looked at him thoughtfully. But she couldn't think of an answer.

'What we could do,' said Pascal, 'is pretend we'd always planned to get married here and that's why we came, then get married on the quiet when we get home. Nobody will know the difference.'

'We couldn't!'

'Of course we could. Why not?'

'What about the certificate of marriage and everything?

My parents would want to see something, to have proof. I know them.'

'*You* could do it,' he said. 'I've seen you do your fancy writing. We could buy paper and ink and do one up.'

'You're joking.'

'Why would I be joking?'

'And why would you even consider this?' she asked. 'You don't have to marry me at all.'

'I want to,' said Pascal. 'I love you. And you're going to have my baby.'

Jenny still couldn't get her head around that part of it. Having a baby was something that had been in her very distant future. But now it was part of her present. She had to think of what was best for her child.

'We could take photos.' Pascal was getting excited by the idea now. 'You could buy a white dress and put flowers in your hair and we could go around loads of places and everyone would assume they were proper wedding photos.'

'But we wouldn't have any of us signing the register or anything.'

'So what?' He shrugged. 'We could say those ones didn't come out. Or that we lost the film. Or something.'

'Oh man . . .' Jenny was beginning to smile. 'But we'd have to buy special paper and pens to fake any kind of legal document. And we're on a budget.'

'I brought some extra traveller's cheques,' said Pascal. 'For emergencies.'

'I don't think this is the kind of emergency you had in mind.'

'Unforeseen circumstances are always emergencies.'

It didn't really feel like an emergency, even though Jenny

knew that being pregnant was a life-altering experience. But truthfully, right then, it simply felt like a big adventure.

They found a higgledy-piggledy stationery shop near the Pantheon that had everything they needed. Jenny felt as if she was in Aladdin's cave as she browsed the shelves stocked with every kind of paper, pen and ink. In addition to a small sketch pad, pencils and an eraser, she bought parchment and ink, a calligraphy pen and some seals. She also bought a postcard that showed a copy of an Italian marriage certificate issued in the 1940s. According to the shop owner, it belonged to two famous Italian opera singers, neither of whom Jenny had heard of. However it was the perfect template to design one of her own. The proprietor of the hotel, who was enchanted by the lovely Irish couple, told her she was welcome to use the old Remington typewriter in the office when Jenny asked if she could possibly type a letter, and so she sat at the rosewood desk and typed the words she didn't understand on to the parchment. Then, in her best formal script, she inscribed in the spaces she'd left for that purpose the information that Jenny Marshall and Pascal Sheehan had been married in the Basilica de San Giovanni on 22 August 1975. She also copied an apostolic benediction from the Pope himself, carefully adding a photo of him at the top of it so that it looked like the one in her parents' house.

The framed certificate and benediction still hung in the hallway of their Dublin home, in full view of anyone who came to visit. They were on the same wall as the photo that a passing tourist had taken of them in their 'wedding' finery beside the Trevi Fountain. Jenny had become so used to seeing them that she'd forgotten they were even there.

* * *

When she finished telling the story, there was a stunned silence and then Charlie guffawed.

'Good on yeh, Jen,' he said. 'You know how to pull a fast one all right.'

There was a chorus of doubtful laughter from the others.

'Jeez, Jen, you had me going there for a moment,' said Sarah.

'My God,' said Paul. 'You can spin a yarn, Jenny.'

'Mum!' cried Roisin. 'This isn't the time for silly jokes. It's a momentous occasion.'

'It's not a joke.' Jenny looked at them all. 'I'm serious.'

'That's the coolest thing I've ever heard,' said Summer. 'You're amazing, Jenny. You're like that master forger guy in the movie with Leonardo DiCaprio! I so want to be like you when I'm your age.'

Carl gave her a dig in the side.

'What?' she said. 'She's old but she's brilliant.'

Alivia stifled a grin although she was as shocked as everyone else by Jenny's revelation, while Steffie looked at each of her parents in turn.

'Mum? Dad? It's not true, is it?'

'Your mum is right,' said Pascal. 'We didn't get married in Rome.'

'But . . . but . . . you must have!' exclaimed Sarah. 'You came home with a wedding ring. You told Mum and Dad. You can't have . . . you can't have lied about it.'

'I'm afraid we did,' said Jenny.

'Those photos,' said Davey. 'Of you in your wedding dress. You *faked* them?'

'They're real photos,' Jenny said. 'I mean, I'm in a white dress and everything, but it's not a wedding dress.'

158

'But your honeymoon in Sorrento!' Lucinda stared at her. 'You told me all about it. About going to Capri. About Pascal giving you a flower. Jeepers, Jenny, you even *showed* me the damn flower!'

'We did all those things,' said Jenny. 'We just weren't married when we did them.'

'I can't believe you didn't run into all sorts of problems at home,' said Sarah. 'Surely someone must have realised your certificate was a fake?'

'I was very shocked they didn't,' admitted Jenny. 'But back then things were a lot less complicated. We never had to produce it for anything important. Let's face it, most of the legal and financial stuff was done by men, in their names. My name wasn't on the mortgage for the house or on our car loan or anything. When the children were born, the hospital registered the births and they simply assumed we were married. After all, I'd been attending as Mrs Sheehan all the time. I suppose it would be a lot harder to do now, with computerised records and everything, but back then it was easy.'

'But why would you pretend?' asked Steffie. 'What was the point in that?'

'I was pregnant,' said Jenny. 'In the seventies. In Ireland. Wasn't that enough reason?'

'I can understand why you wouldn't want to be an unmarried mother,' agreed Sarah. 'But why didn't you get married later on, like you said?'

'You let me think I was the only one,' Lucinda said before Jenny had the opportunity to reply. 'You let me think I was the stupid daughter who'd made a big mistake. You didn't speak out even then!'

'Thanks, Mum,' muttered Alivia. 'Thanks for calling me a mistake.'

'You know what I mean!' Lucinda cried. 'So does she.'

'OK,' said Roisin. 'Are you seriously telling me, Mum, that I went to the trouble of organising a party that's actually celebrating a forty-year-old lie?'

'I'm sorry,' said Jenny. 'I—'

'This is a family matter,' Lillian Kinsella broke in. 'And given that it's obviously something you need to talk about, you won't want lots of people around while you're doing that. Besides, it's still raining out there and the flooding must be getting worse. So, thank you for a wonderful day, Jenny and Pascal. We'll see you again soon, I hope.'

There was a general murmur of assent from the non-family guests that leaving was a good idea despite the fact that most of them would have loved to be part of the unfolding drama. Nevertheless, they moved as a group to depart from the house.

'We'll go too.' Seamus clapped Pascal on the back. 'You don't need our lot here either. But give me a call.'

Pascal nodded as other family members also said goodbye, although Charlie suggested that maybe he should stay and give Pascal some moral support.

'Don't be ridiculous,' said his sister-in-law. 'You came with us, you can leave with us. Besides, Pascal's grand, aren't you, pet?' She looked at him and he nodded again.

'I'll see you at the next community meeting, Jenny,' said Breege. 'Thank you for your hospitality today.'

'Thanks for coming.' Jenny couldn't think of anything else to say.

Pulling the cloak of good manners around her, Roisin saw

160

everyone to the door and watched as the majority of the guests hurried down the driveway. Nobody bothered waiting for their other halves to bring cars from the car park across the road. It was clear that most of them wanted to get away from Aranbeg as quickly as possible. Even when Steffie said that she'd root out some umbrellas from under the stairs to protect them, they all shook their heads and said it didn't matter.

'Do we have to go as well?' asked Daisy, who'd followed her. ''Cos we're supposed to be staying here tonight, aren't we? I have my PJs and everything.'

'I know.' Roisin was reeling from the abrupt end to the party. 'We have to talk to Granny and Grandad first.'

'It doesn't matter that they're not married, does it?' Daisy frowned. 'Loads of people aren't married. Tansy Miller's mum and dad aren't.'

'No, it doesn't matter,' agreed Roisin.

'So they're not in trouble, are they? Or are you angry with them because we've had a party but it's sort of false pretences?'

'Of course they're not in trouble and of course I'm not angry,' Roisin assured her, although inside she was seething. All her effort, all that planning! And in the end her mother had made a fool of her. She shook hands with the last of the guests, Eleanor Sherratt, who was a member of Jenny's art group, and said she hoped that she'd enjoyed herself.

'Wouldn't have missed it for the world,' said Eleanor. 'Great fun. And nobody cares that Pascal and Jenny aren't married, you know that, don't you?'

'I . . . yes,' said Roisin. 'We need to talk about it, that's all.'

She closed the front door. Then she and Daisy walked back into the kitchen, where the remainder of the family, including Bernice and Summer, were still gathered. She wanted to say that they should all leave, but she was afraid of causing more upset, even though she didn't think that anyone other than herself, Steffie and Davey should be here.

'Where are Mum and Dad?' she asked.

'Aunt Jenny went upstairs while you were seeing people out,' said Alivia. 'I think she needed a moment.'

'Dad went after her,' added Davey.

Roisin rubbed her eyes with the tips of her fingers and smudged her mascara.

'Are you all right?' asked Steffie.

'Why on earth didn't they say something to us before now?' demanded Roisin. 'Why would they let us think . . . They must have been laughing at me all day.'

'I'm sure they weren't laughing at you,' said Colette. 'Actually, Uncle Pascal seemed to be having a great time.'

'They should have told us,' said Roisin. 'We deserved to know. I mean basically, right now, the three of us are . . . Well, we're the kids of unmarried parents.'

'That's no big deal,' said Steffie.

'At least your parents are still together,' Alivia added.

'I could kill her,' said Roisin. 'And him.'

Steffie and Davey exchanged glances. Both were wondering whether Roisin was more annoyed at learning of their parents' deception, or at the fact that her carefully planned party had been ruined.

'Somebody should go up and get her,' said Roisin. 'We need to hear an explanation.'

'She's already explained,' said Steffie.

'No she bloody hasn't. She hasn't given us any good reason for keeping quiet about it or for not getting married

162

afterwards.' It was Sarah who spoke, and she sounded angry. 'She allowed our mother to make this huge fuss of her when she had her baby and the truth was it was illegitimate.'

Everybody heard Roisin's sharp intake of breath.

'Sorry, Roisin.' Sarah looked at her apologetically. 'I didn't mean to call you an it. Or illegitimate.'

'Although clearly that's how everyone now thinks of me,' said Roisin.

'We're all in the same boat,' remarked Davey. 'Although illegitimacy isn't relevant these days, is it? Haven't they done away with it as a legal situation?'

'So what,' said Roisin. 'Mum and Dad should have got married and sorted it out properly, for our sakes as much as theirs, and the fact that they didn't . . . well, why didn't they? Do they not love each other enough? Is their entire relationship a sham?'

'Of course they love each other,' said Steffie. 'They've still been together forty years, after all. You wouldn't do that if it was a sham.'

'I do not think this is something that is important.' From her position leaning against the wall, Camilla's clipped tones drew everyone's attention. 'Lots of people don't get married. It shouldn't matter.'

'What matters is they pretended,' said Roisin. 'They lied. For forty years!'

'It was probably for Gran and Grandad,' said Steffie. 'And after they died, it was too difficult to tell the truth.'

'Bit of a shock, though, the way it's happened,' commented Bernice.

'It wouldn't have been as much of one if Jenny hadn't blurted it out when she did,' observed Alivia.

163

'How about I put the kettle on,' suggested Sarah. 'A cup of tea will help.'

'Why do grown-ups always have cups of tea when there's trouble?' asked Daisy.

'It is a social ritual,' said Camilla. 'Social rituals are good at difficult times. Do you want me to help?'

Sarah looked at her without speaking. Then she nodded and they went into the kitchen together while everyone else moved to the veranda. Even though the rain was continuing to fall heavily, the outdoors area was still dry and warm.

I can't believe this has happened, thought Roisin as she stared out into the garden, which was becoming more sodden by the minute. Why on earth couldn't she have kept her mouth shut and not ruined my party? She managed it for forty years. Another few hours shouldn't have been too much trouble!

Chapter 16

Sarah and Camilla made the tea in total silence. Camilla could see that the other woman didn't want to talk, while Sarah was trying to keep a lid on the anger that was bubbling inside her.

She couldn't believe that her sister and brother-in-law (although he wasn't, was he; they weren't related in law at all!) had managed to keep the secret for so long. And it didn't matter that they might as well have been married, that they lived their lives as though they were. What was important was that they had let everybody believe in something that simply wasn't true. They'd played them all for fools. Sarah had sent them a card every year on their anniversary. Sometimes she'd sent flowers too. And they'd never once told her not to bother, it was all a joke.

What was more, they weren't sorry for the deception. Jenny seemed to think it was OK to have conned them all. She'd dropped her bombshell and gone upstairs so that she didn't have to answer legitimate questions about her treachery. Yet they were entitled to question her. They were entitled to know what the hell she thought she'd been doing all these years. They were entitled to know why she'd lied.

And even more than the blatant continuous lies, Sarah thought, as she heated the catering-size teapot that Roisin had acquired for the day, more than that, in pretending to have come home from Rome as a married woman, Jenny had laid out a road map for how she and Lucinda were meant to behave and forced them to follow it. Her actions had coloured everybody's future from the moment she'd walked in the door with her fake ring on her finger, and not in a good way, especially as far as Sarah was concerned. After the initial furore, and when Jenny and Pascal had left the house for his flat, Kay had asked Sarah to put the kettle on for some tea. Then they'd all sat in the small living room while her parents tried to make sense of the situation.

'She should have said what they were going to do before she went,' Kay repeated over and over. 'We would have been able to tell everyone about the wedding.'

'She's pregnant,' Sarah said. 'She was pregnant before they got married. No wonder she kept her mouth shut.'

'It doesn't matter,' Terry told her. 'She's done the right thing now. He's done right by her. We're fine. There won't be any trouble.'

'Well they went a very underhand way about avoiding trouble.' Sarah replaced her cup on its saucer with a bang and splashed tea over the carpet.

'Would you look at what you've done, missy!' exclaimed Kay. 'The good carpet. Get a cloth and clean that up right away.'

Sarah had been stung by the anger in her mother's voice. She knew that most of it was indirectly meant for Jenny, but it wasn't fair that she was experiencing it all the same. She went into the kitchen and returned with some kitchen towel.

'Why are you using that?' demanded Kay. 'There's a perfectly good cloth you can rinse out.'

'What's the point in us having kitchen paper if we don't use it?' retorted Sarah. 'For God's sake, Mam, wake up and smell the coffee.'

'Don't you talk to me like that,' said Kay. 'You're still living under my roof and you'll treat me with respect.'

'But it's all right for Jenny not to respect you, is it?' asked Sarah. 'Because she's left?'

'It's not all right at all,' growled Terry. 'But there isn't much we can do about it now, and her with her apostolic benediction and everything. I doubt she'd have got that if the Holy Father had known she was in the family way.'

'We might be able to pretend,' said Kay.

'Depends on when the baby is born,' Terry said.

'So what you're going to do is cover it all up!' cried Sarah. 'You're going to say that she's married and having a baby and everything is all right.'

'It is,' said Terry.

'That's so damn hypocritical.' Sarah was incensed. 'Not that I think bad things should happen to girls who get pregnant, of course they shouldn't. But you're saying one thing and doing something else.'

'We're not saying one thing,' said Kay. 'We're saying that it's all right to be married and having a baby.'

'You're unbelievable!' Sarah stormed out of the living room, slamming the door behind her.

As well as being annoyed at her parents' hypocrisy, she was equally mad with Jenny because she knew her older sister's actions would have repercussions. And they did. From that day on, whenever Sarah went out, she was quizzed about who she was with and what time she'd be home. From time to time, Kay even phoned the houses of people she said she was with, ostensibly to ask her to pick up something from the shops on the way home, but in reality, Sarah knew, to check that she was where she'd said she'd be. As for boyfriends – they were all vetted carefully, and questions were asked about them as soon as it was clear that there was any kind of relationship at all. Things calmed down to a certain degree for Lucinda, of course. And then Lucinda had gone and got pregnant anyway!

Sarah sometimes wished she'd gone off the rails herself. That she'd rebelled and lied to her parents and got her friends to cover for her. But she hadn't. She'd submitted to all their questioning and all their demands of her and become the daughter they'd always wanted. Compliant and obedient. Never breaking the rules. Always there when they needed her. Yet it hadn't been enough to turn her into their favourite. From the moment Roisin was born, Jenny was back in favour. Kay would sometimes tell Sarah that she'd be lucky to find someone like Pascal, someone who worked hard and cared so much for his wife and child.

'I was angry with them at first,' Kay told her, after Jenny had come home for a visit, during which everyone was convinced Roisin had said the word 'grandma'. 'I thought she'd made a mistake. But I was wrong and I'm glad to be wrong.'

Sarah thought that less than a year after the Roman wedding (as everyone referred to it) was a bit soon to make that call. But she could see that Jenny and Pascal seemed happy together and that both of them cared for Roisin very much.

When she met James Mullens, she knew that she'd found

someone to equal Pascal. James was much better-looking than her brother-in-law and his job as an architect was far more prestigious than that of a mere civil servant. He had plans to build his own house in Blessington, an up-and-coming town about fifteen miles south-west of the city. The site for the house had views over the lakes and was in an immeasurably better location, as far as Sarah was concerned, than the house her sister and Pascal had moved into.

And so, because he was better than Pascal in so many ways, Sarah decided that she would marry James Mullens and that they would have a huge wedding to which they'd invite absolutely everyone. And that it would live in the memories of the entire family, who'd know that she'd outstripped her sister at last.

'They all hate me.' Jenny was sitting on the edge of the bed with Pascal beside her. 'I could see it in their eyes. And the neighbours couldn't wait to leave.'

'Nobody hates you,' said Pascal. 'They're in shock, that's all. And you could hardly expect Breege and Lillian and the rest to stay when you'd dropped your bombshell.'

'I didn't think it would be quite such a big deal,' said Jenny.

'For crying out loud!' Pascal looked at her in disbelief. 'It's our ruby wedding anniversary party, and you're telling them we're not married. Of course it's a big deal. It's huge.'

'I thought . . . I thought that in this day and age they'd be OK with it.'

'I'm sure they will be eventually,' said Pascal. 'But it's a lot for them to take in all the same.'

169

'I know.' Jenny sighed. 'And you were right, like you always are. I shouldn't have said anything.'

'It was hard to listen to all those speeches and know that we'd lied,' admitted Pascal. 'And Jenny, it's been as much my fault as yours that we didn't tell anyone. There were opportunities over the years and I didn't make us take them, even though I know as well as you that you can't keep secrets for ever.'

'I suppose it's astonishing that we weren't found out before now,' said Jenny. 'And of course we still have to—'

'Jen!' He gave her a warning look. 'We've done enough today.'

'But—'

'You can't say anything else. You really can't.'

She covered her eyes with her hands, and when she spoke, her words were muffled. 'I can't not.'

'But not today.'

'If not, when?'

'Tomorrow,' said Pascal. 'When we have Davey and Roisin and Steffie to ourselves. We can talk about everything then. We'll all sit down together, and you and I can explain.'

'I can't wait until tomorrow.' Jenny took her hands away from her face. 'Not after this. I can't go to sleep with another secret. We have to talk to Steffie. Or at least I do.'

'You've already gone rogue on me once today.' He shook his head. 'It's not a good idea to do it again.'

'She deserves to know.' Jenny spoke with a quiet determination. 'I'll do it here. Now. By myself. It'll be easier if it's just the two of us. And then she can decide what to do.'

Pascal took a deep breath and released it slowly.

'If that's what you want,' he said. 'Though honestly, I think you're making a terrible mistake.'

'Pascal . . .'

But he'd walked out of the room and closed the door gently behind him.

Daisy, Poppy and Dougie had decamped to the den, where they were watching *Pirates of the Caribbean* on TV while the adults continued to discuss recent events on the veranda. Daisy hadn't wanted to leave the scene of the drama, but Roisin had insisted she look after her siblings. Daisy had opened her mouth to protest, then seen the expression on her mother's face and headed off to the den with her brother and sister.

'Dad! Are you OK? Is Mum?' asked Steffie.

'More to the point, are we OK?' said Roisin.

'We're sorry,' said Pascal. 'We should've told you before now.'

'It's no big deal, Dad,' Davey said. 'It's a shock all right, but I guess we can live with it.'

'There was no need to keep it a secret from us,' Steffie added. 'It's not like we wouldn't have understood.'

Roisin said nothing. She didn't meet her father's eye but stared out into the sodden garden while she sipped her tea.

'We were wrong,' said Pascal. 'We know that.'

'So when is Jenny going to come downstairs and explain herself?' asked Sarah.

'Before she does, she wants to talk to Steffie.' Pascal turned to her. 'D'you mind going up to her?'

'Me?' Steffie was taken aback. 'Why me?'

'Why her?' asked Roisin. 'Honestly, Dad, I think it's me who—'

'It's Steffie she needs to speak with,' he said.

Roisin clamped her mouth shut.

'Actually it's me and Lucinda she should be explaining herself to,' said Sarah. 'We bore the brunt of her lies. Your lies too, Pascal.'

'We didn't keep on lying.' Pascal kept his voice mild. 'We just didn't correct your assumptions.'

'Hardly a feckin' assumption when you had your so-called marriage certificate framed on the wall!' Lucinda snorted. 'We believed what we were told. I was fifteen, for heaven's sake. How was I to know it was all a crock of shit?'

'Steffie, will you go to your mum now?' Pascal ignored Lucinda's outburst.

'All right,' said Steffie. She gave a bewildered glance at her brother and sister before going into the kitchen, where she took the last bottle of the sparkling rosé out of the fridge. Then she collected a couple of glasses from the table and began to climb the stairs.

Chapter 17

Steffie hesitated for a moment before tapping on the bedroom door. She was surprised that her mother wanted to talk to her and not Roisin, but at the same time she knew that she was closer to Jenny in many ways than her older sister. She'd spent a lot of time as the only child at home, when both Roisin and Davey had left to pursue their own lives. Although she'd missed her brother and sister, she'd revelled in the extra attention she was suddenly receiving from Jenny, and she had some very treasured memories of the two of them sitting curled up in an armchair together watching movies on TV after she'd come home from school. The movies were an occasional treat; most of the time Jenny would tell her to get on with her homework, but it was the fact that every so often she was allowed to forget about it till later that thrilled Steffie so much. That, and her mum's arm wrapped around her as they sat engrossed in the classic melodramas and mystery thrillers that Jenny loved.

She turned the handle slowly and walked into the bedroom. Jenny was sitting in the small wing-backed chair near the window.

'Are you OK, Mum?' asked Steffie.

'I'm not the one who's had a surprise,' said Jenny. 'I knew we weren't married.'

'You certainly made it a surprise party with a difference,' Steffie said. 'But hey, it's kind of cool in an offbeat sort of way.'

'We should have told you before now,' said Jenny. 'It was wrong of us not to.'

'I guess,' said Steffie. 'But in the end the important thing is that you guys have still been together for forty years. Whether you were married or not during that time is pretty irrelevant.'

'Nevertheless, it makes the ruby wedding anniversary a little premature.'

'We were wondering,' said Steffie, 'why you didn't get married. I mean, you could've nipped into a registry office any time.'

'I know,' said Jenny. 'That's what we planned to do. At first we were going to do it before Roisin was born, but you have to give notice and I was afraid someone I knew would see me and wonder what on earth was going on.'

'They probably would've thought you were going to someone else's wedding,' Steffie pointed out.

'I was afraid to take the chance. If your grandmother had had any inkling . . . well, she would've been furious with me. Both for being unmarried and pregnant and for having lied to her. Besides,' she looked a little shamefaced, 'back then the registry office was a horrible place, not a bit personal or elegant or anything. It was as though you were a second-class citizen if you chose not to get married in church.'

'So you wanted to wait and get married in a church?' asked Steffie. 'And you with a fake apostolic benediction already!'

174

'The church part didn't bother me,' admitted Jenny. 'All I wanted was somewhere nice. Which shows you how shallow I am.'

'Ah, no. I understand.' Steffie smiled at her. 'You wouldn't have wanted the real day to be less glamorous than the fake day.'

'Actually, nothing in Ireland could've compared to Rome,' said Jenny. 'Perhaps that's why we didn't do it. And then of course I got pregnant with Davey, so that kind of took our eye off the ball for a while because we had our hands full.'

Steffie nodded. 'But after Davey there was a big gap before I came along. You could've gone to Rome then.'

'We didn't have the money,' Jenny told her. 'Our win on the prize bonds helped with the purchase of Aranbeg, but after that, every spare penny went into renovation. Besides, we were happy enough with the way we were.'

'And after Aranbeg was finished?'

'It took years,' Jenny said. 'Really and truly. Years.'

'But after that? Or after I was born? Why not then?'

'We had other things to worry about,' said Jenny.

'What other things?'

'Something else I should have told you before now,' Jenny said. She picked up the bottle of rosé that Steffie had left on the dressing table and filled the two glasses. She handed one to her daughter and took a deep breath.

'I still can't believe she didn't tell us before now,' Lucinda said to Sarah. The sisters were standing together at the rail of the veranda, looking out into the garden, which was now sodden by the drumming rain. 'I won't forgive her, you know,' she added. 'All our lives she let me think I was the one who'd cocked it up by being unmarried and pregnant. She could have supported me. But she didn't.'

'She couldn't have supported you without telling everyone.' Sarah took a pull from her electronic cigarette. It wasn't as satisfying as the real thing, but at least it gave her the illusion of calmness that she'd experienced as a smoker.

'So she should've told everyone,' said Lucinda. 'All this pretending. Ridiculous.'

'I agree.' Sarah nodded. 'And when I was going through the divorce from James – she could've said something to me too. But no, she had to be the golden girl with her perfect marriage and her perfect children. Living the perfect lie.' She took a deep drag and then put the e-cigarette back into her bag. 'When all the time she was an unmarried mother living with her baby's father. That was fairly monumental back then. She should've come clean. It would've made things easier for both of us. When I told Mum that James and I were separating, I went through hell with her saying that I could work on it a bit more. She used to tell me that Jenny worked on it with Pascal, that they hadn't begun things well but that they were an example to everyone.'

'They're an example of a couple who've stayed together without a marriage certificate,' remarked Lucinda. 'Maybe that's even better.'

'Oh don't you start!' Sarah snorted. 'Make me feel like a total loser, why don't you!'

'I didn't mean that,' said Lucinda. 'Honestly I didn't. I know you tried with James and I don't blame you for splitting up with him.'

'I married him because I thought it would be a grown-up

thing to do,' said Sarah. 'And because I thought that having a massive wedding would be . . .' Her voice trailed off.

'Would be one in the eye for Jenny?' suggested Lucinda.

'Partly,' conceded Sarah. 'I wanted to show her how it should have been done. But ultimately it was rubbish, because James and I weren't suited at all.'

'Oh well. We can't all be as lucky as Jenny and Pascal. Even if he didn't actually put a ring on it.'

'Haven't you ever found anyone, Lou?' asked Sarah suddenly. 'You're a good-looking woman. No reason for you not to have a man in your life.'

'Until recently I wouldn't have trusted anyone not to leave if I got pregnant,' said Lucinda. 'Now, of course, thanks to the arrival of hot flushes, that's sort of irrelevant. But still – George was such a shit, he put me off the whole idea of men.'

'It was a long time ago.'

'Yeah, but you don't forget,' Lucinda said. 'You don't forget the look in someone's eyes and realising that the only thought in their head is getting away from you and away from the trouble you represent.'

Sarah put her arm around Lucinda and hugged her.

'You know what worries me most?' she asked as they stepped away from each other again.

'What?'

'That because of me marrying James for the wrong reasons, I've messed up my kids too.'

'What are you talking about? They're fine,' said Lucinda.

'Um, excuse me? John and Eoin both emigrated. And Colette and Carl have my heart scalded, the pair of them.'

'What's wrong with Colette?' asked Lucinda.

177

'What's right with her! Until the summer James and I split, she was a really easy child. When she came home, she went all goth on me. And she's gone through mad phases ever since. Pink hair, blue hair, gold hair and drama-queen make-up . . . plus three goddam fiancés! She's a freak.'

'Sarah!'

'It's true. She's thirty-two; she's not a stupid teenager any more, so she shouldn't go out looking like one. Look at her get-up today, for heaven's sake. No wonder she can't hold on to a man!'

'Isn't *she* the one who keeps dumping *them*?'

'That's what she says, but who knows? And then, of course, Carl, bringing that Summer woman with him today! Did you ever see anyone more inappropriate for him? And poor Bernice turns up looking so beautiful and elegant. *And* she had to take on her angel-of-mercy role with Poppy while Carl and your wan snuggle up on the veranda. I'm mortified by it, completely mortified.'

'It's Carl who should be mortified,' said Lucinda. 'Everyone else is getting a good laugh out of it.'

'Between him and Colette, though, I'm a laughing stock. I'm not a good mother,' added Sarah. 'And it's all Jenny's fault.'

'You're a normal mother and you can't blame any of your imagined shortcomings on Jenny.'

'See, that's the thing,' said Sarah. 'She had experiences she kept to herself, and if she hadn't – well, everything might have been different for both of us.'

'Her experience was dramatically different from mine, though,' conceded Lucinda. 'There wasn't much she could've done for me. Pascal stepped up to the plate. George legged it.'

'All the more bizarre that she hasn't married him since.'

'Maybe there's a reason,' Lucinda said. 'Maybe he's married already.'

'I think we would have known.'

'Hey, what's one more secret?'

'Don't even go there.'

'Perhaps it was hard to do,' said Lucinda. 'You know how it is with a lie. You get tangled up in it and somehow it seems easier to go along with it than admit the truth.'

Sarah knew what Lucinda meant. But it didn't mean that she still wasn't angry with her eldest sister.

Chapter 18

'So this isn't going to be easy,' Jenny told Steffie.

'Harder than admitting you and Dad never got married?' asked Steffie.

'Yes.'

Steffie was unsettled by the sudden seriousness in her mother's voice.

'Why are you telling me? Why not everyone?'

'Because it concerns you most of all,' said Jenny.

Steffie looked at her in puzzlement.

'How?' she asked.

Jenny took a deep breath.

By the time they'd been together a few years, Jenny and Pascal didn't talk about getting married any more. They were too busy with two children and two homes to give much thought to something that had become vaguely irrelevant to them. Jenny thought that perhaps Pascal had forgotten that the apostolic benediction wasn't real and the rings they wore on their wedding fingers were the cheap ones they'd bought in a shop in Rome. In many ways it was how she thought of it herself. After all, they lived their lives as though they *were* married. What difference would a piece of paper actually make? So she allowed the subject to fade into the background while she busied herself with Roisin and Davey and spent her free time doing charcoal sketches of the children and turning Aranbeg into the place that one day, far into the future, they'd retire to.

Pascal was equally committed to Aranbeg, but he was also doing extremely well at work. Jenny celebrated with him each time he was promoted, and was thrilled when he was chosen to be Ireland's representative at a month-long symposium and study group in Brussels. She brought the children to the airport to wave him goodbye and then decamped with them to Aranbeg, not caring that they were missing the last two days of the school year. Roisin and Davey were delighted to be back in Wexford, while Jenny decided to enrol in an art class to improve her technique. Even though Pascal had insisted they frame some of her sketches, she didn't think they were good enough to be on the walls of the house. Her plan was to have mastered portraits by the time he came home.

It had been a long time since she had done anything solely for herself, and she was excited when she arrived for her first lesson. She listened intently as the teacher, Johnny Macken, talked about the intricacies of the human form, and what they'd be working on during the course. It was only as he described what they'd be doing that she realised they'd be drawing nudes. She was annoyed with herself for feeling slightly embarrassed, and dismissed her thoughts by wondering how difficult it would actually be to draw a naked person.

And then the model arrived and she gasped. Because, fully clothed, he was the most attractive man she'd ever seen in her life. A blond, blue-eyed demigod, in a white T-shirt and ripped jeans. He went behind a screen and emerged wearing nothing more than a small towel around his waist. Jenny knew she wasn't the only one who was stunned by him. She could feel the tension crackling around the room as she studied the lean body and washboard abs so taut they made the Calvin Klein jeans man look flabby and unfit. When she glanced around the room she could see that everyone's eyes were fixed on the model. She wasn't surprised.

Johnny Macken, however, appeared completely unmoved by such perfection. He began the class, talking to them about the line of action and how to sketch in the abs as a single unit before defining them.

'The outer calf is higher than the underside,' he said. 'Don't forget that. And don't forget where your light is coming from.'

Jenny was finding it hard to put out of her mind the fact that, apart from Pascal, the model was the only man she had ever seen naked in her life. Well, almost naked, because the towel was now placed with careful artistry over his groin. She tried to keep her eyes on his perfect face, perfect torso and perfect legs. But they were continually drawn towards the towel and what lay beneath.

After a while, however, she found that she was concentrating on the drawing rather than the man. She worked hard to get the swell of his biceps and the curve of his neck exactly right. And his face – she wanted to capture the expression in his eyes. The one that seemed to be saying that he was a descendant of the gods. She spent a lot of time on his eyes but she was dissatisfied with the result. Compared to the living man, her picture was flat and lifeless. She eventually put down her charcoal in frustration.

'Pretty good, Jenny,' said Johnny when he came to look at her efforts. 'You've captured him very well.'

'But not well enough,' she told him. 'I've got the pose, but I haven't got *him*.'

'That will come,' said Johnny. 'Gregory will be here again next week.'

Jenny didn't know how she'd wait a whole week to see him again. Every inch of him was already seared into her brain. She wondered if they'd have the opportunity to speak with him, but as soon as the class was finished, he disappeared behind the screen and walked out of the back door before they'd even realised he'd gone.

She spent the next few days sketching him, filling her artist's pad with close-ups of his eyes, his nose, his mouth, his torso, his arms and his legs. She concentrated on each individual part of him, hoping that she could bring them all together to represent the complete person. When she arrived at the workshop the following Saturday, she was eager to get it right this time.

He sat in the same pose and with the same expression while they worked with quiet determination.

'Better,' said Johnny when she'd finished. 'Better lines, better definition.'

'I still haven't got the essence of him,' she said in frustration.

'Put yourself inside his head,' said Johnny. 'Think what he's thinking.'

'I don't know what he's thinking, that's the problem.'

Johnny grinned. 'Try to figure it out.'

Jenny considered Johnny's words as she went home. What *was* going through Gregory's mind as he sat in front of them? The past? The present? The future? Someone he'd once loved? Someone he'd lost? What gave him that look of invincibility, of being separate from the rest of the world? Of not needing to be a part of it. Regret? Contentment? She worked her way through all those emotions as she sketched and sketched again.

For the third and final week his pose was different. He stood with his back to them, this time without any towel. It was easier to draw him when she didn't have to think about his expression, Jenny thought, and yet she knew that it was still the same. Still remote and still inaccessible.

'You've nailed it this time,' Johnny said. 'Great work.'

'You think?' She looked at the drawing, not seeing where she'd done well, only the errors she'd made.

'Definitely.'

'Everyone else has done better.'

'Not much,' said Johnny. 'Maybe others are technically stronger. But yours has personality.'

He clapped his hands and thanked them all. Gregory had disappeared behind the screen again, but this time he came back into the room and looked at the drawings.

'They're good,' he said as he studied them. 'Really good.' And then he stopped in front of the one Jenny had done the previous week, of him sitting staring into the distance, and frowned. 'Was that really how I looked?'

'No,' she said. 'I can't get your expression right. I tried very hard. But you're like a male Mona Lisa.'

Gregory laughed. 'I've been called a lot of names, but never Mona Lisa.'

'You're . . . Australian?' she hazarded.

'I'm from New Zealand,' he said. 'Here for a few weeks to study agricultural methods.'

'And sidelining in modelling?'

He grinned. 'I've done it before. Apparently I have a good body to draw.'

'That's true.' She thought she sounded like a groupie and she blushed. 'But that expression . . . What the hell were you thinking?'

'You want to know? You really want to know?'

'Yes.'

'Have coffee with me and I'll tell you,' he said.

It came as a shock to her to realise that she hadn't had coffee alone with a man other than Pascal since before they'd gone to Rome together. She didn't know any men with whom she could have coffee. But it was nothing more than a friendly drink. So she said yes.

Chapter 19

Steffie refilled the glasses as Jenny paused for breath. She hadn't said a word while her mother had been speaking, but now she looked at her with a wary expression in her eyes.

'Do I really want to know what's coming next?' she asked. 'Or can I guess?'

'I never meant to have an affair with him,' Jenny told her. 'I loved your dad, I really did. I still do. But Gregory was like no one I'd ever met before.'

'I guess nude New Zealand sheep farmers aren't ten a penny in Wexford,' said Steffie. 'How long did it go on for?'

'Until just before your father came home from Brussels,' said Jenny.

Their affair had been intense and all-consuming. From the moment they'd walked out of the coffee shop together and she'd driven him to the converted outhouse on a farm about fifteen minutes away, she'd known that she was going to sleep with him. And as soon as they'd stepped over the threshold, they began peeling the clothes off each other, Jenny finally touching the body she'd drawn so many times, feeling the bumps and the curves and the ridges that until now she'd only known in two dimensions.

It was too late to walk away.

Besides, she didn't want to.

'I don't think you should be telling me this, Mum.' Steffie was doing her best to hide her embarrassment. 'You don't need to justify it to me. You had an affair. I'm not happy about it, but I realise that these things happen sometimes. Does Dad know?' A thought suddenly struck her. 'Is that why he never married you? He was too upset?'

'It was a long time ago,' said Jenny. 'Pascal doesn't bear grudges, you should know that.'

'Did you keep in touch with Gregory? Do you . . . do you still love him, is that it? Did you not leave Dad because of us?'

'Of course I don't still love him. What d'you take me for?' Jenny shook her head. 'It's not that at all, Steffie. It's . . . Let me explain.'

The day before he left was a glorious Thursday when the sky was blue, the meadows green and the heat of summer hung in the air. She was lying, sleepy and sated, in the tangle of sheets on his bed when he propped himself up on one arm.

'Are you sure you don't want to leave that old man of yours and come with me to New Zealand?' he asked.

She thought of the dream she'd once had to travel the world, to live in Rome, to be a painter. She'd done none of these things. She'd settled down with Pascal and become a housewife, although not the sort of domestic goddess type that so many other women seemed to be. Her life outside

187

the home was limited, and her paintings merely adequate despite what Johnny Macken might have said about them. Gregory was giving her the opportunity to embrace a new life, to be a different person. To be the Jenny she'd thought she could be.

Or was he? As she gazed at him, she reflected that by going to New Zealand, she'd simply be replacing one man with another. Because she'd be living with Gregory on his sheep farm, wouldn't she, and that surely wasn't any more glamorous than living in Ireland. When he came back from a day doing whatever it was that sheep farmers did, he'd want her to have dinner waiting for him. It was all sultry sex now, but it wouldn't stay that way. She was foolish but she wasn't stupid. Besides, there were the children to think about. Leaving Pascal wasn't impossible, but how could she walk away from Roisin and Davey?

She knew the answer to that.

She couldn't.

She knew that he knew that too. That Roisin and Davey were actually his passport to freedom, because no woman ever walked away from her children. At least, no woman that she knew. And she wasn't going to be the first.

It was late by the time she arrived home. She walked into the kitchen, her hair unkempt and her eyes bright.

'Are you all right, Mum?' asked Roisin. 'We were getting worried.'

'Worried? What on earth were you worried about?'

'It's nearly seven o'clock,' Roisin said, unable to mask her anxiety. 'You're never out at seven o'clock.'

'I'm so, so sorry.' She gathered the two of them to her

and hugged them, inhaling the scent of them, knowing that she would never have left them. 'I met a friend and we were talking and I didn't realise how late it was. Give me a second to comb my hair and then I'll make dinner.'

She went upstairs and looked at herself in the mirror over the sink. Her eyes were red because she'd cried on the way home. She'd known it would come to this, that he'd leave and she'd stay, but she felt as though her heart would break all the same. She told herself that she hadn't really been in love with him, that it had been nothing more than a brief fling, but it had never felt like that. It had been real and glorious and liberating and wonderful. And she was saying goodbye to those feelings because she really didn't have a choice.

It seemed to her that she was always doing things because she didn't have a choice. Because she'd backed herself into a corner so that there was only ever one way out.

'You look a lot better now,' said Roisin when she returned to the kitchen, her hair brushed, her lips glossed and her body spritzed with Nina Ricci.

'I'm absolutely fine,' Jenny assured her.

It wasn't until nearly seven weeks later that she realised she was also pregnant.

Chapter 20

It took a moment before it sank in, and then Steffie stared wide-eyed at her mother.

'Pregnant. With Gregory's baby?'

Jenny nodded.

'Oh my God,' said Steffie. 'So what did you do— Oh!'

It had taken even longer for the full weight of what Jenny had said to register.

'You mean – you were pregnant with me? I'm the baby?' Her words were strangled.

'Yes,' said Jenny.

Steffie could feel the blood draining from her face. Her heart was pumping and there was a rushing sound in her ears. The focus of her vision narrowed so that it seemed that she was looking at Jenny through a tunnel. She felt sick.

'Are you all right?' Jenny's voice was anxious.

Steffie pressed her fingers against her eyes and rocked her body backwards and forwards.

'Steffie?'

'Don't talk to me. Not yet.' She was finding it hard to speak. She couldn't formulate words to encapsulate her thoughts. She wasn't even sure what she was actually thinking.

All she knew was that everything she had ever thought about herself was untrue. Pascal, the man she'd always looked up to, wasn't her father. Roisin wasn't her sister. Davey wasn't her brother. And Jenny, her mother, the person she'd loved and trusted most in the world, had betrayed all of them. She'd betrayed Pascal by sleeping with another man. She'd betrayed Roisin and Davey both by her actions and by her inaction in telling them that she and Pascal weren't married to each other. And she'd betrayed Steffie by all of that and, more shockingly, by only now revealing that Pascal wasn't her father.

Steffie continued to rock silently on the bed as she tried to put order on the chaos in her head. Roisin and Davey were still her half-sister and half-brother, she told herself. They were still related to each other. It wasn't such a big deal. Not really. Yet Pascal. Her dad. But not her dad. She wasn't related to him at all. She wasn't, as she'd always thought, half him and half Jenny. She was half Jenny and half a man who lived on the other side of the world. She didn't want to believe that. She didn't want to believe that Pascal wasn't really her father. It couldn't be true. People often said that she looked like him. They said she had his nose. And his chin. And that she had the same trick of rubbing her fingers across her eyebrows when she was worried. She was doing it now. She snatched her hand away from her face and stared at Jenny.

'Are you positive about this?' Her voice shook. 'The thing is, if you were sleeping with this man but you were with Dad too – well, you could be wrong, couldn't you?' She was saying the words while at the same time knowing that Jenny would never have told her this if it wasn't true.

Jenny shook her head. 'He was away,' she reminded her. 'For a month. The dates didn't add up. And later, I did a test. I'm really sorry, Steffie.'

Steffie swallowed hard a couple of times. She could feel tears welling up in her eyes but she didn't want to cry. Because if she cried, her mother would try to comfort her, and she didn't want Jenny to comfort her. She didn't want the comfort of someone she no longer believed in. She got up from the bed and went to the window, where she stared out over the garden. The rain was pummelling down harder than ever and the mosquito torches they'd placed so carefully earlier looked bleak and forlorn.

'Why didn't you tell me before now?' she asked. 'And why did you choose today of all days to bring me up to speed on your horrible, horrible secret?'

'I didn't know how to tell you,' confessed Jenny. 'There were loads of times when I thought about it and almost did, but . . .' She shrugged helplessly.

'So we go to the trouble of having an enormous party, and instead of managing to go along with it for one more day, you tell everyone about your fake marriage instead!' cried Steffie. 'And then you drag me up here to break my heart.'

'Steffie, darling, I don't want to break your heart.' Jenny was anguished. 'I never wanted to hurt you. Ever. But from the moment we walked in the door and saw you all, I simply couldn't stay quiet any more. I couldn't keep listening to everyone saying what good examples we were to them. I couldn't let people keep believing a lie. And once I'd confessed to that, I couldn't not tell you about . . . about Gregory either.'

'You should've told me years ago. You should have made

it your business to tell me.' Steffie was shaking, but she didn't know if it was from rage or because she was in shock.

'I know,' said Jenny. 'But I couldn't bring myself to do it. I didn't want to cause trouble.'

'You didn't want to cause trouble!' cried Steffie. 'It wouldn't have caused any trouble at all if you'd been truthful before now.'

'I'm a coward,' admitted Jenny. 'I always have been. I've always looked for the easy way out. It's my biggest failing. I worked hard to overcome it, but for this . . . for this I couldn't. Believe me when I tell you how sorry I am.'

'For what?' asked Steffie. 'For being beyond self-centred? For getting pregnant with Roisin? For not getting married? For having an affair? For having me?'

'I'll never be sorry about having you,' said Jenny. 'I love you. I always have and I always will.'

Steffie exhaled sharply. 'And Dad? I mean, Pascal? Do you love him? Does he love you?'

'I love Pascal more than I can say,' Jenny told her. 'And he loves me too, even if I let him down.'

'I suppose he must,' said Steffie. 'After all, you had an affair and you got pregnant and he didn't throw you out. Or . . .' she stared white-faced at Jenny, 'or doesn't he know? You're saying the dates were wrong, but you could have lied to him too, the way you've lied to everyone.'

'Of course he knows,' Jenny said. 'I couldn't keep that a secret. But Pascal . . . when we talked about it, when we were deciding what to do . . . we stayed together and we raised you as our child. Because we both love you. I love you so much, Steffie, and your dad – Pascal – he adores you. You know he does.'

193

Steffie couldn't speak. She swallowed hard, over and over, as she continued to process what her mother was telling her.

'And my biological father?' she said at last. 'The nude model sheep farmer person? What about him? What does he know?'

'I didn't have any forwarding address or phone number for him,' said Jenny. 'I had to let him go. If I'd had a way of communicating with him . . . well, maybe I would have felt obliged to tell him about you, and who knows how things would have turned out. It was important to make a break. He never came looking for me either. Not that I expected him to.'

Although for a while she had. Whenever she drove past the farm, she wondered if he'd be there, waiting for her. Every time the phone rang, she jumped to answer it, her heart pounding in anticipation. And when she saw Johnny Macken, she had to stop herself from asking if he'd heard anything from the nude model.

'So basically you're saying that the man you had an affair with, the man who fathered me, doesn't know I exist. And the man I call my dad has no blood ties to me at all and has only looked after me all these years out of the goodness of his heart.' Steffie's trembling voice broke the silence between them.

'It's not really like that,' said Jenny.

'Seems to me it's exactly like that.'

'Those are the facts,' agreed Jenny. 'The emotions, how people felt, why they did what they did – those are all very different.'

Jenny didn't know she was pregnant when Pascal came home from Brussels. It was the week before the children started back at school and the family had returned to Dublin. She was afraid that her guilt over the affair was written all over her face, but he didn't seem to notice anything amiss. He kissed her and told her that he'd missed her, then hugged the children and told them he'd missed them even more.

'I didn't realise how much I love being with you,' he told her on his first night back. 'And I'd forgotten how important it was for us to have fun together.'

The next day he brought her for a meal in the best restaurant in town, and kissed her in the street afterwards. Quite suddenly she saw him again as the man who'd taken her to Rome. They'd both been passionate people then, although when they'd had to face up to her pregnancy Pascal had gone from being passionate to practical in the blink of an eye. And even though she'd been grateful to him for the way he'd suddenly become a responsible adult, she'd often wished that they'd had more time together with the carefree side of their natures.

That was what she'd rediscovered with Gregory. The Jenny she'd once been. The Jenny she thought she still was. But she could rediscover it with Pascal too, couldn't she? After all, she truly loved him. It was just that their feelings had somehow become secondary to simply getting on with their lives. But not any more. She'd make sure of it. And she'd make it up to Pascal too. Gregory had been an aberration. A mistake. Someone her husband never needed to know about. It suddenly seemed to Jenny as if everything that had happened while Pascal had been away had happened to another person. Gregory had become someone insubstantial to her, conjured up from her imagination. Someone to forget as quickly as possible.

Every so often in the following weeks she would feel faint and light-headed as she thought of how near she'd been to catastrophe. She wondered what had happened to her, why she'd allowed herself to cheat on someone who had never cheated on her. Who wouldn't ever dream of cheating on her because he was a good man. A man who'd stood by her. A man she could trust.

I will never, ever put myself in that position again, she told herself one night as she lay sleepless in the bed beside him. From now on I'll be the perfect wife.

But a perfect wife didn't suddenly realise that she needed to buy another pregnancy test. Nor did she know before she bought it that her husband wasn't the father of her baby. And she didn't have to stand in front of him and confess that she was carrying another man's child.

Pascal was sitting beside Davey in the kitchen. He was listening to his son saying that this was a big fuss about nothing, that it didn't matter that he and Jenny weren't married because as far as everyone was concerned they were. Marriage was just a piece of paper, said Davey, who then glanced involuntarily at Camilla and hoped she hadn't heard him. But his girlfriend was engrossed in a conversation with Bernice and fortunately wasn't listening to him.

Pascal hardly heard him either. He was remembering when Jenny had told him about her pregnancy. He was remembering how surprised he'd been. And how pleased. And then, when she told him the truth about the baby's conception, how betrayed he'd felt.

The betrayal was like a punch in the stomach. He'd put her before everything and this was her thanks to him. The sole excuse he could make for her (and he couldn't believe he was making one at all) was that she'd been lonely while he was away. That she'd been the one left looking after the children and running the house while he was drinking Stella Artois in the bars around the Grand Place and having expenses-paid dinners in the sort of restaurants they normally wouldn't have been able to afford.

But there were no excuses. He himself could have fallen into the arms of the beautiful Amelie Lascelles, a raven-haired beauty from Paris, who'd leaned her head against his shoulder in a bar one night and murmured that she was fed up with being separated from her boyfriend. Or the pretty and vivacious Chiara Benedetti from Naples, who'd played footsie with him under the table at one of the formal dinners he'd attended. But he hadn't even considered it. Because as far as he was concerned, he was Jenny's husband. The fact that they weren't actually married made no difference to him whatsoever.

He was a fool, he thought. He'd had all these notions about doing the right thing by her, and then at the first opportunity she'd made a mockery of him. He didn't care that she was sobbing her eyes out in front of him, telling him that she was an awful person after everything he'd done for her. He knew that already. She was an ungrateful cheating bitch and he shouldn't stay another minute in the house with her.

But leaving her would be leaving everything he'd ever wanted. Because he'd always wanted her. From the minute he'd first seen her striding across the open-plan office in her tartan dress and platform boots he'd been captivated, and he still loved her, even though he was currently so angry that he could hardly be in the same room as her.

He loved that she was different, that she wasn't part of that set of chattering women who seemed to have no conversation other than their husbands and their children and their domestic lives. He loved that she could spend a whole evening marvelling at the iridescence of the oil patch in the driveway or caught up in trying to capture the beauty of a flower petal. He cut her some slack because, unlike him, a plodder, she was artistic. But this was an unbelievable amount of slack to cut. This was something that nobody could be expected to forgive and forget – not that he'd be able to forget anyway, when the evidence of her betrayal would be a living, breathing person. He knew that if he told anyone at all, their advice would be to leave her. But he couldn't. And yet he couldn't be with her either.

In the end it was Jenny who said that she'd go. She told him she couldn't expect him to take on the responsibility for her mistake. She said she understood how badly she'd hurt him and she told him that she would regret forever the fact that she'd cheated on him when he'd always been a rock to her. And then she said that he was lucky he'd never married her, because now he was free.

'Where will you go?' he asked.

'I don't know yet.'

'What about the children?'

'I hoped we could work that out,' she said. 'Joint parenting, isn't that the buzz phrase at the moment?'

'Did you ever love me?' he asked.

'I loved and I still love your kindness,' she said. 'And how you look after me and care for me. I've never had anyone care for me the way you do. I love that about you and I love you too, Pascal. I didn't appreciate you enough, that's all.'

'And him? What more did he give you?'

'He was a fantasy,' she said. 'My romantic fantasy.'

'I was never that,' agreed Pascal.

'I let myself get caught up in something because it was secret and exciting and made me feel good about myself,' said Jenny. 'I was totally in the wrong and I couldn't be more sorry.'

'Sorry for it happening or sorry for having to admit it to me? Because somehow I don't think you'd have said anything at all if it wasn't for the fact that you're . . . you're . . .' He couldn't say it. It was too much.

'Both,' she told him. 'I thought I'd got away with it. For a little while I thought I could keep getting away with it. But you're not a fool. You'd have figured it out.'

'I *am* a fool,' said Pascal. 'I let it happen.'

'I made it happen,' Jenny corrected him. 'Don't try to blame yourself.'

'I don't know if I want you to go.'

She looked startled.

'I mean, right now I'm so angry with you, you need to go. But we've always worked things out, you and me.'

There was a flicker of hope in her eyes. 'You'd forgive me? For this?'

'I don't know,' he said. 'I need some space. For a few weeks at least.'

'I could go to Aranbeg,' she said.

'No.' He spoke quickly. 'Not there. Not without me or the children.'

'There's a three-week residential painting course in Edinburgh starting next month. Before . . . before this I was thinking about it but I thought it would be too long to be away. Not painting nudes,' she added. 'Landscapes. I could go there and come home when it's over and we can decide then if you want me or not.'

He looked at her thoughtfully for a while and then he nodded. And the flicker of hope was there again.

When Roisin and Davey heard she was going away painting, their main concern was who would make the dinner every night. They didn't cry when she left, which made her think that she hadn't been a good enough mother to them, because surely your children should be upset when you went away. She wondered if she'd be any better with the new baby. And if she'd still have a family in which to raise it. Or if this time she was going to be the single mother she could have been twelve years earlier.

Chapter 21

'So you had an affair, got pregnant and then disappeared off to paint?' Steffie looked at her mother in disbelief. 'Leaving Dad . . . leaving Pascal to look after Roisin and Davey?'

'You're making it sound like I was going off to have fun. I wasn't. I was devastated. I didn't want to go but I knew I had to, and at least painting kept me sane.'

'I'm surprised he agreed to it at all, given what happened the last time you took painting classes!'

'Steffie, sweetheart, it was really difficult. This was the solution we came up with. We both needed time to think.'

'And in the end you came home and he lived with what you'd done? Without ever giving you a hard time?'

'I've always said I didn't deserve your dad,' said Jenny.

'You don't. You don't deserve him or us! And what about me?' Steffie's eyes were bright with tears. 'I'm talking about him as though he's my dad, but he isn't!'

'Of course he is.'

'No he's not,' said Steffie. 'I'll always think of him as Dad, you know I will, but I'm not . . . I can't believe you never told me any of this before. I can't believe you're telling me now. And I really and truly can't believe I'm not his daughter.'

'As far as he's concerned you are.'

'I understand all this stuff about your parents being the people who've raised you and nurtured you and loved you, and I accept that. But the thing is, Mum, you've lied to me for twenty-seven years. About you and Dad. And about me. And he might be a forgiving sort of person, but I'm not.'

She got up and walked out of the room. She slammed the door behind her and ran down the stairs. Pascal was standing in the hallway.

'Are you OK, sweetheart?' he asked.

'Thank you for everything you did.' Steffie grabbed the nearest jacket. 'You're an amazing person. I love you and I always will. But you should have told me. You should have made her tell me. And I can't stay in the same house as her any more.'

Then she opened the hall door and walked out into the rain.

'What on earth is going on?' demanded Roisin as she looked out of the window and saw Steffie's car speed down the driveway. 'Where's she going?'

'It's complicated,' said Pascal.

'What could Mum have said to make her rush off like that?'

Pascal hesitated.

'What?' asked Roisin. 'What's going on, Dad?'

'There's stuff we need to talk about,' Pascal said. 'But I don't think this is the right time.'

'How come it was the right time for Steffie, in that case?'

'Because it concerns her the most.'

Roisin ran her fingers through her hair in despair. She'd

planned for just about every eventuality as far as this party was concerned. Yet somehow it had completely slipped out of her control. And she had no idea why.

When Jenny came downstairs, all the adults, who'd gathered in the living room, turned towards her. She flinched beneath their scrutiny and stood beside Pascal, who put his arm around her.

'Where's Steffie?' she asked.

'She drove off,' said Roisin. 'Like the proverbial bat out of hell.'

'Where?'

'I don't know,' replied Roisin. 'How would I? I don't even know *why* she'd head off like that.'

'She's not thinking straight,' said Jenny. 'She's distressed.'

'It's not good that she's driving in the rain in that case,' said Roisin. 'And she had champagne earlier.'

'Oh God.' Jenny's voice was agonised. 'What if . . . what . . .'

'For heaven's sake, Mum,' said Davey. 'Tell us what's upset her so much. There's not much left, is there? You've already done the "actually kids we're not actually married" stuff. The only thing that could be worse is that none of us are really your children at all!'

Jenny covered her mouth with her hand.

'It's not that, is it?' asked Davey, his eyes widening. 'I mean, I was joking, right?'

'Of course not,' Jenny replied. 'But . . .'

'Tell us,' said Roisin. 'You can't keep secrets from us for ever. We need to know. We're *entitled* to know.'

'And *I* need to know Steffie's all right,' said Jenny.

'You started it all today,' Pascal said to her. 'And now you can finish it by telling everyone else.'

Jenny shot her husband an agonised glance, but Pascal's face was grim and set.

So even though she hated having to repeat the story, especially while Steffie wasn't there, Jenny told it again.

There was a shocked silence when she'd finished.

'I remember you going to Edinburgh,' said Sarah slowly. 'I remember you asking if I could help look after the kids while you were away. You said you'd had the chance to be involved in some kind of artists' retreat and exhibition.'

'We were talking about that earlier, Mum. You were cool as a breeze when I mentioned it!' Davey exclaimed.

'I took the children for a few days,' remembered Sarah. 'You didn't see fit to tell me the truth of why.'

'It was a personal matter,' said Pascal, his voice softening as he looked at Jenny's distraught face. 'You didn't need to know.'

'I don't believe it.' Lucinda turned to her sister. 'The golden girl with the feet of clay.'

'Lucinda, please.' Jenny's voice trembled. 'It was a hard time for Pascal and me.'

'I'll bet.'

'I'm not proud of myself,' said Jenny. 'But . . .' she bit her lip to stop it quivering and continued, 'but I am very proud of how Pascal and I worked things out in the end.'

'You worked it out by lying to everyone!' cried Lucinda. 'To me, to Sarah, to your children!'

'We didn't share something very personal,' Pascal corrected her. 'It was nobody's business but our own. And Steffie's, of course. Obviously we should have told her before now. That's as much my fault as Jenny's.'

Jenny shot him a grateful glance.

'Seems to me it's you, Pascal, who made sure everything worked out.' Sarah couldn't keep the bitterness from her voice. 'You're a paragon. You must be so proud of not being married to him, Jenny.'

'Bloody hell.' Davey gave a deep sigh. 'I thought I was part of the most boring, normal family in the world. Turns out I'm living an episode of Jeremy Kyle. My parents aren't married. My sister isn't my sister. Anything else I don't know about? Dad? Mum? Anything else to share?'

Jenny shook her head.

'So you went away, and when you returned, things went back to the way they were.'

'Yes,' said Pascal when Jenny didn't speak.

'But you still didn't get married.'

'No.' Jenny wiped her eyes with the shreds of her already sodden tissue. 'I just . . . I didn't want to force Pascal into anything. And then, when Steffie was born, it didn't seem to matter any more.'

'Brilliant,' said Sarah. 'You have a baby by another man and your partner, who's not even married to you, sticks by you. Whereas James and I, with four children of our own and after a flashy wedding that nearly ruined us financially, couldn't manage to hack it. You must have laughed at me every single day!'

'No I didn't,' said Jenny.

'And while I was struggling to bring Alivia up on my own, Steffie was accepted by Pascal.' Lucinda shook her head. 'How is it you always manage to end up on your feet, Jenny?

The rest of us get slapped in the face by life but you sail blithely on, no mud sticking.'

'I'd hardly call it sailing blithely on,' said Jenny. 'It was the most horrible time of my life.'

'But then Steffie was born and you doted on her,' said Roisin. 'She was spoiled and pampered the whole time. Even you, Dad. You brought her everywhere with you.'

'Overcompensating?' murmured Davey.

'When Jenny and I decided that we were staying together, I knew that we couldn't and wouldn't treat Steffie any differently to the two of you,' said Pascal.

'But you did!' cried Roisin. 'You indulged her like you never indulged us. She always got everything she ever wanted. You kept bailing her out of the financial holes she gets herself into because she's so fecking hopeless. You still do.'

'We had more money by then so it was easier to help her,' said Pascal. 'But if you two had needed the same sort of help we would have done everything we could for you. You know we would. Look, all this was particularly painful and difficult for your mother and me at the time, but we worked it out in our own way. I'm proud of how we did that. I'm proud of her and I'm proud of my children, and although I can't honestly say that I wouldn't change a thing, I can say that we both did our best for all of you.'

There was a silence after Pascal's words. Roisin and Davey exchanged glances but neither of them knew what to say.

'Well that's very noble, Pascal, and I'm sure we're all impressed by your forgiving attitude,' said Lucinda before turning to her sister. 'But Jenny – two unwanted pregnancies, for crying out loud! Why didn't you ever use protection? What were you thinking?'

'Not that I have to answer these intensely personal questions . . .' Jenny was suddenly spirited again, 'but I did. Mostly.'

'Too much information.' Davey winced.

'I know. But everyone seems to think it's OK to find out.'

'I do not think there is anything so terrible in all of this.' It was Camilla who spoke, her precise English sounding calm and reasoned after the agitated comments of the others. 'People make mistakes but it seems to me that Jenny and Pascal have dealt well with everything that has happened. They are happy and brought up their children well together in a strong family unit. There is no need for anger.'

'I'm not angry about the mistakes!' said Sarah. 'I'm angry that over my whole life Jenny and Pascal have been like the perfect couple, with their happy marriage and their lovely kids and their two houses. And now I realise it's all been based on a lie. Two lies!'

'But this is not something you should be upset about,' said Camilla. 'This is their life, not yours.'

'Everyone else in this family has lived in the shadow of their life!' cried Sarah. 'I listened to Jenny's advice when my marriage was going down the pan. I thought someone as happily married as her might have some insights. And now I know what they were. Don't get married, and shag a nude model. Brilliant!'

'Mum.' Carl, who was standing beside her, put his hand on her arm.

'Oh, don't Mum me!' cried Sarah. 'You can't talk about how people should behave when you turned up here and paraded your piece of fluff in front of a girl who has more class than her in her little finger.'

'Mum!' Carl glanced between Summer and Bernice. 'Don't be stupid.'

'Don't call me stupid,' said Sarah. 'You're the stupid one to have cheated on the woman who's been an absolute saint today.'

'Mum.' This time it was Colette who put a hand on Sarah's arm. 'This isn't the time or the place.'

'It's as good as any time and place!' retorted Sarah. 'Let's get all the dirty laundry out there.'

'Thank you for your support, Sarah,' said Bernice. 'But it's OK.'

'It's not OK to me,' said Summer. 'You've no right to insult me. Besides, Carl loves me, don't you, babes?' She leaned her head against Carl's arm.

'Well . . .'

'Of course he doesn't love you,' said Sarah. 'He's doing to you what Jenny did to Pascal. Maybe it's some kind of bad gene in the Marshall side of the family and it's coming out in my kids. After all, Colette's a serial fiancée, and if Carl can't see that Bernice has been an absolute heroine today and is worth a thousand Summers, he's a worse fool than I thought.'

'You're talking complete bollocks, Mum,' said Colette. 'I'm entitled to have as many fiancés as I like, and if Carl brings someone to the party while he and Bernice are on a break, that's his business. Look, everyone's upset, but Camilla is right, none of it is important right now. The best thing is that we allow Pascal and Jenny and the rest of their family to sort things out among themselves.'

Jenny smiled weakly at her niece. 'Thank you.' Then she looked at Pascal. 'We need to find Steffie. We need her to come home.'

Pascal looked grim. 'She said she didn't want to be here,' he said.

'I have to know that she's safe.'

'Wherever she's got to, she'll have a job getting back.' Roisin had gone to the front door to look outside, and now she returned, a worried expression on her face. 'There's a massive flood at the gates. Bernice might have been right about the stream. I think it's turned into a river. And it really has burst its banks.'

'Oh God,' said Jenny and rushed out of the house.

Everyone followed her. Roisin was right. The gates were half submerged by flood water. There was no way in or out.

'She can't have gone far.' Pascal reassured Jenny again 'She won't have done anything silly.'

'In this weather . . . in this rain . . .' Jenny began to bite a nail, a habit she'd given up years earlier. 'And I don't care what you say, she shouldn't be driving after drinking champagne.'

The family had crowded around the doorway and everyone was looking outside. The rain was falling in almost vertical sheets and it was difficult to see even as far as the gate. But it was clear that, in a standard car, the road was all but impassable.

'The end of the road must be completely under water by now,' said Roisin.

'If she turned the other way, up the hill, she should be OK,' said Pascal.

'And what then?' demanded Jenny.

'She could take the back road towards the village,' said Roisin.

'And what would she do there?' asked her mother. 'There's sod all in Castlemoran.'

'She could . . .' But Roisin was unable to think of any words of comfort. Not that she should be comforting Jenny anyway. Everything was her fault. All of it.

'Ring her.' Daisy handed Roisin her mobile phone.

Roisin hit Steffie's number. Everyone waited as the call connected. And then they heard the faint jingle of a phone. Summer, who was nearest the kitchen, walked through to the veranda, where she picked it up.

'Is this Steffie's?' she asked when she rejoined them.

'Bugger,' said Davey.

Jenny was close to tears again. 'It's awful out there and she's upset,' she said. 'What if she has a crash? Or if a tree comes down on her or something?'

'It's not windy,' Pascal told her. 'It's raining, that's all. And,' he added as the sky lit up, 'there's still some lightning in the distance.'

'So it could hit a tree, like in the garden,' said Jenny. 'And that could fall on her.'

'You're obsessed with trees, Jen,' said Paul. 'Don't worry about Steffie. She can look after herself. She'll be fine.'

'She's out there in a rainstorm!' cried Jenny. 'I don't think she'll be fine at all.'

'She's a good driver,' said Davey. 'She'll manage.'

'I'm a good driver but I wouldn't like to be driving around in the rain,' said Jenny. 'Not in that little car anyway.'

'I'll go and look for her,' said Bernice. 'I still haven't had any alcohol.'

'You've just dried off!' cried Jenny. 'I can't ask you to go out again.'

'*I'll* go,' said Colette. 'I haven't had anything to drink either, and the Santa Fe will be able to get through the water.'

210

'You're not going out alone in that,' said Sarah.

'I've driven in worse,' Colette told her.

'I'll come with you,' said Davey. 'When we find her, I might be able to talk some sense into her.'

'I don't mind going with Colette,' said Bernice.

'You've done your good deed for the day already,' Davey said. 'Stay here, stay dry.'

'I'm sure I'd be OK on my own,' said Colette.

'Don't be silly,' said Davey. 'What if you get stuck in a puddle? I know the women have been Amazonian so far today, but you might need a man's strength.'

'It's not safe,' said Sarah.

'I won't get stuck,' Colette said.

'But I'll come with you all the same.' Davey's words were emphatic.

'Do you want me to come too?' asked Carl.

'We'll be fine together.' Davey gave Colette an encouraging look. 'You'll be safe with me.'

Colette gave him a short smile in return, then went into the kitchen and got her bag before running out of the house with him.

'Phone me as soon as you find her!' cried Jenny as Davey opened the door of the 4x4.

'Will do,' he called.

Everyone watched as Colette started the engine and turned the car around. She headed down the gravel driveway and then through the flooded area at the gates, sending up a huge wave of water.

'I hope she knows what she's doing,' muttered Roisin.

'She's competent enough.' But Sarah didn't sound entirely convinced.

211

Chapter 22

The exit had already been partly flooded when Steffie had driven out thirty minutes earlier, and for a moment she'd thought that her grand gesture of storming out of the house would be followed by a pathetic return after abandoning the Citroën at the gate, but she'd made her way through and, keeping in mind what had been said about the lower road being almost impassable, had turned up the hill.

That was as far as her clear-headedness went, because once she'd got on to the road, she wasn't able to think at all. She drove randomly, with no idea of where she was going and what she planned to do when she got there. The only thought going round and round her head was that the foundations of everything she'd believed about her family and about herself had been totally shattered because her parents had systematically lied to her for her whole life.

Whatever their reasons had been for keeping their fake wedding a secret, not telling her about her real father was unforgivable. And that was something she could blame Pascal for too, because he could and should have insisted that Jenny tell her. It would have been a shock, of course, but a damn sight less of a shock than finding out at their surprise ruby wedding anniversary party. If nothing else, thought Steffie as she wiped her eyes with a tissue from the box on the dashboard, it proves that I'm right about surprise parties. They're always a bad idea. Maybe Roisin will listen to me about things like this in future, not that we'll be organising any more anniversary parties for Mum and Dad, given that they don't have an anniversary to celebrate.

Dad, she thought. I shouldn't call him Dad, because my biological father is a New Zealand sheep farmer and part-time nude model. Well, hopefully not a nude model any more, she acknowledged; he had to be in his fifties at least. She couldn't see fifty-year-old models being all that popular on the painting circuit. She shuddered. Anyway, whatever he's doing now, he doesn't even know I exist. Mum never told him. She never even tried to tell him, which was the one part of this sorry debacle Steffie really understood.

She shook her head. Her mother had been totally in the wrong, and despite the fact that she hadn't tried to make excuses, Steffie wanted neither to understand nor forgive her. No matter how hard she tried not to, she couldn't help visualising the man Jenny had described to her. Tall and blond and attractive, with his ripped abs and desirable body. Someone her mother hadn't been able to resist. Someone she'd been passionate about. Passionate about enough to cheat on her husband with. Steffie felt her stomach sink. Her parents had been so solid. And yet that had been nothing more than an illusion. She stifled a sob. Nothing was real. Least of all who she was.

She felt as though she was crumbling inside, that the layers of the person who'd been Steffie Sheehan were peeling away from her and leaving someone else behind. Someone who was different to everyone else in her family. Someone who was a permanent reminder to both Jenny herself and Pascal that Jenny had betrayed him. How can Pascal even look at me without feeling angry? Steffie asked herself. And how can my mother look at me without thinking about sneaking away to have sex with a stranger? How can I be a proper part of the family when I'm nothing more than the cuckoo in the nest?

Tears leaked down her face, blurring her vision even more than the rain beating against the windscreen. It was becoming increasingly difficult to see, even with the wipers on full. Part of her was beginning to regret having driven off, but how could she have stayed, knowing that everyone would be looking at her and realising her cinnamon-blond hair was a legacy from the unknown sheep farmer and not, as she'd always thought, the product of having a fair-haired mother and a dark-haired father.

And is that why Roisin and I are so different too? She sniffed and wiped her eyes with her balled-up tissue. After all, Roisin is organised and capable, like Dad. And Davey has become that way. But the sheep farmer sounds like someone who drifted around, shagging whatever woman came his way. Perhaps that's why I keep hooking up with the wrong men. Perhaps my legacy is not caring enough about the people I'm with. So I've got that from him and from Jenny – well, Jenny was totally selfish. And Roisin often says I'm selfish too. So clearly I'm more like my mother than I realised. I'm destined to live down to people's expectations.

And what are they thinking about me now? she wondered. No doubt they've been told that I'm not who they thought I was. Roisin is probably deciding that it's because I'm not

214

Dad's daughter that I'm not the person she wants me to be. The rest of them – maybe they're feeling sorry for me. Maybe they're thinking that I never properly fitted in at all. I'm not as much a part of the family as I believed. I'm an outsider.

A sudden increase in the volume of rain beating against the windscreen made her gasp and pushed all thoughts of people and their personalities out of her head. Driving in these conditions was scary. She couldn't keep going for much longer. But she couldn't turn back either.

The Citroën's headlights cut through the grey gloom of the evening. Normally, in August, it would simply be dusky at this time, but it was practically dark by now and the shadows of the surrounding trees and hedgerows danced in front of the headlights, while the rain continued to sluice down from the sky. The occasional roll of thunder in the distance made her jump each time she heard it, and she turned on the radio to drown it out.

The station was playing a mournful love song, full of broken hearts and hopeless longing. The plaintive music suited her mood. She suddenly felt like a character in a horror movie – the stupid girl alone in her car not knowing that there are ghouls and vampires and potential murderers on the loose. OK, so she didn't believe in ghouls or vampires, but it was kind of creepy being out here by herself. She wished someone was with her. She wished she didn't feel so completely alone.

Colette turned right out of the gates and towards the lower road. She didn't mind driving in difficult conditions – in fact she enjoyed the challenge – but there was no doubt that this was the most violent rainstorm she'd ever experienced. Nevertheless, she felt secure in the Santa Fe and comforted by the fact that Davey was in the passenger seat beside her.

She glanced at him but he was looking away from her, out of the window. His profile was sharp and defined and his dark hair curled over the collar of his shirt, damp from the brief run from the house to the car. He hadn't changed at all, thought Colette. He was still one of the best-looking men she'd ever known. Better-looking than any of her three fiancés. Better-looking than the most recent guy she'd broken up with, long before there was any talk of commitment or engagements. She wondered how it was that her cousin had managed to evade the clutches of a woman for so long. She thought about the very beautiful Camilla Rasmussen and sighed. She'd realised a long time ago that she didn't have the kind of looks that girls like Camilla had. Her face was simply average, with a nose that was slightly too big and eyes that were a little too narrow. During her goth period she'd festooned her conk with piercings and nose rings and used masses of kohl on her eyes. She still had the marks of the piercings and she still used kohl, although not as extravagantly. Being a goth had worked for her for a few years but she'd grown tired of the entire subculture and hating the world. She'd added pinks and blues to her hair and then eventually had left the whole monochrome look behind. Now she'd gone with rockabilly, which allowed her to embrace her curves and her love of high heels. But nobody would ever call her glamorous or elegant. Not ever. In comparison to his girl-friend, she thought, Davey must think of me as an elephant.

She shot him a glance, anxious that he might be able to somehow read her thoughts. But of course Davey Sheehan had never read her thoughts. Because if he had, he'd have known that ever since the summer she and her brothers had stayed at Aranbeg, she'd been in love with him. Miserable though her unrequited affection had made her, it had been the only saving grace of an even more miserable summer. She'd known there was something wrong between her parents. She'd been convinced that she and the boys had been shipped away to give them time to fight in private. Because it was all they seemed to do those days. Sarah would do something and James would pick a fight over it, and vice versa. It was exhausting and she hated it. But she hated even more being away from them and not knowing what was happening. Aunt Jenny and Uncle Pascal had been kind to them all, but Colette hadn't wanted to be there. And she was driven demented by Steffie, much younger than her and nothing more than a child, who'd wanted to be friends and who questioned her incessantly about everything she did and poked around her room wanting to inspect her clothes, her books and her portable CD player.

That was what had led to the incident in the apple tree, when she'd pushed Steffie and she had tumbled from the branches on to the grass below. Colette had nearly died of fright when she'd seen her fall but at the same time she'd been furious with the younger girl, who'd somehow managed to get hold of her diary. Colette's big fear was that she'd read it. And read what she'd written about Davey.

You are the one, she'd scrawled in her big, looping hand. *You're the one who lights up a room every time you walk into it. You're the one who makes my day better. You're the one who understands me. Because nobody else does.*

It was true. Davey had been lovely to her that summer.

217

Despite being five years older and practically a grown-up, he'd treated her as an equal. He'd sat and talked to her about friends and family, school and holidays, cars and movies. He was easy to talk to. He didn't patronise her like her brothers. He didn't sound perpetually annoyed with her like her mother. And despite their age difference, she'd fallen in love with him and thought that he might have fallen in love with her too. She'd hoped that he'd wait for her until she was the right age for him. She'd almost convinced herself until the day Dervla Murphy had shown up and Davey had told Colette he couldn't go into town with her because he was spending the day with Dervla instead.

Dervla was an elegant brunette who lived in one of the neighbouring houses. Her family had been to the Canaries for three weeks. Now they were back and Colette realised that Davey had been kind and friendly to her, but that he was in love with (or at least fancied) Dervla Murphy. When Davey and Dervla were together, there was a completeness about them that wasn't there when she was with him. She could see it. And it mortified her to think that she had, even for a moment, believed that her cousin could possibly be in love with her. She knew nothing about love. She was an idiot.

And I never really learned, she thought as she slowed down at the flood water. I managed to think I'd found it three times, but I hadn't. Because nobody has ever lived up to Davey Sheehan. Nobody ever will, and the worst part of it all is that he'll never know that.

'Oh my God, she couldn't have got through this.' Davey was staring out of the windscreen at the flooded road.

'If she came this way she must have,' said Colette. 'Otherwise her car would be stuck here.'

'That's true,' he conceded. 'I was being stupid. Thank God you're logical.'

Maybe that had been the problem, thought Colette. She'd treated Davey like a friend. She hadn't batted her eyes or said silly things or looked adoringly at him like Dervla had done. And so he'd never seen her as someone he could love, only someone he could talk to. He saw her as a logical person, not an emotional one. Not that it should matter now. She was, of course, long over him. It was just . . . there were some things you couldn't put behind you completely. And for her, Davey was one of them.

Back at the house, the family had divided up into various groups. Sarah, Jenny and Lucinda were sitting together in the living room. Paul, Pascal and Carl were in the kitchen. Poppy and Dougie were in the small annexe to the living room, watching a Disney movie. Roisin and Daisy, together with Alivia, Camilla and Bernice, were on the veranda. Summer was also on the veranda but she was standing apart from the others, engrossed in her mobile phone.

'D'you think Aunt Steffie is OK?' Daisy asked her mother.

'Of course I do,' said Roisin, who was trying to work out how on earth she could fix everything that had gone wrong today but not coming up with any kind of sensible plan.

'Because Poppy said that you all nearly drowned coming back from the hospital. What if Aunt Steffie nearly drowns too?'

'Poppy was exaggerating. And Aunt Steffie can look after herself,' Roisin said.

'But her car isn't as good as Bernice's,' said Daisy.

'She was silly to go out in the rain but there's no need to worry.'

219

'Your Aunt Steffie will be perfectly all right.' Bernice's words were calm and gentle.

'She should've taken her phone,' Daisy said. 'I never go anywhere without mine. Mum won't let me. She says it's so she can keep track of me. I don't like her always keeping track but it would be a good idea for Aunt Steffie right now.' She looked defiantly at her mother.

'It would,' agreed Roisin. 'But Aunt Steffie is a grown-up. She'll be fine.'

If it was me out there, that'd be true, thought Roisin. Because I can cope. That's what I do. But Steffie – she's hopeless. And I'm not sure she'll be fine at all.

'She'll be fine.' Sarah echoed Roisin's words as she patted Jenny on the shoulder. 'She's a sensible girl.'

'No she's not,' said Jenny. 'She's a dreamy and impulsive girl. She's got her head in the clouds half the time. She does daft things and she's not thinking straight right now.'

'At least you know she gets all that from you and not the nude model.' Lucinda couldn't help herself.

'Oh shut up, Luce,' said Jenny tiredly.

'You should've told us the truth about you and Pascal,' said Sarah. 'It would've made such a difference.'

'How?' asked Jenny.

'I mightn't have married James, for a start,' replied Sarah.

'And I wouldn't have felt that I'd let Mum and Dad down,' added Lucinda.

'It's not my fault.' Jenny wrapped her arms around herself. 'You can't blame me for your choices.'

'We always had to measure up,' Sarah said. 'And we were always falling short.'

220

'Please don't say that,' begged Jenny. 'Please don't blame me for everything that's gone wrong in your lives. And for how you feel about it.'

Sarah opened her mouth but saw Lucinda's warning look. And so she didn't say anything else.

Alivia was watching her mother and her aunts. She could tell by Jenny's face that whatever was being said wasn't what she wanted to hear, and she felt sorry for her. Today was meant to have been a huge celebration but it had turned into a total disaster. Which, if it wasn't for everything that had unfolded, might have been funny, because Roisin had been her usual self in micromanaging everything and it had been amusing, on one level, to see the expression on her face when Jenny had dropped her bombshell. But Steffie . . . Alivia's heart went out to her younger cousin. It must have been an awful shock for her to find out about her father like that. No wonder she went haring off into the rain. All the same, who would've thought it of Jenny? An illicit love affair. An unexpected pregnancy. And all that on top of the fake wedding in Rome! We all think, Alivia mused, that the older genera-tion lead much duller lives than us, but the truth is that everyone has their own crisis to deal with.

She took out her phone and frowned. No messages from Dermot even though she'd sent him a couple of selfies taken in the garden, and had then texted him to say that he was missing out on major drama at Aranbeg but that she'd fill him in later. He usually liked drama and scandal. She knew he was probably busy at the charity event but that didn't mean he couldn't send her even one text in reply to all of hers. Her main concern was that Sophie Fisher was at the event too, because she and Dermot were both patrons of the charity. There was no reason for Alivia to think that there was anything more than a professional relationship between them, but as far as everyone else was concerned, Sophie and Dermot were still a happily married couple. And despite what she'd said to Steffie earlier, Alivia wasn't comfortable with the deception.

'It is clear that Davey and Colette haven't found Steffie yet.' Camilla spoke as Daisy left the adults to get a drink, and drew Alivia's attention away from her mobile, which she put back into her bag. 'He would've called by now if they had.'

'I guess so,' Alivia said. 'It might not have been such a good idea to go chasing after her. She's an adult. She can look after herself.'

'This is not what Davey says about her,' Camilla said.

'Really?'

'Or Carl,' added Bernice. 'He always says that she has her head in the clouds. Like Jenny.'

'She's not as dopey as everyone's making out,' said Alivia. 'She has her own business, for goodness' sake.'

'But she doesn't make any money,' said Camilla. 'It is important if you have a business to know how to generate profit, don't you think?'

'Well . . .'

'Davey told me she set up her business because she couldn't find anything else. But that if it weren't for her parents she would have no money because she's living in their house rent-free.'

'Not completely rent-free,' Alivia pointed out, although she only had sketchy knowledge about Steffie's financial affairs. 'Besides, it takes time to build a business. It's good of Pascal and Jenny to help her out while she finds her feet.'

'I don't disagree,' said Camilla. 'But I don't know if she'll ever find her feet, as you say. It seems to me that she's a nice girl but not a businesswoman.'

'You hardly know her,' protested Alivia.

'I don't need to,' said Camilla. 'It's easy to see.'

'Not everyone has to be a ruthless businesswoman,' said Bernice. 'Sometimes it's good just to be nice.'

'Not if you're trying to earn a living.' Camilla shrugged. 'I am not trying to be critical of Steffie. After all, I believe that there is more to life than simply making a profit. But you have to make some money to survive.'

'Hopefully Steffie's business will make money one day,' said Alivia.

Camilla said nothing.

'Anyway, my sister's career choices are hardly the most pressing issue.' Roisin had kept quiet while everyone was analysing Steffie. 'Where she's gone and how she's feeling are more important.'

'She is embarrassed,' Camilla said. 'But there is nothing for her to be embarrassed about. So her father is not her father. And you are her half-sister. She will get over that. I have half-brothers and sisters. It is normal.'

'Not for us,' said Roisin.

'It doesn't matter who your biological parent is.' Camilla was dismissive. 'It is who *you* are that counts.'

Easy to say, Roisin thought. Not always as easy to accept.

Davey and Colette were debating about whether to go back to Aranbeg. They hadn't seen Steffie's car. In fact since they'd been out looking for her they'd only seen one other vehicle, a green Land Rover heading in the direction of McGovern's farm.

'She might have made it to Wexford,' Davey said. 'In which case we could be driving around for hours without spotting her.'

'Does she have any money with her?' Colette looked at him thoughtfully. 'She left her phone behind; maybe she left her bag behind too. And that means she can't stay anywhere.'

'Why did she have to be such an idiot!' exclaimed Davey. 'I know she was upset, but running away never solves anything.'

'Yet you did,' said Colette.

'Excuse me?'

'You left Ireland after you split up with that girl, didn't you?'

'I left because I got a job in Denmark,' Davey said.

'But would you have taken it if you'd still been going out with Emily.'

'How on earth do you know the name of my very ex-girlfriend?' Davey asked in astonishment.

'I'm female,' said Colette. 'We remember these things.'

'Mother of God.' He shook his head. 'I hardly remember her name myself.'

'I talked to Steffie about it before,' explained Colette. 'She told me she'd always felt a little guilty because she was the one who'd mentioned that she'd seen Emily with someone else.'

'You women are incredible.' Davey was still taken aback. 'I didn't even think you and Steffie were in touch with each other.'

'We're not that close,' Colette said. 'I bumped into her in town one day and she mentioned it.'

Colette didn't add that Steffie had only told her because she'd specifically asked how Davey was. When she'd heard, she'd had to stop herself phoning him to ask him if he was OK.

'I certainly didn't run away because of her,' Davey said. 'I admit that I was a bit hurt. But I would've taken the job regardless.'

'And would Emily have come with you to Denmark?'

'How would I know? It's not something I ever even thought about.'

'How is it that men get over things so quickly?' she asked.

'Hey, you get over things quickly yourself,' he returned. 'Three fiancés?'

Colette was silent.

'Sorry,' said Davey. 'I didn't mean it to sound as though I was getting at you.'

'You're not,' she said. 'You're right. Three of them and I don't regret any of those break-ups.'

'Why did you split with them all?' he asked.

Because none of them were you, she thought. Although that wasn't what she said. Instead she joked that she liked engagements but not weddings, which made him laugh. And then they discussed again what to do about Steffie.

'Tell you what,' said Davey. 'We'll go back up the road, past the house. I've just remembered there's a garage about two kilometres further along, on the way to Castlemoran. We'll ask if anyone's seen her. If not, we'll give up and hope she's found somewhere in Wexford to stay.'

'Does she have any friends there?' asked Colette.

'She could have,' said Davey. 'I wouldn't know, but perhaps Mum and Dad do. I'll phone them and ask.'

It was Roisin he called, and she told him that Steffie hardly spent any time at Aranbeg these days and that she didn't know of any friends, but to hold on while she asked their parents. When she spoke again, it was to say that neither Jenny nor Pascal were aware of friends in Wexford, but that Steffie could, of course, have gone back to Dublin. They knew that her best friend there was called Brianna but they didn't know her number.

'I tried checking her phone,' said Roisin. 'But there's a code and I don't know it. I had two guesses, neither of which was right, so I stopped before I locked her out.' The frustration in her voice was evident.

'OK,' said Davey. 'Colette and I will give it one last shot and let you know.'

'Good luck,' said Roisin.

'How's Mum?'

'So-so.'

'And Camilla?'

'She's fine,' said Roisin. 'Why wouldn't she be?'

'Well, it's not what you'd call a great introduction to the family for her, is it?' said Davey. 'She'll think we're all complete nutters.'

'And she'll be right,' said Roisin.

Davey disconnected the call while Colette turned the car around and began to head back towards Aranbeg. The flood at the end of the road was as deep as ever, but she drove through it quickly and fearlessly. Then she took them past the house and up the hill.

'The garage is on the left,' said Davey as they peered

through the windscreen. 'A few minutes after the crossroads.'

'I remember it,' Colette said. 'There was a shop there when we were kids. We used to buy ice creams. You introduced me to the Wobbly Wobbly Wonder.'

'Did I?' Davey grinned. 'It was my favourite.'

'I liked Brunch,' she told him.

'A good one too.' He nodded.

They fell into an almost companionable silence as they each recalled their childhood summers. And then, about half a kilometre before the garage, Colette gave a cry and brought the Santa Fe to a stop. She and Davey exchanged worried glances.

Because in the ditch at the side of the road was Steffie's blue Citroën.

The passenger door was wide open.

And there was no sign of her.

Chapter 23

Steffie couldn't decide if her blurry vision was due to the tears that were continually welling up in her eyes, the rain beating against the windscreen of the car, or the fact that she'd been drinking champagne earlier. In her frenzied dash out of the house, she'd forgotten about the alcohol, and even though she'd switched to cranberry juice later, she was uncomfortably aware that it would be better not to be driving at all. Which meant that she should really turn around and go home. But even if she wanted to, turning around in the narrow country road was impossible. She remembered a garage further up the road that would be a better place to stop. With a bit of luck she could get some hot coffee there and drink a gallon of it before . . . Well, she wasn't sure what she wanted to do or where she wanted to go yet. Maybe she'd be in a better frame of mind to figure that out after the coffee.

She sniffed a couple of times and rubbed the back of her neck. Her eyes were hot and stinging and her head ached. The rain drummed even harder against the windscreen and Steffie had to squint to see through it. Then she shrieked in disbelief as a dark shape shot across the road in front of the car. She yanked the steering wheel to avoid what she supposed was a fox or a cat (and hoped wasn't a ghoul or a murderer) and felt the Citroën skid on the surface water. With an increasing sense of horror, she realised that she wasn't in control any more and that she was heading for the ditch on the opposite side of the road. She tried desperately to correct the skid but the wheels had lost traction, and despite her turning into it as she once remembered being told to do, the car wasn't responding. She couldn't believe that she was about to crash. Yet there was nothing she could do to stop it. The Citroën hit the grass verge with a jolt and for a second she thought that everything was going to be all right because the impact hadn't been forceful enough to deploy the airbags. But then she felt the ground give way beneath her as the vehicle toppled slowly and inexorably into the ditch, taking her with it.

Her seat belt kept her anchored in her seat, although her head bumped sharply against the driver's door window when the car tilted sideways, stunning her for a moment. When her vision cleared, she could see the hedgerows and grass of the ditch through the window. She could also see that the ditch, normally dry, was full of water, which was already trickling into the footwell of the car. She felt a rising sense of panic as she scrabbled frantically at her seat belt without managing to release it. She recalled again her childhood fantasy of pretending to be a drowning princess, lying in water with her hair spread out, about to be rescued. But that had been in the safety of the bathroom, knowing her family was nearby. Who was going to rescue her now? Even as she felt around for it, she remembered with a sense of despair that she'd left her mobile phone at Aranbeg. She couldn't call for help. Her mind was swamped with images of people finding her dead body anchored in the car, and the type of story that might be on the evening news. She imagined Sophie Fisher reporting on the devastation wreaked by the storm. Sophie was always good with the tragedy stories. Her lyrical voice with its soft cadences sounded both sympathetic and reassuring. Perhaps Alivia would do a programme on the storms too, full of human interest and drama and the sad story of her drowned cousin. And after the TV reports, there'd be a photo in the paper and an interview with her grieving mother . . . At the thought of Jenny talking about how much she loved her, Steffie gritted her teeth.

Pull yourself together, she told herself. You're not dead yet. And you're not going to die either. The water isn't even in the car yet, for crying out loud. All you have to do is to stop panicking, undo the seat belt and get out. Having given herself the lecture, she immediately felt a bit better. She took her time with the belt, finally managing to release it, then clambered across the centre console of the car to open the passenger door. It took some effort but she eventually succeeded. She pulled the jacket she was wearing more closely around her – it was a man's jacket that she'd taken on her race from the house and it didn't fit her properly, but it offered some protection from the relentless rain.

A moment later she was standing at the side of the road, looking at the car and thinking that she'd been lucky to get out when she did, because the rising water had now covered the floor beneath the driver's seat. She was trying to figure out precisely where she was, because she was confused about which direction the car was now facing. She hoped her disorientation was simply due to shock and not the bump on her head, which was now throbbing fiercely. She looked around her, trying to spot a landmark. In the distance, along the road to the right, she thought she could see a faint glow of light. That must be the service station, she thought with relief. She'd be fine once she got there.

She started to walk, the slight heels of her sandals unsteady on the uneven surface of the country road. The further she went, the more she began to think that she'd made a mistake and that she was walking in the wrong direction. But there was definitely light ahead. The best thing to do was to keep going until she reached it.

Davey and Colette spent ten minutes searching the immediate vicinity of Steffie's car to make sure that she hadn't collapsed anywhere nearby because of an injury.

'She must have got out herself,' Davey said. 'The windscreen is cracked but intact, so she wasn't thrown out.'

'Maybe someone helped her,' suggested Colette.

'I guess. But she would have let us know, wouldn't she?'

'Not necessarily,' Colette replied. 'Should we call Roisin, d'you think?'

'Let's go to the garage first,' suggested Davey. 'If Steffie's there, or has been there, at least we'll have something more useful to tell her.'

Colette nodded and the two of them set off in the 4x4 again. They were both thoroughly soaked by now, and as Davey turned the heat up, he felt a wave of anger towards his younger sister. My younger half-sister, he corrected himself, if we're being technical about it. And suddenly his anger disappeared, replaced by a surge of sympathy for her. It had been a shock, no doubt about that. He couldn't really blame her for wanting to get away for a while. It was just a pity that she'd hared off on the worst night of the year. And that she'd managed to crash her car – the very thing that Jenny had been so worried about. Davey didn't think Steffie had been drunk, but she definitely shouldn't have been driving. And whatever condition she was in now, she clearly shouldn't be wandering around dark, narrow roads in this weather. He hoped she'd made it to the garage. He hoped she was still there.

But the attendant behind the till shook his head when they asked whether a rain-soaked fair-haired girl had come into the garage any time within the last forty-five minutes.

'It's been dead quiet,' he told them. 'Not a sinner. Not that I'm surprised in this weather.'

'Well look, if she does come in, will you get her to call me?' asked Davey. 'She doesn't have her phone with her and we're worried.'

'You need to contact the police,' said the attendant. 'Nobody should be out in that.'

Davey and Colette exchanged glances. Calling the police would make it seem so formal. It would be admitting that something really had happened to Steffie, and he wasn't ready to accept that. But perhaps it was time he did.

'Let's get back to Aranbeg,' said Colette. 'We'll talk to your parents before calling in the guards.'

'OK.' Davey was glad that Colette was with him. She was so solid and sensible, despite the mad hair and the bumblebee dress. But then she'd always had a strong streak of common sense running through her. He remembered thinking the same thing when she'd stayed at Aranbeg all those years ago during her parents' horrible break-up. When she'd spoken to him about them it had been with a despairing practicality that he'd found refreshing.

He strapped himself into the passenger seat again and let her drive him home.

The lights were further away than Steffie thought, and by the time she reached them she had blisters on her feet and was wet through and shivering. She'd definitely managed to get lost, because the building in front of her wasn't the service station she'd been expecting, but a converted two-storey house with a cube-shaped extension to the front. It was well lit and welcoming and she recalled that a long time ago it had been Mulligan's pub. But now there was a large sign outside that said 'Cody's'.

Cody's. She frowned. That was the restaurant her parents had been supposed to go to tonight. The restaurant owned by Liam Kinsella. He must have transformed the old pub into his high-class eatery. It wouldn't do his image any good for her appear on his doorstep like a survivor from a ship-wreck. But she couldn't go anywhere else. She was too tired and too cold. And apart from a few houses she recalled further down the road, there really wasn't anywhere else *to* go.

She walked up the steps to the door, then pushed tenta-tively against it a couple of times. It didn't budge and she feared that, despite the lights, the restaurant was closed. She felt a wave of despair as more tears stung her eyes. She couldn't walk any further. She really couldn't. Then she gave the door a tug. It flew open and she wobbled on the threshold before regaining her balance and stepping inside. Her first emotion was one of relief at being out of the interminable rain. She looked around the small entrance hallway, which contained a coat rack, a small desk and a large mirror. Another door, of frosted glass, with 'Cody's' etched on it, led into the cube and what had to be the restaurant itself.

She hesitated for a moment, then opened the door. The room in front of her was intimate, with about a dozen tables cosily arranged around banquette seating. However, there were only two diners, seated at a table in the corner. She stared at them in astonishment.

'Bobby,' she said. 'Tom.'

Her cousin Bobby and his partner, Tom, had left the party at the same time as most of the other guests. They must be staying nearby, she thought, although why they'd come out for something to eat on such a horrendous night and when there'd been plenty of food at the party was a mystery to her.

'Steffie, sweetheart!' Bobby put his knife and fork on the table and looked at her in astonishment. 'What on earth are you doing here?'

'And what in God's name happened to you?' asked Tom.

'I . . . um . . .' She felt herself wavering on her feet as the warmth of the restaurant and the sight of familiar faces overwhelmed her.

'Are you OK?' Both of them spoke at the same time.

She didn't answer. She couldn't. She swayed on legs that had turned to jelly beneath her. It was Bobby who jumped out of his seat and caught her as she fell.

When she opened her eyes again, she was on a chair, with Tom holding her hand and Bobby's arm around her shoulders. And when she eventually raised her head, she also saw Liam Kinsella standing in front of her. He was dressed in his chef's whites and was wearing a pair of bright green Crocs on his feet.

'Glad you're back with us,' he said. 'How are you feeling?'

'I . . .'

'You need to change out of those wet things,' said Liam. 'And then I'll get you something hot to eat.'

'I'm fine. Really. There's no need to get me anything.'

'You fainted,' Tom said. 'You're not fine.'

'And you're soaked. You'll catch your death unless you get out of those clothes and have something to warm you up,' Bobby added.

'I'm OK,' she said and then shivered. 'I don't have anything to change into.'

'I've spare stuff,' said Liam. 'A bit big for you but much better than staying in wet things. Give me a minute and I'll get it for you. You can change in my flat upstairs.'

'Oh look, I don't want to cause trouble,' she said through teeth that were starting to chatter.

'Don't be silly,' said Liam. 'It's no trouble and you'll catch pneumonia otherwise.'

She didn't have the energy to argue with him.

'Are you all right, sweetie?' asked Bobby when Liam disappeared into the kitchen. 'Is everything OK at Aranbeg?'

'I will be.' She rubbed her arms as briskly as she could. 'And yes, more or less they're fine at home. What on earth are you two doing here?'

'Eating dinner,' he replied.

'But . . . but there was a ton of food earlier. How can you possibly be hungry now?'

Bobby looked guiltily at her. 'We don't really do mass catering,' he said.

'Bobby Sheehan!' Steffie felt her strength returning. 'That was good food, not mass catering.'

'Sorry, sorry,' said Bobby. 'I meant . . . well, we don't like turkey and ham salads, that's all.'

'There were vegetarian options too.'

'We didn't have very much,' said Tom. 'And when your mum dropped her bombshell and everyone left early, we decided to see if we could find somewhere to eat. Mrs Brannigan in the guest house told us about this place, and it's so close it seemed like a good idea. Did you know that Cody's is considered the best restaurant for miles? And that Liam has won awards?'

'Yes,' she said. 'Mum and Dad were supposed to eat here tonight, but because of the party they had to cancel. At least, Roisin cancelled for them.' She looked around her. 'Which I'll bet Liam wasn't too happy about. It doesn't seem to be very busy.'

'The weather,' said Liam as he walked back into the dining room carrying a bundle of clothes. 'We had plenty of early diners but most of the later sittings cancelled. I don't blame them. I wouldn't come out in this myself. So I sent the staff home and I was going to close the kitchen when these guys showed up. Here.' He proffered the clothes, some T-shirts and chef's trousers. 'It's spare gear we keep in the kitchen,' he said. 'If you'd like a jumper or socks as well, I have some upstairs.'

'These are great,' she said. 'Thank you.'

'This way.' He led her through a door at the back of the restaurant and pointed at a narrow flight of stairs. 'First on the right at the top,' he said.

'You're sure it's OK?'

'Of course.'

'Thanks.'

She climbed the stairs, conscious that she was dripping rainwater on to the pale hessian carpet. She opened the door to Liam's flat and stepped into a small living room furnished with a couple of two-seater sofas either side of a rectangular coffee table. She had to lean over some brown cardboard boxes to draw the curtains across the windows. She supposed that during the daytime Liam would have a view of the chequered green valley that stretched towards the town, but in the blackness of the night and with the rain beating against the glass, it was hard to see past the car park.

She didn't want to undress in the living room, so she opened the first door she saw but closed it quickly when she realised she was looking into a small room dominated by an enormous bed. When Liam had spoken about the flat, she hadn't thought he actually lived here.

The bathroom was as compact as the rest of the flat and she peeled off her wet things awkwardly before putting on a T-shirt and loose chef's trousers from the freshly laundered selection Liam had given her. After towelling her hair and running her fingers through it, she felt marginally better. She wished she'd had the wit to bring her bag with her when she'd stalked out of the house, because her face could have done with some repair work – her make-up and mascara had smudged in the rain, and after washing it off she looked pale and wan. She pinched her cheeks and bit her lips a few times to bring some colour into them, then went downstairs again.

'Better?' asked Bobby as she walked into the restaurant.

'A lot.' It was true. She didn't think she was going to keel over any more and she felt warm for the first time since she'd stormed out of Aranbeg.

'Good.' He slid along the red banquette so that she could sit beside him.

'You look better,' observed Tom. 'You scared the living daylights out of me when you walked through that door first. I thought you were a ghost.'

Steffie smiled faintly. 'You're a desperate man for the exaggeration,' she said.

'He's not,' Bobby told her. 'You looked awful. But, like he said, a lot better now. You're totally rocking the trainee chef look.'

'Don't think I'd make it in the kitchen somehow,' said Steffie.

'Oh, we could train you up, no bother,' said Liam, as he placed a bowl of steaming soup in front of her. 'Here. Get this into you.'

'I'm not hungry.' She'd remembered again why she was there in the first place. The reason she'd left Aranbeg in a daze. Her stomach flipped.

'Of course you are,' said Liam. 'Have a little. It'll warm you up.'

'I'm not that cold now,' she said truthfully. Nevertheless, she picked up a spoon, because despite her unsettled stomach, the aroma of the French onion soup in front of her was totally irresistible.

'My own secret recipe,' Liam told her as she took a tentative taste.

'Oh my God,' she said. 'It's the best soup I've ever had in my life.'

Liam looked pleased. 'Glad you like it.'

'It's amazing,' she said. 'I wasn't hungry, but . . .'

'When you've finished your soup, you can tell us how come you've walked in here looking like Ophelia,' said Bobby.

'I'll leave you in peace,' said Liam. 'It's obviously a family matter.'

'No, don't.' She reached out and touched his arm, then withdrew her fingers quickly. She'd touched Liam Kinsella before, high-fiving him at a rounders game or giving him a sympathetic pat on the back when he'd been run out. It hadn't been a big deal. But brushing her fingers against his skin now seemed suddenly and shockingly intimate.

She took another sip of the soup. While she ate, Bobby and Tom talked inconsequentially about the B&B they were staying in. Steffie was grateful to them for the chatter. She wasn't ready to tell them about her mother's affair yet. Still less that she was the result of it. She was still coming to terms with it herself.

She didn't feel quite as shaky as she had earlier when she finally finished the soup and put the spoon down. The men on the opposite side of the table gave her encouraging smiles as she cleared her throat and began to speak. Their expressions changed from encouragement to shock as she told them about Jenny and Gregory and the fact that it was Gregory, and not Pascal, who was her biological father. Bobby took her hand and squeezed it.

'And of course Liam doesn't know the other part,' she added. 'That Mum and Dad weren't even married in the first place.'

'What?' Liam was completely gobsmacked. 'But it was their anniversary party, wasn't it?'

239

'It wouldn't have been if they'd been truthful with us from the start,' said Steffie.

'You poor pet.' Tom reached across the table and squeezed her other hand. 'It's been a tough day for you, hasn't it.'

'I feel I should be OK,' said Steffie. 'I mean, although it's totally bizarre, the wedding thing isn't such a big deal really. The important thing is that they're happy together. But . . . but finding out about Gregory . . . that's hard.'

'I'm not surprised you keeled over,' said Liam. 'I wonder did anyone know about your mum and him back then.'

'Oh God!' The thought had never occurred to Steffie. 'You mean everyone could have guessed already? They might have been talking about it – and me – behind our backs!'

'I doubt it very much.' Liam backtracked on his words when he saw the distress on Steffie's face. 'I never heard any rumours about your parents, and you know what it's like around here. Everyone knows everything.'

'In which case they probably *do* know,' Steffie pointed out.

'I shouldn't have said anything,' said Liam. 'I've upset you even more and I really don't think there's any need. As far as the anniversary is concerned, my mum and dad were thrilled to go to the party and I know Mum wouldn't have been able to keep it secret if she'd suspected even for a second that your parents weren't married. And Steffie, if anyone thought your dad wasn't your dad . . . well, surely there would have been some gossip about it before now.'

'Perhaps you're right.' Steffie rubbed her fingers across her eyebrows.

'Anyway, your biological father isn't important,' Tom told her. 'Pascal's always been your dad. You know that.'

'Yes, I do,' she said. 'But that's not the point, Tom. They

lied to me all my life. And I know he'll always be my dad, but . . . but he's not part of me. I used to like it when people said they could see him in me because everyone always banged on about how much I took after Mum whereas Roisin and Davey are the spit of Dad. And now I find out I'm like her because I don't have any of Dad's genes at all. Everything I have comes from a nude sheep farmer in New Zealand.'

Bobby laughed. He couldn't help it.

'It's not funny,' she said, although her mouth twitched involuntarily.

'It's the image,' said Tom. 'I see him in a kind of *Brokeback Mountain* way, rounding up the sheep on a horse in his pelt.'

'Stop.' Steffie was smiling now, although her eyes were bright with tears again.

'Steffie, who *you* are is more important than who your parents are,' said Liam. 'And you're a smart, attractive woman with her own business. That comes from you yourself.'

'I think you're exaggerating the smart, attractive and business elements,' she said. 'But thanks all the same.'

'Would you all like coffee?' Liam stood up. 'Or tea?'

'Coffee, please,' replied Bobby, and Tom nodded in agreement.

'How about you, Steffie?' asked Liam.

'Coffee would be nice,' she agreed.

He went into the kitchen, leaving her alone with Bobby and Tom.

'Where did you say you were going when you walked out?' Bobby asked her. 'Did they try to stop you?'

'They couldn't have even if they'd wanted to,' she answered. 'I didn't tell them anything.'

'It might be a good idea to let them know where you are.' Tom spoke gently. 'I'm sure they're worried about you.'

Steffie snorted. 'Why? They weren't worried about me when they kept secrets from me.'

'They wanted to tell you,' said Bobby. 'I guess they didn't know how.'

'Oh for God's sake!' she exclaimed. 'They had twenty-seven years to figure it out.'

'Nonetheless,' said Tom, 'you should ring them and put their minds at rest. After all, it's a horrible night and there are floods all over the place.'

Steffie sighed. 'I don't want to talk to them. And,' she added, 'I left my phone behind.'

'Let me.' Bobby took out his phone. 'I have Roisin's number,' he said. 'She's probably the best one to talk to anyway.'

Chapter 24

'Oh, thank God.' Jenny had come back downstairs again and was sitting at the kitchen table when Roisin took the call and told them all that Steffie was with Tom and Bobby. 'They're both sensible people. They'll look after her.'

'They're in Cody's,' continued Roisin.

'Cody's!' exclaimed Pascal. 'What on earth made her go to Cody's?'

'She had car trouble,' Roisin said. 'She stopped off there.'

'I knew she'd end up in some sort of trouble,' said Jenny. 'When's she coming home?'

'He doesn't know yet,' said Roisin after a quick conversation with Bobby. 'He says he'll call again later.'

'Tell him I want to talk to her,' said Jenny.

'I'm sorry.' Roisin looked at her mother. 'She doesn't want to talk to you.'

Jenny crumpled back into the seat, although the relief in knowing that Steffie was all right meant that her face had lost the haggard look of earlier.

Roisin ended the call and then dialled another number.

'Davey,' she said when the phone was answered. 'We know

where Steffie is. And I think you should go there and bring her home.'

'That's a relief,' said Colette when Davey shared the news. 'Jeez, though, there she is living it up in the best restaurant in the area while we're out like total eejits in the rain looking for her.'

'I've never been to Cody's,' said Davey. 'At least, not as a restaurant. It used to be Mulligan's pub, on the back road, so it's pretty close to where she abandoned the car.'

'Crashed the car,' Colette corrected him.

'There was no talk of crashed cars from Roisin,' said Davey. 'Which is why I didn't say anything. I'm glad we didn't call when we found it.'

'Let's go get her.' Colette put the Santa Fe into gear and set off for the restaurant.

The rain had eased off a little, although a steady stream of water ran alongside the road, occasionally flooding across it and causing Colette to swear softly under her breath. When they reached the restaurant she stopped as close as possible to the entrance, then both she and Davey sprinted from the car to the door.

They heard the laughter before they went inside and they exchanged glances. Davey's expression was grim as he pushed the door open and saw Steffie, Tom, Bobby and Liam Kinsella sitting around a table drinking the Irish coffees that Liam had decided would be a good idea in addition to the regular kind.

'Glad to see you're enjoying yourself,' he said to Steffie. 'You've had us all worried sick.'

'What on earth are you doing here?' She looked at him

in astonishment. 'Bobby phoned home to let Mum and Dad know where I was. You didn't have to come haring out after me.'

'Colette and I have been looking for you for the past hour,' said Davey. 'Everyone was concerned about you being upset, being out in such awful weather and having had too much to drink. Not that it seems to be stopping you from having more!'

'Oh Davey.' Steffie looked stricken. 'I'm so sorry, I'd no idea.'

'I brought out the Irish coffees.' Liam stood up and faced Davey. 'Steffie didn't ask for one.'

'She should have more sense,' said Davey. 'And we were right to be worried because Colette and I saw her car in a damn ditch a kilometre down the road.'

'Steffie!' Bobby looked at her in horror. 'You didn't say you'd crashed.'

'It wasn't a proper crash,' she told him. 'The car slid in some water, that's all.'

'I thought you were wet from standing outside,' said Tom. 'Which, now that I think about how drenched you were, is ridiculous. Oh Steffie, you should've said.'

'You didn't injure yourself, did you?' Liam turned to her.

'No. No. I'm fine,' she said. 'A couple of blisters on my feet, that's all.'

'Come on,' said Davey. 'It's time to go.'

Steffie shook her head.

'Don't be stupid,' he said. 'You've got to come home.'

'I don't want to go back to Aranbeg,' she said.

'Steffie, for crying out loud!' Davey was infuriated. 'The

rain might have eased off but the floods haven't lessened. The roads are in a terrible state. You've got to leave now.'

'I can't go back there. I don't want to see her right now.'

'You're behaving like a child,' he said. 'Get your things and come home.'

'Davey, please.' She looked at him anxiously. 'I just can't.'

'Leave her.' Colette put her hand on his arm. 'If she needs a little time, she's entitled to it. You can't force her to come with us.'

'Thank you,' said Steffie.

'Mum's very upset,' said Davey. 'So is Dad. The least you could do is come back and talk to them.'

'I can't,' said Steffie. 'Not now. I'd only say things I'd regret.'

'I know it's difficult for you,' he said. 'But we all love you, Steffie. Nothing has changed.'

'Everything has changed,' she said. 'Everything.'

Davey gave her a despairing look. He understood that she was upset but there was no need. He didn't think of her as anything other than his sister. He didn't think of his parents as anything other than the happily married couple they'd always appeared. He wanted her to feel the same way.

'I'll run her home when she's ready,' said Liam. 'Don't worry, Davey.'

'You're Liam Kinsella, right?' Davey looked at him quizzically. 'You used to come to the house to pick up . . . Michelle, wasn't it?'

'Yes,' he said. 'I own the restaurant. I promise you I'll get Steffie home safely.'

'It's nice to see you again, Liam,' said Colette. 'You

246

probably don't remember me from visiting Aranbeg. You look great, by the way.'

'Of course I remember you,' said Liam. 'You look great too.'

'She *is* great.' Davey ignored Liam and gave Steffie a reproachful look. 'She's been doing all the driving while we've been searching for you.'

'Oh God, Colette, I'm sorry,' said Steffie. 'I never thought anyone would come after me.'

'You ran away in the middle of the worst storm in years,' said Colette. 'Of course we came looking for you.'

'I didn't think . . .' Stefie squeezed past Tom, got up from the banquette and hugged her cousin. 'Thank you for coming out in such filthy weather.'

'That's OK.' Colette held her for a moment, then patted her on the back. Steffie felt her eyes well up with tears but she blinked them away. She wasn't going to start crying again.

'And knowing the trouble we went to, you still won't come home?' Davey asked when she and Colette had stepped apart again.

'I need some time on my own. That's all,' she said.

'You're hardly on your own.'

'We'll look after her,' Bobby promised. 'Don't worry.'

Davey sighed, then frowned as he focused on the wet jacket hanging over the back of a chair.

'Is that my jacket?' he asked.

'Oh, it's yours?' Steffie looked at him apologetically. 'I grabbed the first one I saw when I was leaving the house. I'm sorry. Hopefully it'll dry out OK.'

Davey took the jacket and patted the pockets.

'I didn't touch anything,' Steffie assured him.

247

He took his wallet from the top pocket and then went through the jacket again.

'Honestly,' she said. 'Whatever was in it is still in it.'

'Not everything,' he said.

'I threw it on the back seat of the car,' she said. 'If you've lost keys or something, that's where you'll find them.'

'For fuck's sake, Steffie!'

'I'm sorry,' she repeated.

'Is everything OK?' asked Colette.

'Oh, for Steffie it is,' said Davey grimly. 'Come on, we'll leave her to her merriment and be on our way.'

He strode out of the door, Colette following him.

It banged closed behind them.

'What's the matter?' asked Colette as they got into the Santa Fe. 'What's missing from your jacket?'

Davey shook his head. He couldn't trust himself to speak. If Steffie had somehow managed to lose the engagement ring he'd planned to give Camilla, he'd kill her. And then, he thought angrily, she wouldn't have to worry about who her damned father was.

'Stop here,' he said to Colette as they approached the Citroën. 'I need to check inside.'

She pulled in close to the ditch, leaving her hazard warning lights flashing in case another vehicle came along the road. Davey got out of the Santa Fe and clambered into Steffie's car, which was now about half a metre deep in muddy water. It was entirely possible, he thought, that the box containing the engagement ring had fallen out of his jacket pocket when the car slid into the ditch and had now been washed away. But with only the car's feeble interior light, and given the awkward angle it was at as well as the flood water, it was difficult to search. He was getting more and more stressed and more and more angry with Steffie. Yes, she had a right to be upset. But she'd caused more chaos than anyone tonight by storming out of the house, crashing her damn car and losing his engagement ring. Thinking about it being lost made his heart palpitate. It wasn't simply the expense of it; it was the fact that he'd spent so much time choosing the perfect one. Admittedly his plans to give it to Camilla in a romantic haze of happiness during his parents' anniversary party had been shot to pieces. But the idea of not being able to give it to her at all was making his head spin.

'Can I help?' Colette poked her head around the open door.

'I don't think so,' he said. 'I've looked everywhere and I can't find it.'

'What exactly are you looking for?' she asked. 'Maybe whatever it is has fallen out of the car.'

'It's a bloody engagement ring in a box!' Davey hadn't intended to tell anyone about the ring, but Colette had been brilliant tonight, and besides, perhaps a woman would see what he'd missed.

'An engagement ring?'

'Yes,' he said. 'It was in my jacket pocket. I was going to ask Camilla to marry me.'

'Oh.'

'Oh indeed.' Davey didn't see the expression on Colette's face. Nor did he notice the bleakness in her voice. 'Really and truly I want to throttle Steffie. She's ruined the party and she's ruined my plans too.'

Colette sank to her knees and looked in the wet grass around her. There was no sign of a box.

'What colour was it?' Her words were jerky.

'It's a diamond,' Davey said.

'I meant the box.'

'Oh. Blue.'

Colette returned to the Santa Fe and took out a large Maglite torch. The beam cut through the darkness.

'You're fantastic,' said Davey. 'Shine it in here.'

But even with the light of the torch they couldn't find the box, either in the car or in the surrounding area.

'Maybe it fell out earlier,' suggested Colette faintly. 'Back at the house.'

'Maybe.' Davey sounded defeated. 'I wanted it to be perfect, you know. And now it's all ruined. I'll kill Steffie. I really will.'

Colette said nothing. Then Davey's phone rang.

'Yes, yes,' he said. 'We're on our way now. No, Roisin, she's not with us. She's knocking back Irish coffees in Cody's.' He thrust the phone into the pocket of his trousers.

'If you don't find it tonight at the house, we can come out tomorrow and look.' Colette's voice was a little stronger. 'Perhaps we'll see it when the water recedes. Or it could have fallen underneath the car, which is going to have to be hauled out anyway.'

'You're a brick.' He gave her a quick hug. 'I'm glad you're with me tonight.'

'No problem,' said Colette as they got back into her car.

She started the engine and drove towards Aranbeg. It was weird, she thought, how her heart was feeling positively squeezed right now. After all, she shouldn't be surprised or upset that Davey had decided to ask Camilla to marry him. He was living with her, after all. It was just . . . She realised with a shock that a small part of her had always hoped that one day Davey might realise how much *she* meant to him. That he would fall for her in the same way as she'd fallen for him all those years ago. Every time she'd got engaged, she'd waited for Davey to phone her and say that he was devastated by the news. But he hadn't. And he never would. He was her cousin, after all, and he was in love with someone else. He wanted to get engaged to Camilla. And he wasn't doing it to make some kind of statement to Colette as she'd done, fruitlessly, to him.

Maybe he'll think that losing the ring is a sign. The thought came to her as they approached Aranbeg. After all, I was always looking for signs during my engagements. That's why I had so many of them. But men don't look for signs. Men don't write pages and pages in their diaries about unrequited love. Men don't get engaged three times because they want to show someone else that they're wanted and desired. God almighty, she thought, how could I have been so stupid all my life?

The flood at Aranbeg's gates was even deeper than when they'd left.

'Nobody else is going to get in or out of here tonight,' Colette told Davey as she negotiated the water. 'It would be crazy even to try. You should text Steffie and tell her to stay with Tom and Bobby. We don't want another accident.' She couldn't believe that she was speaking so naturally, as though he hadn't delivered a hammer blow to her hopes and dreams. She couldn't believe he didn't know how she was feeling.

251

She stopped the car and the two of them got out. Davey pressed the doorbell and they stood side by side, waiting for someone to answer. It was Bernice who finally opened the door. As the warm light from the hall spilled on to the porch, Colette saw the blue box. It was sitting among the flowers in the huge planter to the right of the door. It must have fallen from the jacket pocket when Steffie had swung it over her to protect herself from the rain.

She looked at Davey but he'd already stepped over the threshold. She picked up the box and put it in her handbag.

'Is she all right?' was the first thing Jenny asked Davey when he walked into the house.

'Not a bother on her,' he replied. 'She was sculling back Irish coffee when we found her.'

Jenny looked startled.

'Having too much fun to come home?' asked Roisin.

'Looked that way,' said Davey.

'Oh Davey, she's very upset.' Colette couldn't let him downplay Steffie's distress. The fact that her cousin had been drinking Irish coffee wasn't the key issue. Colette had felt Steffie tremble as she'd hugged her. She wondered if Davey had even noticed that she hadn't been wearing her pretty floral party dress but had changed into a too-big T-shirt and chef's trousers. And her feet had been bare.

'She's looking for attention, like she always does,' said Roisin.

'I do not think you can make that assumption.' Camilla's tone was brisk. 'She has had a shock.'

'We've all had a shock,' said Roisin.

'But for Steffie it is a bigger one.'

'Camilla's right,' said Bernice. 'It has to be difficult for her right now.'

'That's right,' muttered Carl. 'You girls stick together. Steffie is an idiot.'

Bernice ignored him.

'Well I would've run away too if it had been me.' Summer spoke and startled them all. She'd been very quiet ever since Steffie's dramatic departure from the house, melting into the background and staying out of the family conversation. 'It's not nice to discover that your dad isn't your dad.'

Everyone looked at her in surprise.

'Did that happen to you?' asked Bernice. Her tone was neutral as she studied Summer curiously.

'Oh, I don't know who my dad is,' said Summer. 'I was a one-night stand, not even a love child like Steffie.'

'I'm not sure love child is the appropriate word for her,' said Lucinda. 'But I'm so sorry, Summer. I know how you must feel. Alivia's dad didn't hang around either.'

'But at least I know who he is,' said Alivia.

'Not that he's worth knowing,' Lucinda told her.

'Mum!'

'He abandoned us,' Lucinda said. 'The same way Summer's dad abandoned her. Men are such shits.'

'Not all of them,' said Bernice. 'Pascal has been sort of amazing really.'

Pascal looked embarrassed.

'My dad wasn't amazing,' Summer said. 'But I don't care. Me and my mum are good. She was sixteen when she had me, so we're more like friends really, even when she comes over all motherly and concerned if I stay out late without telling her.'

253

'How old are you now?' asked Roisin.

'Twenty-one,' said Summer.

Roisin realised with a shock that Summer's mother was younger than she was herself. She suddenly felt very old. If a bad day could get worse, she thought, it just had.

'I'm so sorry.' Jenny spoke into the sudden silence. 'This is all my fault. I should've told everyone about Pascal and me before now. And I should very definitely have told Steffie about her father a long time ago.'

'It's not your fault,' said Pascal. 'The two of us are to blame for that.'

'But you weren't the one who blurted it out. And you weren't the one to have the affair!' Jenny got up from her seat and walked out of the room.

Daisy looked at Roisin. 'Granny is really upset, isn't she?'

Her mother nodded. 'But she'll get over it. We all will. It's just one of those things, pet. Now, will you take your brother and sister and go to bed.'

'Bed!' Daisy gave her a withering look. 'It's not bedtime yet.'

'It's been a long day,' said Roisin. 'I'd really like it if you took the others upstairs. Poppy must be worn out with her sore arm. I'll come up shortly and see that everyone's settled. If you're still awake then, you can come back downstairs.'

'Oh all right,' said Daisy. 'But you owe me.'

She opened the door again and stalked out of the room.

'I'll go up too,' said Pascal. 'Jenny needs me.'

There was an awkward silence when he'd left the room. Nobody wanted to talk about the day's revelations, although they were the only thing any of them could think about.

'Anyone like a drink?' It was Paul who finally spoke. 'Given that Steffie is OK and nobody else seems to be going anywhere tonight, we might as well relax.'

There was a general easing of the tension in the room as most of them clustered around the table, which was still littered with bottles and glasses. Summer offered to make cosmopolitans with the vodka and Cointreau she'd found earlier.

'What the hell,' said Alivia. 'Let's make this party rock.'

'I hardly think you can still call it a party,' said her mother.

'All the bad news is out of the way,' Alivia told her. 'There's no point sitting around mired in gloom.'

'You're right.' Lucinda gave her a smile and told Summer she'd also have a cocktail.

'I wasn't expecting to be spending the night under the same roof as you again just yet.' Carl, who was sticking to beer, unexpectedly found himself beside Bernice. Having avoided alcohol because she'd expected to be driving home, she'd now decided to have a glass of wine.

'Clearly not,' she told him. 'Considering you brought my replacement with you.'

'She's not your replacement,' said Carl.

'Seems like it to me,' said Bernice. 'In any event, you're going for beauty over brains this time.'

'And you're being very judgemental,' said Carl. 'She's actually quite smart.'

'You're right, I am,' agreed Bernice. 'But that's me, isn't it? Judging her, judging you. I forgot you don't like being judged.'

'I don't want to fight with you,' said Carl.

'Good.'

'Why did you come today?'

'Because I like Jenny and Pascal. Because they invited me.'

'They invited us.'

'Yes. Carl and Bernice. Not Carl and Summer.'

'Not Bernice without Carl either,' he pointed out.

'What were you expecting?' asked Bernice. 'That she'd get the immediate seal of approval from the family and thus validate your choice of bed partner for the future?'

'Ber!'

Bernice sighed and said she was sorry. Then she shook her head. 'Hell, no. I'm not sorry. As much as maybe I shouldn't have come, you shouldn't have brought her. It's not fair on Jenny and Pascal.'

'They have other things to worry about,' said Carl. 'I feel sorriest for Roisin. She went to so much trouble . . .'

'She'll get over it. So will your mum.'

'My mother?'

'Can't you see what a state she's in too?' asked Bernice. 'She always resented how good Jenny seemed to have it compared to her. Now she's having to reassess everything.'

'She never resented Jenny. That's ridiculous.'

Bernice held up her hand. 'You're right. I shouldn't make comments. I'm not a part of it all any more, despite my eight years of being hauled to your family's events.'

'We're taking the break for a reason,' said Carl.

'I know. And I shouldn't have come,' said Bernice. 'I should've stayed away and taken my punishment, just like you wanted.'

'I'm not punishing you.'

'Whatever.'

'I deserved to know what you were up to,' he said.

Bernice looked away from him. Summer was still happily

256

dispensing cocktails to most of the women in the room, laughing and joking with them as she handed them the glasses.

'I was trying to find out where the problem was,' she said as she turned back to face him. 'But you're right. I shouldn't have gone behind your back.'

'I guess it's because you're a nurse. You couldn't leave well enough alone.'

'I wanted to know for me,' she said. 'For us too, but mostly for me.'

'And did you find out in the end?'

'Of course,' she said.

'And?'

She thought of the paper she'd put so carefully in her bag earlier.

'You're not my date today,' she said. 'You're with Summer. So it doesn't really matter to you any more, does it?'

She took a mouthful of wine, put the glass on a nearby table and walked away from him.

'I'm trying to think of worse days in my life.' Jenny was sitting on the edge of the bed again. It seemed to her that she was spending a lot of time closeted in her bedroom today. 'But I haven't come up with one so far.'

'Not the day you realised you were pregnant with Roisin?' asked Pascal.

Jenny shook her head.

'Or when we realised we couldn't get married in Rome?'

She shook her head again.

'Or when you discovered you were pregnant with Steffie?'

He kept his tone mild.

'No,' she said. 'All of those things were traumatic. Being pregnant with Steffie the most traumatic of them all. If I had to pick a second worse day, the day I had to tell you about it would be way up there. And the reason is because both that day and today are about me hurting other people. Finding out about Roisin, not being able to get married – those things mainly affected me. I know that learning I was up the spout affected you too, but it didn't hurt you. Telling you I was pregnant with Steffie did. Telling Steffie about it hurt her. You both matter so much to me, I shouldn't do anything to hurt you. And yet I did.'

'Not telling Steffie is as much my fault as yours,' said Pascal. 'You wanted to when she was much younger and I said no. At the time, I told you that we should wait until we could tell her the full story. I said it was important she knew it. But I was lying to you, Jen. I didn't want you to tell her because I didn't want her to know I wasn't her dad.'

'What?' Jenny looked at him in astonishment.

'I love her,' said Pascal. 'And I'm only saying this because it's between you and me and nobody else will ever hear it, but . . . but I find her easier to get on with than Roisin. I know that's awful. Roisin is my own flesh and blood and I love her equally. But Steffie's more fun.' He rubbed his eyebrows. 'I know she's not my daughter, but I've always pretended to myself that you were wrong and that the test was wrong too. That she is. Telling her would have changed that.'

'Oh Pascal.'

'Soppy, huh?' He gave her a wry smile.

'Not at all,' said Jenny. She put her arms around him and held him close to her. 'Not at all. I'm so sorry for everything, Pascal. I really and truly am.'

'Oh, look . . . we'll be better before we're twice married.'

She smiled at the expression. It was one her mother had used a lot. Everything bad that happened to her, in Kay's view, would be better before she was twice married.

'What a bloody awful day,' she said as she rested her head on his shoulder. 'And it's not even our damned anniversary!'

He kissed the top of her hair. 'One day we *will* get married. And when we celebrate our anniversary, we'll definitely be the ones who do all the organising.'

'Promise?'

'I promise,' he said. And this time he kissed her on the lips.

Chapter 25

Steffie was relieved that Davey had left her in Cody's. She'd been afraid for a moment that he was going to drag her forcibly to the car. She was surprised at how angry he'd suddenly become. If someone had told him he wasn't who he thought he was, she was quite sure he wouldn't have been able to continue on as though everything was OK. Because right now, nothing was OK. She knew she was the same Steffie who'd got out of bed that morning, who'd driven down with the anniversary cake in her car, who'd laughed and joked with everyone at the party . . . but she was a different Steffie too. She was a Steffie who wasn't as closely linked to everyone as she'd thought. And who wasn't linked at all to Bobby, who was sitting across the table from her. Although, weirdly, Bobby had been the one she'd ended up confiding in. She felt the sudden ache of missing something that, strictly speaking, hadn't even existed in the first place.

She took the final sip from the Irish coffee that Liam had insisted on bringing out to them after they'd finished the regular ones. She'd demurred at first, saying that she'd had more than enough to drink already, but Liam had said they weren't very strong and that the warmth would do her good. And it had looked so pretty with its smooth cream topping that she hadn't been able to resist. She had to admit that the whiskey combined with the coffee had worked exactly as Liam had predicted and had spread a warm, relaxing glow through her body.

'Feeling better?' Bobby asked her.

She nodded.

'You look it,' Tom said. 'You've got some colour back in your cheeks.'

She smiled at him.

'So what d'you want to do now that you've given Davey the boot?' Bobby asked.

'I can't go back to Aranbeg,' she said. 'Not yet. It's too hard.'

'I understand,' said Tom.

'D'you think there's a room for me at your guest house tonight?' she asked.

'Oh pet, I wish there was.' Bobby's voice was full of sympathy. 'But it's a case of no room at the inn. It's full. Like everywhere around.'

'Don't you want me to drive you home later?' asked Liam. 'I don't mind doing that for you.'

'Um – that's not going to happen. Not tonight, at any rate.' Tom, who was looking at his mobile, interrupted her. 'I've just had a text from Davey. The entrance to Aranbeg is impassable.'

'You're joking!' Steffie was shocked.

'Apparently it's completely flooded,' said Tom. 'He says you're not even to try to get home.'

'Has everybody else left? Or are they marooned there?' she asked.

Tom glanced at the phone again. 'He doesn't say.'

'Crikey.' Steffie grimaced. 'Roisin will be going ballistic at how her party has turned out.'

'It wasn't Roisin's party,' said Bobby. 'It was your parents' party.'

'Not as far as Roisin was concerned,' said Steffie. 'You know what she's like, Bobby. She was the one who insisted on the whole surprise thing. If she'd told them what she was planning to do, they'd have baulked at it and none of this would ever have happened.' Her voice trailed off. It wasn't fair to blame the day's events on Roisin, but it gave Steffie a fleeting moment of *Schadenfreude* in thinking that she herself had been right about the surprise party not being a good idea.

'It'll certainly put the poor girl off party planning for a while.' Tom grinned. 'Can you imagine them all stuck back at Aranbeg? Where are they going to sleep, for one thing?'

'Oh, she'll have that organised already,' said Steffie. 'All the same, I should've used my brain before I got all huffy and stormed off.'

'I'm glad you're thinking like that,' said Bobby.

'I'm saying it, I'm not sure I'm actually meaning it,' Steffie confessed.

'I wish you could stay with us,' said Tom. 'But I doubt Mrs Brannigan would let you kip down on the sofa.'

'You can stay here, of course,' said Liam.

'Here?' She stared at him. 'In the restaurant?'

'In the flat,' he said.

'But . . . there isn't room,' she said.

'Of course there is. You can take the bedroom and I'll sleep on the couch.'

'Liam! I can't—'

'Yes you can,' he interrupted her. 'It's only for a night.

262

And it's not like I've been run off my feet this evening and need to collapse in my bed.'

She hesitated. She'd been enough of a bother already. But Liam had sounded sincere in his offer and she couldn't think of an alternative.

'That's really nice of you,' she told him. 'You've been beyond good to me already. But I'll be the one to sleep on the couch.'

'Steffie—'

'Honestly. There's no need to be all self-sacrificing and macho about it. I'm the one who barged in so I'm the one who should take the couch and be grateful.'

'OK.' He shrugged. 'Whatever you like.'

'At least it's somewhere for you to stay,' said Bobby. 'And tomorrow . . .'

'I've no idea what I'm going to do tomorrow,' said Steffie.

'Things will have settled down a bit by then. You'll feel differently,' said Tom.

'You think?' Steffie's tone was bleak.

'You'll be better in yourself,' he amended.

'Tom's right,' said Bobby. 'Tomorrow is another day, as the magnificent Scarlett O'Hara in the best book and movie in the world would say. In the meantime, could you bring us the bill, Liam? We'd better go, it's getting late.'

'It's on the house,' Liam said.

'Absolutely not.' Bobby looked horrified.

'My treat,' said Liam. 'At least you guys kept me busy this evening.'

'Hardly,' said Tom.

'I'd have been sitting around like an eejit otherwise,' Liam said. 'I much prefer that I was able to cook for someone.'

'And rescue a damsel in distress,' added Steffie.

Liam grinned. 'You can't say that your family haven't kept me occupied tonight.'

'Though I really shouldn't stay either,' said Steffie.

'You've already accepted my limited hospitality,' said Liam. 'You can't run away again.'

'Please let us pay.' Bobby stood up and took his wallet from his jacket pocket.

'No,' said Liam. 'You can spread the word about my wonderful restaurant instead.'

'I'd do that anyway,' said Bobby. 'It was a fantastic meal. Thank you.'

'You're welcome.'

Liam walked with the two men to the door of the restaurant and handed them a giant golf umbrella before waving them into the night.

'It's normal Irish rain out there now,' he told Steffie when he returned. 'Heavy, but not sheeting it down. So hopefully they'll only get a bit wet, not totally drenched.'

'Perhaps I could get to Aranbeg after all. Although . . .'

'If the gate is flooded, it'll stay flooded,' Liam pointed out. 'It hasn't actually stopped raining. Anyway, we've agreed you'll stay here.'

'You're being incredibly good to me,' she said.

'I'm known for my compassion towards rain-sodden maidens.' He grinned. 'Do you want to go upstairs to the flat? Have another coffee? Tea? Whatever?'

'I'd better not have any more coffee or I'll start walking on the ceiling,' she said. 'If you have stuff you need to do, please go ahead.'

'I need to tidy up a little,' he said. 'Why don't you go on up and relax?'

Steffie felt slightly awkward about being in Liam's flat alone, but she realised that he had things to do and that she'd be in the way. So she nodded and left him to his own devices.

It was very difficult, she thought, to be in someone else's home and not have a nose around. As she'd observed earlier, the living room was small and sparsely furnished, but the cardboard boxes were probably full of possessions that Liam hadn't yet arranged around the flat. The one personal item she could see was a family photo of Liam, Michelle and their parents. Liam and Michelle were still children in the photo and it had been taken long before he'd embarked on whatever diet had seen him lose his excess weight. She picked it up and studied it. His eyes were the same, she decided, still that intense indigo blue. And his hair was as dark as ever. But otherwise he was almost unrecognisable from the boy in the photo. Steffie didn't want to be fattist; while being slender herself, she didn't think everyone should look the same, but there was no doubt that the weight loss suited Liam.

'I've changed.'

His voice, in the doorway of the flat, startled her so much that she almost dropped the photo.

'Sorry,' she said as she replaced it on the shelf. 'Sorry.'

'Good catch,' he said as he walked into the room. 'Not entirely surprising, though. I remember you being pretty OK at ball games and rounders when you were younger.'

She laughed, although she was still shaking from having been caught with the photo in her hands. 'I'd forgotten the rounders,' she admitted. 'I'd forgotten that you bothered to play with us.'

'My mum insisted.' He made a face. 'She thought the exercise would be good for me. I was crap.'

Steffie nodded. The games had been played at Liam and Michelle's house. Two families, both with children around the same ages, lived nearby and Mrs Kinsella had often invited them, along with Steffie, to play. Steffie couldn't remember who organised the rounders but it was a constant feature of being at the Kinsellas'. She recalled the excitement of hitting the ball high into the air, and pelting around the garden trying to score runs. She'd covered the ground well because of her long legs, and despite her being the youngest everyone had wanted her on their team. Her desirability was in contrast to Liam, whose hand-to-eye co-ordination was awful and who pounded from post to post, often getting hit out. She hadn't thought much about how he'd felt when the kids would shout at him to try harder, or indeed what it was like to be picked last every time.

'You'd probably be better at it now,' she said.

'I doubt it,' he told her. 'I'm still absolutely useless at anything that requires hand–eye co-ordination. Except chopping things with a knife.'

'All the same, you're fitter.'

'And you're very polite.' He smiled. 'I had to get fitter. I was eating myself into an early grave. By the time I left school I wasn't just fat, I was obese.'

'Oh, I don't think—'

'I was,' he said firmly. 'And I was having all sorts of health problems. But in college I met with a dietician and worked out a plan. Then I started exercising.'

'What exercise do you do?'

'Boxing,' he said.

'Boxing? You? Seriously? Doesn't that require really good co-ordination?'

'It's not the same as rounders or cricket,' he replied. 'I'm surprisingly adept at it. Maybe there's something buried in my psyche that means I like hitting people on the jaw.'

'I hope not.'

'Ah, no, what I do is very technical.' He grinned. 'Obviously you're punching someone but it's not as aggressive as you think.'

'Hmm.'

'I work out in the gym too,' he said. 'I have to confess I'm not great at that. I prefer the competitive thing.'

'You weren't one bit competitive as a kid.'

'I hadn't found the right thing to be competitive about.'

'And so . . .' She walked to one of the sofas and sat down. 'You then went into a business that must be a terrible temptation to you every day.'

'Not really.' He sat on the sofa opposite. 'I had a dysfunctional relationship with food but now it's much healthier. And in the restaurant I try to make healthy taste good. It's not that I don't use butter or cream or anything like that, but I like to make my meals nutritionally good without going overboard on the sugary, fatty stuff.'

'It's obviously working if you're winning awards,' she said.

'My new-found competitive nature.'

'The French onion soup was amazing,' she said.

'You should try my Moroccan roast lamb. Or my Basque chicken.'

'Perhaps sometime,' she said.

'Definitely.'

They sat in silence. But it was a companionable silence. And Steffie felt the most relaxed she had all day.

Chapter 26

Colette was in Aranbeg's upstairs bathroom. She'd filled the sink and every so often she splashed water around so that anyone walking by would hear it. But she wasn't washing her hands. She was looking at the ring that Davey Sheehan had bought Camilla Rasmussen, and which she was currently wearing on her engagement finger.

It was a rock, no doubt about it: a large centre diamond surrounded by six smaller ones set into golden petals, so that the whole thing looked like a glittering flower. Beneath the halogen light of the bathroom cabinet it sparkled and shimmered, throwing pinpoints of colour on to the sink below. It was the most beautiful ring she'd ever seen. Far more beautiful than any of the three she'd been given herself. When she'd been younger she'd imagined what it would be like to be engaged to Davey and had visualised herself wearing the ring he'd given her; when she'd seen the one he'd planned to give Camilla nestling in the blue velvet of the box, she hadn't been able to help herself. She'd sneaked away to the bathroom and slid it over her finger, thinking that it wasn't a bad fit although possibly half a size too small for comfort. But it suited her. It was the perfect shape for her long fingers.

She held her hand out in front of her and looked at her reflection in the bathroom mirror. And she felt her heart splinter. If only Davey had bought it for me, she thought. If only he'd thought I was the one who deserved such a magnificent piece of jewellery.

But it isn't you, she told herself, even as she moved her hand so that the diamonds continued to sparkle gloriously beneath the light. It wasn't back then, when we were kids, and it isn't now when we're grown-ups. It doesn't matter that he insisted on accompanying you in looking for Steffie. He's in love with someone else. He loves her so much he wants to marry her. He bought this magnificent ring for her. As far as he's concerned, you're just the sad little cousin who used to come and stay.

She sat down with a thud on the toilet seat and put her head in her hands. She knew she was being foolish but she couldn't help herself. Her childhood crush on Davey Sheehan had always been a lot more than that as far as she was concerned. She'd fallen in love with him even though he was her cousin and, God help her, she was still in love with him. And the madness was that he didn't know – he'd never know – how much he meant to her. That she measured every man she ever met against him and found them wanting. That because of him, she was still single. Despite the three engagement rings of her own.

A thump at the bathroom door startled her.

'Colette? Are you in there? Are you OK?' It was Alivia's voice.

'Yes, fine,' she called. 'Trying to make myself presentable, that's all.' She sniffed, stood up and looked at her wet hair. Presentable was almost impossible.

'There's a hairdryer in Steffie's room if you need it,' said Alivia through the closed door.

'Thanks.'

'Sure everything's all right? You've been up here for ages.'

'Yes, of course. Um – do you want to use the bathroom, Liv?'

'No. It was just that Davey noticed you'd disappeared and he was wondering about you.'

Colette felt her heart beat faster.

'I'm grand,' she said.

'OK. Well, on the basis that nobody's going anywhere tonight, Paul is dispensing drinks and Summer – fair play to her – is mixing more cocktails. So don't spend too long on beautifying yourself or you'll miss out.'

'Won't be long,' said Colette.

She leaned against the bathroom wall and exhaled slowly. Davey had asked about her. He cared about her. He wanted to know that she was OK. Even hearing that made her feel a million times better. But knowing it also seemed to flick a switch in her head. Davey cared because he liked her and because she was his cousin and because she'd driven around in the rain and the dark tonight. He didn't care because he had any other feelings for her. If he had, he wouldn't have crawled into Steffie's half-submerged car looking for Camilla's engagement ring. If he had, he wouldn't have bought it for her in the first place.

I'm being very stupid, thought Colette. I've been very stupid for years.

She looked in the bathroom mirror again. She held her hand against her face so that she could see the ring on her finger one more time. It was pointless comparing it to any of hers. It outshone them by a considerable distance. Perhaps if any of her ex-fiancés had given her a ring like this, she might have stuck with them. And then she reminded herself that she wasn't as shallow as all that, that she'd honestly thought she loved each of them while deep down knowing that her heart was bound to someone else. But his heart . . . she looked at the ring again . . . his heart was taken and it was time she accepted that fact.

You're such a fool, she told herself as she began to remove the ring from her finger. And it's as well that nobody knows it. She twisted the ring to get it over her knuckle. It wouldn't move. She pulled it a little more but it remained stuck. She told herself to be calm, that she'd got it on to her finger and she could get it off again. But she couldn't. It didn't want to budge.

'Don't panic, don't panic,' she hissed to herself as she pumped soap from the dispenser and rubbed it around the ring. 'All you need is to take it easy and then it'll come off. No problem. No bother.'

She inhaled and exhaled slowly and rhythmically. Then she gently tugged the ring.

It was still completely and utterly stuck.

'There you go.' Paul handed Roisin the last of Summer's cosmopolitans.

'Thanks.' Roisin took the drink even though she hadn't officially lifted the cocktail ban from earlier. But it was too late now. The party had spiralled completely out of her control and cocktails were the least of her worries.

'What are you thinking about?' asked Paul as he came around from behind the table to join her.

'Where we're all going to sleep, of course,' she replied. 'None of these people are meant to be here – least of all her!' She glanced at Summer, who'd also abandoned the table and was sitting on the sofa beside Carl.

'Give the girl a break and chill out with your cosmopolitan.' Paul nodded at the glass in her hand.

Roisin began to speak but then changed her mind and took a sip of the drink.

'Not bad,' she admitted reluctantly. 'In fact, it's pretty good.'

'She works in a bar,' Paul said. 'So she knows what she's doing.'

'I thought she said she was a model.'

'That's more aspirational than actual,' said Paul. 'She mostly does corporate events – you know, the kind where they need an attractive young girl to hand over an award or a prize. It's not exactly London Fashion Week or whatever, is it?'

'I don't know what's worse. Wannabe model or actual cocktail waitress.'

'It's time to lose the chip on your shoulder about her, Roisin.' Paul looked at his wife with exasperation. 'She's a nice girl and being a cocktail waitress is as good a job as any.'

'I suppose you fancy her.'

'Now you're being ridiculous.'

'She's young and fun and makes a mean cocktail.' Roisin sipped again. 'What's not to love?'

'Her cocktail skills are second to none,' agreed Paul. 'But she's not my type, Rosie. You know that.'

'Do I?'

'Of course you do. But I'm flattered that you might have been even the teeniest bit jealous.'

'I wasn't.'

'You were!'

'Oh, shut up.' But she suddenly smiled at him. 'I'm sorry, but I can't help seeing her as a future contestant on some kind of reality show. And you know how I feel about them.'

'Just as well she isn't part of one today,' Paul said. 'Mind you, the ratings would've gone through the roof.'

Roisin shuddered and allowed her gaze to flicker around the room. 'I can't believe all this has happened. And I still have to find somewhere to put everyone. Given that Steffie is gone for the night, I was thinking that maybe Sarah and Lucinda could share her room and I could move the girls into ours, along with Dougie. Davey and Camilla should take his room, I suppose. But where does that leave Carl? And Summer? And what about Alivia and Colette? Bernice too? We don't have room for everyone.'

'None of them particularly look like they're ready for bed,' said Paul. 'They'll be fine, Roisin.'

'Fine now,' she said. 'But later, when everyone's tired, they'll need somewhere to sleep. I have to work it out.'

'There are plenty of sofas.'

'You can't ask people to sleep on sofas.'

'There isn't much of a choice.'

Roisin sighed. 'After all the trouble I went to,' she said, 'this has been the most disastrous night of my life.'

'Ah, they'll get over it,' said Paul.

'You're not denying it's a disaster,' she said.

'As a celebratory party it is,' he agreed. 'But as an exciting night out – you couldn't have done any better if you'd tried.'

'Don't be silly,' she said. 'It's not just the party that's disastrous. It's everything to do with Mum and Dad. And Steffie.' Her voice wobbled.

'You've a right to be upset,' agreed Paul. 'Especially after all the effort you put in.'

'I wanted it to be perfect.'

'I know. And it's not at all your fault that things turned out the way they did. You're a great organiser, Ro.'

'Thank you.' She looked up at him. 'I'm sorry if I get snappy sometimes. Especially that I always seem to get snappy with you. It's just . . .'

'You're a perfectionist,' he said. 'I knew that when I married you. I like that you want everything to be just so. And even if you go over the top a bit sometimes, we'd be lost without you.'

'Truthfully?'

'Of course,' said Paul. 'You're the one that keeps it all together. And even if today didn't work out the way you expected, you all had to know about Pascal and Jenny sooner or later.'

'You realise Mum lied to me too, don't you?' she asked.

'I thought the whole thing was that she lied to everyone?'

'Yes, but she always let me think that she and Dad got married because of me,' said Roisin. 'They didn't. They didn't think I was worth getting married for.'

'You're being silly now,' said Paul. 'They wanted to get married, she said so. The fact that they couldn't is irrelevant.'

'They could have later,' said Roisin. 'If it had really mattered, they would have found a way.'

'Your mum has already explained that.'

274

'Saying that they never found the right moment isn't really a good enough explanation.'

'It's understandable, all the same.'

'I still—'

'Roisin.' Paul's voice was gentle. 'Leave it. It doesn't make any difference. It really doesn't. To you, to me or to them. There's been enough for Jenny to deal with this evening. She doesn't need to be punished by another daughter.'

'I wasn't going to . . .' Roisin's words trailed off. She'd intended to have a go at her mother but she suddenly realised that Paul was right. It wouldn't serve any purpose to heap more anger on Jenny. 'All I wanted was to fix things,' she said.

'You can't fix everything,' Paul told her. 'Sometimes you have to leave it to other people. And there are some things, Rosie, that can't be fixed at all.'

Camilla was also enjoying one of Summer's cosmopolitans, although Davey had stuck with beer. They'd moved to the veranda, where they were sitting beside each other on the bamboo sofa. Davey said that it was almost like their holiday in the Caribbean, what with the warmth and the rain and the cocktails. Camilla laughed and told him that the Caribbean had been a lot more tranquil. Then she asked him what the matter was.

'What d'you mean, what's the matter?' he asked.

'You've been like a cat on a hot tin roof since you returned,' she said. 'You're tense and edgy.'

'Are you surprised?' He made a face. 'My parents dropped the biggest bombshell of my life today. I spent ages out in the rain looking for my runaway sister. We're now trapped in the party from hell. And . . .' He checked himself. He'd almost blurted out that he'd lost an engagement ring worth more than three months' salary and that if he'd had the courage of his convictions and asked her to marry him sooner, they could have been sitting here together as an engaged couple. But instead he allowed his words to trail off.

'It's not the party from hell,' said Camilla. 'It's a far more exciting party than the last one I was at.'

He looked at her questioningly.

'You remember?' she said. 'The drinks reception with Ivar.'

Davey nodded. He hadn't wanted her to go to any social function at which her previous boyfriend would be in attendance, particularly a social function he wasn't personally invited to, but he hadn't said anything because Camilla wouldn't have understood how he could be jealous about a man she considered to be in her past. As far as she was concerned, over was over. She didn't tie herself into emotional knots about things. Which, generally speaking, was great and made her easy to live with; but sometimes, Davey thought, sometimes he'd like to know exactly what she was feeling.

'Now that was a boring party,' she said. 'All of them standing around with their glasses of wine and yammering on about the critically acclaimed books they were reading and the art-house films they'd seen and me knowing that it was all bullshit because Ivar prefers crime fiction to literary work and is pathetically addicted to kids' movies.'

'Kids' movies?' Davey was startled.

'Oh yes,' said Camilla. 'Cartoons and comic book hero stuff. Spiderman and the Avengers.'

'I don't see him like that,' said Davey. 'I imagined him as the arty type.'

'Because he likes to be seen as the arty type,' said Camilla. 'Whereas I'm not arty and nobody would consider me arty.'

'And that's a good thing.' Camilla smiled at him. 'That is why I'm with you, Davey Sheehan, and not Ivar Nygaard.'

'And why you're putting up with the party from hell.'

'I keep telling you it's not from hell,' she said. 'Although your poor mother must be exhausted.'

'I suppose so,' acknowledged Davey. 'It's been stressful for her.'

'And for you, out there in the rain, looking for Steffie.'

He nodded. 'When we found her car in the ditch, I felt sick,' he admitted. 'I thought she'd be in it. I was relieved when she wasn't and then terrified of what might have happened to her.'

'But nothing bad did,' said Camilla. 'So everything is all right.'

Except that I've lost your engagement ring. He couldn't keep the thought out of his mind for long. He wanted to tell her, but of course he couldn't do that. The problem was, he didn't really know what to do.

He was still wondering about it when he saw Colette. She'd dried her hair and was now wearing a pair of fluffy pink slippers, which, teamed with the yellow and black striped dress, made her resemble a character from *Sesame Street*. He waved at her and she crossed the room hesitantly.

'Davey says you were fantastic tonight,' said Camilla before he could say anything.

'All I did was drive.' Colette knew that she sounded like a sulky teenager, so she gave her cousin's fiancée a wide smile to make up for it. Camilla looked slightly startled.

'Can I get you a drink?' asked Davey. 'You deserve something nice after your Trojan work earlier. I might be able to persuade Summer to rustle you up one of her cocktails.'

'Oh, don't bother with that. A beer would be nice though,' Colette told him.

Davey got up and went inside. Left alone with Camilla, Colette couldn't think of anything to say. But then Camilla started talking about Steffie and Jenny and saying that people were overreacting but it was understandable when everything had come as such a shock to them all. Colette didn't need to say anything. All that was required of her was a nod from time to time as she listened to Camilla's logical viewpoint on the mess that was Pascal and Jenny's anniversary party. But she didn't really hear much of what Davey's girlfriend was saying. She was too busy thinking of how fabulous the engagement ring would look on the Danish woman's finger. She closed her left hand around it. Despite having spent another fruitless five minutes trying to remove it, all her efforts had done was cause her finger to swell up even more, making it impossible to get off. So she'd turned the stones around until they were facing her palm and all that could be seen on her engagement finger was a narrow band of gold.

'So this is a very close family?' Camilla looked enquiringly at her and Colette tried to stop thinking about the fact that she was wearing the other woman's engagement ring.

'Not really,' she replied. 'This is the first time we've been together in a long time.'

'Davey says that you came here a lot when you were younger.'

Colette explained about summers at Aranbeg. 'But when we were kids. It's different now.'

'You remain close to Davey's parents?'

Colette shrugged just as Davey returned with a bottle of Corona. She was careful to accept it with her right hand, keeping the left out of sight.

'Cheers,' he said. 'Thanks again for the brilliant driving earlier, Colette.'

'It was the car, not me,' she told him.

'Funny, I never saw you as a four-by-four sort of person.'

'Oh? What sort of person am I then?'

'A Volkswagen Beetle,' he said. 'Or maybe a Fiat 500.'

'Comedy cars,' she said.

'Quirky,' he amended.

'You think I'm quirky?' As she spoke, she looked down at the stripy dress and the fluffy slippers and gave a rueful smile.

'They're cars with personality,' said Davey. 'You have tons of personality, Colette.'

She wished he'd said that years ago.

'I don't have a car,' said Camilla. 'But if I did, it would be a Leaf.'

'Environmentally friendly,' Davey agreed.

'But not exactly designed for ploughing through flood water,' said Colette.

'If more people don't drive environmentally friendly cars, there will be more floods in the future,' said Camilla.

'That's true,' said Davey.

He and Camilla began to talk about environmental issues. Colette listened for a moment or two and then, realising that they were becoming more and more engrossed in their own conversation, left them to it.

'You know what the worst of all this is?' asked Pascal.

He and Jenny had come downstairs and were alone in

the front room. She was standing in front of the sketches she'd done of the children, remembering the feel of the charcoal on the paper, remembering how back then they'd believed she was invincible. She turned from the sketch of Steffie to look at the man she'd always thought of as her husband.

'What?' she asked.

'We're stuck with that lot till tomorrow,' said Pascal.

Jenny smiled. She couldn't help it. Pascal had sounded totally indignant at the idea of interlopers spending the night in his home.

'We were already expecting a full house,' she reminded him.

'But not this full,' he said. 'Not nieces and nephews, girl-friends, ex-girlfriends and the unexpected new model.'

'True.'

'And they're all getting sloshed now because they've no place to go.'

'Surely not.'

'Summer is making cocktails and they're going down a treat.'

'Oh well,' said Jenny. 'I suppose anyone stranded here needs something to cheer them up. It's pretty grim.'

'One day Roisin will learn to ask before she does things.'

'It wasn't her fault,' said Jenny. 'And it was hugely thoughtful.'

'Hmm.'

The two of them were silent. The sounds of muted conver-sation drifted towards them.

'You know what?' Jenny stood up straighter and looked at her husband.

'What?'

'You're right. We're stuck with them. And they're stuck with us. But the thing is, they came to celebrate. Not to sit around having boring conversations about us and feeling embarrassed and miserable.'

'Nothing we can do about that now.'

'Of course there is,' she said. 'It's supposed to be a party, isn't it? Let's get in there and turn it into one.'

'Huh?'

'I've spend enough time crying and sniffing and moping,' said Jenny. 'There are things I have to deal with, of course, but I can't do it all now. I know Steffie is OK. We have guests in the house. The least we can do is look after them.'

Pascal stared at her.

'So come on,' she said. 'Let's go inside and be the perfect host and hostess and insist that they have a good time.'

This time Pascal grinned. 'OK,' he said.

But when they walked into the living room, Jenny realised that she was too late. Because the guests were being organised into having a good time already. Roisin had inserted the SingStar disc into the PlayStation and told them that it was time to have some party fun.

'Oh, good,' said Daisy, who'd come back downstairs a few minutes earlier, telling Roisin that her brother and sister were asleep and that she was bored. Roisin had expressed surprise that Daisy could possibly be bored, since she usually spent hours chatting to her friends on her smartphone whenever she was alone, but Daisy admitted that she wanted to know what was going on. Roisin realised that it was both unfair and unnecessary to banish her teenage daughter upstairs again, and so Daisy had curled up in one of the living-room chairs.

'We should divide into teams,' Roisin said. 'Write your names on pieces of paper and we'll draw them.'

'This is very professional,' murmured Camilla.

'It's Roisin in her element,' Davey murmured back as he wrote his name. 'Can you sing?'

'Not well,' she replied.

'It'll be a competition,' he told her. 'Everything with the Sheehans is. So do your best.'

She was startled by the intensity of his voice.

'Right.' Roisin put the slips of paper into a bowl and began to call out the teams.

'I've never done SingStar before,' said Summer, who was on the same team as Carl. 'It'll be fun.'

Bernice, who was on the third team, snorted loud enough for Carl to hear.

'OK, hun,' said Roisin, who was on the same team as Daisy. 'You're up first. Give it socks.'

Daisy got up and gave a very good rendition of Carly Rae Jepsen's 'Call Me Maybe', which left her with a Superstar score.

'Excellent,' said Roisin. 'Glad you're on my team. OK, up next . . .' she looked at the list, 'Aunt Sarah.'

'Oh well, you all know my party piece,' said Sarah. She threw back her head and belted out 'I Will Survive', accompanied by much cheering and whooping by everyone else.

'She's robbed my song,' Bernice muttered to Alivia. 'It's the only thing I feel like singing right now.'

'Of course you'll survive.' Alivia squeezed the other girl's arm. 'You're doing great today.'

Bernice said nothing as Alivia took out her mobile and checked it again. Still no response from Dermot to her texts. She didn't know whether to be annoyed or concerned.

Paul was up next and to everyone's amusement he opted for 'I'm Every Woman', which he sang out of key but with lots of enthusiasm.

'Full marks for interpretation,' Roisin assured him as he sat down again. 'Now you, Camilla.'

Camilla stood up and took the mic gingerly. She cleared her throat a few times and then, as the music blasted out, started to sing Lady Gaga's 'Poker Face'. She accompanied it with a selection of athletic dance moves that left everyone looking at her in awed amazement.

'I thought you said you couldn't sing?' said Davey when she'd finished to rapturous applause.

'You were distracted by the dancing,' replied Camilla breathlessly. 'I had to learn that song as part of a team-building exercise at work. It's the only one I know.'

'You're unbelievable.' He grinned at her.

'Summer!' cried Roisin when the applause for Camilla died down. 'It's your turn. C'mon, do our team proud.'

Summer beamed as she took hold of the mic. She fluffed out her blond hair, struck a confident pose and then began.

'Wow,' whispered Alivia as Summer's tuneless voice filled the room. 'Even Paul was better than her. She makes Cameron Diaz sound like Celine Dion.'

'Don't.' Bernice's shoulders were shaking with laughter. She looked up. Carl's face was a mask of horror as he watched his date for the night.

Summer's score was awful but she didn't care.

'I know I can't sing,' she told them cheerfully. 'But if I

283

ever get a big break I can release something anyhow. They'll auto-tune it or whatever and it'll sound perfect. It's all about the performance really.'

'Right.' Roisin looked grim as she told them that Davey was up next. She'd been counting on Summer to get a good score for the team, especially after Camilla had wowed for the opposition. But Carl's girlfriend had totally bombed. It was unbelievable that such a terrible sound had come out of her mouth.

'And now Colette,' she said when Davey had finished singing 'New York, New York'.

Colette wasn't a particularly good singer and usually tried to get out of karaoke nights, but as nobody could be worse than Summer, she got up and grabbed the mic. She'd chosen 'Girls Just Want to Have Fun', and as she sang, she lost herself in the words and skipped around the room, not caring that she was still wearing the pink fluffy slippers. It didn't matter. Having fun was the most important thing and what was wrong with that? She needed to throw off the shackles of thinking that she was in love with Davey Sheehan and embrace life on her own terms. Which she was going to do. Right now. She was going to have her own walk in the sun.

She bowed low as she finished the song and her happy mood evaporated almost immediately. Because in her singing and jumping and skipping around the room, Camilla's engagement ring had somehow turned on her finger so that the magnificent diamonds were clearly visible. Using the mic to shield her hand, she turned it around again, hoping that nobody had noticed. But when she looked up, she realised that her hopes had been in vain. Because Davey had. And he was looking at her with an expression of utter disbelief on his face.

Chapter 27

Steffie would have been relieved to know that she was missing out on SingStar. She had Summer's voice without Summer's confidence, so she never even got close to sounding good. The last time she'd been forced into joining in, at one of Daisy's birthday parties, she'd sworn never to get involved again. It was mortifying to sound like a hippo on heat in front of everyone and know they were creased up in hysterical laughter wondering how it was she was so tone deaf when the rest of the family could all keep in tune.

The music that Liam was playing in the flat wasn't for singing along to. It was mellow lounge music and it was making her feel very chilled as she reviewed the events of the day in her mind. Her initial fury at Jenny had finally begun to dissipate and she was now feeling a certain sympathy for a woman who'd twice found herself in the situation of having an unplanned and unwelcome pregnancy. She remembered Roisin once remarking that it was disconcerting to think that her mother's first reaction when she thought she was pregnant with her had doubtless been one of unmitigated horror.

'It's not a nice feeling,' Roisin had said, 'to know that

your mother was probably thinking you were the worst thing that had ever happened in her life.'

Steffie had told her not to be silly, that although Jenny must have been shocked, she'd also been happy enough to marry Pascal and become a family and so Roisin had simply hurried the inevitable along. But now Steffie was experiencing her sister's feelings herself (half-sister, she told herself again) and she wished she'd been more sympathetic and more understanding when Roisin had spoken about it before. Basically, Steffie thought, the only one of us who was born without background drama was Davey. And who knows if they planned him either?

So Steffie allowed herself to feel a smidgen of sympathy for Jenny and her pregnancies, but that was as far as it went because there was no doubt in her mind that her mother should have told her about her biological father years ago. She was also upset that Pascal hadn't insisted on it. It had been a wonderful gesture on his part to raise her as his own daughter, but the truth was that she wasn't. She was someone else's. And she should have been told.

She also finally understood Alivia's need to meet her own father, despite Lucinda having been so set against it. It was all about knowing who you were, thought Steffie. Where you'd come from. She'd been secure about it before. Now she felt lost.

'You OK?' Liam turned to her as her breath escaped in a low sigh. She nodded and told him what she'd been thinking.

'I can imagine it's difficult to deal with the fact that everything you thought you knew has changed,' agreed Liam. 'But *you* haven't changed, Steffie. You're still the same person.'

'Am I?' She furrowed her brow. 'I want to think so, and yet part of me feels different already.'

'You suddenly know all about sheep farming?' He raised an eyebrow. 'Or nude modelling?'

She gave a faint smile. 'Well, no, obviously. Thing is, Liam, I've always felt a little different from Roisin and Davey. I thought it was because of the age gap between us. Now I can't help thinking it's because we really are different.'

'Don't overanalyse things,' said Liam. 'Of course nature and nurture explain some differences. Like why you're so devastatingly gorgeous whereas Roisin is . . . well, not as pretty.'

'Liam! That's an awful thing to say.'

'I'm pointing out a fact, that's all,' he said. 'You're a really attractive girl, Steffie. And your biological father had to have been good-looking too, given the modelling thing.'

Steffie said nothing.

'But outside of that,' Liam said, 'you're still the person you always were. Nevertheless, if you want to look for your biological dad, there's bound to be help you can get from various agencies.'

'I hadn't even thought of it,' she said. She told him about Alivia's search for her own father and how that had impacted on her relationship with Lucinda.

'It's funny how proprietorial we get over people,' said Liam. 'We want them to react in the way we want. But that doesn't always happen. We hurt them and we don't mean to. They hurt us and they don't mean to. Yet we end up feeling bad all the same.'

'Have you had any hurtful experiences?' asked Steffie.

'I'm thirty-three years old,' said Liam. 'It'd be weird if I hadn't. But the way I look at it, I've just had to get on with my life.'

'And you've made a real success of it.'

'I'm doing what I want to do,' he said. 'Which I reckon is the most important thing of all.'

'And do you share that with someone special?' she asked.

'Not right now,' he said. 'There has been from time to time, but when you're working all the hours God sends, it's difficult to juggle the relationship thing. You'll understand that, working for yourself too.'

Steffie nodded, although she'd never really got to the stage where she was working all the hours God sent.

'Of course in the restaurant you see all sorts of relationships going on,' he added with a grin. 'Which can cloud your view sometimes.'

'Given that Cody's is sort of upmarket, I guess they come for their big night out.'

'And we do our best to make sure they have the best possible time,' he told her.

'Have you ever had people propose in the restaurant?'

'A few times,' he replied. 'You get the guy who wants us to do a special dessert and include the ring in it. We say no. We did it once and the girl said she didn't want dessert. He insisted and she said he wanted her to get fat again. They ended up having a row.'

'No!'

'And then there are the ones who organise the champagne for directly after the big moment but she turns him down.'

'Oops. Does that happen often? That the girls say no?'

'Not often. But they're usually embarrassed. We sometimes wonder if they say yes just to get it over with then break it off immediately afterwards. I remember one guy whose girlfriend refused him. He stayed and drank the bottle of champagne and she went home alone.'

288

'I suppose there wasn't much left for him to do,' said Steffie. 'Anyhow, you've managed to destroy all my ideas of romantic proposals over dinner.'

'Sorry.'

'And my parents have destroyed my ideas of romance generally.'

'How?' he asked.

'I always thought of their Roman wedding as being impossibly romantic,' she confessed.

'Maybe we all have impossible ideals when it comes to romance,' he said.

'Do you have ideals?' she asked. 'Do you already know what you want from your perfect girlfriend?'

'Perfection is impossible,' he said.

'True. But do you have a list of requirements?'

He laughed. 'I've never sat down and thought about it like that. But I have to say that Scarlett Johansson pushes a lot of my buttons.'

'I wonder if she's any good in the kitchen?'

'I don't want women fussing around my kitchen,' he said firmly. 'Scarlett would be perfectly welcome to disport herself gracefully in the bedroom while I go about my business with the meat cleaver and seasonings.'

'Now you sound like the lead in a horror movie.'

'A sort of Jack Nicholson hacking down the door to bring you fillet steak.'

'I shouldn't have brought up the subject of horror movies while I'm sitting above a restaurant with a selection of chef's knives,' said Steffie. 'Now I'm picturing someone breaking into the kitchen and butchering us while we sleep.'

'Good God, woman.' Liam looked at her in amusement. 'You have a fertile imagination.'

'I don't really,' she said. 'Roisin is always telling me I've none whatsoever. Horror movies scare me, that's all.'

'You're creative, that probably has something to do with it.'

'It's a different sort of creativity,' said Steffie. 'And what I have, I've channelled into a work environment rather than an artistic one.'

'Graphic design, you said?'

She nodded, and when he asked her to tell him more about it, she gave him a summary of how she'd got to where she was and then told him about her anxiety over the branding project.

'A pretty chequered employment history,' she finished.

'Varied,' amended Liam. 'Don't be despondent because you haven't heard about the branding project yet either,' he added. 'I'm sure they'll be in touch soon.'

'I'm trying to be positive,' Steffie said. 'They didn't definitely say it would be this weekend, just that they hoped to decide by this weekend. All the same, I've got ants in my pants! Every time my phone rings, I jump a mile. Although,' she added ruefully, 'that didn't stop me dropping it earlier and forgetting it when I left the house.'

'You were stressed,' said Liam.

'I keep wondering if I overreacted,' confessed Steffie. 'And I'm beginning to feel awful for walking out in a strop. Yet right now, I know I'm still too annoyed to go back, even if I could.'

'I'm glad you're forgiving them.'

'I'm only thinking about it for some time in the distant

future,' she said. 'I'm definitely not in the right frame of mind to talk to either of them yet.'

'It's a start.'

'I guess.' She sighed. 'I wish I hadn't forgotten my phone. The company might have emailed about my design proposal.'

'On a Saturday? And it's a little late for an email, don't you think?' asked Liam. 'But tell you what, I'll get my laptop and you can check.'

'Thanks.'

She allowed herself to relax into the comfortable sofa as he left the room. Liam was a nice guy, she thought. And so different to the younger person she'd once known, not only physically but also in his manner. When they were kids, he'd been grumpy and dismissive. She remembered muttering that he wasn't one bit jolly like fat people were supposed to be. Her mother had overheard her and scolded her, saying that Liam Kinsella was a very nice boy but a little shy. He wasn't now, thought Steffie. He was full of self-confidence, which wasn't surprising given the success he'd made of his life.

He came back with the laptop and opened it. The home page on his browser was the Cody's webpage, and Steffie looked at it for a moment before logging in to her webmail account.

'No news,' she told him. 'Although if I give my bank account number to someone in Nigeria, they'll send me a few million dollars.'

He laughed.

She closed the email and looked at the Cody website page again.

'You could improve this,' she said. 'Not that I want to speak out of turn or anything, but it seems clunky and static.'

'I know it's not very exciting,' said Liam. 'It's good enough for me, though.'

'Would you say that a meal was "good enough"?' she asked, and he looked at her abashed. 'Can people book online?' she continued.

He shook his head. 'Too complicated to get it right.'

'Don't be silly,' she said. 'It's easily done. And you should . . .' She stopped. 'Sorry. I get carried away sometimes.'

'Can I see your own site?'

'Of course.' She opened the page for him and handed him the laptop.

'Oh wow,' he said as he looked at the image of a butterfly on a leaf and then began to click on the links. 'It's excellent. I love the font, too. It's really clear.'

'I'm having a bit of a love affair with Helvetica Neue at the moment,' she told him. 'Which is what that font is. It looks good on lots of different designs.'

'Would my site look better if I changed the font?' asked Liam.

'You could, of course,' Steffie said, 'but honestly it wouldn't be great. Why don't I do up a few designs for you, see what you think? You don't have to go with any of them.'

'What are your rates?' asked Liam.

'I wouldn't dream of charging you,' she said. 'Not after everything you've done for me tonight.'

'And I wouldn't dream of not paying you,' said Liam.

Steffie shook her head. 'You've been lovely to me. It would be a thank you.'

'We're both professional people,' said Liam. 'This is your livelihood. If you do this for me, I'd like it to be a business arrangement.'

She didn't want his business just because she'd given him a sob story about what a precarious state her finances were in. She didn't want charity.

'I understand,' she said. 'But you took me in and fed me and you're letting me stay here, so it's a less formal business arrangement than I have with my other clients. I'd be happy to do this for you.'

He considered it for a moment. 'How about you do up something and if I like it and want you to develop it a bit more, I pay you then?'

'Agreed,' she said and suddenly sneezed.

'God bless you.' His words were automatic.

'Thanks.' She sneezed again. And again.

'I hope you haven't caught a cold from your walk in the rain.' There was a note of concern in Liam's voice. 'How about I make you a hot lemon and honey drink?'

She shook her head. 'Thanks, but it's allergies. D'you have a cat?'

'Not as such,' said Liam. 'But Grizzly, Mrs Brannigan's tortoiseshell, occasionally sneaks in through the back door.'

Steffie sneezed again. 'I have a spray that's really good, but I left my bag at Aranbeg,' she said. 'However, I also have a Zirtek on my keyring.'

'On your keyring?' Liam looked at her in puzzlement.

'It's a tiny pill case,' she explained. 'Holds one tablet. It was a token from a Christmas cracker and it's surprisingly useful. Normally I keep a paracetamol in it for emergencies, but I put the Zirtek in this morning in case a day in the garden was too much for me.'

'That's fortunate,' said Liam.

'Thinking ahead is not normally one of my strong points.'

Steffie rubbed her eyes, which had begun to water. 'I think I left my keys downstairs.'

'I'll go and get them for you,' said Liam.

'It's OK, I'll go myself.' Steffie stood up. 'I can take the tablet down there. I'm a total wuss about swallowing pills without water.'

'Sure?'

'Absolutely. Unless you don't want me wandering around your restaurant on my own?'

Liam grinned. 'That's not a problem. The lights are out, though. The switch is on the left as you go down the stairs. Try not to think about axe murderers.'

'Idiot.' She sneezed a few more times in quick succession. 'Sorry about this. It comes out of the blue sometimes.'

She hurried out of the room in her bare feet, rubbing her nose and willing the sneezing to stop. Her eyes were itchy and beginning to water. She wondered if the cat was somewhere in the building.

She found the switch and flooded the restaurant with far more light than when she'd been sitting there with Tom and Bobby. Then the table had been lit by candles and a much fainter glow from overhead. She hurried over to the table and saw her keys sitting on it. She picked them up and opened the tiny case that contained the Zirtek. Really and truly, she thought as she looked at it, I should simply swallow it down. But I need a drink.

She walked through the swing doors to the kitchen. It was a professional kitchen, no doubt about it. The metal surfaces gleamed and there wasn't a single thing out of place. Pots and pans had been put away, and the multitude of knives were carefully placed in their blocks. She tried very hard not to think of axe murderers. Then she reminded herself that she wasn't imaginative and that nobody was going to come into the kitchen and stab her to death. She opened a couple of the cupboards. Most of them were filled with flour and spices and salt and pepper. But eventually she found one with some measuring cups and a few glasses. She took one of the glasses and filled it at the sink. She'd turned away from the sink and was just about to take a sip of water when the lights went out.

She shrieked and dropped the glass, which shattered on the floor beneath her.

The lights had gone out at Aranbeg too, although thanks to the lanterns on the veranda, the blackness wasn't as all-enveloping as in the kitchen at Cody's.

'Oh crap,' said Alivia, who'd taken the mic from a still flustered Colette. 'Just as I was about to share my vocal talents. Now you'll never know what you've missed.'

Roisin got up and started lighting more candles, while Paul suggested that the power cut was due to the flooding.

'If that's the case, we could be without electricity for ages,' said Jenny. 'I wonder if it's local or if it's all over the town.'

'God knows,' said Pascal. 'Actually I'm surprised it didn't go earlier. It's after midnight now, it's been raining for hours.'

'We should go to bed,' suggested Roisin. 'It's been a long day.'

'Let's give it a few minutes,' said Alivia.

'Where did you want us to sleep, Roisin?' asked Colette.

'I haven't entirely worked that out yet.'

'Anyone want another drink?' asked Paul.

'I think we've all had enough,' said Roisin. 'Even if nobody can get home tonight, they'll be driving tomorrow.'

'I guess you're right,' he conceded, as he thought of the hangover the unaccustomed cocktails would probably leave him with.

Colette murmured something about getting some water and went into the kitchen. Her hands were shaking as she poured herself a glass and then moved to the veranda. She knew that Davey would be looking for her. For the first time in her life, she wanted to avoid him.

Steffie stood immobile in Cody's kitchen, afraid to move in case she stepped on one of the shards of glass. The darkness seemed to wrap itself around her like a shawl. No matter how wide she opened her eyes, everything around her was shadowy and insubstantial. Except, she thought, for the knives on the worktop opposite her. Knives that could be wielded by the marauding thieves who'd cut the power lines so that they could gain access to the restaurant unseen.

'Steffie! Are you OK?'

Liam was coming down the stairs; she could hear the tread of his footsteps as he descended.

'Yes. More or less.'

A thin beam of white light forced its way through the dark. He had a torch.

'Come on,' he said.

'I can't.'

'Why not?'

'I broke a glass. I'm sorry.'

'Don't worry about it,' he said. 'This way.'

'I can't move because I'm not wearing any shoes,' she explained. 'And there's glass everywhere.'

'Oh,' said Liam.

He walked around the worktop to where she was standing and flashed the torch on to the floor. The glass had scattered out around Steffie in small and large pieces.

'It's as well you stayed put,' said Liam. 'Otherwise it could've been a bloodbath that Jack Nicholson would've been proud of down here.'

'My shoes are in the restaurant,' she said. 'Well, sandals actually. I put them at the door to dry.'

'I wouldn't imagine they're dry yet.' Liam, wearing trainers, stepped carefully over the shards. 'Hold this.'

He handed her the torch. And then he put his arms around her and lifted her.

'Liam, stop! What are you doing?'

'Rescuing my damsel in distress.' His voice bubbled with laughter. 'From the dangers of my kitchen. Hold tight.'

His arms held her securely as he turned around.

'You can put me down now,' she said when they reached the bottom of the stairs.

'Oh, let me do my Action Man thing.' He started to climb, still holding her.

'Liam, you're being daft!'

'I know.'

'I can walk.'

'But that's not as much fun.'

He was puffing slightly as he finally walked into the flat and lowered her gently to the floor.

'Did you find your keys?' he asked, his arms still around her.

'Yes.'

'The tablet worked.'

She hadn't taken it. But she wasn't sneezing any more.

He smiled at her and pulled her closer.

Her eyes met his. She stared at him for a moment.

Then he kissed her.

She felt the warmth of his breath and the gentle touch of his lips on hers. His scent was musk and he tasted faintly of coffee. He swung her into his arms again. She didn't say anything at all as he carried her into the bedroom. But when he looked at her queryingly, she said yes.

She said yes the second time too.

Chapter 28

Colette had been right. It was less than a minute before Davey was standing beside her on the veranda. She was conscious of how close he was to her, close enough that she could hear him breathing. She wondered if he could hear her breath too, ragged and nervous.

'Do you have any reasonable explanation for wearing Camilla's engagement ring?' His voice was icy.

She turned to face him. His expression matched his tone.

'It's a mistake,' she said.

'Too right it is,' said Davey.

'I didn't mean to . . .' She exhaled slowly, trying to calm herself. 'I saw the box when you were going into the house. It had fallen into one of the planters.'

'So why didn't you give it to me?' he asked.

'You were talking to Camilla. I was waiting until you were on your own. And then . . .' She didn't know how she could say it without appearing incredibly stupid. She *felt* incredibly stupid, of course, but she didn't want him to realise how much of an idiot she was.

'Then?' His eyes were steely.

'I know I shouldn't have looked at it,' she said. 'But I

did. I was in the bathroom, cleaning up and drying my hair, and I saw the box in my bag and I couldn't help myself.'

'I realise you have a certain ongoing interest in engagement rings.' He didn't try to hide the mocking tone of his voice. 'But how did you move from looking at it in the box to wearing it in front of everyone?'

'It's the most beautiful ring I've ever seen.' She glanced down at her finger. The ring was still turned so that the stones were facing her palm. 'I couldn't help myself. I tried it on.'

'It's my *girlfriend's* engagement ring,' Davey hissed. 'You'd no right to try it on. But even if you did . . .' he stared at her, 'even if you did, why are you still wearing it now? In front of me and in front of her? What sort of perverted thing is going on in your head to make you do something like that?'

'I can't get it off,' explained Colette. 'I tried and tried with soap and everything but it won't budge.'

'What!'

'It's true.' Colette tugged at the ring. 'It's completely stuck, Davey. I'm so, so sorry.'

'It can't be stuck. Let me try.'

'Ouch!' she cried as he pulled at it. 'I'm telling you, it won't come off. I know it will eventually. Maybe with the help of butter or something. But I couldn't raid the kitchen for slabs of butter without people wanting to know what I was doing.'

'So you decided to show it off anyway?'

'I didn't decide anything. Alivia was banging on the bathroom door and wondering what I was doing in there for so long. I had to come downstairs.'

'For crying out loud!' Davey was getting more and more frustrated as he continued to try to get the ring of

Colette's finger. 'If the damn thing went on, it should come off.'

'I think it's like getting your head stuck in railings,' said Colette miserably. 'Easier one way than the other.'

'I'd quite happily shove your head through some railings now,' muttered Davey.

'If it meant the ring would come off, I'd let you,' said Colette.

'Right.' Davey abandoned his attempts at removing the ring, although he was still holding Colette's hand. 'We need to do this in private, with Vaseline.'

'Do what in private with Vaseline?'

Neither of them had heard Camilla walk on to the veranda, so they both jumped guiltily at the sound of her voice.

'Not whatever you might be thinking,' said Davey, as he moved rapidly away from Colette.

'You've no idea what I'm thinking.'

'Perhaps not, but—'

'I'm thinking that you and your cousin have a very strange relationship,' said Camilla. 'You spent hours together driving around in the rain. And now you're holding hands.'

'We're *so* not holding hands!' cried Colette. 'Honestly, Camilla.'

Camilla's attention was caught by the sight of the ring on Colette's finger. She looked from her to Davey, complete astonishment on her face.

'Really and truly not what you think,' repeated Davey. 'But something we don't want everyone to know about.'

'From your perspective, I guess not.' Camilla turned and walked away from them.

'Shit,' said Davey and hurried after her.

*   *   *

301

SingStar having had to be abandoned, Roisin was now busy sorting out the sleeping arrangements. Despite it being a logistical nightmare, the effort of trying to find places for people to bed down was helping to relax her, and when Jenny walked into the den where she'd been standing, she gave her mother a brief smile.

'There are two other camp beds in the utility room.' Jenny knew what her elder daughter was thinking about. 'That'll help.'

'Oh, I hadn't thought of them!' Roisin tutted in annoyance. 'I'd forgotten how many people stayed here in the past.'

'At least then it was always part of the plan.'

'I know.'

'I'm sorry, Roisin,' said Jenny. 'For messing up what was a lovely day. And for allowing ourselves to be in a situation where it could get messed up.'

'It's OK,' said Roisin.

'It's not,' said her mother. 'Maybe it will be, but right now it's as far from OK as it's possible to be.'

'Because Steffie shot off like a scalded cat and left us all frozen with worry.'

'Because I've made you unhappy,' said Jenny. 'Because I've let you down.'

Roisin was horrified to feel a lump in her throat. She said nothing. She didn't want Jenny to know how she felt.

'When I found out I was pregnant with you, I couldn't believe it,' Jenny told her. 'Even though I was young and naive, I knew I loved you more than anything in the world. Before you were born and afterwards.'

Roisin couldn't speak.

'Not marrying your dad wasn't some kind of disrespecting of you,' Jenny continued. 'I think you feel it might have been. There were loads of reasons we didn't. None of them good enough in hindsight.'

'What about after Steffie? Why didn't you get married then? Was it because Dad was too angry with you? Or that he didn't love you any more and you only stayed together for all our sakes?'

'I didn't want him to feel obliged to marry me,' said Jenny. 'I wanted to give him the option to leave if he felt he couldn't put up with the situation. He wouldn't have left because of you and Davey. You both meant the world to him. But I didn't want him to feel trapped.'

'So you just drifted along?'

'More or less,' said Jenny. 'And then, when we realised it was working, we thought – why change? You know how it is, you read all these things about celebrities who've been together for twenty years and then a year after they get married they split up. We didn't want to be those people.'

'I wish you'd said something before now.'

'So do I.' Jenny's words were heartfelt.

'I don't like to think that you cheated on Dad.'

'It was the worst thing I ever did,' confessed Jenny. 'It was a terrible, terrible mistake and I never really paid the price for it. Maybe I'm paying it now.'

'Not on my account,' said Roisin. 'I'm still angry with you, Mum, but I suppose I'll get over it.'

Jenny smiled. 'Thank you.' She held out her arms and Roisin allowed herself to be hugged. It wasn't something she and Jenny had much time for these days. Mainly because Roisin was always too busy to give her mum more than a cursory peck on the cheek when she was saying goodbye to her. But it was nice to feel the warmth of Jenny's embrace and to know that, no matter what, they loved each other.

Then her thoughts returned to more practical matters and she asked Jenny about extra bedlinen.

'Don't worry about me,' said Alivia, who walked in at that moment. 'I don't need fancy linen to stretch out on the sofa in the living room.'

'We've found camp beds,' said Roisin.

'Doubles?' asked Alivia. 'For Carl and Summer?'

'Oh please!' Roisin's face was agonised. 'I don't even want to think about that.'

'I'll get the sleeping bags,' said Jenny. 'You can have one of those, Alivia. Thank God I never took Pascal's advice to throw them out.'

The three women returned to the living room, where some of the guests were relaxing in the candlelight. Roisin outlined her thoughts about sleeping arrangements.

'If you leave the sleeping bags and bedlinen or whatever here, we can work it out between us,' said Bernice. She glanced at Carl. She'd be sleeping in the same house as him again. And his girlfriend. Who, she realised, wasn't actually here at the moment. Davey and Camilla were missing too.

'Where has everyone gone?' asked Roisin. 'Honestly, it's like rounding up a bunch of kids.'

'D'you want me to check?' Alivia giggled. 'I could knock on doors and ask them if they're decent before I open them.'

Roisin made a face at her as Jenny returned with a variety of blankets and sleeping bags as well as a couple of torches.

'The lanterns are great,' she said. 'But it's a good idea to have torches too.'

'Oh, Aunt Jenny, it's just like when we were kids!' cried Alivia. 'I feel like I've stepped back twenty years.'

'So do I,' said Sarah, who was looking at the mound of bedding. 'Especially as you're making me share with Lucinda.'

'Did you share before?' asked Alivia.

'When we were children, of course,' replied her mother. 'Your granny's house only had two bedrooms.'

'Really?' Alivia looked surprised.

'Yes. Me and Jenny and Lucinda in one, Mum and Dad in the other. Me and Lucinda shared a bed then.'

'You were probably delighted when I left,' remarked Jenny.

'I had to wait around for both you *and* Sarah to leave before I had any privacy,' said Lucinda.

'I left to get privacy,' said Sarah. 'But all I did was get the wrong husband.'

The three sisters looked at each other.

'That's what you think?' said Jenny.

'That's the actual fact.' Sarah spoke slowly. 'I never really thought about it like that before. But I guess the reason I wanted to be married and have kids – leaving aside my jealousy of you and your perfect life, Jen – was so that I could have a place of my own.'

'You do realise that I never had a perfect life?' said Jenny.

'I thought you had.'

'Nobody does,' said Lucinda.

All of the women were silent.

Jenny thought about the mistakes she'd made and the effect they'd had on other people. Her sisters had resented her, she realised, but she hadn't realised it. Because she'd been the only one to know that the picture she'd painted hadn't been true.

'But we do the best we can,' said Alivia to break the silence. 'Everyone does.' Even as she spoke, she checked her mobile. Still no reply from Dermot to her last text. She sighed. She was doing her best too. But now she wondered if it was going to be enough.

Camilla had fled upstairs and locked herself in the bathroom, ignoring Davey's calls to her to wait and let him explain. She didn't want to hear some kind of made-up story when it was perfectly obvious to her that there was something going on between him and his cousin. She'd wondered earlier, when she'd seen the way Colette had looked at him, a repressed longing in her dark eyes. Camilla knew that look. She'd worn it herself in the past. When she'd been in love with Mikkel Hansen. She'd been sixteen at the time and Mikkel, a friend of her half-brother's, had never even noticed her, but her longing had been expressed in her face every time he came to the house. She knew that because her mother had laughed at her one day and told her she was like a lovesick cow pining after a bull. Camilla had been horrified that her secret, innermost desires had been clear for everyone to see (everyone except Mikkel himself, who continued to ignore her). She resolved that in the future she would be self-contained, clearheaded and emotionless. She knew that she wasn't actually emotionless, that it was impossible not to have feelings, but she'd grown very, very good at hiding them.

Now, sitting on the edge of the bath, her eyes adjusting to the fact that the room was illuminated by a single tea light on the windowsill, she wasn't hiding her emotions at all.

Tears were streaming down her face and she couldn't stop them. She hadn't realised she was going to cry. She hadn't realised that it mattered to her that Davey Sheehan was her boyfriend. She'd thought he was someone she cared deeply about; someone she could, perhaps, marry if she felt that way inclined, but someone who would be easy to leave if she didn't. She'd been completely and utterly wrong about that because now she was devastated. Devastated at the idea that there was someone else in his life. Devastated that he'd hidden it from her. Devastated at realising she didn't know him at all.

'For God's sake, Cam, open the door.' Davey waited until his mum had disappeared downstairs again with an armful of blankets before he banged on the bathroom door.

'I don't want to talk to you,' she said.

'I have to talk to you,' he told her.

'You don't.'

'I do.'

'No,' said Camilla.

'Please,' said Davey. 'You've got it all wrong.'

'I don't think so,' she said.

Davey leaned his head against the door. He'd planned everything about today and how he'd ask Camilla to marry him, and he'd tried not to imagine what it would be like if she said no, but never in his wildest dreams had he envisaged the way things would turn out.

'Camilla, it's me, Colette.' Colette had hesitated before following the two of them up the stairs but she hoped she'd be able to help.

'Go away,' said Camilla. 'Both of you.'

Davey looked at Colette in desperation.

307

'She needs some time,' said Colette. 'She doesn't want to hear what she thinks are lies.'

'But they're not lies,' said Davey. 'I want to tell her how much I love her. That it's only ever been her. That there's no one else in my life and there never will be. I want to ask her to marry me.'

His words were like a whip lashing across Colette's face. But they were words she knew were true. And she was glad that he was speaking them. She was also glad that the landing outside the bathroom door was in almost complete darkness.

'I had a crush on you,' she said rapidly. 'When we were kids. Well, I was a kid, you were a teenager. I fancied you. That's why I tried on the ring.'

'You're joking.' He sounded appalled.

'You were nice to me when nobody else was,' she said. 'When I had the fight with Steffie, when she fell out of the tree, it was because I'd written about you in my diary and I didn't want her to see it.'

'Oh my God.'

'I was afraid she'd make fun of me. Or tell you.'

'I had no idea,' said Davey. 'I never thought . . .'

'People don't, I suppose, when you have crushes,' said Colette.

'But it wore off, right? I mean, you've been engaged three times.'

'Because I kept thinking I'd find something of you in them,' said Colette.

Davey didn't know what to say.

'But I'm over it now.' She smiled faintly at him.

'Now? Since when?'

308

'I guess there's always been a bit of something in the background,' said Colette. 'But today. Since I tried on the engagement ring. It's gone.'

'There was no something from me.' Davey's voice was firm. 'I'm sorry if that breaks your heart or anything, but . . . Colette, you were a kid. I never, ever thought . . .'

'I realise that,' she said. 'I always knew it. It was a dream, that's all.'

He groaned.

'Not any more,' she said. 'I promise. It was silliness.'

Davey rubbed his head. 'Maybe I can talk sense into Camilla. Maybe she'll understand. But listening to you, Colette, my faith in the sense of womankind has been fairly shattered.'

'I can see that.' She twirled the ring on her finger. 'I do. I wish there was something I could . . . Oh!' She looked at him in surprise as it suddenly slid free. 'Oh my God. It's come off. Just like that.'

'Give it to me,' said Davey.

She handed it to him. In the darkness it was nothing more than a piece of yellow metal. The diamonds weren't able to glitter.

'I'll wait here till she comes out,' he said. 'And then . . . well, we'll see.'

'Good luck, Davey,' said Colette. She moved to kiss him on the cheek but then drew back. 'I'll keep my fingers crossed.'

'Thanks,' said Davey as she turned around and walked back down the stairs.

Chapter 29

Steffie was lying in the crook of Liam's arm, but she was thinking about Steve. It seemed like an eternity since she'd felt hurt by his decision not to come to the anniversary party and then decided to break up with him. But she hadn't actually said anything to him before she'd jumped into bed with another man. If he knew where she was, he'd say she was cheating on him. But circumstances altered the facts. Didn't they?

Her mother had said that to her earlier when trying to explain about her fake marriage and her fling with Gregory. Steffie hadn't wanted to believe that when presented in a particular way people's actions could seem callous and unthinking, but that they were in fact influenced by what was going on around them and maybe even understandable. Not that Jenny having an affair was remotely understandable, or forgivable, but Steffie wondered if, twenty-seven years ago, her mother had been swept away by the same feelings that had taken over Steffie herself tonight. An overwhelming desire for someone that was simply irresistible. A feeling that what you were doing was inevitable and right.

Not that what Jenny had done could ever have been

considered right. Fair enough, thought Steffie, she herself might have technically cheated on Steve, but at least she wasn't supposed to be married to him. Jenny didn't have that excuse. The fact that she wasn't actually married to Pascal was completely irrelevant.

Steffie shifted slightly in the bed and Liam pulled his arm from beneath her. But he didn't roll away as she'd expected, just turned so that he was curling up behind her, pulling her close to him.

'Okay?' he whispered.

'Yes.'

'You know you were amazing earlier.'

'So were you, to be honest.'

He chuckled in the darkness.

'I never thought I'd sleep with you, Steffie Sheehan. Never even dreamed about it.'

'You weren't exactly on my radar either.'

He didn't answer. His breathing became deep and steady and Steffie realised that he'd fallen asleep. Men did, she thought, after making love. She'd read somewhere that it was because of hormones or something. Men slept but women . . . She couldn't remember what she'd read about women, but she knew that it took her ages to fall asleep after being with someone for the first time. Not that there had been all that many notches on her bedpost. She wouldn't be breaking any records. But she had a bit of experience. Enough to know that making love to Liam Kinsella was in the number one position by a mile. That first time had been phenomenal. And the second even better. So where did that leave her, she wondered, in the emotional stakes? Because she wasn't the sort of girl, experienced or not, who normally put out on a first date. A minimum of three was where she set the bar. With Steve it had been four, because the first date didn't really count; they'd gone for something to eat after working late, nothing more. And this thing with Liam – well, it wasn't even a first date, plus he'd made it clear earlier that he didn't have time for relationships because he was so caught up with running the restaurant. Which was fine. Tonight had been a one-off, sparked by the situation they'd found themselves in. She wasn't expecting anything from Liam. It was too complicated. But the idea that they wouldn't do again what they'd done tonight was heartbreaking.

Was that what Jenny had thought about Gregory? That it had been so good she couldn't say no? Despite Pascal and despite Roisin and despite Davey? Had Gregory been her Liam Kinsella? Steffie wrinkled her nose at the thought. She really didn't want to compare herself to her mother, especially when the subject was their sex lives. She didn't want to think of Jenny's sex life even for a nanosecond. And yet she herself was the result of it. Of Jenny's days of wild abandon. She was the result of a passionate fling. She supposed the newspapers would call her a love child.

At least there was no chance of there being a pregnancy from her own passionate sex with Liam. They'd been upfront about protection, and although she'd briefly wondered how many times he'd had the conversation before, the only thing she'd cared about was how wonderful being with him was.

Tomorrow I'll get up and walk away, she said to herself. But tonight – if for no other reason than it was the best sex of my life – I'm very glad I was here.

'People are going to bed, Camilla,' said Davey. 'They'll be wanting to use the bathroom. You can't stay in there.'

There was no reply. He leaned his head against the locked door and sighed. Then he almost fell as it opened inward.

'I'm leaving the bathroom so that no one is inconvenienced. I don't want to talk to you,' said Camilla as he steadied himself.

'I have to explain—'

'I do not believe in explanations,' said Camilla. 'People trying to justify themselves. Trying to come up with something that will make other people happy.'

'I'm not coming up with anything,' said Davey. 'All I want is to tell you what happened.'

'I don't want to know what happened.'

'Yes, you do.' He caught her by the wrist and she stood perfectly still. For a moment he thought she was going to snatch her hand away and accuse him of assaulting her, but they heard voices on the stairway and both of them hesitated. Davey opened the door to Roisin's bedroom, which was the nearest, and pulled Camilla inside. It took a couple of seconds for their eyes to adjust to the almost total darkness. Davey could see his nephew curled up asleep in the middle of the big double bed.

'You've got it all wrong about Colette and me,' he whispered to Camilla. 'And I can't let your stubborn pride allow you to think there was anything at all going on between us. I'm not making up stories so that you feel better. I'm telling you the God's honest truth. If, after you hear it, you're still mad at me and never want to see me again, that's fine. But you have to hear me out.'

'OK,' murmured Camilla, after a short pause. 'Say what you have to say.'

So Davey did and Camilla listened.

'You're saying that your cousin has been in love with you all her life?' asked Camilla, when he'd finished.

'Not in love with me,' amended Davey. 'In love with some kind of ideal that she thought I represented. She was only a kid when she stayed with us that summer. Her parents' marriage was crumbling. She was miserable. I guess she saw me as some kind of romantic figure.' He could sense, rather than see, the sceptical expression on Camilla's face. 'I was a lot younger and better-looking back then,' he added.

'A heart-throb,' said Camilla.

'To an impressionable young girl,' said Davey.

'And now?' asked Camilla.

'Like I said, she's been engaged three times,' Davey told her. 'She's looking for something and someone but at last she knows it isn't me.'

'It's hard to believe,' said Camilla.

'Because in it I'm some kind of sex symbol?' Davey sounded rueful.

'Maybe real life is always harder to believe than things people make up,' said Camilla.

'Maybe.' He peered anxiously at her. 'So . . . do you believe me?'

'Oh yes,' said Camilla after a pause. 'It's too ridiculous not to be true.'

'In that case – are we OK again?'

Camilla didn't answer straight away. She was reliving the emotions she'd felt when she'd seen Davey and Colette together, when she'd rushed to conclusions about their relationship. The jealousy was still like a dagger of ice in her heart. She knew now that she loved Davey and wanted him for herself. Which went against everything she'd ever believed in before – being detached, being cool, being in control. She'd been proud of how she'd cultivated that personality. How she never crumbled. How she'd changed after her mother had joked about how emotional she'd been. It had been important to her for a long time. But perhaps it was different now. Perhaps it always should have been different. Perhaps she, Camilla Rasmussen, was different too. She allowed her head to rest on Davey's chest.

'We're OK,' she whispered. 'I shouldn't always jump to conclusions.'

'The talk about Vaseline didn't help,' murmured Davey, and felt Camilla giggle. A wave of relief washed over him. The woman he loved believed him. Believed in him. Enough to stay with him for ever?

It wasn't how he'd planned it, of course. But then nothing ever worked out the way he planned. He reached into the pocket of his trousers and took out the engagement ring.

'I wanted this moment to be special,' he said softly. 'I wanted it to be memorable. I had all sorts of plans for how it was going to be. But the only thing that matters now is to ask you. Will you marry me, Camilla?'

She took the ring from him. The ring that she'd seen another woman wearing. She supposed that if you were the sort of person who looked for omens and portents, it might mean something. If you allowed yourself to become emotional about things. But even if she was allowing herself to be more emotional than usual tonight, she was, and always would be, a practical woman and the ring was beautiful. She slid it on to her finger. It fitted perfectly. She looked at Davey and smiled.

'Of course I'll marry you,' she said and kissed him.

'Oh yuck.' Dougie sat up in bed. 'You're kissing. In my bedroom. That's totally disgusting.'

'This takes me back,' said Lucinda as she and Sarah sat on the end of Steffie's bed, a selection of tea lights flickering on the dresser in front of them.

'How many years?' asked Sarah.

'Since we shared a room? Gosh it must be thirty-five . . . no, oh my God, Sarah, it's thirty-seven years!'

'That makes me feel old.'

'Me too.'

'But then we are old. We're in our fifties.'

'Fifty is the new thirty,' said Lucinda. 'So they say.'

'Hmm. They were never around to say that when I was thirty,' said Sarah.

'Me neither.'

The two of them laughed.

'I don't feel all that different,' Sarah said. 'I still think the best years of my life are ahead of me. But they can't be, can they? Being realistic, there's more years behind than in front now.'

'No reason why the ones in front can't be the best,' remarked Lucinda.

'Do you actually believe that?'

Lucinda sighed. 'I wish I did. If that was the case, I'd meet someone gorgeous and baggage-free and live happily ever after with him.'

'Unlikely,' said Sarah. 'I suppose if there is a gorgeous, baggage-free man out there, he's looking for a gorgeous, baggage-free woman. And let's face it, neither of us count on that score!'

316

'True.'

'So maybe we need to adjust our expectations.'

'It would be good to think there was someone out there who wasn't weighed down by his past,' said Lucinda. 'But by our age the baggage is huge, isn't it?'

'Mine came spilling on to the carousel earlier,' said Sarah. 'First when we got here and everything seemed so perfect. And more when Jenny told us her secrets and we realised it wasn't. I managed to blame her both for getting nothing wrong and for getting nothing right.'

'Poor Jenny. I feel sorry for her tonight.'

'I've never felt sorry for her in my life,' said Sarah. 'Truthfully, I don't think I ever will. But today has to have been a nightmare for her.'

'She'll get over it,' said Lucinda. 'But nothing will be the same again.'

'And what about Steffie? Will she forgive Jenny?'

'I like to think children forgive their parents. I want to think that Alivia forgives me for not understanding when she went looking for her dad. I gave her an unnecessarily hard time. I thought I was losing her but in the end I think I was driving her away. And I know I can be clingy, but the thing is, Sarah, she might have been my greatest mistake, but she's also my greatest joy.'

'I suppose everyone makes at least one tremendous mistake in their lives,' said Sarah. 'The trick is learning from them. I don't think I've quite nailed that yet.'

'You can't go back,' said Lucinda. 'You can't erase your mistakes. You can't start over. All you can do is move on and live with them.'

'From tomorrow I'm going to try to do that.' Sarah

yawned. 'We never talked like this before we went to bed when we were younger.'

'We didn't have such dramas to talk about.'

'We probably did, over boyfriends or something, but of course those so-called dramas all fade into insignificance eventually.' Sarah began to peel off her clothes. 'I suppose everything does. You won't be offended by the sight of me in my bra and knickers, will you?'

Lucinda laughed. 'Not a bit of it. As long as you're not offended by me either.'

'Right so,' said Sarah. 'I'm getting in first. Will you blow out those tea lights? I don't want to burn the house down.'

Lucinda extinguished the lights then got into bed beside her sister. 'I hope you don't snore these days,' she said.

'Like a trooper,' Sarah assured her.

'It doesn't matter.' Lucinda's voice was already drifty. 'I'm so tired and this bed is so comfortable. G'night, Sarah.'

'Good night, baby sister.'

The two of them closed their eyes.

They were asleep within five minutes.

With the exception of Summer, who'd abruptly flaked out on the sofa and was lost to the world, nobody who'd been offered blankets, camp beds or sleeping bags was making any move to sleep. Carl covered his girlfriend with one of the lightest blankets and then went into the kitchen, where Alivia was sitting at the table scrolling through her text messages. He poured himself a glass of water, then walked back through the house. Colette was curled up in an armchair in the living room drinking a glass of wine. Bernice was also curled up with a glass of wine, although in her case she was on the veranda.

'Mind if I join you?' Carl asked.

'Where's your girlfriend?'

'Sleeping.'

'Lightweight.' Bernice sipped her wine.

'If I'd known you were coming, I wouldn't have asked Summer,' said Carl as he sat down beside her.

Bernice raised an eyebrow.

'I'm not a total dick,' said Carl.

'Bringing that girl to this party was definite dickdom,' Bernice said. 'It was awkward for everyone, not just me.'

'She got on with all of them,' protested Carl. 'She's a sweet person.'

Bernice said nothing.

'I wanted some fun, that's all,' said Carl.

'I didn't realise that life with me was so fun-free.'

'It became that way.'

Carl's words lodged between them.

Bernice ran the tip of her finger around the rim of her glass before Carl spoke again.

'I thought by now I'd be tucked up in bed at the guest house. I reckoned I'd have left early because Mum would've done my head in.'

'You were never keen on family gatherings.'

'No,' he said. 'I wasn't.'

Bernice didn't add anything. She was trying not to think about the last time they'd been together as a couple and the suppressed anger that had crackled between them. She'd asked if they were breaking up and he'd said he needed some space. She'd asked what sort of space, and he'd said he didn't know; then she'd said that he could leave if he wanted because they weren't committed to each other, and he'd told her, quite sharply, that he had been committed to her but that she'd gone behind his back.

Despite the fact that they'd agreed to give it three months, she'd felt as though they were over as soon as he'd walked out the door. She hadn't expected him to come back. Indeed, he'd waited until she was at work before he'd emptied his wardrobe and taken things that had always been his. As well as the Blu-ray player and the small TV from the bedroom. And it had broken her heart.

'You always got on with everyone,' he said when she didn't speak. 'They all love you. They were delighted to see you today. Happier to see you than me, I reckon.'

'I doubt that. You're family. I'm not.'

'You were great earlier,' he continued. 'Looking after Poppy. Driving to the hospital in the rain. A real angel of mercy.'

'I didn't realise the floods would be that bad, to be honest,' she said. 'If I had, I probably would've let someone else drive.'

'But you *did* drive,' said Carl. 'Everyone was impressed by you. They always are.'

'It's my job,' she said.

He took a deep breath and turned to face her. 'We always said it would be a joint decision. That we'd go together.'

'I don't want to have this argument again, Carl.'

'It's not an argument.'

'That's what it became. Every time.'

'Because you wouldn't see my point of view.'

'I know exactly what your point of view is,' she said. 'You were relieved each time I didn't become pregnant.'

'Not relieved,' he said. 'It was just . . . Having a baby is a such a big responsibility, you know.'

'Yes, I do know. I realise that you weren't ready for it. I'm sorry. I kind of thought that at the age of thirty-five and with eight years behind us, you would have been.'

'I'm responsible about the things that matter,' he said.

'And this mattered to me.'

'It's heavy stuff. Going to get tested. Seeing if it's me or you that was the reason.'

'And grown-ups have to deal with heavy stuff,' she said. 'But the truth is, you didn't even want to be responsible for breaking up with me. You couldn't say it out loud.'

'Is that what you think?'

She gave him a resigned look and nodded.

'It's not true,' said Carl. 'I needed time to think about it. I said so.'

'And your time to think made you decide that what you really needed in your life was someone like Summer,' said Bernice.

'You made me feel like a machine,' he said. 'That I was only there to provide sperm for you. As though all you wanted was a baby, not me.'

'That's not true.'

'You agreed with me about kids at the start. You changed.'

'Perhaps I thought you'd change too. Seeing you with Summer has made me realise what a big mistake that was. I'm sorry.'

'So being sorry . . .' He looked at her. 'Does that mean you want things to go back to the way they were?'

'Of course not.' She sipped her wine. 'It's too late for that. I want a family. I wanted it to be with you, but it's not what you want. That's what I'm sorry about.'

321

'I haven't had a great experience when it comes to family life,' he said. 'Mum and Dad . . .'

'You're not the only person whose parents had a crap marriage,' she told him. 'And you lived with me, in reasonable stability, for eight years.'

'We could still be together,' he said.

She raised an eyebrow. 'How would Summer feel about that?'

'I like her a lot. But you can see yourself that she's not the settling-down kind.'

'Which must be ideal for you, because if I recall correctly, you told me that's what you didn't want to do.'

'I said I didn't want to be the sort of married-with-kids couple my parents were.'

'Well, no chance of that when you wouldn't talk about our fertility issues either.'

'I didn't want to be bludgeoned into going through tests and God knows what else when I wasn't ready. And I didn't like you going behind my back to get yourself checked out either.'

'I was looking after my own health,' she said. 'Which I was perfectly entitled to do without you behaving as though I'd signed up for IVF on the spot!'

'It was supposed to be a joint thing.' His tone was stubborn.

'I know you're angry about what I did,' said Bernice. 'But it's my body.'

'Is it my fault?' he asked abruptly. 'Am I the reason?'

She thought again of the piece of paper in her bag. The results that she'd brought, not knowing if she'd intended to give them to him or not. Thinking that if she did, it would be a real jaw-dropping moment for everyone at the party.

322

She got up from her seat and looked at him.

'If you want the answer to that question, you should go and get tested yourself,' she said. Then she turned away and walked back into the house.

Chapter 30

When Steffie woke up, she was alone in the bed. She had no idea of the time, but there was a faint light filtering into the room. She sat upright, listening for sounds of Liam moving around. But the flat was silent and so she pushed the covers away, got out of bed and opened the curtains. It had stopped raining, although there were still some large grey clouds in the sky. Even as she stood there, however, the rising sun flecked them with a warm orange glow and the patches of blue between them grew bigger. But the road outside was still wet and the potholes remained full of water. She wondered if it had receded in the ditch where she'd abandoned her car. She'd have to deal with that as soon as possible.

Her discarded underwear was on the floor beside her and she picked up her bra and knickers before going into the tiny bathroom. She realised the power must still be out because the water from the electric shower was nothing more than a cool trickle. She hopped around beneath it for a minute before switching it off and drying herself with one of the two bath towels on the rail. Then she put on her party dress again. She pulled her fingers through her curls and walked downstairs, once again in her bare feet.

Although it was only six thirty, Liam was already in the restaurant, mopping the floor. At first she thought he was simply cleaning it, and then she saw that the entire floor was under water.

'Oh my God,' she said. 'Don't tell me you've been flooded! You're on a hill here; how on earth did that happen?'

Liam rested his chin on the handle of the mop. 'Not from the ground up,' he told her. 'From the top down. The roof is leaking.'

Steffie glanced upwards.

'That's the trouble with flat roofs,' said Liam. 'Water can gather and if there's a weakness it'll find it. I'm surprised it didn't happen sooner.'

'Did it do much damage?' asked Steffie.

'It's not too bad,' replied Liam. 'But the banquettes are soaked and they'll take some time to dry. I'll send emails to the diners who had reservations for today. It won't all be dried out in time, and besides, I've no power.'

'What about the food?' asked Steffie. 'Won't it spoil?'

'The temperature in the cold storage room will stay low for a while yet,' said Liam. 'But I'm hoping they'll have it restored soon. Either way, though, I'm closing for today.'

'Will that be very costly for you?'

'It's just one day,' he said. 'A pity it's a Sunday, but there's nothing I can do about it.'

'Can I help with anything?'

'Are you good with a mop?'

She grinned. 'It wouldn't be my number-one thing. But I'll manage.'

'There's another one in the cupboard over there,' he said.

They spent the next half-hour in silence as they worked

on cleaning up. At least it wasn't muddy flood water, Steffie thought as she squeezed the mop into her bucket. It wouldn't take long to get the restaurant back to normal. When they'd finished, Liam told her he'd make some pancakes for breakfast.

'I thought you had no power,' she said as she followed him into the kitchen, which he'd already cleared of broken glass.

'It's a gas hob,' he explained.

'Of course. I'm an idiot.'

He smiled at her.

'Do you want me to do a notice?' she asked as she watched him get the ingredients together.

'What sort?'

'To stick on the window. In case people come to the restaurant anyway.'

'That would be useful,' he agreed. 'There's a little office through that door. You'll find paper in the printer tray and pens in the cup on the desk. Tomorrow is our day off, so we won't be open till Tuesday.'

Steffie went into the office, returning a short time later with some A4 sheets on which she'd inscribed the words 'Closed Due to Flood Damage. Business as Usual on Tuesday' and sketched a line picture of a man with a mop.

'That's fantastic,' he said as she stuck them up. 'You'd think it was printed.'

'Hopefully you *will* be able to open on Tuesday.'

'Fingers crossed. Here you go.' Liam handed her a plate on which he'd placed three pancakes and a small ramekin of whipped cream, along with a variety of chopped fresh fruits.

'This looks gorgeous,' she said.

326

'It's meant to.'

'I don't normally eat much for breakfast.'

'You should, you know. It's the most important meal of the day.'

'So the experts say. But I'm not usually one for food until at least ten. And being honest with you, I don't see six thirty in the morning very often.'

'It's not my thing either,' he admitted. 'But I woke up and I thought I heard the sound of dripping water so I came downstairs to investigate. Although,' he added, 'I would've much preferred to stay where I was. I could've done far more interesting things there.'

She felt herself blush as her eyes met his. Neither of them spoke, and then he leaned over and touched her cheek. She felt a jolt of electricity run through her as his finger glided across her skin and came to rest on her lips. They remained immobile for a moment and then she closed her mouth around it.

'You taste of sugar and strawberries,' she whispered.

'Is that a good thing?'

She nodded. 'Why don't we delay breakfast?'

Liam took the plate from her hand and put it on a table. Then, as he'd done a few hours earlier, he picked her up and carried her up the stairs.

'Sure?' he asked as he placed her gently on the bed. 'In the cold light of day?'

'It's the warm light of morning,' she said. 'And I'm certain.'

'I need to sort everyone out.' Roisin had already been up half an hour before Paul opened his eyes. 'I don't know what people want to do about getting home.'

'They can just go,' Paul mumbled from beneath the duvet, where Dougie was still sleeping. 'You don't need to do anything else for them.'

'I have to say goodbye,' said Roisin.

'Why?'

'It's good manners.'

'What time is it?' asked Paul.

'A little after nine.'

'What! We've only been in bed a few hours. They'll all still be asleep.'

'Maybe. But I can tidy up.'

'Around them?'

'Whatever.'

'You go and sort things if you want,' said Paul. 'I'm staying here for a bit longer.'

He pulled the covers further over his head.

Roisin opened the bedroom door and walked quietly down the stairs. The first person she saw was Summer, stretched out on one of the two sofas, a blanket around her shoulders. In sleep, she looked almost as young as Daisy, her face unlined and untroubled, her long dark lashes sweeping her dewy cheeks.

Bernice, on the other hand – and on the other sofa – was managing to look tired despite being asleep. Her red hair was tangled and her eyes were smudged with mascara. Roisin thought she'd been crying and her heart hardened against Carl. She was convinced that the whole 'on a break' thing had been his idea.

There was nobody in the kitchen. She filled the kettle and switched it on, then realised that the power was still out. She poured herself a large glass of water and began to tidy up, putting empty beer cans into one plastic bag for recycling and empty wine bottles into another, and then stacking glasses in the dishwasher for later. She'd just closed the door when Colette walked into the room wearing her now crumpled black and yellow dress but looking, Roisin thought, happier than she'd seen her in ages.

'I'm going to head back to town,' Colette told her.

'I can't offer you tea or coffee before you go because there's no electricity,' said Roisin.

'It doesn't matter,' said Colette. 'I'm not the sort of person who needs caffeine in the morning to get going.'

'Plus you weren't drinking last night so you're not hungover. Lucky you.'

'Indeed.'

'I was going to make some sandwiches,' said Roisin. 'I thought people could do with some food inside them before they go. Though perhaps not if they have particularly sore heads.'

'You should chill a bit, Roisin,' said Colette. 'You don't have to look after everyone. If they have sore heads, it's their own fault.'

'It's what I do,' said Roisin.

Colette smiled. 'It always was,' she said. 'I remember when we were kids and the boys and I stayed here. You were always rushing around the place doing things. You were so efficient and grown up. Glamorous too, of course.'

'Glamorous? Me?' Roisin snorted. 'I don't think so.'

'You were what – eighteen, nineteen back then?' Colette recalled. 'Of course you seemed glam to me. And you had a part-time job too, which made you properly important.'

'Stacking shelves in the local supermarket,' said Roisin. 'Not at all glam or important.'

329

'To me it was. And you were so together, that was the thing. Nothing seemed to bother you.'

'I'm sure plenty of things did,' said Roisin.

'If they did, you never let it show. I wanted be like you but I couldn't.'

'Like me?' Roisin was flattered.

'Of course. You were the eldest. You were super-cool. And I was . . . well, not in a good place back then.'

'It was a tough summer for all of you,' said Roisin.

'And I let it get on top of me,' agreed Colette. 'But you – you never let things get to you. You're like – like Superwoman.'

Roisin smiled.

'Except you don't have to be all the time,' added Colette. 'Like now. You need some time to yourself after everything that's gone on.'

'It won't change anything,' said Roisin. 'Besides, I have me time when I'm tidying up and stuff.'

'It's not quite what I meant.'

'I know, but it works for me. Anyway, thanks for everything you did yesterday.' Roisin took some butter from the lifeless fridge.

'No worries,' said Colette.

'Um, one other thing. I hope you don't mind me asking – did you and Davey have a row about something last night?'

'It was a misunderstanding, that's all,' said Colette.

'I saw him talking to you and he seemed so angry. It was odd after you'd driven through all that bad weather together.'

'Nothing to worry about. All sorted.'

'Sure?'

Colette nodded.

330

'You and I don't see each other enough,' said Roisin. 'We should do coffee sometime.'

'I'd like that,' said Colette. 'Keep in touch, Roisin. I'm off now. Give my good wishes to your mum and dad. Tell Davey I said goodbye.'

'OK.'

'And go easy on Steffie when she comes home. It was a big shock for her.'

'Oh, I know.' Roisin put some glasses in a cupboard. 'I always seem to be making allowances for Steffie, even when she does something that scares us all witless.'

'I always make allowances for Eoin because he's my younger brother,' said Colette. 'Even though he can be a right eejit. Steffie's not a bad person, and yesterday's news was a really big deal as far as she was concerned.'

'It was a big deal for all of us.' Roisin flicked a cloth across one of the worktops. 'Oh, you're right, Colette. Her stuff is harder. It's just . . . there's always something with her, that's all. And for some reason everyone thinks she needs support while I'm supposed to manage by myself.'

'I understand,' said Colette. 'I feel that way too sometimes.'

'You do?'

'You and I are life's copers,' said Colette. 'You do it by organising and cleaning and I do it by looking bizarre outside when I feel churned up inside.'

'Oh Colette! I never thought – you always seem totally happy and together to me.'

'I think I'll be better in the future,' said Colette. 'Funnily enough, last night made me see some things differently myself.'

Roisin looked at her enquiringly, but when she realised that Colette wasn't going to say any more, she simply asked her if she'd like a sandwich before she went. When her cousin said no, she put her arms around her and hugged her.

Colette had just picked up her bag prior to leaving when Davey and Camilla appeared.

'Don't go yet,' said Davey. 'We want to celebrate.'

Colette looked between them. Camilla held up her engagement finger.

'It looked so good on you, I had to have it for myself,' she said.

'Oh my God, Davey!' squealed Roisin, who, in the excitement of seeing the ring on Camilla's finger, hadn't listened to what she'd said. 'I don't believe it! Today of all days!' She threw her arms around her brother and then around Camilla, who hugged her tentatively in return.

The sound of their raised voices soon brought everyone else into the kitchen, where Camilla showed off her ring amid delighted whoops. When Jenny and Pascal, awakened by the noise, came downstairs themselves, they found their only son and his new fiancée the centre of attention.

'It's wonderful news,' Jenny repeated over and over. 'Simply wonderful.'

'The best anniversary present you could give us,' said Pascal.

'Um, it's not actually your anniversary,' Roisin reminded him.

'Whatever,' Jenny said. 'It's the best news, Davey. I can't tell you how happy you've made me.'

'You're some woman, Camilla, taking on this family,' said Paul.

'She's seen us at our absolute worst,' Davey told him. 'I'm hoping in the future she gets to see us at our best.'

Carl clapped him on the back and told him that he was a crafty sod not to have said anything before. He wished him lots of happiness and then glanced across the room to where Bernice was standing, her face totally expressionless. Summer was missing out on the commotion as she was still asleep on the sofa, oblivious to the excitement of the moment.

'I'm glad we have something to celebrate,' Roisin said. 'After all, a celebration is what this party was supposed to be.'

'When do you plan to get married?' asked Lucinda.

'I don't know yet,' replied Camilla. 'But as soon as possible, I think.'

She smiled. She couldn't believe how happy she felt and how much enjoyment she was getting from the fact that people were crowding around her, wanting to look at her fabulous ring and being delighted for her and Davey. Such unbridled joy had never been part of her life before and it was exhilarating. It was equally exhilarating, too, to allow herself to realise that she really and truly did love Davey Sheehan and that she wanted to be married to him. She was also looking forward to being part of his family, even though he kept apologising for the debacle of the day before. She'd never seen so much emotion on show in her life, and although he told her that this wasn't normal for them, she couldn't help feeling that she was part of something bigger than just her and Davey. That although there were clearly issues to be sorted out among the Sheehans, they would talk them through. Her own parents had never talked about anything.

'We'll have to go to Copenhagen,' Jenny said. 'See where you live and meet your parents, Camilla.'

'Give us a chance, Mum,' said Davey. '*I* haven't even met her parents yet.'

'They will be happy for me, I know,' said Camilla.

'And the wedding? Here or in Denmark?' asked Roisin.

'I haven't thought about the wedding at all yet,' said Camilla. 'Only that Davey and I are going to get married.'

'I'm delighted for you,' said Colette. 'I really am.'

She was telling the truth. She didn't quite understand why, but Davey and Camilla's engagement had lifted a weight from her own shoulders. He wasn't available any more. He belonged to someone else. He would be living a different life. And she was glad about that. It freed her up to think about men as people in their own right, not simply to be found wanting against Davey Sheehan. Maybe the next time I get engaged to someone – always providing there is a next time – I won't mess it up, she thought as she looked at the ring sparkling on Camilla's finger. Maybe it'll work out for me.

'OK, I know everyone's driving home and you can't be lashing back more alcohol,' said Pascal. 'But there's one bottle of champagne left and I think we should all have a tiny drop. To toast the engaged couple.'

'The engaged couple!' cried everyone when he'd filled the glasses.

And that was when Steffie arrived home.

Chapter 31

Steffie and Liam had met Tim, the garage owner, at her car before coming to Aranbeg. When she saw the little Citroën askew in the ditch, she'd cried.

'We'll get it out of there, don't you worry,' said Tim. 'And I'll do a complete check on it. It'll take a few days, mind.'

'I understand.' Steffie sniffed. She'd been thinking mean thoughts about the car as she'd driven from Dublin in the sweltering heat, but seeing it looking like a wreck was really upsetting her. On the up side, though, she hadn't been injured, which in the light of day seemed a total miracle.

'I'll phone you with an estimate on the repairs,' Tim said. 'I won't be able to get it to you today, but with a bit of luck your insurance will cover the most of it.'

She nodded as she looked mournfully at her car.

'Here are the lads.' Tim nodded in satisfaction as a tow truck arrived and two mechanics began to haul the Citroën out of the ditch.

Steffie watched and winced as they righted it and hooked it up to the truck, then she and Liam got into his van and set off along roads that were still partly flooded to Aranbeg. As they passed the GAA car park, Steffie could see a river of water running from one end to the other, although the vehicles themselves seemed to be unscathed. The gates to her parents' home were still under a little water, but it was possible to drive up to the house. When she stepped out of the van, however, she could see how drenched everything was.

'They got it worse here than up the road,' remarked Liam.

'I suppose we're lucky that the gardens slope away from the house,' said Steffie. 'But it certainly looks like the stream flooded. That's never happened before.'

'At least you don't have a flat roof like the restaurant,' said Liam. 'So no internal damage.'

She nodded as she got out of the car and inserted her key in the door. Liam stayed outside as she walked into the house.

'Aren't you coming in with me?' she asked.

'I'll wait here.'

'Come in,' she said. 'Please.'

He followed her into the hallway and then to the kitchen, where she stopped and looked at the scene in front of her in surprise.

'Steffie!' It was Davey who saw her first. 'You're back. Here, have a glass of champagne.'

'Champagne?' She stared at him. 'At this hour?'

'We're celebrating,' he said.

'Camilla and Davey are engaged,' explained Roisin, who realised that this wasn't an appropriate time to give Steffie an earful for running away even though she desperately wanted to.

'What!'

'I asked her last night and she said yes.' Davey couldn't contain his excitement.

'Last night?'

'After we left you at Cody's. Hi, Liam,' he added. 'Thank you for bringing her home like you promised.'

'No bother,' said Liam.

'You'll have a taste, Liam?' asked Jenny. 'We don't normally neck back alcohol before noon, but we're just having the tiniest sip to celebrate.'

'No thanks, Mrs Sheehan,' replied Liam. 'If you have some sparkling water, that'll do me.'

'Water is enough for me too,' said Steffie. 'Congratulations, Davey. And Camilla.'

Roisin filled a glass and handed it to Steffie, who raised it to her brother and his fiancée. She was glad Davey had found the right time to ask his girlfriend to marry him, and equally glad that Camilla had said yes. She hadn't been a hundred per cent confident that the Danish girl wanted to marry him, and yet she was certain that she was perfect for him.

'Are you OK, Steffie?' Jenny's look was anxious.

'I'm fine,' she said, avoiding her mother's eyes. 'Liam looked after me and he's driving me back to Dublin. I only came to get my things.'

'It'll be a few days before Steffie's car is roadworthy again,' explained Liam. 'I've had to close the restaurant today because of flooding and the power situation, so I offered to drive her home.'

'That's very nice of you.' Alivia's eyes darted between her cousin and the chef.

'Pascal and I were supposed to eat at Cody's last night,' Jenny told him. 'I hope we can do it later in the week.'

'I look forward to seeing you,' he told her.

337

'I'm going upstairs to change,' said Steffie. 'I'll be ready in a couple of minutes, Liam.'

She put the glass on the table and walked out of the room. She heard the buzz of chatter continue as she climbed the stairs. She went into her bedroom and quickly changed into fresh underwear and the cotton dress she'd worn the previous day on the drive from Dublin. After that, she stripped her bed, putting the bedlinen into the wicker laundry basket on the landing. Then she paused for a moment and leaned against the bedroom wall. Her head was spinning, both from her slight hangover and from the surprise of Davey's engagement. And, of course, from the fact that since she'd arrived at Aranbeg yesterday, everything in her life had changed.

She heard footsteps on the stairs and glanced up. Alivia was standing there, looking speculatively at her.

'Hi,' said Steffie.

'Hi yourself. How are you doing?'

'I'm all right,' said Steffie.

'Really? No ill effects from crashing your car?'

'It wasn't a proper crash,' Steffie said. 'It sort of slid off the road, that's all.'

'We were worried sick about you until we heard you'd ended up in Cody's,' said Alivia.

'There was no need to worry,' said Steffie.

'It was when we realised you didn't have your phone and the rain was getting heavier and heavier that we all got concerned. Obviously when Davey and Colette came back and said you were living it up in Wexford's finest restaurant, we relaxed.'

'I wasn't living it up,' protested Steffie.

'You were lucky the restaurant was open.'

'And that Liam gave me soup and dry clothes and a bed for the night.'

'And he's bringing you back to Dublin.'

'Yes.'

'So,' Alivia looked at her speculatively, 'you slept with him?'

'Alivia Marshall!'

Alivia raised an eyebrow.

'What makes you think that?'

Alivia raised her eyebrow even higher.

'OK, OK.' Steffie made a face at her. 'He has a tiny flat. I slept there.'

'With him.'

'How can you be so certain of that?'

'It's written all over your face,' she said.

'I hope not.'

'Possibly only visible to someone with my sensational empathic abilities.' Alivia grinned.

'Yeah, well. No need to spread the word.'

'That's mainly what I'm asking if you're OK about,' said Alivia. 'You're not usually a one-night-stand sort of girl.'

'Maybe it's not a one-night-stand sort of thing.'

'Steffie! Really?'

Steffie shrugged.

'Because you're hurt and vulnerable right now and I don't want to see you even more hurt and vulnerable later.'

Steffie gave her cousin a slight smile. 'At least if I get hurt this time it's 'cos I'm doing it to myself. But I won't. Yes, it was probably a sympathy shag, but I don't care. I needed someone and he was there and that's it.'

'So you're not looking for anything from him?'

'Absolutely not.'

'But he's driving you home.'

'To be sure I get there!'

Alivia nodded. 'Men are like that. They take you into their lives, use you and move on.'

'We're being unfair,' said Steffie. 'Liam was exactly what I needed last night.'

'I'm not really talking about Liam,' confessed Alivia. 'It's Dermot. He spent the night with Sophie.'

'No! But you said . . . I thought . . . How d'you know?'

'I sent him a million texts yesterday,' said Alivia. 'And after a while he stopped replying. This morning I got one from her.'

'Oh my God. What did it say?'

'She told me to keep away from her husband.'

'Alivia!'

'I don't believe it.' Alivia bit her lip. 'He swore to me. Promised. But he was lying. And now, if it gets out, my career will be on the line. How could I have been so stupid?'

'He won't want it to get out,' Steffie assured her. 'It wouldn't do him any good either.'

'It's different for men,' said Alivia. 'It shouldn't be, but it is. This story breaks and I'm the home-wrecker. But he's the playboy.' She gritted her teeth.

'I'm sorry,' said Steffie.

'I'm such an idiot,' Alivia said. 'I thought I was different. But it's never different, is it?'

'Oh Alivia.'

Alivia straightened her shoulders. 'But I'm strong, right? That's the thing. I'll come through it.'

'Of course you will.'

Alivia nodded and the two girls hugged. Then Steffie went downstairs again.

'Here's your phone,' said Jenny, handing it to her. 'Sweetheart, before you leave, perhaps you and I could have a talk.'

'I'm not ready to talk to you,' said Steffie.

'Please,' said Jenny.

'Why?' asked Steffie. 'Do you have anything else you want to confess to me? Any other skeletons rattling in your closet?'

Everyone looked uncomfortably at the two of them.

'No,' replied Jenny. 'I think all of them came rattling out yesterday. But it would be good for us to chat about it.'

'I have nothing to say to you,' said Steffie. 'Not now, and possibly not for a long time.'

'Steffie, honey . . .' Pascal moved so that he was beside her.

'I *will* talk to you,' she said. 'But not today. You should have told me even if she didn't. But as far as I can see, you're still the only one who comes out of it all with any credit. I truly wish I was your daughter.'

And then she picked up her bag and walked out of the house.

'You don't think you were unnecessarily harsh?' asked Liam, after he and Steffie had driven for more than ten minutes in total silence.

'Maybe,' she conceded. 'I couldn't help it. I'm so angry with her and I still feel . . . lost inside.'

'I understand,' said Liam. 'And I know it's a cliché, but time heals things, Steffie.'

'Can we not discuss it right now?' she asked. 'I have a headache.'

341

She closed her eyes and relaxed back into the passenger seat. Seeing Jenny had made her feel unanchored again, reminded her that the essence of who she was had changed. It was an uncomfortable feeling, like standing on a slippery surface, not knowing when you might lose your balance and fall. No matter what had gone on in her life before, she'd always felt secure in herself. Even when work was going badly, or her relationships were rocky, there had been the knowledge that her parents were solidly, unconditionally behind her, loving her and supporting her. If it wasn't for them, she thought, she wouldn't be able to cope. And yet it had all been based on a much bigger lie than them not being married. And she didn't know if she could ever truly trust either of them again.

The sudden sound of Oasis blasting through the speakers shocked her into sitting bolt upright again.

'Oops, sorry.' Liam lowered the volume. 'That wouldn't have done your head any good. And sorry for my musical choices too.'

'I like Oasis,' she told him.

'Betraying my age.'

'I loved "Wonderwall" when I was a kid,' she said. 'I used to sing it all the time. Unfortunately I'm a tune-free zone, so it drove everyone around me crazy.'

'In that case, sit back and allow yourself to be transported.'

She closed her eyes again. Suddenly she was back in the kitchen of the house in Dublin. Her mother was making cookies and singing along with her as they shaped the mixture on to greaseproof paper. Jenny hadn't told her that she hadn't got a note in her head. She'd just joined in with her. Steffie had loved those moments with her mother in the kitchen as much as she'd loved curling up in front of the TV with her. She'd felt protected and loved. And now she didn't know how to feel.

Liam allowed her to wallow in her thoughts and it wasn't until they were on the M50 and close to Tallaght that he asked her which exit to take.

'Oh, sorry, next one,' she said, and then continued to direct him to the neat semi-detached house where she'd grown up. 'Number 25,' she added. 'About halfway down the street. And watch out for kids running out in front of you; they seem to appear out of nowhere.'

Liam drove slowly, allowing plenty of time for the group of boys playing football in the middle of the street to jump out of the way. Then he pulled into the short drive in front of the house.

'I can't thank you enough for bringing me home,' said Steffie. 'You're a lifesaver.'

'You're welcome,' said Liam.

They sat side by side in the van. It seemed wrong to Steffie to simply jump out and wave goodbye to him. She'd made love to him three times in less than twenty-four hours, after all. There should be something more than leaving him as though he was just someone who'd done her a good turn by driving her home. But she wasn't sure what she should say or do.

In the end she fell back on the reliable means of asking him if he'd like a coffee.

'In fact,' she added after glancing at her watch, 'it's gone lunchtime. Would you like something to eat before you head off home again?'

'That'd be lovely.' He smiled at her and got out of the van.

She unlocked the door to the house and he followed her inside. Almost immediately her eyes were drawn to the fake marriage certificate and apostolic benediction, as well as the photo of Jenny on the boat from Capri. She wanted to rip them from the wall but she pretended not to see them and walked straight into the kitchen, glad that she'd moved the pile of clothes for ironing from the table before she'd left for Aranbeg. And then it hit her again, that sense that everything she'd known about herself had shifted. That in all the times she'd been in this kitchen before with Pascal and Jenny, they'd been keeping secrets from her. That the building blocks of Steffie Sheehan weren't what she'd always believed. Those memories and that realisation hit her like a physical blow. She stumbled for a moment and leaned against the table for support before sinking on to a kitchen chair, her head bowed.

'Steffie! Are you all right?' Liam looked at her in concern. She nodded without speaking.

He hunkered down beside her, taking her hands and holding them between his own. He leaned towards her so that their heads were touching. He didn't say anything.

Eventually she took a deep breath and sat upright. He straightened too, still holding her hands.

'I'm sorry,' she said. 'You must think me an awful eejit.'

'No,' said Liam. 'I don't.'

'I've had plenty of time to get used to it,' she said. 'But coming back here, walking into the house . . . Yesterday, I thought all I had to worry about was my job. Getting that contract. I comforted myself by thinking that if I didn't, at least Mum and Dad would be supportive of me. They always are, no matter how much I mess up. And now . . .'

'Now they'll still support you,' said Liam.

'But they're not Mum and Dad any more.'

'Your mum is still your mum,' said Liam. 'And as for your dad . . .'

'Oh Liam, I know you're going to say he's as much my dad as ever and that there are loads of people who've had much worse traumas in their lives. I don't blame you for thinking I'm a total drama queen. It's just . . .' She started to cry. She hadn't wanted to, but she couldn't stop herself in time.

Liam put his arms around her and held her tightly.

'I'm sorry,' she murmured through her tears. 'I really am. This is nothing. Nothing.'

'Steffie, sweetheart, it's not nothing. It's a fundamental thing about who you are.'

'Yes, but you hear about people who find out they're adopted or something, and they don't run away and crash their cars and do stupid things.'

'Maybe some of them do,' Liam said. 'Who knows? Everyone's different. I understand how you feel. If someone told me my dad wasn't my real dad, I don't know how I'd react either.'

'But my dad, Pascal, has always been great to me.' Steffie raised her tear-streaked face to him. 'So being upset about it is being really disloyal to him.'

'No it's not.'

'He took me fishing.' She sniffed. 'In the river. And he paid for my car and he assembled my office furniture.'

'Sounds like a good dad to me,' said Liam.

'I know. He was. He is. But still not my dad.' She dropped her head on his chest again. She desperately wanted to stop feeling like this. She wanted to put it all behind her. To move on. People talked so much about moving on these days. You weren't allowed to be upset for too long. You had to face things and get on with life. And she wanted to. But how could she when she felt so rudderless right now? Rudderless except for Liam, who was still holding her tightly to him.

He kept holding her tightly until she exhaled slowly and raised her head again.

'I think I'm OK now,' she said.

'Sure?'

She nodded and grabbed some kitchen towel from the roll on the wall. She dabbed at her eyes, then blew her nose and disposed of the towel in the waste bin.

'Sorry,' she said again.

'You've nothing to be sorry about,' he told her. 'It's quite cool for me to have a girl weeping on my shoulder. It's never happened before.'

'Hopefully I won't do it again,' she said. She brushed her eyes with the backs of her fingers. 'So, you know, I was going to make you some coffee. And I made this rash offer about something to eat too.'

'It's rash because?'

'I'm guessing frozen crispy pancakes wouldn't be one of your main food groups?'

'Tell me you're joking.'

She opened the freezer and took six boxes of pancakes out of the bottom drawer.

'Oh my God,' said Liam. 'I don't know how you're still standing.'

346

She smiled slightly. 'It's awful, isn't it. I have some frozen French bread pizza too.'

'Steffie Sheehan! Have you bread? Or anything in the fridge?'

'Friday's bread. Some tired salad, tomatoes . . .'

'Why don't you let me look after the food and you can do the coffee?'

'You're my guest,' she said.

'I don't want to be your food-poisoned guest.'

'The pancakes and pizza won't poison you,' she pointed out.

'They'll poison my soul,' he said. 'Let me at your fridge.'

Her smile was a bit stronger this time.

'OK,' she said. 'I'll just go upstairs and splash my face with water.'

'Fine.' Liam's attention had already turned from her and towards the fridge. He was standing pensively at the open door when she went upstairs.

She went into the bathroom and looked at herself in the mirror over the sink. Her face was blotchy, her eyes slightly pink. She splashed cold water on her cheeks, then used eyedrops on her eyes. After that, she went into her bedroom, slapped on some tinted moisturiser and changed from her dress into a plain white T-shirt and cropped jeans. She sat on the end of the bed for a few minutes, not thinking of anything, simply staring into space. And then the smell of bacon wafted towards her and her stomach rumbled. She hadn't realised she was hungry. She stood up and brushed her hair before spraying herself with Clinique Happy and going downstairs again.

'Hi,' Liam greeted her. 'You look good.'

'And that smells good,' she said.

'I can't honestly say I'm cooking up a storm here,' he said. 'You only had rashers, tomatoes and milk in your fridge.'

She looked shamefaced.

'So it's a tomato and bacon all-day breakfast,' said Liam. 'Fortunately you had bread and herbs, so we can make it something a little more appetising.'

'Will I do the coffee?' she asked.

'Go ahead.'

She switched on the machine. By the time the coffee was ready, Liam had loaded up plates with toasted bread piled with fried tomatoes sprinkled with herbs, and topped with chopped bacon.

'Funnily enough, my rasher and tomato sandwich doesn't ever look like this,' she said. 'Or taste like it either. Jeez, Liam, what did you do to it?'

'It's the herbs and seasoning,' he said.

'Wow.' She cut another piece and popped it in her mouth. 'You're a handy man to have around a kitchen.'

He laughed. 'And you're not bad with coffee,' he said after tasting it. 'It's pretty good.'

'Mum and Dad . . .' She faltered slightly and then continued. 'Well, they're big into coffee. She says they got a taste for it in Italy.' Thinking of her parents in Italy made Steffie grimace. 'Anyhow, long before the whole coffee thing took off here, we were a family with a machine.'

'A proper one,' he said. 'That grinds the beans and everything.'

She nodded. 'We have one at Aranbeg too. Mum says the one thing she can't compromise on is coffee. It's a pity,' she added, 'that she seems to be able to compromise on pretty much everything else.'

348

Chapter 32

Back at Aranbeg, the power had been restored and Roisin had put the kettle on so that they could have tea and coffee before going home. She didn't bother with the sandwiches but decided to cut Pascal and Jenny's anniversary cake instead.

'You really are something, Ro.' Davey gave his sister a hug. 'Out of nowhere we're having a family coffee morning.'

'Ha ha.' She made a face at him.

'Seriously,' he said. 'You're amazing. Thank you.'

To her horror, Roisin felt her eyes well up at the fact that at least one member of her family appreciated her efforts.

'Fabulous cake,' said Alivia, who was comfort-eating after the text from Sophie Fisher.

'It's pretty good all right,' mumbled Colette as she crammed the last of her slice into her mouth. 'But I'd best be off now.'

'I'd like to go too,' said Sarah. 'But we can't leave yet, Carl, can we? We're still waiting for Summer to make an appearance.'

'Where on earth is she?' asked Roisin.

'Asleep in the living room,' replied Carl.

'What?' Colette looked at her brother in astonishment.

'How can she possibly have slept through a champagne cork popping and all of us congratulating Davey and Camilla?'

'She sleeps well,' said Carl.

'I'll bet,' muttered Bernice.

'Go and wake her,' commanded Sarah.

'I tried,' admitted Carl, 'but she's out for the count. The thing is,' he added, 'she's really used to staying up late and then getting up late the next day.'

Colette laughed. 'She was asleep before me last night. Although maybe she'd just passed out from all her home-made cocktails.'

'There's no need to be like that.' Carl gave her an irritated look.

'No, indeed,' said Bernice calmly. 'She's a young girl and she needs her rest. Jenny, Pascal, I'm away now. Thank you for all your hospitality.'

'Thank you, Bernice,' said Jenny, 'for looking after Poppy and being so capable in a crisis.'

Poppy herself, who'd been methodically demolishing her slice of cake, got up from the table and hugged Bernice with her good arm.

'You were brilliant,' she said. 'I love you.'

Bernice smiled at her.

'We owe you one. Or two. Or three,' said Roisin. 'Poppy's right. You were more than brilliant. Give me a shout some-time you're free and we'll meet up.'

'Will do,' said Bernice. She picked up her bag and slung it over her shoulder. 'Bye, everyone.'

They all chorused their goodbyes and watched her drive away.

'You can come home with me if you like, Mum,' said

Colette. 'Save you waiting until Summer decides to wake up.'

'That would be nice,' said Sarah.

'She'll be up soon.' As far as Carl was concerned, all the attention that had been lavished on Bernice before she left was calculated to insult him and Summer. And now his sister was adding to it by offering to drive their mother home.

'But Colette is awake and ready to go now,' said Sarah. 'I'm fairly certain that even when she does wake, it'll take Summer a significant amount of time to get herself together.'

'There's no need—'

'We'll go now,' said Colette firmly.

'And so will we,' said Lucinda. 'OK with you, Alivia?'

Alivia agreed and went to collect the car from the GAA car park. Lucinda was at the front door, saying goodbye to Jenny, when she returned.

'Great party,' she told her sister. 'Best fun I've had in years.'

'And now us.' Davey turned to his mother. 'We have to be at the airport in a couple of hours.'

'It was so lovely to have you here,' said Jenny. 'And I couldn't be happier about your news.' She hugged Davey and then Camilla. The Danish girl returned the hug and said that she'd had a wonderful time and that she hoped to see them all again very soon.

'Who knows,' she quipped. 'We might even get married here.'

Davey looked at her in astonishment and she winked at him. Then the two of them left.

'Only Carl and Summer to go now,' said Roisin.

'I'll get her up,' said Carl.

'Don't worry on my account,' said Jenny. 'Let the girl sleep if she wants.'

But Carl was feeling ever more pressured by his sleeping girlfriend. He went into the living room and shook her hard. Summer rolled over, pulling the light blanket more closely around her shoulders.

'For crying out loud, Summer,' hissed Carl. 'Open your feckin' eyes, would you?'

Eventually she blinked a few times and looked sleepily at him.

'What time is it?'

'Nearly twelve,' he told her. 'Everyone's gone except us.'

'I'm exhausted,' she said.

'Get up,' he told her. 'We're leaving.'

Summer yawned widely and finally sat up. Her golden hair tumbled messily around her face but her make-up, which she hadn't bothered to remove before going to sleep, was still flawless. She looked around for her high-heeled sandals and put them on before smiling widely at Carl and saying that she desperately needed coffee. They went into the kitchen where Jenny, Pascal and Roisin's family were sitting around the table.

'I'm up!' Summer gave them a cheery smile as she plopped down on a seat beside Daisy. 'How are you, sweetie?'

'I'm OK. You look fabulous,' said Daisy.

'Thank you. Oh, and thank you too,' she said to Roisin, who offered her a cup of coffee. 'Carl told me everyone was gone.'

'Except us,' said Poppy. 'We're always last. Mum has to make sure everyone has gone before us.'

'Poppy!' Roisin gave her an irritated look.

'Well, you do,' said Poppy. 'And everyone *is* gone, except Carl and Summer.'

'It's my fault,' Summer said. 'I was so sleepy, Carl couldn't wake me.'

'That's OK,' said Jenny. 'It was a long day yesterday.'

'I'm used to long nights,' Summer said. 'It's long days and long nights together that are the trouble.'

Jenny laughed.

'I know it's very naughty of me, but I'll just have a quick smoke in the garden before I go,' said Summer. 'I treat myself to one cigarette a day, in the morning. It helps me to motivate myself.'

Roisin frowned as Daisy said she'd go outside with her. Poppy and Dougie, who'd been eating cereal, said they were going out too. They wanted to look at the stream, said Poppy, to see if there were any fish.

'Please don't get wet,' said Roisin as they trooped out. She wasn't at all happy at the idea of Summer smoking in front of Daisy, but there was nothing she could do about it now without appearing like a total killjoy and control freak. But she was going to remind Daisy about the evils of cigarettes on the way home. And she'd warn her that Summer's beauty would be ruined by her smoking habit.

'I'm sorry, Aunt Jenny.' Carl looked at her sheepishly. 'I guess Summer might not have been the best person to bring along.'

'Why on earth did you?' asked Roisin before her mother could speak.

'Oh, look, it was a party,' said Jenny. 'It doesn't matter who you brought.'

'Except that he was supposed to be on a break from Bernice,' Roisin said.

'I like Summer,' Jenny said. 'She's fun and uncomplicated and from what I can gather she makes a damn good cocktail.'

'Mum!' Roisin glared at her. 'Bernice practically saved Poppy's life!'

'There's a time for life-saving and a time for cocktail-shaking,' said Jenny. 'Of course you have to decide which works best for you, Carl. But it's your life and your choice.'

'Thank you,' he said. 'You might not be married for forty years but you certainly sound like someone who is.'

'What happened between you and Ber?' asked Roisin. 'Why did you need the break in the first place?'

Carl sighed. 'We want different things,' he said.

'Will you always want different things?' asked Jenny. 'Or is this a temporary situation?'

'I don't know.' Carl glanced through the patio doors to where Summer was chatting with Daisy. 'I really don't know.'

When Summer had finished her cigarette, the two of them left. Before they went, Summer kissed Daisy on the cheek and promised to send her a goody bag of make-up she'd got for free. Roisin was afraid she might choke with the effort of saying silent. But finally they were gone and she and her family were the only ones left at Aranbeg with Pascal and Jenny.

'I suppose we should hit the road too, and leave you in peace,' she said.

'I'll get the car,' said Paul. 'Roisin, are you going to leave with us or stay a little longer?'

Roisin had almost forgotten that she'd driven down separately. Being able to go home later would give her more time to talk to her parents, she thought, which would be a good thing. But then Poppy said that she wanted to come home with her and so they decided to leave at the same time.

'Thank you for everything,' Jenny said as she hugged her daughter.

'You're probably fuming with me,' said Roisin. 'If I hadn't wanted to surprise you . . .'

'You had the best of intentions,' said her mother. 'I should've kept my mouth shut yesterday, then told you all properly afterwards.'

'It would've been easier,' Roisin said. 'But it's good to have it all out in the open, even if it's going to take us a bit of time to come to terms with everything.'

'And as far as you and Pascal are concerned, Jenny, it's really not such a big deal.' Paul, who was eager to leave, didn't want his wife and her mother to get into another discussion about the non-marriage. 'It's a matter of formalising things, that's all.'

'Which is how I always looked at it,' agreed Jenny.

Roisin said nothing.

'I know it bothers you, darling,' Jenny said to her. 'But please believe me when I tell you that your dad and I were all set to tie the knot in Rome, for your sake as much as ours.'

'It's OK.'

Jenny's expression, as she looked at her elder daughter, was regretful. She knew that Roisin was burying her hurt by being busy and practical, but she didn't know what to say to make things better. So in the end she simply wished them a safe drive home and said she hoped to see them again soon.

'Are you still angry with Granny?' asked Poppy as they turned on to the main road.

'Of course not,' replied Roisin.

'You sound it,' Poppy said. 'You sound like you do when you're angry with me. Like when I fell out of the tree.'

'I'm not angry with Granny and I'm not angry with you either,' said Roisin. 'Although I expect you to listen to me in future and do what you're told.'

'I expect you want Granny to do what she's told too,' said Poppy, before taking a book out of her rucksack and settling back in the passenger seat to read it.

'I'm glad we have the house to ourselves again.' Jenny sank into the sofa in the living room and pulled her legs up beneath her.

'Me too,' agreed Pascal. 'I thought they were never going to go.'

'I guess we shouldn't think like that about the girl who only wanted to provide us with a memorable day,' said Jenny. 'Which she did, of course, but not the way she intended. Poor Roisin. I'll bet she had it planned to precision.'

'Of course she had.'

Jenny sighed. 'I'm sorry,' she said.

'You've said that about a million times.'

'To Roisin. To Davey. To Steffie. And to all our guests. But not to you.'

'Oh, you must have included me in an apology at some point.'

'Perhaps. But I truly am sorry, Pascal. Sorry that I got pregnant when I was twenty-one. Sorry I kind of forced the whole getting married thing on you. Sorry I haven't been a better . . . well, not wife, but a better person to live with. So, so sorry about Gregory. And about not telling Steffie when you told me I should. I'm sorry for being weak and foolish and always putting myself before others.'

'And are you sorry for being hard on yourself too?' he asked.

'I'm not being hard on myself,' she said. 'I've often allowed myself to feel that life's been hard on me. But it hasn't. I have you and the children and I'm luckier than most of the women I know. Sarah and Lucinda are sort of right about me. I'm nothing but trouble yet I always land on my feet.'

Pascal gazed past his wife and out over the garden. The flood water had receded and the grass was visible again. The sun, emerging from behind the clouds, lit up the still damp leaves and flowers, so that they dazzled beneath its rays. It was serene and, despite the black stump of the tree that had been struck by lightning, very beautiful. Jenny had helped to make it that way, just as she'd turned Aranbeg into an oasis for him.

When he'd first told her about the money he'd won on the prize bonds, she'd talked about how many things it would help them with. Putting proper central heating in at home had been high on her list. The houses had been built with warm air heating that had never worked properly, and Jenny had always wanted radiators. Yet when he'd told her of his desire to have a bolt-hole in Wexford, she'd immediately abandoned all notions of an upgraded central heating system and told him that it was a wonderful idea. She'd been thinking of a small cottage. Or even a mobile home. She'd never expected a place like Aranbeg, which had inevitably been a money pit in the early years. Yet she'd never complained, even when he disappeared at weekends without her to do some extra job on the house, leaving her in town with the children. She'd never questioned him or nagged at him or told him that she was fed up having to cut back when the white elephant of Aranbeg was eating lumps out of their available funds. She had always said that one day the house would be perfect, and when all the structural work had been completed, she'd turned her talents to the interior design and to the gardens. She was the one, Pascal knew, who'd made his dream a real home.

Naturally, when it was habitable, she'd loved staying there too, but she'd had faith in him that he'd be able to turn it into somewhere habitable in the first place. If she'd had doubts, she'd never expressed them. In fact, over their entire life together, she'd always fallen in with his wishes no matter what he wanted to do. Of course there was the issue of the summer of Gregory, as he'd come to think of it in his own mind. He doubted he'd ever have known anything about it if she hadn't got pregnant, and he sometimes wondered if that would've been a good thing. As far as he was concerned, Jenny had fallen for Gregory, the model, not Gregory the sheep farmer. It had been an infatuation. And it was over. She swore to him it was over and he believed her.

He was aware that had they known, many people would've told him to walk away or throw her out. Yet how could he have done that? What would it have done to his own children? What would it have done to Jenny herself, especially as Gregory was on the other side of the world and she had no way of contacting him? Afterwards, when Steffie was born and Pascal had fallen in love with her, Jenny called him a saint. But he wasn't. He was someone who knew what he wanted and who had what he wanted. His family was

358

important to him. And he was prepared to make hard choices to keep it.

The thing was, thought Pascal, those choices had been the right ones. Now, more than ever before, he and Jenny complemented each other. They'd come through the bad times and they were still together, with lots of good times in the bank too. As far as Pascal could tell, they were the most complete couple of anyone they knew. They deserved their forty-year anniversary party. They deserved to be celebrated. No marriage ceremony or certificate could give them what they already had.

Chapter 33

After Liam's simple but incredibly tasty lunch, Steffie made more coffee, which they drank in the back garden because the clouds had completely disappeared and the sky was a brilliant blue again. Then, at his request, she brought down her laptop and showed him more of her design work.

'I've seen this before,' he said as he looked at one of the images.

She nodded. 'It's the packaging design for an eco-friendly hot-water bottle made by an Irish company. They're sold in a lot of big stores now.'

'And you created it?'

'Not the hot-water bottle.' She smiled at him. 'The design on the box. But it works very well.'

'It's eye-catching,' he said. 'The fact that I recognised it proves it. What else have you done?'

'For the same company . . .' She clicked forward and stopped at another design. 'This is for some candles they do.'

'I've seen them before too. You keep telling me you're barely keeping things going, but you've got some good clients, Steffie.'

'All the same, I need to keep them coming,' she said. 'And

times have been tight. But if I get the rebranding contract, that'll open more doors for me. Speaking of which . . .' She reached into her bag and took out her mobile. 'Hopefully they haven't tried to ring,' she said. 'I just realised that I haven't charged it since the day before yesterday. It's dead as a dodo.'

'They'll hardly ring on a Sunday.'

'I know. I'm being super-hopeful. Plus I feel like my arm is cut off when my mobile is out of action. Although,' she added, 'given that I'd forgotten about both the project and the phone until right now, I mustn't be quite as addicted as I thought.'

'Mobiles are a tyranny,' he agreed. 'I know you're anxious about your bid, but I can't imagine you'll get a call on a Sunday.'

'You're right. And I'll prove to myself I can live without it by not charging it yet.' She left the phone on the garden table and went back to looking at the laptop with Liam, showing him her drawings for the illustrated book, as well as rough designs and the eventual finished product.

'When we talked before about you doing a design for my site, I didn't realise it would entail so much work,' he said. 'Regardless of what you do for me, I want to pay you.'

'Maybe some things are harder work than others, but I already have an idea for you,' she told him. 'If you like it and we develop it, you can pay me. Otherwise it's absolutely and utterly on the house. And I don't want you to say another word about it!'

'OK. OK.' He held up his hands in mock surrender and she was laughing at him when she heard the sound of the doorbell.

Her immediate reaction was to look for a football, because normally the only time the doorbell rang on a Sunday in summer was when one of the kids next door had kicked a ball over the wall, but she didn't see anything. She went to answer it.

'Steffie, my sweet.' The man on the doorstep leaned forward and kissed her on the lips. 'How are you? How was the party?'

'Steve.'

'That's me.' He walked past her into the house. 'I rang you a couple of times but I kept getting your voicemail.'

'My battery's flat,' she said as she followed him. 'I didn't charge my phone. Steve, I wasn't expecting you to come around today.'

'Truth is I was feeling bad about yesterday,' he told her. 'I finished work earlier than I thought and I kept telling myself that I should've come to that party with you. I nearly did.'

'Really?'

'Yes. Then the weather changed and it started pelting with rain and so I didn't bother. I thought you might still be in Wexford actually. But I had to drop some stuff in to a friend so I thought I'd call by and check if you were home. I thought I'd wasted my time when I didn't see your car in the driveway. Who's Cody, and why is his van there instead?'

They'd made it as far as the kitchen, where the plates from lunch were still on the table. Steve glanced at them before his eyes were drawn to the open door and to Liam sitting outside.

'Um, he is. Sort of,' replied Steffie.

Steve looked at her enquiringly.

362

'My car is out of action so he gave me a lift home,' said Steffie.

She was acutely aware that two men she had slept with were now in her house and that she really didn't want them to meet at all. And now I'm feeling like some kind of scarlet woman, she thought, even though I'm not.

'Hi, buddy.' Steve stepped outside and nodded to Liam. 'Steve O'Donnell. Steffie's boyfriend.'

'Liam Kinsella.'

'Liam rescued me after the car broke down,' said Steffie.

'So Blue Betty has finally given up the ghost,' said Steve. 'I told you she'd eventually choke and die.'

'It wasn't her fault,' said Steffie. 'I drove her into a ditch.'

'What!'

'In the storm,' she explained.

'Are you all right?'

'I'm fine.'

'And you came to her rescue?' His eyes narrowed as he looked at Liam.

'In a way.'

'You were lucky someone was around,' Steve told Steffie.

'I know.'

'So where's Blue Betty now?'

'In a garage in Wexford.'

'Is she repairable?'

'I hope so,' Steffie replied. 'The garage owner seemed to think he'd be able to do something for her.'

'Why didn't you ring me this morning?' asked Steve. 'I would've picked you up.'

Steffie shrugged. 'I thought you were busy. And Liam offered to drive me.'

'Did he do such a terrible job of driving that you punished him by giving him lunch?'

Steffie gave him a weak smile. 'Liam's a chef. He made lunch for me.'

'Wow. I'm sorry I turned up too late to share,' said Steve.

'Another time, perhaps,' said Liam as he stood up. 'Steffie, thanks for the coffee but it's time I got going.'

'Oh don't,' she protested. 'Stay for a little longer.'

'Better not,' said Liam.

'Don't go on my account,' said Steve. 'Anyone who looks after my girl deserves at least another cup of coffee.'

'You're very kind,' said Liam. 'But I need to get back to my restaurant and see how it's drying out. Storm damage,' he added for Steve's benefit.

'I'll see you to the door,' said Steffie.

She led Liam through the house to his van.

'I'm sorry,' she said. 'I wasn't expecting him to call around.'

'No problem,' said Liam.

'We're not . . . I mean . . . we were, but we're not . . .'

'You don't have to explain,' he said. 'We all have busy lives with lots of people in them.'

'Yes, but . . .'

'You're a grown-up, Steffie. I didn't expect you to be without boyfriends.'

'Of course not. But all the same . . .'

'And I don't want to mess up any relationship you do have. Which I'm sure you don't want to do to me either.'

She exhaled sharply.

'It was fun,' Liam continued. 'I'm glad we spent some time together. I enjoyed . . . well, I enjoyed being with you.

I hope you'll come back to Cody's some time in the future. And in less dramatic circumstances.'

'Liam . . .'

He took his keys from his pocket and unlocked the van. 'It was fun,' he repeated as he stood by the open door.

Steffie had told Alivia she was OK with it being a one-night thing, but suddenly she realised she wasn't. Yet Liam clearly was. And she didn't want to make a fool of herself over him.

'I guess it's . . . just thank you,' she said. 'For everything.'

'You're more than welcome.'

'I don't know which bit to thank you for most. Yesterday or today.'

'One all-encompassing thank you was more than sufficient,' he said.

She didn't want him to go. But she didn't know how to make him stay.

'Everything all right?' Steve was behind her. He put his hand on her shoulder.

'Great,' said Liam. 'I'm off now. Goodbye, Steffie.'

'Goodbye,' she said and watched him drive away.

'So tell me all about the party. And about your car,' said Steve. 'And Sir Galahad there too.'

They were sitting at the garden table. Steve had taken a beer from the fridge and began to drink as Steffie gave him an edited version of her exploits the previous evenings.

'That sounds scary,' he commented. 'But why on earth did you go out in such awful weather in the first place?'

She wasn't prepared to tell him that. She didn't want to

talk to him about her family's issues. So she simply said that they'd needed to collect something.

'From the restaurant?' asked Steve. 'That's where you were going?'

'Mmm.' She didn't want to tell him a direct lie, but the truth would take for ever.

'So were your parents really surprised by the party?' he asked.

She nodded.

'And how about your sister?'

'You know, if you cared all that much about it, you would've come,' she said.

'Whoa, Steff!' He looked at her. 'I'm trying to be nice.'

'Well there's no need,' she told him. 'You didn't want to come and that's that.'

'But like I said, I feel bad about it.' He leaned towards her. 'Honestly I do. I was too caught up in my own stuff to think about you. And I'm sorry.'

She was taken aback. The fact that Steve rarely apologised for anything was something that usually drove her mad. When he was late for a date, as he frequently was, he'd simply turn up and greet her as though nothing was amiss. If they were having a disagreement about anything, he never admitted he was wrong, even when he was. But now he was actually apologising. Without her suggesting that he should.

'It doesn't matter.'

'It kinda does,' he said. 'When I talked to you on the phone yesterday and you were in the bath and everything, I was thinking, why am I putting my job before my girlfriend? And I don't know the answer to that because you're a really important person to me, Steff.'

366

She stared at him. He was saying the kind of thing she would've liked him to say before. Only now . . . now it was too late. She didn't want to hear it.

'Anyway,' he said, 'I wanted to bring you out to make up for it. I was going to take you for something to eat, but if you've already had a gourmet lunch cooked by a chef, you might not be up for that now. '

She shook her head. She wasn't hungry, and the idea of food was making her stomach heave.

'I'm starving, though. How about we stay here, I'll order pizza and we'll download a movie?'

'I'm really tired,' she said. 'I don't know if—'

'I came all the way over,' he said.

Steve lived in Newbridge, which was almost fifty kilometres from Steffie's house, although an easy drive on the motorway.

'OK,' she said. 'We'll watch a movie.'

'Excellent.' He took out his phone and dialled Domino's. 'Pizza will be here in half an hour,' he said when he'd placed the order. 'And I bet you'll want some of it too. It's all very well having a chef cook for you, but it can't beat a twelve-inch pepperoni, can it?'

'Probably not,' she agreed as she brought the coffee cups back into the house. 'Probably not.'

Chapter 34

Roisin was relieved when they finally got home and she could relax in her own living room without having to worry about an assortment of other people, although she did have to spend some additional time reassuring her children that their grandparents weren't in some sort of trouble for not being married, and that Aunt Steffie had got over her upset.

'I think Aunt Steffie's situation is sort of cool,' Daisy told her later that night when both Poppy and Dougie had gone to bed. 'I mean, it'd be pretty exciting for me to think that my dad was someone more sort of exotic.'

'Thanks,' said Paul.

'You know what I mean,' Daisy said. 'Like you think you're one person and then you find out you're way different.'

'Aunt Steffie isn't different,' said Roisin. 'She's the same person she always was.'

'Yeah, but with a good story,' Daisy insisted. 'If I follow my dream and become a model like Summer, it'd be an advantage to have a good story behind me.'

'Summer isn't really a model,' said Roisin.

'Of course she is. She's done loads of stuff, and just because you don't see her in the papers every day doesn't mean she's not doing a good job.' Daisy looked at Roisin indignantly. 'She told me all about it. You can't diss her because you don't like her, Mum.'

'I didn't say I didn't like her.'

'Huh, you made it obvious,' said Daisy. 'You kept giving her dirty looks. But she's nice. I like her. And I'm going to be friends with her on Facebook.'

Roisin knew that to say anything else would only make Daisy support Summer even more. And maybe her daughter was right. Maybe she was being unfair on the model . . . cocktail waitress . . . whatever.

'I hope she'll be able to give you good advice,' she said, biting back the comment about smoking that she'd wanted to make.

'I hope so too,' said Daisy.

Roisin was relieved when her daughter eventually went to bed, and was happy to head off herself shortly afterwards. When Paul climbed in beside her, she'd already turned out her bedside light, having been unable to concentrate on the book she'd brought with her.

'You OK?' Paul asked as he turned out his own lamp.

'Exhausted,' admitted Roisin. 'I'm never organising a party again.'

'Good,' said Paul.

'Good?' Roisin rolled over so that she was facing him, even though it was too dark to see his face. 'Why would you say that? Excluding yesterday, what's wrong with my parties?'

'You think you have to do everything,' he said. 'You had that party planned with military precision. You stressed over the food and the drink and the fact that you'd put Steffie in charge of the invitations. You had me driven demented. And in the end nothing went according to plan anyway. So I'm glad you're going to give it a miss in the future.'

'That was the exception. Besides, someone has to co-ordinate things.'

'It doesn't always have to be you,' said Paul.

'But without me it wouldn't have happened.'

'And that might have been a good thing.'

'Well thanks a lot.'

'I'm sorry. I didn't mean it like it sounded.' Paul put his arm around her. 'It's just that I can't bear to see you getting so revved up all the time. You don't always have to be the one in charge. Let Davey or Steffie do it once in a while.'

Roisin snorted at the idea of either of her siblings being responsible for any type of family do. Even if Paul was right, and even if he was echoing what Colette had said earlier, it was still her job as the eldest to look after things. And she wasn't going to blame herself for the current fiasco. Nobody could have predicted that. Not even the best organiser in the world.

She closed her eyes. As she was wondering how much help Davey and Camilla might need with their wedding plans, she was suddenly overcome by the exhaustion of the last forty-eight hours, and fell so deeply asleep that not even Paul's snoring disturbed her.

It was late, too, by the time Davey and Camilla reached their apartment in Østerbro. As they climbed the winding stairway, Davey felt a sense of relief at being home at last. It was the first time he'd ever truly thought of the apartment as home, but now, away from the drama of his family, he felt himself relax. The last forty-eight hours had been the most stressful of his life – and that included the job interview for his current company, in which he'd sat in front of a board of five men in suits who'd practically filleted him in the detailed questions that they'd asked.

He put the key in the lock and pushed open the door. There was a tranquillity about the apartment, too, about its Nordic simplicity, its clean lines and its functional furniture. It returned to Davey the sense of order that had totally vanished from his life while he'd been in Ireland.

'That's what I meant when I said we were hopelessly chaotic,' he told Camilla when they were sitting on the white Karlstad sofa, drinking decaf. 'Even when we plan things, someone always throws a spanner in the works.'

'A spanner?' she queried. 'I saw lots of things in your parents' house but not a spanner.'

'It's an expression.' He grinned. 'It's good to know that your English isn't quite perfect yet. It means that someone does something to mess things up.'

She nodded. 'I understand. I can see what it means. It's a good expression.'

'And apt for the Sheehan family,' said Davey. 'Every single time we get together, something unexpected happens. There was a pretty memorable dust-up at Alivia's twenty-first birthday too. And there was one Christmas my dad and Uncle Seamus nearly came to blows about something – I've no idea what. That time Colette pushed Steffie out of the tree . . .' His voice trailed off.

'Colette seems to be a large part of your family's activities,' said Camilla.

'Not really,' Davey said. 'When we were kids, she and her brothers stayed with us, that's all.'

'And this weekend she was a key part of everything.'

'I don't have feelings for her.' Davey wanted to reassure Camilla. 'Not those sort of feelings anyhow.'

'I know,' said Camilla. 'I'm being a little silly.'

'You don't have to worry about Colette. Honestly.'

'Clearly.' Camilla stretched her hand out in front of her. 'After all, I am the one wearing the ring.'

Davey grinned. 'Indeed you are. And it looks wonderful on you. I'm very glad you said yes, Cam.'

'So am I.' Camilla smiled in return.

'When do you want to get married?'

'I don't know. I'm getting used to being engaged. Which is nice too.'

'We should have a party ourselves to celebrate,' said Davey.

'Here? In Denmark?'

'Well, we had a celebration in Ireland,' he said. 'Admittedly a glass of champagne the morning after the night before isn't what I'd ideally have had in mind, but nevertheless the important people were there to congratulate us. So we should do something here too.'

Camilla nodded slowly. 'Our good friends will want to celebrate with us.'

'And your family.'

'Not all of them,' she said. 'They would not want . . .'

'Camilla! Don't be silly. Of course they would.'

She gave him a wry smile. 'There have been lots of engagements and weddings in my family,' she reminded him. 'It's not exactly a new thing.'

'It is for you,' he said. 'And for me. So we'll have people around for drinks and canapés and it can all be very quiet and sophisticated and not at all like the party at Aranbeg.'

Camilla grinned. 'The party at Aranbeg was fun.'

'Nevertheless,' Davey said. 'Let's go for something a little less dramatic.'

'OK.'

They put their cups in the dishwasher and went to bed. Davey, as he always did, fell asleep almost immediately after they'd made love. But Camilla spent another hour awake, gazing into the darkness and wondering how it was that she suddenly felt happier than she'd done in years.

Jenny was sitting on the sofa staring into space when Pascal walked into the living room, a large mug of hot chocolate in his hand.

'Here,' he said. 'To help you sleep.'

It was a joke between them. Jenny was a light sleeper who woke regularly through the night but who nonetheless was always bright and cheerful the next morning, whereas he, who always had a good night's sleep, was a grouch until well after ten.

'Thanks.' She took the hot chocolate and gazed out over her bedraggled garden. The water from the flash-flooding of the stream had completely disappeared, as had the puddles of sodden grass. But the garden looked sad and careworn. Rather like me, she thought, it can't cope with unexpected shocks.

Pascal sat beside her and rested his arm on the back of the sofa. He'd always known this day would come, when everything would be brought out into the open. He'd hoped that it would be at a time of his and Jenny's choosing. And in some ways it had been of Jenny's choosing, although he wished she hadn't blurted out her confession of their

373

deception in front of everyone like that. Yet he was relieved that she had. He'd always felt guilty about the anniversary cards that arrived every August, wishing them well and expressing delight at how long they'd been married. It had all been a pretence and Pascal didn't like pretences. But as the years went on, it became harder and harder to admit to the truth. As for Steffie . . . Pascal sighed. He'd dreaded her birth, expecting that despite what he'd promised Jenny, he'd feel differently towards the child who wasn't his own. And yet from the moment he'd seen her, wrapped in a white blanket, a tuft of golden hair on her head, he'd loved her unconditionally. And he never for a second thought of her as another man's daughter. To him, Steffie was, and always would be, his own.

Deep down, he liked to believe that she was. From the moment he'd decided that he was keeping the family together, he'd also decided that Steffie was his. Her sunny, accepting nature always lifted his spirits, and even when things weren't going well for her – like when she'd lost her job over the jewellery ad – she took it on the chin and got on with life. And, of course, she had that artistic, dreamy streak that he so loved in her mother, that way of thinking that everything should turn out OK in the end because she wanted it to. They were more alike than either of them realised and he hoped that they'd reconcile soon. More than anything he wanted to have his family back together again, and the sooner the better.

But he had a feeling that it would take longer than he'd like for that to happen.

He hoped he was wrong.

The Wedding

Chapter 35

The snowflakes that were drifting languidly past the window landed gently on the ground beneath, before slowly melting. As she peered anxiously skyward, Steffie hoped the snowfall wouldn't get any heavier and the roads would stay clear. Otherwise the trip to Wexford would be far more fraught than she already expected. She wasn't a fan of driving in snow, and even though her little Citroën hadn't given her a moment's trouble since it had been rescued from the ditch in Wexford more than three months earlier, she didn't want to risk another mishap with it.

The smattering of snow hadn't been entirely unexpected. Immediately after the previous night's chilly weather forecast, she'd looked up half a dozen weather sites in the vain hope that they'd be somewhat more benign than Met Eireann, but they'd confirmed the sweep of Arctic air and heavy cloud advancing southwards from Siberia. And all of them had mentioned the possibility of snow while hedging their bets by saying that it might be confined to higher areas. At least Camilla will feel at home, thought Steffie, as she allowed herself to be mesmerised by the swirling flakes. It'll be properly Nordic today.

She shivered, then tightened her fluffy robe around her. The central heating had come on an hour earlier, but it was still cool in the house. She hoped it would be significantly warmer in the restored hall of the castle, which was the venue for the winter wedding. She wasn't entirely convinced about that, because despite it being a stunning building, it could be draughty. The restoration a few years previously hadn't allowed for the installation of central heating in the two-storey hall, which was the only remaining building in the original castle complex where Steffie used to play when she was younger.

Following the restoration, the castle had become a very popular venue for cultural evenings, but an even more popular choice for wedding ceremonies. On the rare occasions when she'd thought about getting married, Steffie thought it would be a wonderful place to tie the knot. But she'd been beaten to it now and would have to find an alternative venue for her hypothetical wedding. Not that there was any chance of that happening any day soon, she thought, as she turned back into the bedroom and looked at her outfit hanging on the door of her wardrobe. Her life had been a man-free zone of late and she was content to keep it that way.

She held the green silk dress she'd bought at the tail end of the summer sales against her body. It was very pretty, but not exactly made for warmth. Her new green angora jacket would help to keep the chill out, but the truth was that she'd put style before comfort for today's ceremony. She wanted to look good at the first family occasion since the anniversary party. She wanted to feel good too. And although there'd been no wedding date fixed when she'd bought the dress, it was totally appropriate for the day. Provided she didn't die from hypothermia.

She went downstairs and took a packet of rashers and a couple of tomatoes from the fridge. It would be a long day and she needed something hot and filling to keep her going, which was why she planned to make the tomato and bacon dish that Liam Kinsella had rustled up for her the day he'd driven her home from Aranbeg. It had become a staple meal for her – she regularly made it for breakfast, brunch or a light snack, and every time she did, she marvelled at how such simple food could taste so great.

If nothing else, she thought, Liam had made her rethink the contents of her fridge for ever. And weaning her off frozen crispy pancakes was as dramatic a change in her life as everything else that had happened since the day of the anniversary party. It was the one good thing sandwiched between the awfulness of the party and the even greater awfulness of the day after she got home.

She shuddered as she remembered. It had been the ringing of her mobile phone plugged in beside her bed that had woken her from more a coma than sleep that morning. She'd lain beneath the duvet, not wanting to be awake and not wanting to feel the pain of remembering. Not only the events of the party, but also the pain she'd felt when Liam had walked out of her house, clearly untroubled by the fact that she seemed to have someone else in her life. In fact, she'd thought bleakly as she curled up in the bed, possibly even relieved that Steve was there so that he wouldn't have to extricate himself from a relationship he didn't really want. Men are different, she'd mused. Having sex isn't the same to them as making love. They can walk away and not care. And then she'd reminded herself that she too had wanted to walk away and not care. But the problem was, she did. It didn't matter how stupid it was to think there was something between her and Liam Kinsella after just one night. It didn't matter that she told herself it was the circumstances of the storm and the power cut that had drawn them together. That it was a temporary thing. A one-off. It made no difference that she'd told Alivia she'd be fine. When Liam had walked out of her house, she'd felt as if a part of her had left with him. And it had been awful sitting beside Steve, knowing that she'd already distanced herself from him but not wanting him to think it was because of Liam, because she didn't want to make him feel bad. And then thinking that he wouldn't feel bad anyway. And worrying about that too.

In the end, after he'd finished the pizza and before he'd had the chance to open another bottle of beer, she'd told him that he couldn't stay with her that night. He'd looked at her in complete astonishment.

'I'm sorry,' she said. 'I really appreciate that you came here, Steve. But it's not going to work.'

'What's not going to work?' he asked.

'You and me.'

He stared at her and an expression of disgust crossed his face.

'Don't tell me it's because of restaurant van man. That you went behind my back and—'

'It's not because of Liam.' She knew she was on shaky ground but she was comforting herself with the fact that she'd planned to break it off with Steve long before she'd hopped happily into bed with Liam. All the same, she thought, I clearly take after my mother in the cheating department. I deserve everything that's happened to me.

'Oh come on.' He snorted. 'I saw the way he was looking at you.'

'What way?' Even as she asked the question, she wanted to think that Liam cared, even a little bit.

'He wanted you,' said Steve. 'Anyone could see that.'

Steffie tried to keep her face as expressionless as possible. Liam might have wanted her. He'd already had her. Three times. And he'd still walked away.

'It's nothing to do with him,' she said. 'It's about loads of stuff, Steve. It's not you. It's me.'

'For crying out loud.' He stood up. 'You're parroting those stupid women's magazines. "It's not you. It's me." What a load of horseshit.'

'But it is!' she cried. 'Steve, all sorts of things happened at the party. Family things. I don't want to talk about them again, but—'

'Again?' he said. 'You didn't talk about them at all to me. All I got was a litany of how annoying your sister was and how mad some of your relations were. Is it any wonder I didn't want to go to the party in the first place? And now you're blaming me for not being there and using something I don't even know about as an excuse for breaking up with me. Well if that's how you feel, that's fine. I don't need to be messed around. I'm out of here.'

And she'd watched as another man she'd slept with walked out of her house.

That was when she'd started on the wine. It had done the job. When she eventually went up to her bedroom, she'd passed out, but not before remembering to plug in her phone. When it had buzzed insistently the following morning, she'd ignored it and the ping of a voicemail being left. It was nearly two hours later before she crawled from beneath the duvet and looked at the number of the missed call. When she realised that it was from the company to which she'd submitted her branding and logo proposal, her heart started to beat faster even as the pounding in her head increased. She pressed the dial button and then disconnected. It would be better to listen to the voicemail first.

'Hi, Steffie, this in Gerald Morton,' she heard. 'I'm ringing to say that the management group really liked your proposals. They were very fresh and interesting. But on this occasion we've decided to go with a different company. Thanks for all your hard work.'

Her stomach plummeted and she thought she was going to be sick with disappointment. She'd tried and tried ever since she'd submitted the proposal not to get too excited about it. But she hadn't been able to help thinking about what it would mean to get the job. She hadn't been able to push out of her mind images of her logo on their corporate website, on their headed paper, on everything they did. She'd told herself not to get carried away, but she'd really believed in her design. And now they were telling her it wasn't good enough. That *she* wasn't good enough.

Why? When Roisin was so damn capable, when even laid-back Davey was now settled in a good job and engaged to the gorgeous Camilla, why was she still the utterly hopeless one in the family? She didn't get it from her mother. Jenny wasn't hopeless. She'd managed to work things out in her favour even when she'd totally messed up. So was it the fault of the nude sheep farmer? Had he been utterly hopeless too? But no matter what, he couldn't have been as hopeless as her. She'd messed up with two men in as many days. She hadn't landed the contract. She couldn't go to her parents for support any more. She was on her own and useless with it.

She'd thrown the phone, with its already cracked screen, across the room, then pulled the covers back over her head. Some days simply weren't worth getting up for. At that moment, she didn't feel like ever getting up again.

'It's snowing, Mum!' Dougie squealed with delight as he looked out of the window.

Roisin turned from the cooker where she was preparing breakfast. It was a full Irish – sausage, bacon, eggs, potato cakes and beans. Roisin was proud of her cooked breakfasts, which always went down well with both Paul and the children. But she knew that everything, even food, paled into insignificance for Dougie in comparison to snow.

'It's not much,' said Paul, who was looking out of the window too. 'And it's not sticking. It won't be a problem.'

'I want to build a snowman!' cried Dougie.

'I don't think we'll get enough for that, pal,' his dad told him. 'But if we do, then you and I will definitely build one.'

'I'm crossing my fingers.'

'Please don't,' begged Roisin. 'We can't have snow today. Can you imagine if we don't make it to Aranbeg? We can't miss the wedding. That would be a nightmare.'

'I don't want snow either,' said Daisy. 'I'm looking forward to wearing my dress and my shoes and everything. And doing my make-up.' She peeped at her mother from beneath her sweeping black lashes, but Roisin was busy turning sausages and didn't reply.

'Ooh, we might get stuck at Gran and Gramps'. Like in the summer.' Poppy was thrilled at the prospect.

'I sincerely hope not.' Roisin began to load the plates with food. 'Getting trapped at Aranbeg again is something I don't want to repeat.'

'But it was fun,' said Poppy.

'Y'see.' Paul walked away from the patio doors and slid his arms around his wife's waist. 'Our children look back on that day with pleasure.' He nibbled the back of Roisin's neck.

'I don't.' She relaxed into the warmth of his body instead of wriggling free as she'd first intended. 'However, I appreciate that I might have been a teeny bit stressed at the time.'

'No need for you to be stressed today, though.'

'Not at all.'

'You don't sound convinced.'

'It's just that given that the weather is bad, I think we should set off earlier than we originally planned,' she told him.

He groaned and released her from his arms. 'I don't want to be faffing around in that draughty old castle for ages.'

'You won't be,' she promised. 'We'll get there half an hour or so before the ceremony, no more than that.'

'Aren't we going to Gran and Gramps' first?' asked Daisy.

'No,' said Roisin as she put the plates on the table. 'We're going to go straight to the castle. Which won't be a bit draughty.' She shot an exasperated look at Paul.

'It's very exciting, isn't it?' Poppy rubbed her hands together. 'This will be my first wedding. It's good practice for me.'

'Practice?' Paul looked at his daughter enquiringly.

'For my own,' said Poppy. 'I need to check out dresses and stuff.'

'I thought you didn't like dresses.'

'Oh Dad. You're so lame. Of course I do.'

'Right.' Paul scratched his head, then turned his attention

to his breakfast. The female mind continued to mystify him. Up until the end of the summer Poppy had been a complete tomboy who only wore dresses when she was forced into them by Roisin. Now she was planning her wedding. And, he suddenly realised, she'd become a lot more girlie over the last few weeks. She didn't slide down the banisters any more. He recalled her having an argument with Daisy over nail varnish. Thank God for Dougie, he said to himself. Otherwise I'd be completely outnumbered by the female psyche.

'Tamarin will be here shortly to do our hair,' Roisin told the girls. 'So as soon as you've finished your brekkie, hop upstairs and have your showers. You can use my special shampoo if you like.'

'That's very nice of you, Mum,' said Daisy. 'But I have the one Summer gave me.'

'So you do,' said Roisin.

'I'll use your shampoo, Mum,' said Poppy.

'Me too.' Dougie spoke through a mouthful of fried egg.

Roisin's smile didn't quite reach her eyes. Despite Paul's assertion that there was no need for her to be stressed, she was tense anyway. But that was because today's events were completely outside her control. The wedding invitation, while not unexpected, had come much sooner than she'd imagined. And when she'd asked if there was anything she could do to ensure that the day went as smoothly as possible, she'd been told that this was one day on which she would simply be a guest. That she was to enjoy herself without worrying. That everything was already in hand.

Maybe it was, she conceded as she rinsed plates under the tap before stacking them in the dishwasher. But it felt weird not to have any input into something as momentous as this when all her life she'd been the one in charge.

'All you have to do is see that we're suited and booted and ready to go at the right time.' Paul put milk and butter in the fridge beside her. 'Enjoy being one of the crowd for a change.'

'How did you know what I was thinking?' she asked.

'We've been married fifteen years,' he reminded her as he closed the fridge door. 'And guess what – given that we can't count Pascal and Jenny as a married couple, we're the ones who've been married the longest in the family. We're the ones with the most experience of marriage!'

She turned to look at him. 'I've never thought about that before.'

'I think about it a lot,' he said.

'You do?'

'Yes. And you know what I think?'

'What?'

'That I was lucky the day I married you.'

'Paul.' She felt a lump in her throat. 'That's so . . . so . . .'

'Unlike me?'

'That too,' she said. 'But romantic is what I was going to say.'

'I can manage romance from time to time,' he whispered, and kissed her.

'Oh, gross.' Daisy got up from the table, followed by her brother and sister. But Roisin didn't notice. She was caught up in the fact that she'd been lucky in love. Lucky with her choice of husband. And even though she sometimes felt that marriage was a damn sight harder than she'd ever thought it could be, she knew that she'd always love Paul. He was her soulmate. It was funny that it had taken today to remind her of that.

386

Chapter 36

Camilla laughed with delight when she saw the snow. Because Denmark was surrounded by sea, the snowfall there wasn't usually as heavy as in other Nordic countries, and she always felt childishly excited by it. But, like everyone else, she was hoping that it wouldn't come down any heavier and disrupt people's travel plans. She and Davey had arrived the day before and driven down in crisp bright sunshine. Bright sunshine would probably be better than snow, she conceded, but it would be magical if it started to fall properly after everybody had arrived. She'd visited the castle when she and Davey had returned to Ireland a month after his parents' party and she'd been enchanted by it, remarking that it was an ideal wedding location. Davey had looked enquiringly at her and they'd taken photos so that they could think about it when they got back to Denmark.

'What's so funny?' Davey walked into the bedroom and she told him about the snow.

'It's more like sleet,' he said. 'Fortunately. Can you imagine if people were snowed in and couldn't get here? After everything?'

387

Camilla told him about her desire for it to snow when they were all in the castle.

'And then everyone would definitely get stuck here. We're crap at snow,' said Davey.

'Would that be such a bad thing?' she asked. 'If we got stuck?'

'Are you kidding me? After the last time?'

'Maybe some things that were problems then could be resolved today.'

'Ever the optimist.'

'I can't believe that Steffie and your parents haven't spoken since,' said Camilla.

'According to Mum, they've exchanged the occasional email and text,' Davey said. 'But Steffie hasn't been to Aranbeg and they haven't come up to Dublin. Which is tough on Mum, because she used to meet Steffie whenever she came to town to do some shopping. Apparently Steffie doesn't want to see her, and she doesn't want to turn up uninvited for fear of making things worse.'

'They will move on,' said Camilla confidently.

'I hope so. But it seems the Sheehans aren't as good as your family in the moving-on department,' Davey said.

'You care about them a lot, don't you?'

Davey shrugged. 'This thing with Steffie is a complete disaster. I feel sorry for her but I feel just as sorry for Mum.'

'Steffie hasn't done anything about tracing her father, though, has she?'

'Not as far as I know.'

'Then she should get over it.' Camilla's voice was firm. 'There is no point in revelling in misery.'

'And that's why I love you, Camilla Rasmussen,' said Davey

as he pulled her into his arms. 'You get to the nub of things every single time.'

Camilla smiled but she didn't reply. She was too busy kissing him.

Sarah had called Lucinda to ask her what she was wearing to the wedding. When Lucinda replied that she hadn't yet decided, Sarah sent her a photo of the suit she'd bought – a biscuit-coloured skirt and jacket trimmed with dark brown fur – and told her to steer well clear of anything even remotely similar. Lucinda sent back a smiley face in return and, a week or so later, a picture of the blue velvet dress she was going to wear. Sarah was congratulating herself on her own choice today as she watched the snow spiral dizzily from the sky. A winter wedding was a nice idea, she thought, but it was a bit of a fashion nightmare. There were plenty of stunning cocktail dresses in the shops to cater for the Christmas party season, but none of them were really wedding material, what with their low-cut necklines and thigh-high splits, which didn't work for someone her age. Especially when she had to take into account the time they'd be spending in that freezing wreck of a castle. Jenny had assured her that the conservation committee allowed portable heaters, and that it would be plenty warm enough, but she'd said that before temperatures had plunged to their current below-zero levels. Sarah was thankful that the ceremony wouldn't take too long.

She was standing in front of the mirror in her bedroom, admiring her reflection, when the doorbell rang. She hurried down the stairs to open it. Colette was standing on the step, melting snowflakes glittering on the collar of her white coat.

'Come in, come in,' said Sarah. 'I was just about to put the kettle on. Would you like something?'

'Coffee would be nice,' said Colette as she removed the coat and hung it over the banister.

'Oh Colette!' Sarah stared at her daughter. 'You look beautiful.'

'Thank you.'

'I mean it,' said Sarah. 'Your hair. That dress. And you look so . . . so fit all of a sudden.'

'I'm going to the gym,' said Colette. 'It's paying off.'

'It's not the gym,' said Sarah. 'It's you. You're glowing.' Her eyes widened. 'Is it a man? Are you engaged again?'

Colette laughed. 'I do manage to live my life without getting engaged every few months,' she said. 'So no, it's not that. It's just . . .' She hesitated, uncertain how to continue.

'Now that I think about it, you've been a lot brighter in yourself for a while now,' said Sarah. 'Ever since Jenny and Pascal's party, in fact.'

'It was a bit of a catalyst for me,' agreed Colette.

'You were brilliant that day,' Sarah said. 'But I never expected you to blossom like this. It's definitely not a man?'

'Not everything has to be about men!' Colette was both amused and exasperated by her mother's comments. But she appreciated the compliments Sarah was paying her. She knew that she looked good. Her hair was now a burnished copper, the closest to her natural colour it had been in years, and she'd had it cut into a shoulder-length bob that emphasised her heart-shaped face. She'd given up on the rockabilly fashion too and had chosen a more elegant style for today – a well-fitted purple dress that suited her colouring. But it wasn't her changed appearance that was the most important thing

390

for Colette. It was the sense of peace and purpose she'd found in herself. Since the night of driving around with Davey Sheehan, and the announcement of his engagement to Camilla Rasmussen, she'd stopped thinking about him whenever she was alone. She'd stopped wondering, stopped imagining, stopped caring. She'd worried a little that it would suddenly start to matter again, but so far it hadn't. She was, of course, slightly concerned about today and how she'd react to seeing him and Camilla together. But she was pretty hopeful that it wouldn't affect her, that he was part of her past and she'd continue moving on. She was banking on it. It would be awful to relapse into the unhappy person she'd been for so many years. Not when everything was going so well for her.

She'd been promoted at work. Her immediate boss had been astonished by the change in her, and how she'd become so much easier to work with. Her changed attitude had meant a change in the way the team worked too, and productivity had increased. When Colette had approached Mike and told him that she was applying for a more senior position, he'd been happy to recommend her. And the feedback had been that she'd done an excellent interview. In the past, she'd been let down by her combative attitude.

Colette felt that she was in a good place. And she was more content with her life than she ever remembered.

'Have you been talking to Steffie?' asked Sarah as she handed her daughter a mug of coffee.

Colette shook her head. 'Not recently.'

'I wonder how she's feeling.' Sarah sat at the table with a coffee of her own.

'I'm sure she's fine.'

'But she and Jenny still haven't resolved their differences.'

'It's more than just differences,' Colette pointed out. 'It's a kind of fundamental thing for Steffie.'

'If I could get over everything your aunt did to me—'

'Mum! It's totally different.'

'Hmm.'

'It is,' repeated Colette. 'And I really don't want to hear you yakking on all day about how she ruined your life. It was bad enough back in August.'

'I don't yak.'

Colette grinned. 'No?'

'Well, maybe a little,' admitted Sarah.

'And you're not to get upset with Aunt Lucinda either,' said Colette.

'Why on earth would I be upset with Lucinda?' Sarah's voice was one of injured innocence.

'Bringing a boyfriend?'

'That doesn't upset me.'

'Doesn't it?'

Sarah shook her head. 'I'm happy for her.'

'Really?'

'Really.' Sarah drained her cup. 'Come on,' she said. 'Let's stop with the gas-bagging and hit the road. We can't be late. Especially if it starts to snow.'

'We won't be,' promised Colette. 'And you already know that I'm an expert at driving in crappy weather.'

Chapter 37

In the end, Steffie travelled to Wexford with Roisin and her family. Paul had phoned her when the snow flurries began to get heavier, saying that it was ridiculous that she should travel on her own when there was plenty of room in their SUV. Which would certainly be a safer and more comfortable drive than the Citroën if the weather worsened.

'Just because I went off the road in the rain doesn't mean I'll do it again,' Steffie protested.

'It's not because of that,' Paul told her. 'It makes sense for you to come with us. And Roisin would feel happier.'

Because that way she knows I'll definitely be there, thought Steffie. She didn't say that out loud.

'Besides,' Paul added, 'it's more fun for us all to travel together.'

Which it sort of was, Steffie agreed, as she sat in the back of the car with her nieces and nephew. She was stunned at how grown-up Daisy looked in her chocolate-coloured dress covered by a lace skirt decorated with tiny sequinned stars. Her hair was messily arranged on her head and held in place by gold clips, and if Steffie hadn't known better, she'd have thought her niece was at least sixteen. It was a shock to realise that the little girl she'd babysat, who'd wrapped her arms around her in delight when she'd arrived at the house, who'd confided her secret dreams (of being an acrobat, a tennis star, a surfer, a hairdresser, a model), would soon be making real decisions about her life. And that although people like Steffie would be a part of it, she wouldn't be regarded as the fount of all wisdom that Daisy had believed she was before. It must be hard, Steffie thought, for Roisin to watch her daughter grow up and grow away, even though she'd surely be proud of her too. And she wondered if that was how Jenny had felt as her three children had grown. If she had looked at Steffie and been awed by her and scared for her in equal measure, as Steffie now was for Daisy.

She breathed deeply through her nose and exhaled slowly through her mouth. She was anxious about seeing her parents for the first time since the end of the summer. Although part of the reason for not seeing her mother was the anger that still bubbled within her over the secrets that Jenny had kept, another part of it had been the fact that she'd been extremely busy. The busyness had been down to the sudden explosion of work that had come her way a couple of days after the disappointment of not getting the rebranding contract. Sometimes, even looking at her healthier bank balance and knowing how much work she was doing, she still couldn't quite believe her luck.

She'd been sitting at the kitchen table a week after the party, unable to even feign interest in anything, when her friend Juliette had dropped by to talk about the second illustrated book. Steffie had all but forgotten about it (truthfully she hadn't been entirely convinced it was going to happen), but Juliette showed her the contract, bubbling with excitement and saying that the publishers could do way more with the story of the princess in the lake than she'd been able to do by herself. Steffie's headache had disappeared and she'd been infected by her friend's enthusiasm, so that they spent a happy couple of hours talking about the story and discussing ideas for illustrations. By the time Juliette left, Steffie had become fired up with creative thoughts, not only about the book, but also about a couple of the smaller projects she was supposed to be working on but for which she simply hadn't been able to find inspiration. She was totally caught up in a stationery design when her phone rang. She picked it up without even noticing who was calling.

'Hi, Steffie, Gerald Morton again,' said the voice at the other end.

'Hello, Gerald.' He'd rejected her branding project, so she wondered what he could possibly have to say to her now.

'Sorry I didn't get to speak to you before,' he said. 'I hate leaving messages that sound like bad news.'

'I was disappointed not to get the contract,' she admitted.

'That's what I'm calling about now,' said Gerald. 'The company we're going with has a strong message for us and we think it suits our ethos most closely. But as I said in my message, we really liked your work. And we have something else in mind that we'd like you to be involved in. It's an internal development plan. We think you'd be the ideal person to help with some of the material.'

'You do?'

'Yes,' said Gerald. 'So I was wondering if you'd like to drop by our offices this week and we can discuss it.'

She told herself that it was more than likely a minor project and not to get too excited. But Gerald's company was a prestigious one, and even something small for them would be fantastic to have on her resumé. Trying not to sound too eager, she suggested the following morning for their meeting. He told her that suited him perfectly. When she ended the call, she realised that she was literally shaking with anticipation.

She didn't sleep that night. But it was the first time since the party that it wasn't because she was agonising over her relationship with her mother. Or because she was thinking about Liam and Steve and feeling foolish. This time, sleep was an impossibility because she was too busy deciding on the image she wanted to project to Gerald Morton the next day. She kept going over and over ideas she could bring to whatever it was he wanted her to work on. This was an opportunity that she definitely wasn't going to let slide by.

The following morning, she dressed in her smart navy suit, tied back her wayward hair and got a taxi to the company's head office on the Airton Road. She didn't allow herself to feel intimidated by the modern glass and steel building with its air of quiet efficiency. When she was brought up to Gerald's office, she held back on the jokes she usually made about big business and how it was ruining the world. She listened to what he had in mind, nodded a few times and then told him that she could do a good job for him. They agreed terms there and then – she tried not to look too delighted at the money he was offering – and he promised to have a contract to her within a couple of days.

'I'm delighted we get to work together,' he said. 'I really did like your designs.'

'I'm thrilled too.' She forgot to be cool and businesslike

then and gave him a wide smile, which he returned as they shook hands.

The great thing about the project was that it had a six-month time frame. The even greater thing, from her perspective, was that it included some travel to the company's international headquarters in Singapore. Steffie hadn't been able to contain her excitement when she called Roisin to tell her about it.

'You're not serious!' Roisin had been totally taken aback by the news. 'They're actually sending you to Singapore? By yourself?'

'They sure are,' Steffie replied. 'And I'm not slumming it in economy either! They've sprung for a better seat.'

'You lucky thing.'

'It's work.' Steffie had tried to keep her voice serious. 'It's not a holiday, you know.'

'It doesn't matter!' cried Roisin 'You're being sent to Singapore! On business. You! I can hardly believe it.'

Steffie couldn't either. She'd been beyond excited checking in at the airport, even though she kept telling herself that millions of people travelled for business every single day and she wasn't anyone special. But she felt it all the same.

Jenny had texted her to say congratulations and to wish her a safe journey. When Steffie got the message, she was tempted to call her mother and share the excitement with her. But she didn't. Talking to Jenny would inevitably mean having to deal with their personal situation, and she didn't want to allow a complicated conversation to interfere with how happy she was right now. So she simply texted thank you in return. During her four-day stay in Singapore, she sent group picture messages to her family, including Pascal and Jenny, to let them know how she was getting on. But that was as far as she was prepared to go. She still wasn't ready to talk, or to meet them face to face.

It occurred to her when she was in Singapore that she could get a flight to New Zealand from there and try tracing her biological father. But it was a fleeting notion and she knew that she'd have to put in a lot more research before actually embarking on something like that. Besides, she admitted to herself, it wasn't something she really wanted to do. Unlike Alivia, who'd been very firm about her desire to meet her biological dad, Steffie didn't feel the need to make contact with the nude sheep farmer. Somewhat weirdly, given how she'd felt when she first found out about him, she was growing less and less concerned about him every day. Although not less concerned about the fact that her parents had kept him a secret. That was still a struggle.

The snow had begun to fall more heavily and was coating the roads with a dusting of white by the time they arrived at the castle.

'Absolutely on time,' said Roisin with satisfaction.

'We're half an hour early,' objected Paul.

'We have to be there before the bride and groom,' Roisin said.

'We're the first to arrive!'

'Maybe,' Roisin conceded. 'But I'll bet the others will be here soon.'

Even as she spoke, a car turned in to the small car park outside the castle and Alivia got out. She was wearing a fuchsia-pink coat with matching high-heeled shoes.

'Oh my goodness, Liv, you look gorgeous!' cried Roisin as she too got out of the car.

'It's freezing.' Alivia rubbed her hands together and wished she'd invested in the pretty leather gloves she'd seen in the window of Brown Thomas the previous day. 'What's the chances of it being warmer inside?'

'Fingers crossed,' said Roisin. 'Where's your mum?'

'She's coming with the new boyfriend.' Alivia grinned. 'We're all staying at Roselawn B and B, which to be honest makes me feel slightly gooseberry-ish. I'm hoping I don't hear them at it in the middle of the night.'

'Alivia!' Roisin made a face. 'Not in front of the children.'

Alivia laughed. 'The kids are fine,' she said. 'Hey, Steff! How are you?'

Steffie hadn't seen Alivia in the flesh since the party, although they'd talked a number of times. She got out of the car and hugged her.

'I'm grand,' she said. 'Busy.'

'So you are.' Alivia smiled. 'Jet-setter!'

'Ah well, it's not as glam as it sounds, but it's a brilliant contract and I've got more work off the back of it. So much,' she added, 'that having to take a day off for a wedding is a bit of a chore.'

'I really hope you don't mean that, Steffie Sheehan,' said Roisin. 'Especially when it's such an important day.'

'I'm ferociously busy,' Steffie said. 'But I'm not complaining. Not at all.'

'Can we go inside, Mum?' asked Daisy. 'It's really cold out here.'

Roisin nodded and they walked into the castle building.

The hall had been laid out with chairs either side of the red carpet that ran the length of the flagstone floor. The thick walls were painted white and the vaulted ceiling was supported by timber beams. Iron candle holders hung from the beams while two enormous candles flickered at the top of the hall, either side of a huge wooden table. A stained-glass window was recessed into the wall behind the table. During the summer, the coloured light from the glass reflected across the floor, but today, as the snow continued to fall, the light from both the candles and the glow of electric lighting suffused the wall with a gentle lilac hue.

'It's not exactly brass monkeys indoors,' murmured Alivia. 'But not tropical either.'

'I guess back in the day they had a big fire going somewhere,' said Steffie.

'And they were roasting an entire pig on it.' Alivia laughed.

The sound of conversation from the entrance to the hall made them turn around, and they waved in greeting as Colette and Sarah walked in.

'My God, Colette,' said Roisin. 'I've never seen you look better.'

'Thank you.' Colette kissed her cousin on the cheek. 'You look great too.'

'I've made an effort,' agreed Roisin, 'but I haven't undergone a complete transformation like you.'

'Colette manages to transform herself on a regular basis,' said Sarah, 'but I have to say this is her best look yet.'

'Mum!' Colette gave her an exasperated look.

The castle manager, who'd been making some adjustments to the sound system, came over and welcomed them, and then, as the remainder of the guests arrived, the registrar walked up to the table.

'The bride and groom are outside,' she said. 'So if you could all take your seats . . .'

The group did as they were asked, and suddenly music echoed around the hall. Beside her, Steffie heard Roisin sniff, and she began to well up herself as the tenor started to sing. It was 'Some Enchanted Evening', a song that she knew was her mother's favourite.

Everyone was turning around to see the bride. And the groom. Because Jenny and Pascal had decided to walk up the aisle together. Jenny had told him they'd been a couple for forty years and she wasn't going to do a solo run now. Pascal had been happy to agree.

She was dressed in red silk. The dress was cleverly cut, and complemented by a matching bolero jacket, so that she appeared taller and slimmer than usual. On her head was a neat pillbox hat with a short net veil. But what made her look beautiful was the smile on her face. At least that was what Camilla whispered to Davey as Jenny and Pascal walked by them.

'I will have to up my game in the summer to make it as romantic as this,' she murmured.

Davey chuckled and squeezed his fiancée's hand. Their wedding would be the following June, in Denmark. When Jenny had rung to ask him if they'd set a date and explained that she and Pascal had decided that the time had come for them to get married too, both Camilla and Davey had been happy to let his parents have their ceremony earlier. Camilla said that she wouldn't feel in the least put out. And Davey joked that he would feel better knowing that his parents had got married before him.

Roisin was now sniffing into her tissue. She'd come prepared with plenty of them because she'd known that she'd cry, although she'd hoped she'd last until her parents were actually married. But it was good to be prepared.

Steffie was staring straight ahead. She didn't want to turn around and look at Pascal and Jenny walking up the aisle. My mother and her husband, she murmured to herself, although of course he wasn't her husband yet. And he'd never be her father. But, she thought, as they walked past her, she'd been totally unable to stop thinking of him that way. And after they were married, it would be even harder.

'It's a nice day,' whispered Alivia, who was standing beside her. 'You should be happy for them.'

And I am, thought Steffie. I really am. I just wish that they weren't the two people who took what I thought was my life and ripped it up in front of me.

Her emotions were mixed as she saw Jenny stand in front of the big table. They were even more mixed as the registrar talked about love and happiness and being together. Then Pascal and Jenny read their vows.

'When you walked into my life, you lit up my world,' said Pascal. 'I loved you then, I love you now and I will love you for ever.'

'You have been with me through good times and bad,' Jenny said. 'Through ups and through downs. Through joy and through sorrow. I loved you then, I love you now and I will love you for ever.'

Dammit, thought Steffie, they're doing their best to make me cry. And I don't want to cry. But beside her Alivia was dabbing at her eyes, while Roisin had taken another tissue out of her bag. Even Camilla was sniffing.

Steffie knew she couldn't hold out any longer. The tears slid from her eyes. She didn't try to stop them.

Chapter 38

As soon as Pascal and Jenny were pronounced man and wife, the guests broke into applause and rushed from their seats to embrace them.

'Mind my hat!' cried Jenny as she was hugged enthusiastically by Lucinda and Sarah. 'It's the first time in my life I've ever worn one!'

Pascal's brothers were patting him on the back, and so were the neighbours who'd crowded around the couple. Roisin had pushed forward too, wanting to hug her mother, but Steffie stood to one side while she struggled to compose herself. Usually at weddings her emotions were all to do with happiness for the bride and groom and good wishes for the future. But it was different this time. Pascal and Jenny had managed to live together for forty years, raise a family, work their way through the worst sort of betrayal and still stay together. They didn't need good wishes for their future. They'd already lived it. Even though she was happy for them, Steffie wished she didn't still feel a part of their big betrayal. Part of the reason they hadn't got married before now.

'You OK, sis?' Davey stood beside her.

'Yes.' She nodded. 'It's weird all the same, isn't it? You

don't expect to see your mum and dad walking up the aisle. At least not at our age.'

'I know,' said Davey. 'The whole thing . . . it was all a shock. And for you, Steffie, a bigger one than for the rest of us.'

'Yes.'

'How are you doing with it?' he asked.

She looked at him in surprise. She had never, in her entire life, had a conversation with Davey about feelings. Her words caught in her throat.

'I love you, Steff, you know that,' he said when she didn't speak. 'Mum and Dad love you too. There's no need to feel . . .' he grimaced slightly, 'well, whatever you might be feeling.'

'Thanks,' she said. 'I don't know what I feel, to be honest. Probably because I haven't quite figured out how to deal with it yet.'

'I might have been a bit abrupt with you before,' he said. 'I didn't understand why you ran away. I do now, and if there's anything I can do to help . . .'

'Oh Davey, that's really good of you. But I think I need to sort it out in my own head.'

'Hopefully you can,' he said. 'But if you can't, and if I can't help you, there are places to go.'

'Professionally?' She looked at him in surprise. 'You think I need to see a shrink?'

'There's no shame in it,' he said. 'If you can't work it out on your own, why not let someone else help you?'

'I never thought of that,' she said.

'Well, do think about it.' He gave her a quick hug. 'You know, if you decide that you never want to speak to Mum or Dad again, that's your right. If you want to trace your dad, you're perfectly entitled to do it. All I care about is that you're happy.'

Steffie felt a rush of love for her brother. It was the first time since Jenny had detonated her bombshell that she felt she wasn't being pushed into trying to forgive and forget as quickly as possible so that everyone could resume the lives they'd had before.

'And what about you and Camilla?' she asked after a moment. 'Don't you mind that the parents have stolen your thunder?'

Davey laughed. 'Not in the slightest,' he said. 'I told Mum I was happy that they'd be married before us. Makes me feel less like a boring conservative while they live out some wild-child hippy dream.'

'Jenny is dazzling in red,' said Camilla, who had joined them. 'It's such a good colour on her.'

'What colour will you be wearing on your wedding day?' asked Steffie.

'I think I will go for something traditional,' said Camilla. 'It wasn't my original idea but now . . . well, it will be very beautiful in Denmark in June and I want to be a lovely summer bride. Does that sound silly to you?'

'Not at all,' said Steffie. 'I'm really looking forward to it. I was looking forward to it before Jenny and Pascal skipped ahead of you in the queue.'

'Photo call!' Pascal's brother Seamus, who was one of the witnesses, clapped his hands to get everyone's attention, while the local photographer began to organise the guests behind the oak table.

'I should stand this way.' Summer, who was wearing a

cream mohair coat over a gold lamé dress, turned to face the camera.

'You were fine the way you were, pet,' said the photographer.

'This is better,' she insisted.

Colette, beside Carl at one end of the line, glanced at him, but he was looking straight ahead, expressionless. Bernice, at the other end, was equally stony-faced.

After the group pictures, the photographer took some of Jenny and Pascal with their brothers and sisters, then others with nieces and nephews, and finally he asked Steffie, Davey and Roisin to pose with their parents.

'Can you swap places with your sister?' he asked Steffie, so that she was standing between Jenny and Roisin. They were so close that they were touching each other; she could feel her mother's arm resting on her back. I wish I could get over it, she thought. But I don't know how. Maybe Davey is right. Maybe I do need to talk to a professional about it.

She was relieved when the photographs were finished and she plunged back into the crowd without saying anything, though she was conscious of Jenny's eyes on her and she felt that she should congratulate her.

'We'd better leave now,' said Seamus. 'We were due at the restaurant fifteen minutes ago.'

There was more chatter and movement from the guests as they made their way to the door.

'Oh!' gasped Daisy as she looked outside. 'Oh my goodness. It's snowing. Properly.'

She was right. In the time that it had taken to pronounce Jenny and Pascal husband and wife, the landscape had been transformed into a picture-postcard snowscape. And it was beautiful.

The newly-weds had reserved Cody's for their celebration dinner, something else that had made the day particularly tense for Steffie. They didn't know (she assumed) that she'd slept with Liam Kinsella. They didn't know that he'd left her house because another man had arrived, and that their sole communication since then had been short and professional. In some ways a professional relationship had suited Steffie, because the unexpected contract from Gerald Morton's company had taken over her life. But she also knew that if Liam Kinsella had wanted to be part of it in a personal way, she would have made room for him without a second thought.

She'd designed the new logo for Cody's on her flight to Singapore. She'd been mulling over her original idea when it suddenly crystallised in her mind and she'd started working on it straight away. By the time the flight had landed, she'd built a brand identity around an apron graphic that she thought would fit perfectly with Cody's. She'd emailed it to Liam before she'd gone to bed that evening, telling him that she'd promised to do some preliminary work for him, that she was now too busy to do anything more and that he could do what he liked with the logo and the suggestions of how to use it. She'd also sent him a link to a website developer who might be able to help him with the restaurant's site.

It was a few days later before Liam replied, telling her he really liked the design and he'd have a think about how it could be implemented. He wanted to know how much to pay her. She reminded him that they'd agreed her initial design was free and that she'd only charge him if she was going to do more work for him. But as she couldn't, he didn't owe her a thing. She added that she was currently in Singapore working on a major project.

She hadn't received any more emails from him after that. She'd tried very hard not to think about him either. But now, standing in Cody's, the only thing going through her head was that the double doors leading to the kitchen was all that separated them. She wanted to barge through them right now and wrap her arms around him. She wanted to talk to him, to tell him that she loved him, that she couldn't stop thinking about him. Because it was true. She thought about him all the time, even when she was busy doing other things. And she wished that it had worked out differently between them.

She was wondering why it was that life never took the route you expected when Bernice came to stand beside her. Carl's still ex-girlfriend had reprised the look she'd had for Jenny and Pascal's anniversary party, with her hair in luxurious curls and her face perfectly made up. She was wearing a deep burgundy satin dress with flared skirt and narrow waist. Seeing her tense expression, Steffie was struck by the fact that she wasn't the only one at today's event who had issues. Bernice had been through the mill too. She glanced around and saw Carl talking to Davey.

'How are you keeping?' she asked Bernice, who was also looking in Carl's direction.

'Oh, you know. Getting there,' replied Bernice. 'It was sweet of your mum and dad to invite me.'

'Of course they were going to invite you,' said Steffie. 'You're family.'

Bernice grimaced. 'I used to say that to myself all the

time,' she admitted. 'When I was living with Carl and we'd come to events, I believed I was part of it. I know we weren't married, but we might as well have been. Not unlike your mum and dad, I suppose.'

'I suppose.' Steffie had never thought of that before.

'And then Summer came along and I felt like I'd been wrenched out.'

'I'm stunned that they're still together,' admitted Steffie. 'I always thought she was a fling. His summer fling,' she added wryly.

'Yeah, well, so did I until . . .' Bernice's fingers tightened around the champagne glass as she spoke. 'They haven't told anyone yet, but she's pregnant.'

'What!' Steffie almost dropped her own glass. 'I never thought . . .'

'Neither did I.' Bernice gave her a tight smile. 'These things happen, right?'

But she hadn't expected them to happen between Carl and Summer. When he'd phoned her with the news, she'd gone into complete shock.

'I thought I should give you a heads-up,' Carl said, 'although we're keeping it quiet for the moment. It wasn't planned, Bernice. Nowhere near planned. But I guess this means that I wasn't the problem as far as we were concerned. Which on the one hand I'm glad about. But I'm sorry for you. I really am.'

And yet he didn't have to be sorry for her. Because the result of Bernice's test, the one she'd brought with her to the anniversary party with the intention – perhaps – of handing it to Carl as a kick in the teeth, had been that she was perfectly normal and healthy and there was no medical reason why

409

she shouldn't conceive. Which meant, from her point of view, that Carl was the reason she hadn't got pregnant. Believing that had given her a certain confidence at the ill-fated anniversary party. It had made her feel superior to him and allowed her to have condescending thoughts towards his silly relationship with Summer. Yet now he'd proved that he was perfectly fine, achieving something with his new girlfriend that he hadn't with Bernice, despite the fact that there'd been no physical reason they couldn't have had a baby after all. The news had shattered her.

She'd thought about not accepting the wedding invitation, uncomfortable at the idea of seeing Carl and his pregnant girlfriend there. And she wondered how it was that Summer had got pregnant so quickly when they weren't even planning it, while she'd tried for nearly a year without success. Maybe I wanted it too much, she thought now as she watched the younger girl chatting to Daisy. Maybe the very fact that I cared worked against me somehow.

'You'd never know,' said Steffie. 'She still has her figure.'

'I'm hoping she balloons up like a walrus.' The words were out of Bernice's mouth before she could stop them, and Steffie couldn't help laughing.

'I'll drink to that,' she said, and clinked her glass against Bernice's.

From the other side of the room, Sarah was watching Bernice and Steffie talking together. She was aware that Carl was watching them too. She couldn't for the life of her understand why he was still with the flibbertigibbet. Summer wasn't his kind of girl. She really wasn't. He'd told her that it was nothing more than a bit of fun, and Sarah had hoped that after the silly 'on a break' thing was over, he'd go back to Bernice. But somehow he was still with Summer. When the wedding invitations had come and Sarah realised that Carl and Summer would be going as a couple, she was gutted. She hadn't known then if Bernice would be invited too, so she'd called her, and when Bernice said that she had been but that she was in two minds about it, Sarah had told her that she simply must come. She'd been certain that when her son saw Bernice again, he'd realise what he was missing. But so far he hadn't appeared to have spoken to his ex-girlfriend at all, while being unnecessarily solicitous towards Summer. The girl was perfectly capable of looking after herself, thought Sarah. She was a tough cookie despite her frothy exterior. She knew what she was doing. She watched as Summer refused champagne and instead had her glass refilled with sparkling water, and suddenly understood why. Her heart sank like a stone, before treacherously lifting again almost at once at the thought of her first grandchild.

My children are still nothing but heartache to me, she thought as she allowed her own glass of champagne to be topped up. Why can't I have an easy life with them? She was ready to concede that of late Colette was less of a worry than before, but Carl was more than making up for her now. Especially if she was right about Summer. Which she knew she was.

'Hey, Sarah, penny for them.' Lucinda pushed her way to her sister's side.

'Nothing very exciting,' said Sarah.

'You were looking at Carl as though you wanted to shoot him.' Lucinda's eyes danced with merriment. 'Give him a break, sis.'

'I think she's pregnant,' said Sarah.

411

'Who? Oh!' Lucinda's eyes widened and she looked across the room. Summer was still talking to Daisy. 'Are you sure?'

'Pretty sure,' said Sarah. 'She's drinking water and . . . and she's put on a bit of weight.'

Lucinda studied Summer and nodded slowly. 'You might be right.'

'She's trapped him,' said Sarah. 'I should have guessed she would.'

'Don't be so old-fashioned.' Lucinda made a face at her sister. 'Girls don't trap men any more. If they ever did. Even if I'd wanted to, I didn't trap George, did I?'

'You're right. I'm sorry.' Sarah shook her head. 'The relationship between Carl and Summer is none of my business. I have to butt out. That's what Carl told me when he first had problems with Bernice, and he's right. I wanted to help, but it's not up to me, is it? They have to work it out themselves. It's taken me a long time to realise that.'

'Oh, look, none of us ever work it out properly,' said Lucinda. 'For ourselves or for the people around us.'

'But you're working on working it out.' Sarah smiled slightly. 'You and the man!'

Lucinda had introduced Frank to Sarah at the church.

'Isn't he a pet?' She beamed. 'I met him at a concert. I suppose it's a sign of my advancing years that it was a stage and screen musical celebration and not a rave somewhere. We hit it off straight away. He's divorced, two grown-up kids, everything fairly amicable, at least by now.'

'Is it serious?' asked Sarah. 'You've only known him a couple of months.'

'Time moves faster in your fifties,' said Lucinda. 'I don't have the luxury of faffing about.'

'So it *is* serious?'

'I like him a lot,' confessed Lucinda. 'If I decide to marry him, I can't hang around for forty years like Jenny.'

Sarah looked at her keenly. 'It's on the cards?'

'I don't know,' admitted Lucinda. 'He's the first man I've had in my life in any kind of serious way since George. That's sad, don't you think? That I wasted thirty feckin' years keeping them at arm's length. I guess after talking to you at Jenny and Pascal's do, I realised that I couldn't be like that for ever. That time really is marching on. And so when Frank asked me out, I didn't get all defensive like I usually do, and I said yes. I'm glad I did.'

'I'm glad for you,' said Sarah. 'And I hope you'll have lots of happiness with him, no matter how long you decide it's for.'

'Thank you.' Lucinda was pleased at her sister's remarks. In her experience, Sarah had always been the most bitter of them, a glass-half-empty sort of person. Yet today, even though she was clearly rattled about Carl and Summer, she was very definitely trying to be more positive.

Perhaps weddings do that for you, Lucinda thought as she waved at her new boyfriend, inviting him to join them. Perhaps they bring out the optimist in all of us.

Chapter 39

Although Steffie was at the same circular table as her parents, she was seated between Daisy and Dougie, and too far away to have to engage in direct conversation with them. Whoever had decided on the layout had been very thoughtful, she decided, although sitting among the children made her feel that she wasn't fit for adult conversation. Which she knew was somewhat paranoid. However Daisy was keeping her up to speed on her efforts to become a top model – Summer had sent her a surprise package of make-up samples the previous week, with tips on how to apply them; while at the same time Dougie started to tell her about the hat-trick he'd scored at his football match the previous weekend, where he'd been given the man-of-the-match award, so she had to devote all her attention to them.

They were both so hopeful, she thought, so excited about their lives and their futures. I used to feel like that all the time too. And I did again when Gerald Morton rang me. But until I resolve my issues with my mother, I can't honestly feel right about anything again. Yet it's so much easier to say than to do.

She pushed her prawns around her plate, unable to eat despite the general consensus that they were utterly sublime.

'It's by far the best restaurant in the south-east,' Jenny was telling Camilla. 'Pascal and I come here all the time. They don't normally cater for private functions like this, but when we asked them, the owner couldn't have been nicer about it.'

Steffie felt herself glow in Liam Kinsella's reflected niceness. I'm perfectly capable of being happy, she told herself as she realised she was smiling. I just need to stay that way. At the moment I'm like Dougie at his most petulant. Worse, in fact, because he's only six.

She made herself eat one of the prawns. Everyone had been right about them. They were the best she'd ever tasted.

This time, Jenny didn't hesitate before she and Pascal cut the cake that had been baked for the occasion. It was a traditional wedding cake, in two tiers, with royal icing and little figures of a bride and groom on the top.

'Comic figures,' Jenny pointed out as she held the knife over the cake. 'We can't possibly take ourselves too seriously at this point.'

But inside she believed they'd done a serious thing. And she felt a wave of relief wash over her that she was finally, as she'd always thought of herself, Mrs Sheehan. Married to Pascal. No more pretending. No more worrying that people who mattered would discover their secret. A secret that both lessened and grew with the passing years. Lessened because it didn't matter to her that they weren't married. Grew because the longer they went without confessing, the harder it became to tell anyone. The trouble with secrets, she thought, is that they start to take over our lives. They take on a life of their own. They change

415

us. They make us change to keep them. And it's not always a good thing.

She looked at Steffie, who was clapping along with the rest of the guests. Her daughter was smiling, which was an enormous relief. Jenny had hoped to have made her peace with Steffie before today, but she knew that she had to do things at her daughter's pace. The group texts and emails had been a start, but Jenny ached for the easy relationship they'd had before.

The wedding itself had been another source of anxiety. Following the fateful anniversary celebration, she and Pascal had decided they should get married as soon as possible. But Jenny was concerned about arranging it before the situation with Steffie had been resolved.

'Putting things off before didn't exactly work out how we planned,' Pascal told her. 'Let's do it now, Jen. And you never know, if we haven't sorted it out beforehand, perhaps it will help to heal things.'

Although she'd agreed with him that they should go ahead, Jenny's greatest fear had been that Steffie wouldn't come to the wedding at all. Her absence would have been a gaping wound that no clapping or congratulating or champagne could have healed, so she'd been very relieved when her daughter had sent an acceptance card, even if it arrived at the last possible minute.

The fact that she's here is the main thing, thought Jenny, as Pascal got up to make his speech. And he was right, as always. Waiting wouldn't have made things any better. She listened to her husband's words, which were both wise and humorous, and she knew that she was lucky to have him in her life.

Davey, as Pascal's best man, got up to speak too. Both of them were cheered wildly before the small local band began the music for the evening, and the waitresses moved the tables to make room for dancing. Pascal led Jenny to the centre of the floor and the guests gathered around them, applauding them.

'I feel an awful fraud again,' whispered Jenny. 'After all, we're supposed to have done all this before.'

'We never had the party,' he murmured. 'We're entitled to the party.'

She laughed and he kissed her.

Observing them from the edges of the crowd, Steffie felt her eyes brim with tears. It was a happy occasion. It was good to know that people could come through difficult times and stick together. Yet she felt as though she was suffocating in the universal goodwill. Each of the guests wanted things to be back to normal. They wanted Pascal and Jenny to be married, to forget the inconvenient truth that they'd lied to everyone here. They wanted Steffie herself to forget the even more inconvenient truth that she'd been the result of her mother's affair. They wanted things to be the way they'd always believed. Not the way they really were.

She watched Davey and Roisin clap and cheer and she envied the genetic bond that bound them together. Roisin had told her a million times that having a different father meant nothing. Whenever Davey spoke to her these days he called her sis, which he'd never done before. They would always include her, there was no doubt about that. The problem was, she didn't feel she had the right to be included. She knew it was silly. But she couldn't help how she felt.

She was too hot. And the buzz of conversation, as well as

417

the music, was making her head ache. She needed to be on her own for a few minutes. She needed some peace and quiet. She took her angora jacket from the back of her chair and slipped out of the restaurant door. The snow was still drifting slowly from the sky, turning the dark countryside into a single white expanse, and the icy coldness of the air took her breath away.

She shivered as she stood beneath the half-shelter of a spreading silver fir tree. The snow muffles everything, she thought, as faint traces of music seeped from the restaurant. Even your feelings.

Colette was the only one who'd noticed Steffie stepping outside. She thought about following her to check if she was OK, but then decided that Steffie probably needed some time to herself. She understood that it was a difficult day for her cousin. She'd been prepared for a difficult day herself, having to see Davey and Camilla again. She'd worried that all her old feelings for him might suddenly come rushing back. But they hadn't. When she'd met him at the castle and said hello, it was as if she'd never spent hours and days and months and even years pining for him. He was just Davey. Someone she'd known when she was a kid. Someone she felt comfortable with. Not awkward. Not anything. And that was that. In fact, she thought, it was almost frightening how her feelings for him had disappeared. He'd overshadowed her life for so long, it seemed incredible that that wouldn't continue to be the case. And yet here she was, watching him dancing with Camilla and not feeling a thing. It was very liberating.

'Hi.' A man was standing beside her. He was holding two glasses of champagne, one of which he offered to her. 'I saw you were without a drink,' he said. 'I thought I'd bring one to you.'

'That's very kind of you.' She smiled at him. 'It'd never do for me to be a champagne-free zone.'

'Sean McGettigan,' he said, proffering his hand. 'I work with Pascal.'

'Accountancy?' hazarded Colette, who knew her uncle was doing some kind of part-time work but had no idea what.

'Is it that obvious?'

'There's a look of an accountant about you.' She chuckled. 'Maybe it's the suit.'

'All the men are in suits,' he protested.

'But you wear yours with a greater sense of ownership.'

'Dammit,' he said. 'I clearly have to try harder to throw off the shackles.'

'Perhaps if you danced,' she suggested. 'Loosened up a bit, you know?'

'You think?'

'I do.' She put her glass on the table and moved towards the centre of the floor. The band was playing a mid-tempo tune, but he put one hand on her back and swung her into a quickstep.

'Oh crap,' she said. 'You really *can* dance. You're putting me to shame.'

'Follow my lead,' he said. 'You'll be fine.'

And she was. She let him twist her and turn her and manoeuvre her around the floor, and she realised that she was having more fun than she'd had in ages. Which was why, when the music stopped, she sat down beside him to catch her breath and didn't think of Davey, or Camilla, or Steffie at all.

Chapter 40

The wedding party, fuelled by limitless champagne, had moved into a slightly more raucous phase. Davey and Camilla were jiving in the centre of the floor and doing – as Alivia said – a surprisingly good job of it. The Danish girl was letting her hair down both literally and figuratively, as she'd taken out the clips that held it into her customary updo and it was now falling in loose waves around her face.

'She did a great Lady Gaga impression at the anniversary party,' Bernice reminded Alivia. 'I think she'll be fun at gatherings in the future. Not that I'll be at any more of them,' she added.

'I'm sorry, Bernice,' said Alivia.

'It's time for me to move on,' Bernice said. 'I can't keep picking at the remains of a failed relationship. I only came today out of respect for Jenny and Pascal. I know I said that's why I came to their anniversary party too, but actually I turned up there with the idea of humiliating Carl. In the end, I was the one who was humiliated.'

'No you weren't,' said Alivia. 'You were the heroine of the hour, rushing Poppy to A and E through the floods.'

'She would've been fine anyway,' said Bernice.

'Well, yes,' agreed Alivia, 'but you were still the one who looked after her. You're a good person, Bernice.'

'I'm not thinking particularly good thoughts,' she said.

'You and I are the sad singletons at this affair,' remarked Alivia. 'Even my mother has found herself a man before me! We should socialise more. Go on the hunt together.'

Bernice laughed. 'It's a bit difficult with you in Galway.'

'I'm moving to Dublin later in the new year,' Alivia told her. 'I've been offered a new gig after the current show ends and I'm going to take it. But it's totally hush-hush, I haven't told a soul. Not even my mother. So keep it under your hat.'

'That's wonderful news,' said Bernice. 'Your mum will be thrilled for you.'

Alivia hoped so. Now that Lucinda had a man in her life, she'd become a lot less reliant on her and a lot more like the person Alivia was sure she'd been when she was younger. Alivia couldn't help feeling sad that her mother had poured all her love and attention into Alivia herself, without any thought of having a life of her own. It seemed to her that Lucinda had wasted a lot of years when she could have been out there having fun. But she was doing it now. And even if things didn't work out in the long term with Frank, at least Lucinda had changed her outlook. Which was, her daughter felt, a very good thing.

And I'm making changes myself, she thought, which is also good. Getting the new series was a major coup for her, and going to Dublin and being out of Dermot Falconer's circle as a result was even better. I was an idiot about him, Alivia said to herself. But I got over him. As you do. As you always do when you let yourself. She sighed. Allowing yourself to feel OK again was often the hardest part of a break-up.

421

'Where's Steffie?' It was Roisin who came over to Bernice and Alivia, a worried frown on her face. 'I haven't seen her in ages.'

'Nor have I.' Alivia thought about it. 'She was chatting to that woman who's on some local committee, but that was at least half an hour ago.'

'She's nowhere around,' said Roisin. 'I hope she hasn't done anything silly.'

'Like what?'

'I don't know,' Roisin admitted. 'But everyone's having such a good time, Mum and Dad are really happy . . . I'm afraid it might have been a little too much for Steffie.'

'You don't think she's run off again?' Bernice looked horrified. 'Into the snow instead of the rain this time?'

'She can't have,' said Alivia. 'She was fine earlier.'

'Everything all right?' Colette, on her way to get another drink, realised that there was a confab going on. Bernice told her of their concerns about Steffie.

'I saw her going outside a while ago,' said Colette. 'I thought she might have needed a bit of a breather.'

'Outside! But it's freezing. And that light dress she's wearing won't keep her very warm.'

'I assumed she came back in after a few minutes,' said Colette.

'But nobody's seen her,' Bernice said.

'Bloody hell.' Colette frowned. 'She seemed fine, Roisin, honestly. I didn't think . . . I couldn't . . .'

As the three women exchanged worried glances, Jenny came over to them.

'Have you see Steffie?' she asked.

Roisin was going to lie and say that her sister was in

422

the loo, but she knew there was no point. Jenny would know she wasn't telling the truth. She'd always been able to tell.

'Colette said she went out for a breath of air,' Bernice said.

'When?'

'A while ago.'

'I haven't seen her for ages,' said Jenny.

'You've been keeping an eye on her?' asked Roisin.

'I always know where my children are,' said Jenny.

'Perhaps she needed some down time.' Colette didn't want to think that Steffie had done anything foolish. Not at her mother and father's wedding. Although part of the problem, from Steffie's perspective, was that she still hadn't accepted the fact that Pascal wasn't her father. Shit, thought Colette. I should've gone after her. But I got caught up in dancing with Sean McGettigan. And I'm wishing that I was back dancing with him now instead of worrying about my cousin.

'Maybe she's gone back to Dublin.' Jenny bit her lip. 'But it's snowing, and—'

'And this is like the anniversary party all over again,' said Roisin. 'How can she be so damn thoughtless.'

'Didn't she drive down with you, Roisin?' asked Alivia. 'She doesn't have her car here, does she?'

'No, she doesn't. You're right.' Roisin allowed herself to exhale with relief. She'd been envisaging her sister in a ditch again. Although perhaps not being as lucky this time as before.

'She could have decided to walk to Aranbeg,' said Colette.

'In the snow? In high heels?' Jenny looked aghast. 'She wouldn't have got more than a few metres.'

'That might be what's happened,' said Alivia. 'She decided

to walk somewhere, she slipped on the snow and she twisted an ankle.'

'Mother of God,' said Colette. 'If she's out there with a broken ankle in the snow . . .'

'We'd better go and look,' said Bernice.

'Before we do . . .' Alivia took her phone out of her bag. 'I'll try calling her.'

But the call went directly to Steffie's voicemail.

'You stay here, Aunt Jenny,' Colette said. 'The three of us will have a look.'

'You can't possibly,' said Jenny. 'You're all dressed up. You're equally likely to break an ankle yourselves. And anyway, I'm not letting you go outside on your own.'

'You do realise that she might be quite happily having a break outside the door,' said Bernice.

'I need to be certain.'

'Best not go in a big group,' said Roisin. 'People will wonder what's up and we don't know anything's actually wrong.'

'I'll go outside with Colette,' said Bernice. 'You two follow us after a minute. Unless we come back with her straight away, of course.'

'OK,' said Jenny.

She watched as her two nieces retrieved their coats and went outside. She couldn't believe that Steffie might have run into trouble again and that her wedding to Pascal might have triggered it.

'It's not your fault,' said Roisin.

'It is,' said Jenny.

'No.' Roisin shook her head. 'I'm as entitled as Steffie to be upset, you know. After all, I found out that my mother,

424

who I always believed was perfect in every way, had an affair! That she left me and my brother to our own devices that summer while she had hot sex with a male model. I'm really entitled to be angry about that, Mum, but I've put it to one side because . . . because . . .' She released her breath slowly. 'Because it doesn't matter. You can't plan your life. Everyone does something they regret.'

'You never have,' remarked Jenny.

'I regretted giving up my job,' said Roisin. 'I always felt I should've stuck with it. But it was too complicated after Dougie was born. So sometimes I regretted having him. Only because of that,' she added hastily. 'Not because I don't love him to bits. Sometimes I think I had it all worked out, except it didn't happen the way I wanted and I had to adapt.'

Jenny nodded. 'You're such a good girl, Roisin,' she said. 'Of all my children, you've never given me a moment's worry.'

'Really?'

'Without a doubt.'

Roisin smiled. She was pleased to hear that. Pleased to know that she was, in at least one aspect, the favourite child.

'It doesn't look like Steffie is nearby,' she said. 'Neither Alivia nor Colette has come back.'

'Dammit,' said Jenny, and the two of them went out of the restaurant together.

'Oh my God, it must be below zero out here.' Roisin's breath formed clouds in front of her mouth as she spoke. 'She can't have gone far, she really can't.'

'I called her,' said Alivia. 'But there was no reply.'

'There are faint footsteps over here.' Colette pointed at

indentations in the snow. 'They're heading off towards the trees.'

'Why would she have gone there?' Jenny's teeth were chattering. She didn't have a jacket, and although the sleeves of her dress were three-quarter length, the scoop neck meant she was exposing a lot of skin to the elements.

'I don't know,' said Colette.

The women followed the footsteps, which stopped beneath a tree.

'There are more here,' said Alivia as she looked at a jumble of prints. 'So it's like she met someone. But then they disappear into one set again. It looks like they're going to the back of the building.'

Her words were met with a horrified silence.

'Maybe we should call the police,' said Bernice.

'Or maybe she met someone she knew,' pointed out Colette. 'Was there anyone at the party she might have hooked up with?'

'Oh.' Alivia put her hand over her mouth.

'What? Someone?' Jenny looked at her intently. 'D'you know who, Alivia?'

'The kitchen's at the back of the building, isn't it?' said Alivia.

Jenny's eyes met her niece's in a flash of understanding. 'I didn't think there was anything in that.'

'Neither did I,' said Alivia. 'She said there wasn't.'

'In what?' asked Roisin.

'The chef,' Alivia said. 'She slept with the chef.'

'Liam Kinsella!' Roisin was shocked. 'I know she stayed with him when she ran away the last time, but she never said . . . She couldn't have . . . I don't believe it.'

426

'She said it was probably a one-off.' Alivia was studying the footprints. 'These aren't Steffie's, but they're the only ones going anywhere.'

'We need to check them out,' said Jenny.

They followed the prints, which led to a closed door at the back of the restaurant.

Jenny moved ahead of the others and grasped the handle. Then she took a deep breath and opened the door.

Steffie had been standing beneath the silver fir tree when she felt someone's hand on her shoulder. She jumped with fright and gave a small scream.

'Hey Steffie, don't yell. It's me.'

She turned to see Liam Kinsella standing in front of her. He'd changed out of his chef's whites and was wearing jeans, a checked cotton shirt and a pair of Timberland boots, which were far better suited to the snowy conditions than her high heels. His dark hair was tousled, as though he'd pulled the shirt over his head without bothering to undo the buttons. His expression was friendly but concerned.

'What on earth are you doing out here?' he asked. 'Are you OK?'

'Of course I'm OK,' she said, her voice still sharp because of the fright. 'You shouldn't creep up on people like that.'

'I didn't mean to creep,' he said. 'I thought you'd hear me.'

Snow muffles sound as well as feelings, she thought. And it was true: the music from the restaurant was muted, absorbed by the white blanket around them. But still, he could have been anyone creeping about in the dark. She said so.

He laughed. 'Fortunately I'm not just anyone,' he said. 'Why on earth are you out here?'

'Why are you?'

'I like to walk outside after I've finished work,' he said. 'And then I saw you. A snow princess beneath the tree.'

She smiled. 'Hardly.'

'A snow princess with icy-cold feet, I bet.' He looked at her elegant shoes.

'Slightly,' she admitted.

'Want to come back inside and warm them up?'

'I don't want to return to the party yet,' she said. 'I came out to be on my own for a bit.'

'I understand.' He nodded. 'But there's no need to freeze your buns off. You can warm up in the office while the staff finish up in the kitchen.'

'I . . .'

'Come on,' he said. 'Allow me.' And once again, Liam Kinsella lifted her into his arms.

'I don't need to be carried,' she told him.

'I can't let my little snow princess freeze to death.' There was amusement in his voice. 'Nearly there now anyway.'

She leaned her head against his shoulder as he climbed the steps to the wooden door and opened it. Once they were inside, he allowed her to slide from his arms.

'Thank you.'

'And now my snow princess is melting,' he said as the snow that had stuck to her hair began to form tiny pools on the tiled floor.

'Sorry.'

'Don't be. You were lovely out there,' he said. 'And you look lovely in here too.'

428

She blushed. She'd enjoyed being carried by him and was enjoying his compliments too. But she was also remembering that she'd slept with him and he'd walked away.

'Thanks for agreeing to my parents . . . to Pascal and Jenny having their reception here. Roisin told me it's the first time you've ever done that.'

'I felt a certain proprietorial interest in it,' said Liam equably. 'And it doesn't hurt for me to do special events from time to time. It's good money for the staff, too.'

'Maybe you should do more of them,' suggested Steffie. 'Themed nights could be fun. Or black-tie evenings.'

'I hadn't actually thought of that,' said Liam. 'A couple of minutes in your company and I've got new ideas already.'

'I didn't think you were interested in my ideas,' she said. 'Not that you have to be, of course, but you didn't get in touch to say you were going to go ahead with it with someone else.'

'I loved the design,' he told her. 'But I didn't want anyone else to work on it, and you were too busy with your trip to Singapore. How amazing was that, though!'

'It was only for ten days,' she said. 'But yes, imagine me as an international businesswoman! It was brilliant.'

'I'm so pleased for you,' said Liam. 'You work hard. You deserve success.'

'Thank you. And thank you for everything you did for me before.'

'You're welcome.'

I slept with you, she thought during the silence that followed. I made love to you three times in twenty-four hours. I was wild and wanton and abandoned with you. And I told myself that it was great fun but a one-off thing because that was how you seemed to want to play it. Especially after meeting Steve. But it was so wonderful being in your arms just now. And I want to sleep with you again. Not only because of how much fun it was before, but because I feel connected to you. I wish you felt connected to me.

'D'you think we can set up a business meeting?' Liam had put a pod into the coffee machine on the sideboard beside his desk and switched it on. 'So that we can get things moving with that design of yours? I love the line of aprons to click on the website.'

'They were a fun idea really. I wasn't sure they'd be appropriate, because you're a high-end restaurant and I was afraid you were thinking something a little more formal.'

'We try to do the best food possible,' said Liam. 'Doesn't mean we don't want to have fun with it. Besides, I don't want my customers to feel intimidated by us.'

He handed her a mug topped with froth. 'Hot chocolate,' he said. 'To warm you up.'

'Thank you.' She took the mug from him and sipped. 'It's very good.'

'I can make a better one from scratch,' he told her. 'But on the basis that your lips were blue with the cold, I thought I'd better go for speed over speciality.'

She smiled.

'And that's nice,' he said. 'Seeing you smile. Seeing some colour in your cheeks.'

'It was a bit mad to go outside,' she admitted. 'Seemed like a good idea at the time, though.'

'I'm remembering the last time I carried you,' said Liam.

'Another rescue,' she said.

'Rescuing you might be going a little far,' said Liam. 'You turned up on my doorstep, after all.'

'You rescued me,' she said, 'because you made me stop thinking of myself and my problems, although to be honest, I've still been horribly self-absorbed.'

'You're being hard on yourself.' His voice was warm and comforting. 'You'd had a shock. And I'm sure it's still difficult for you.'

'I keep saying that to myself. That's it's been hard. That I need time.' She put the mug on the desk. 'And it has been very . . . unsettling. But I can't stay unsettled for ever, can I?'

'I told you before, Steffie. You're still you. You're still the same person you always were.'

'I thought that perhaps I should go looking for him,' she said. 'My biological father.'

Liam nodded slowly.

'But I don't want to.'

'That's your choice.'

'But still. You hear so much about people having this need to seek out their real parents. So I thought there was something wrong with me that I didn't feel that way.'

'Pascal and Jenny are the sort of people who'd support you no matter what.'

She sighed. 'I'd been going through a time when I was feeling guilty about all the financial support they were giving me. Living in the house. Always there if I needed them. And I thought maybe that it was because they felt guilty. That they were trying to make it up to themselves.'

'Oh.'

'And I don't know how I should be now,' she said.

431

'Sometimes I want to hug them and tell them how much I love them and appreciate every single thing they've done for me, and sometimes I want to scream at them for keeping secrets from me. I guess I'm totally conflicted.'

'In which case, today must have been difficult for you.'

'I'm happy for them and I want to say that to them, but I don't want them to think that everything's OK,' she confessed. 'I'm a horrible person really.'

'No you're not,' he said. 'You never were. You never could be.'

'You thought I was.' She had to say it. She couldn't not. 'You walked away from me because of Steve.'

'And I'm not exactly proud of myself over that,' said Liam. 'I keep going over and over that day in my head. How I reacted when he came into the house with you. All proprietorial and marking his territory. I got a bit stroppy, to be honest. The thing is, I'm not someone who's good at muscling in. I never was.'

'You didn't have to muscle in,' she told him. 'He was already on the way out.'

'Because of me?' He looked at her sceptically.

'Actually, no,' she confessed. 'Because I'd worked out he wasn't the one. Admittedly only a few hours earlier, at the party, but still, in my head it was over and it was nothing to do with you. But that's why I didn't mind getting down and dirty with you, Liam Kinsella. As far as I was concerned, I'd already left Steve. If I'd been in love with him, I certainly wouldn't have jumped into bed so eagerly – and so often – with you!'

'I was a little bit of a spoiled child about it,' said Liam. 'He was so much the boyfriend, I felt . . . oh look, I thought I was the proverbial notch on your bedpost.'

'You're joking, right?' she said. 'It's girls who usually have those sort of thoughts. Men are proud of their bedposts, aren't they?'

'We do like to boast,' agreed Liam. 'But at the same time we can be as insecure as women. Why would you think otherwise?'

'I don't know.' She spoke slowly. 'I guess it's because you always seem to be the ones in charge.'

'Maybe some men are,' agreed Liam. 'But Steffie, I'm used to being the last man picked for things. Remember? And just in case you're thinking I'm a bunch of neuroses and stuff, I'm pretty OK with my life. Except I struggle with the relationship thing sometimes. With what I'm supposed to do and how I'm supposed to do it.'

'You didn't struggle with it very much when I was here before,' Steffie pointed out. 'In fact, if I remember correctly, you knew exactly what you were doing.'

'I did, didn't I?' He grinned. 'And . . .'

'And?'

'How about I do it again?' he suggested as he put his arms around her.

'Oh!' exclaimed Jenny.

Behind her, Alivia, Colette and Roisin's mouths had also formed circles of surprise as they looked at Steffie and Liam, locked in their kiss.

'Hello, Mrs Sheehan.' Liam raised his head. 'Is there a problem with something?'

'I . . . um . . . no.' Jenny's hands were at her cheeks. 'I'm . . . sorry. I didn't mean to barge in here.'

'But you did.' Steffie, who'd been shocked into complete

silence when she saw her mother, followed by her sister and cousins, found her voice again. 'What on earth d'you think you're doing?'

'We noticed you were missing, Steff.' Alivia's voice bubbled with amusement. 'We saw footsteps in the snow. We thought you'd been abducted.'

'Abducted!' Steffie stared at her. 'That's the lamest thing I ever heard.'

'It's true, though,' said Roisin. 'I'm sorry, Steffie. We were worried about you.'

'You thought I'd kidnapped her and brought her back to my office to do what with her?' asked Liam.

Four pairs of female eyes looked at him.

'We couldn't know it was you,' said Roisin. 'We thought . . . we were afraid . . .'

'I did indeed meet Steffie outside, although not by prior arrangement.' There was a hint of laughter in Liam's voice. 'And then I suggested she'd be better off in the warmth than in the snow.'

'Well look, Steffie, as you're obviously OK, I'll leave you to it.' Jenny wondered if there were any more ways in which she could embarrass her daughter and make her hate her. Because so far, she thought, I'm managing to do a great job.

'You can use that door, Mrs Sheehan.' Liam pointed behind him. 'It leads directly to the dining room.'

'Thank you,' said Jenny.

'Thanks, Liam,' chorused the other three.

They followed Jenny out of the office.

Steffie and Liam were left alone. They looked at each other wordlessly for a moment.

And then they began to laugh.

434

Chapter 41

Back among the crowd of revellers, Jenny sought out Pascal and told him what had happened. Her husband's mouth twitched and she gave him a stern look.

'It's not funny,' she said. 'If we'd walked in a few seconds later, God knows what would've been going on.'

'They were only kissing, weren't they?'

'Yes, but . . .' Jenny sighed. 'It's like everything I do regarding Steffie turns to dust. Things were bad enough before, but she's never going to forgive me now.'

'You're overdramatising,' said Pascal. 'The good news is that she seems to be getting it together with Liam Kinsella, who's one of the nicest men I know. He looked after her when she was out in the storm and he looked after her tonight too. He obviously has some kind of feelings for her and she could do a lot worse than have a relationship with someone whose accomplishments in the kitchen exceed beans on toast.'

Jenny smiled weakly. 'You always look on the positive side.'

'What's not to be positive about?' asked Pascal. 'She's finding happiness, Jen.'

'Or else this is some kind of fling and he'll break her heart and—'

'And that's what happens in life,' Pascal interrupted her. 'We kept things hidden from our kids partly for our own sake, but then because we thought it would be easier to wait till they were older – and in the end that was a complete disaster. She's had a lot to deal with. Whether it's a fling or something else with Liam Kinsella, it'll do her good. Although,' he added, his tone suddenly grim, 'if he breaks her heart, I'll break his bloody neck.'

'I was beyond mortified,' Roisin said to Davey, who she'd been telling about the encounter.

Davey roared with laughter. 'I can't believe you went looking for her in the snow,' he said.

'We were all worried. This is a difficult day for her.'

'Why on earth should it be?' asked Davey. 'It's not about her, it's about Mum and Dad.'

'Yes, but . . .' Roisin shook her head.

'Steffie will be fine,' said Davey. 'All she needed was a good man in her life to sort her out.'

'Davey Sheehan! Don't be so damn sexist! I bet you wouldn't have said that if Camilla was nearby.' Roisin's eyes scanned the crowd. Her brother's fiancée was chatting to one of the neighbours.

'Probably not,' Davey admitted. 'She has me under the thumb all right. But I like being there.'

'Hopefully your wedding will be a less fraught event,' said Roisin.

'I hope so too,' said Davey. 'But Rosie, every family has its own problems, not just the Sheehans. With five marriages between them, Camilla's parents bring a lot to the table in that regard.'

436

'You're right.' Roisin sighed. 'All I want is for everything to be sorted.'

'And eventually it will be,' Davey told her. 'Even if it's not exactly how you'd like it.'

Bernice didn't know how she'd ended up standing beside Summer. One minute she and Alivia had been giggling like school kids about Steffie and Liam, the next she'd turned around and Summer was at her elbow. Bernice felt her stomach sink. The mother-to-be was as pretty as ever, her face flawlessly made up, her golden hair curled and adorned with a sparkly comb, her dress not completely figure-hugging despite the fact that she didn't seem to have a shadow of a bump yet.

'I believe congratulations are in order.' Bernice knew that her clichéd words were stilted and awkward, but Summer smiled at her.

'Thanks,' she said. 'It was a surprise for both of us.'

'Are you keeping well?'

'I was sick as a dog at first,' Summer confided. 'I thought I was going to die. But the last couple of weeks have been better.'

'Have you and Carl made any plans?'

'What sort of plans?'

'Marriage?'

Summer shook her head. 'That's not on the agenda yet.'

'I hope you'll be very happy.'

'I hope so too,' said Summer. 'But it's difficult when the father of your child doesn't really know his own mind.'

'In what way?'

'You all think I'm an idiot,' said Summer. 'You think that

because I like to have a good time and because I work – well, worked – in a bar, and because I do some modelling, and most of all because I'm blonde, even though you also know it's not natural – well, you think I'm a fool. But I'm not.'

'I never thought—'

'I'm not an idiot, and I know you and Carl had a long history and that everyone here loves you and tolerates me. I know that Carl still loves you too.'

'He doesn't.' But Bernice could feel her heart beating faster.

'He thinks he does,' amended Summer. 'He feels bad that the whole on-a-break thing ended up with me getting pregnant and no big showdown with you. I sometimes think he started going out with me to spite you. But I've got a lot of skin in the game now and I have to look after my future and my child's future. I don't know what's going to happen between me and Carl, but I think we have a shot. We have fun together. I'm good for him. And I think he'll be a good dad too.'

Bernice was silent.

'I don't know if it'll work with Carl and me in the long term, but for the sake of our child I have to give it a try. So what I'm saying, Bernice, is butt out.'

It took Bernice a few moments to get her thoughts in order. And to accept this harder side of Summer.

'I wanted a baby,' she said. 'He didn't. That's what it was all about.'

'I know,' said Summer. 'And I'm sorry for you that I got knocked up and you didn't. But there's not a lot I can do about that now other than make the best of it. Which is what I intend to do.'

438

'Good luck with that.' Bernice tried and failed to keep an edge of bitterness from her voice.

'I'll need it,' said Summer. She turned away from Bernice and plunged into the crowd again.

Bernice watched as she spoke to Poppy and then Alivia and then began to talk to Sarah. Carl's mother had a fixed smile on her face but then Summer said something to her and she laughed. Dammit, thought Bernice, she knows what she's doing. And if she's managing to get Sarah on side, she's a smarter operator than I ever gave her credit for. She watched as Carl joined them and put his arm around Summer's waist. Maybe he wasn't entirely happy with the situation, Bernice thought, but he was accepting it. If I'd managed to get pregnant, he would have accepted that too. But I didn't. And it's over. It was over from the moment we went on a break.

She dragged her gaze away from her ex-boyfriend. Time for me to accept it, she thought. Time to acknowledge that this is the last Sheehan family party I'll ever be at. And given the way most of them tend to turn out, maybe that's a good thing.

'So what are you doing next weekend?' Sean McGettigan asked Colette.

'No plans.'

'Fancy dinner with me?'

'Could be fun.'

'You're in Dublin and I'm based in Wexford,' said Sean. 'How about we meet in Avoca? I know a lovely place there for dinner, and we could stay over if you like.'

'Sounds like a plan.'

Sean grinned at her. 'Excellent.'

Colette grinned in return. 'Excellent,' she said too.

Alivia was talking to Frank. She hadn't had much opportunity to speak to her mother's boyfriend before, but she was finding him an engaging person with a wide range of interests.

'So you and Mum,' she said, when there was a pause in their conversation. 'How's that going?'

'Daughters are so upfront,' said Frank. 'My own asked me the very same question yesterday.'

'She did?'

He nodded. 'Sandra's always looked out for me. She doesn't want me to fall into the clutches of an unsuitable woman.'

'I hardly think my mum is unsuitable.' Alivia thought this Sandra sounded a bit of a dragon.

'Ah, she cares about me. Same as you care about your mum. And you need to know how much I care about Lucinda too.'

'You care about her a lot?'

'Of course. Why d'you think I'm seeing her?' Frank's voice was light, but there was a serious tone behind it. 'I like being with her. She likes being with me. We're enjoying life.'

'But are you looking for more than that?'

'Have you ever seen those articles about divorced and widowed men? We all want to get married again. We need good women to keep us on the straight and narrow,' Frank told her, a hint of amusement in his voice.

'And you think my mother fits that bill?'

'If she wants to,' said Frank.

'Don't mess with her,' warned Alivia. 'Just don't.'

'I love her,' said Frank. 'Maybe when you're older you have a different perspective on what love should be. I'm prepared to give it time if that's what she wants.'

But as Lucinda came over to them and kissed Frank on the cheek, Alivia knew that her mother didn't need any time at all.

Steffie rejoined the party a little later, while Liam divided his time between the kitchen, the bar and the guests. Nobody said anything to her about her disappearance into the night, and she took part in the celebrations with a lighter heart than she'd had for a long, long time. Every so often Liam would join her for a while, and each time he did, she felt herself fall in love with him a little more. Although maybe that's because it's a wedding, she told herself. It envelops you in all sorts of soppy romance, and I can't let myself be carried away by romance.

But it was hard not to.

The party broke up after one, and the waiting staff began to clear the tables. The taxis Pascal had arranged to take the guests to the hotel most of them were staying in had arrived, and people were transferring their cases from their own cars, then coming back to hug Pascal and Jenny and thank them for a lovely day.

'I'll be in touch,' said Sarah. 'Maybe we could do a girls' day, you, me and Lucinda.'

'Sounds good,' said Jenny.

'Fabulous party,' said Summer. 'Hope to see you again soon.'

Everyone was telling them it was a fabulous party. Everyone

441

was saying what a good time they'd had. And Jenny supposed that it had been a great day, if you discounted the fact that she'd messed up with her younger daughter before she'd even resolved their first crisis.

'You're staying in the B and B next door, aren't you?' Roisin said to Steffie as she came back from her own car with Steffie's overnight bag. 'With Bobby and Tom.'

Steffie nodded.

'Here you are.' She put the bag down in front of her.

'Thank you,' said Steffie. 'What time are you heading back to Dublin tomorrow?'

'I was hoping you'd all come for brunch.' It was Jenny who spoke, her voice hesitant. 'You and Davey and Roisin – and your other halves and families, of course. Around half-eleven, twelve? I was going to do a full Irish.'

'Sounds good to me,' said Davey. 'I'm trying to wean Camilla off soused herring and on to sausages.'

'He hasn't succeeded yet,' said Camilla.

'I don't have herring,' said Jenny. 'But I have cold meat and cheese.'

'Perfect,' said Camila.

'And we'll be there too,' Roisin told her mother.

'Steffie?' Jenny looked at her younger daughter.

'I don't know yet,' she said.

'You're coming home with us,' Roisin pointed out. 'So you should be there. Save us having to detour to pick you up.'

'I'll text you,' said Steffie.

'That's grand.' Pascal put his arm around Jenny. 'We don't have to have everything set in stone now when we're all exhausted after a long day. Hopefully you'll make it, Steffie.

I'm sure Bobby or Tom would be happy to drop you off at Aranbeg.'

'I'm sure they would,' she said.

'We'll expect you,' said Pascal. 'But don't panic if it doesn't work out. Liam, you're welcome too. We'd be delighted to see you, especially after you did us so proud today.'

'Thank you, Mr Sheehan,' said Liam.

'Our taxi is here, so we'd better go,' said Pascal.

Roisin and her family, Davey and Camilla, and Pascal and Jenny went outside. The snow was still falling, but half-heartedly now, barely making a difference.

'See you tomorrow,' said Pascal as he helped Jenny into the car.

'See you tomorrow,' said Steffie as they drove away.

'I suppose I'd better make tracks to Mrs Brannigan's,' Steffie told Liam when everyone had gone. 'Tom and Bobby have a key to the guest house, but I didn't get one because Roisin insisted on going straight to the castle.'

'So where's your stuff?' asked Liam.

'Oh, I took my overnight bag from her earlier,' said Steffie. 'It's behind the coat stand.'

Liam glanced around and saw it.

'So I'll head off now,' said Steffie.

'I bet they've all gone to bed,' said Liam. 'Mrs Brannigan won't thank you for ringing the doorbell at this hour.'

'I told Bobby to wait up for me,' Steffie told him.

Liam gave her an enquiring look.

'He and Tom were going to have a cup of tea before turning in for the night,' Steffie said. 'Apparently it's their ritual.'

'I have a much better ritual than that,' said Liam. 'At least, when gorgeous ice princesses are around.'

'Oh?' she said. 'What would that be?'

'Do you really have to ask?'

She looked at him.

'Text Bobby,' said Liam. 'Tell him you're staying with me.'

'Are you sure?'

'Of course I'm damn sure,' said Liam. 'I've never been surer of anything in my whole life.'

He waited while she tapped out the message. Almost immediately, her phone pinged with a reply. It was a thumbs-up emoji.

'Now that we have that . . .' Liam scooped her into his arms again. 'I have plans for you tonight, Steffie Sheehan.'

'I look forward to helping you fulfil them,' she said as she wrapped herself around him and he carried her up the stairs.

Chapter 42

Despite the fact that it was after two before they got to bed, both Jenny and Pascal woke at their usual time of eight o'clock the following morning when the central heating gurgled into life. They snuggled up to each other for a while before Jenny finally got out of bed and pulled her dressing gown around her. She looked out of the window. The rising sun was casting a pale pink light over the snow-covered garden, where a small flock of birds were feeding on the bread that she had thrown out for them when she and Pascal had arrived home the previous night.

'You OK?' he asked as he stood behind her and put his arms around her.

She nodded.

'It was a good day yesterday,' he said.

'I hope it'll be a good day today.' She turned to him. 'D'you think Steffie will show up?'

'Even if she doesn't today, she will eventually. All she needs is time.'

'I know. But life's short, Pascal. And it's such a shame to waste it being angry. Not that I don't understand it, of course. If only . . .'

'If only,' he said. 'Two of the most futile words in the English language.'

'You're right.' Jenny leaned her head against his shoulder. 'Doesn't stop me wishing things had been different.'

'And that's a waste of your energy,' he told her. 'As you've told me on any number of occasions.'

She smiled suddenly. 'I'm usually the one offering the clichéd advice,' she conceded. 'And you're right. I need to deal with things the way they are, not the way I want them to be. All the same . . .'

'Give her time,' repeated Pascal.

'If we hadn't barged in on her and Liam Kinsella . . .' Jenny sighed. 'Mind you, I don't know who was more embarrassed, me or her.'

Pascal chuckled. 'Parents are there to embarrass their children,' he said.

'I always thought I'd be the sort of parent who didn't,' Jenny told him. 'I wanted to be cool and understanding and down-with-the-kids. I guess I've turned into my mother after all.'

'You're nothing like your mother,' Pascal assured her. 'And even if you're not down-with-the-kids now, you were a pretty cool mum to them when they were small. Maybe it's more commonplace these days, but back then, no other mum allowed their kitchen walls to be painted with their offspring's handprints.'

'God, yes, that could've been a terrible disaster,' recalled Jenny. 'But it actually looked quite good in the end.'

'Steffie will remember the good,' Pascal said. 'She will, really.'

'I'd like to think so,' said Jenny. 'But whenever I think of my own mum, I remember her for the things she wouldn't

446

let me do rather than the things she did. And I'm afraid that Steffie will always remember me for the lies I told her.'

'You did what you thought was right,' said Pascal. 'We both did. Hopefully she'll see that.'

'Hopefully,' said Jenny.

But she wasn't feeling all that hopeful at eleven thirty, by which time Davey and Camilla, as well as Roisin, Paul and their children, were seated around the kitchen table, eating buttery toast and looking at each other's photos of the previous day. The ones in the castle were particularly striking, and the group photo outside in the snow was spectacular.

'Totes brilliant,' said Daisy.

'Please, Daisy.' Roisin looked at her daughter. 'Use real words.'

'English is an evolving language,' said Daisy. 'It totes is.'

Jenny hid a smile as Roisin put her head in her hands. And then all of them looked up as the doorbell rang.

'Are you going to answer it?' asked Roisin. 'Or do you want me to go?'

'No, I will.'

Jenny walked to the hallway and opened the door.

Steffie was standing alone on the step.

'Hi,' she said.

'I'm so glad you came,' said Jenny. 'I really am. Is Liam not with you?'

'Sunday lunch,' said Steffie. 'He has to work today.'

'Of course.' Jenny hesitated as she realised that Steffie hadn't yet crossed the threshold. 'Are you coming in?'

Steffie glanced back at the road. At her own request, Liam had dropped her outside the gate and she'd walked up the driveway alone. But he was waiting on the snow-covered road outside in case she changed her mind about brunch at Aranbeg. She raised her hand in a half-wave, then turned back to her mother.

'Yes, I'm coming in,' she said.

She stepped inside, and as Jenny closed the door, Steffie's phone beeped. She took it out of her bag and looked at the message.

Good luck, she read. *I love you.*

He'd said it last night too. And she'd told him that they hardly knew each other really, so maybe it was too soon to say things like that, and he'd said that they'd known each other since they were children, what more did she want? And she'd laughed and so had he, and he'd kissed her and she'd known that she was completely in love with him. And then he'd said it again and she'd cried and he'd said not to be an idiot as he kissed her tears away.

'Everything all right?' asked Jenny.

'Yes,' she said.

She followed her mother into the kitchen, where everyone was gathered around the table. They smiled at her as they greeted her.

'Hungry?' asked Pascal.

'Starving,' she said.

Liam had offered to make her pancakes for breakfast, but she'd declined. Partly because she was nervous about the prospect of brunch at Aranbeg. Partly so that she'd be hungry when she got there.

Pascal loaded a plate with sausage, bacon and tomatoes and handed it to her. 'No egg,' he said. 'Right?'

'Yes. Thanks.' She took the plate and sat down.

Steffie sat beside Pascal and said nothing as everyone else took up the conversation, including her, as easily as they ever had before. She watched Paul grimace but say nothing as Roisin began to give Davey and Camilla advice on their wedding, even though it would be happening twelve hundred kilometres away. She saw Pascal slip an extra piece of toast to Dougie. She noticed her mother smooth Poppy's hair. They're all my family, she thought, as Davey pushed the cafetière of coffee towards her. They all matter to me. And I suppose I matter to them too. Slowly and tentatively she joined in the conversation. She laughed at one of Paul's jokes. She told Davey that she couldn't wait to visit Copenhagen. She took Daisy's side in a dispute with Roisin over the best mascara in the world.

After a while, she excused herself from the table and went upstairs to her old bedroom. She leaned her head against the cold window pane and wondered if she'd forgiven her parents without realising it. And then she realised that she'd thought of them as her parents again. Not Jenny and Pascal. Not her mother and Pascal. But her parents. The people who'd always been there for her. And who still were, whether she wanted them to be or not.

There was a light rap at the door. She waited for it to open, but it remained shut.

'Come in,' she called.

Jenny walked into the room, her expression anxious.

'Are you all right?' she asked.

'Yes. Just, you know, taking some time out.'

'Thank you for coming today,' said Jenny. 'It means a lot.'

'You always did a fantastic brunch,' said Steffie.

'I know.'

They stood in silence, neither knowing exactly what to say.

'I hope one day you'll forgive me.' It was Jenny who spoke first.

Steffie had never heard such desperation in her mother's voice before. In the past, she'd been the one asking for forgiveness. For wading into the river in her wellington boots. For using Jenny's newest and best lipstick as a crayon on the kitchen wall. For staying out much later than she was supposed to one night so that Jenny hadn't been able to sleep for worrying about her. She remembered those times of waiting anxiously for Jenny to say it was all right, that it didn't matter. That she wasn't to do it again. And then her mother would put her arms around her and hug her and tell her that it was OK.

'What am I supposed to forgive you for?' she asked. 'The affair? Getting pregnant? Not telling my father about it? Not telling me?'

Steffie could almost see Jenny gather her thoughts before she spoke.

'Your father – Pascal – has forgiven me for the affair and for getting pregnant,' she said. 'He's the only person who needs to forgive me for that. As for Gregory . . . perhaps I should have told him and perhaps one day you'll try to find him and he'll need to forgive me. I don't know. What I'm asking your forgiveness for is hiding it from you. At first it was for the best of reasons. But it was still wrong. And I'm sorry.'

'It's not just keeping it a secret,' said Steffie. 'It's letting me think I was the same as Davey and Roisin.'

'You *are* the same,' said Jenny.

'I'm not.' Steffie shook her head. 'And you know what, I've always felt a bit different. I thought it was because of the age gap, but maybe it's because of . . .'

'I wish you didn't feel like that,' said Jenny. 'Pascal and I wanted you to be as much a part of the family as the others. Well, to us you absolutely are. From the moment you came home with us, you were our cherished daughter. That has never changed. It never will.'

The thing was, Steffie thought, she knew that already. She knew they'd never treated her differently. She knew how much Pascal loved her. She knew Jenny loved her too.

'I've talked to your dad a lot about this, and if you want to search for Gregory, we'll help you,' continued Jenny. 'We totally understand that you might want to do that and we won't stand in your way.'

But I don't want to find him, thought Steffie. He isn't important to me and I don't need to meet him. I already know who I am. Who I'm supposed to be. Besides, what right would I have to turn up in his life now, when he's probably forgotten all about Mum and their summer of love. Or lust. Or whatever.

Mistakes, she thought. Everyone makes them. Even the people you think never do. And everyone needs forgiveness. Everyone has the power to forgive.

'I'm sorry too.' She looked at Jenny. 'I was shocked and I was hurt and I've taken it out on you ever since. But you and Dad have been nothing but great parents to me. So I should be able to forgive you. It's just that sometimes it's easier to allow yourself to stay angry.'

'I understand, I really do. And I truly wish that I'd handled it better. I was thinking of me, not you, when I told you everything at the party.'

'Oh, you couldn't have kept quiet, not after saying you weren't married,' Steffie said. 'If you'd left it a few weeks to tell me, I would've been even madder.'

'I'm sorry for yesterday, too.' Jenny winced. 'It was lunatic to think you might have been kidnapped. I don't know what was going through my head. I think I panicked.'

'*You* panicked?' Steffie raised an eyebrow. 'When you and the girls barged into Liam's office, it was me who was panicking.'

The two of them shared a smile.

'D'you think you need counselling or anything?' asked Jenny 'Roisin was showing me a site where—'

'I might have guessed Roisin would come up with a plan to sort me out.'

'Roisin always has a plan,' Jenny said.

'Yes, she does.' Steffie nodded. 'Davey actually asked me about counselling too. But I'm fine, Mum. Really.'

And she was, she realised. Not perfect. Not entirely at ease with everything. But getting there. And she knew she'd be all right. She had her parents behind her, after all. The rest of her family too. And, of course, she had Liam.

The funny thing was – the thought flitted through her mind fully formed – that if it hadn't been for Jenny's confessions, she wouldn't have fled from the house and she wouldn't have driven through the storm and she wouldn't have ended up soaked and bedraggled at Liam's restaurant. Which meant he wouldn't have kissed her and she wouldn't have stayed the night, and if she hadn't stayed the night, she wouldn't have fallen in love with him. And he wouldn't have fallen in love with her.

So because of Jenny, she'd met the man she loved.

And what more could she ask from her mother than that?

By late afternoon, everyone had finally left Aranbeg.

Jenny and Pascal flopped on to the sofa in front of the TV.

'I never thought,' said Jenny, 'that we'd have a day like today. Or yesterday either, come to think of it.'

'Which was better?' asked Pascal.

Jenny thought about it. 'I'm glad Steffie is starting to be OK with everything,' she said. 'I'm glad we had today to sort it out. I hope we would've done it eventually. But yesterday was our day. The one where I told you I loved you and I meant it. And so, in all the days we've spent together, Pascal Sheehan, I think that was the very best.'

'Come on.' He pressed the remote and turned off the TV.

'What?'

'Bed,' he said.

'But it's only five o'clock.'

'Did that ever stop us before?'

She laughed and followed him up the stairs and into the bedroom. And stopped in amazement, because the duvet was strewn with silk rose petals.

'Pascal Sheehan!' she exclaimed. 'When did you do this? How come I didn't know?'

'I have my moments,' he told her as he pulled her on to the bed.

Jenny kissed him. Then they moved together with the easy familiarity of forty years. The familiarity of knowing that they loved each other. And of knowing that somehow, maybe even despite their best efforts, they'd managed to get it right.

BONUS MATERIAL

An interview with Sheila O'Flanagan

An exclusive sneak peek at the first chapter of
Sheila's new novel, THE MISSING WIFE

An interview with Sheila O'Flanagan

What do you enjoy most about life as a full-time writer? Do you miss any aspects of your old job in the world of banking?

I like the fact that I can spend time staring into space thinking about people and call it work! I've always loved creating people and putting them into situations outside of their comfort zone and now I can do it for a living. I enjoy taking the idea and working on it to turn it into a book that people want to read. So that's the best thing – but I love not having to be in the office for 7am meetings and not having to buy loads of business-y suits either. The only thing I miss about my banking days is my briefcase. I had a really stylish leather one that I loved, but I don't need it anymore.

Where do you find inspiration when you're creating characters for a new novel? Do you plan what sort of people they'll be and how they'll look before you start writing?

457

Sometimes I find inspiration in simply seeing a person in the street, when something about them makes me wonder about their lives. Other times a particular situation sparks the idea. To be totally honest, I'm not 100 per cent sure. I have vague ideas about the characters before I sit down to write but they develop their own personalities as the novel develops and that can also change the outcome of the novel itself. However I usually do have a fairly good idea of their appearance at the very beginning, as I can't write about someone I can't see in my head!

Do you find it quite different creating male characters rather than female characters? If so, why do you think this is?

Not really. I worked with seventeen men on a trading desk for a long time so I think I have a handle on how their minds work . . .

Can you tell us your dream cast list if there was a film or television drama based on MY MOTHER'S SECRET?

That's hard, although I think I'd have to go with Irish actor Saoirse Ronan as Steffie. I think she'd be able to get to the heart of Steffie's character. And maybe Amy Schumer could be Summer, the cocktail waitress! As for Liam – perhaps Liam Hemsworth would step into his shoes quite easily.

Aranbeg has a vivid, magical presence in the novel. Is it based on a house from your own childhood? Are there places you spent childhood summers in that are still special to you now?

Aranbeg itself is a figment of my imagination but there are lots of lovely Irish houses in the same kind of rural setting which I know quite well. I think Aranbeg is probably a mixture of all of them. When we were small my parents used to rent a couple of mobile homes in the seaside village of Rush in north county Dublin. They were in a private field near the beach, and my English cousins used to come and stay with us there during the summer. We ran wild and I have great memories of those summers. Rush has become a town in the commuter belt now, so it's not quite the same whenever I go back!

When Jenny and Pascal finally reveal the secret at the heart of the novel, their children get a glimpse into their parents' past that some people never have. Have you ever learnt something about older members of your family or friends' families that has surprised you?

Frequently, although nothing in anyone's past really surprises me any more. We tend to forget that our older relatives had lives before we were born and that they made the same mistakes as we did, and others of their own. There are times when someone reveals a secret they've been keeping and you see their current lives in a different light – sometimes things about them become clearer and you understand them better.

In MY MOTHER'S SECRET Steffie is very close to her sister Roisin but their relationship is fractious at times, too! Why do you think the relationship between sisters can often be turbulent, and do Steffie and Roisin handle this well?

It's certainly true that sisters can have rocky relationships, but it's possibly because they know each other so well and don't tend to make allowances in the same way as they'd do for other people. I think Steffie and Roisin will always have an edgy relationship because they look at life differently and have very different personalities, but there's also a strong bond between them and they will always be there for each other.

Part of MY MOTHER'S SECRET is set in Rome. What do you think it is about the city that makes it such a romantic setting for a novel?

Everything! There's so much history there, so many great monuments and buildings and houses. Every street seems to resonate with people's stories and lots of them are love stories. Rome is one of the most vibrant places I've ever been and there's nothing nicer than sitting at a pavement cafe sipping the best coffee in the world (or maybe having a lovely gelato) while watching impossibly pretty women and equally handsome men walking by. It's totally inspirational.

You currently divide your time between Ireland and Spain. What are your three favourite things about life in each place?

I love the greenery of Ireland, it really is an emerald island and I miss the lushness of the grass when I'm away. I love the people too – you can strike up a conversation with almost anybody on practically any subject and they'll have an opinion. It's not so much the opinion that will surprise you, it's the way they can back it up with all sorts of information! I realise it's probably a cliché but I also love our pubs – you don't get the same communal atmosphere in any other country. Of course the greenery comes at a price and the one thing I don't miss when I'm away is the rain, consequently I really like the dry climate in Spain. And there it's the outdoor life – being able to eat on the terrace or at the beach without having to plan for four seasons in a day is wonderful. So is the food – Serrano ham with figs, cheese and honey is amazing.

We're already looking forward to your next novel, THE MISSING WIFE! Can you tell us a little bit about it?

Imogen is on a business trip to Paris when she makes the decision not to go home. Until the point she gets on a bus going in the opposite direction to the airport, she isn't certain she's going to go through with her plan to disappear without a word to anyone. Of course she has her reasons for what she's doing, although they're not immediately clear. Those reasons are mainly a result of her marriage to Vince, but Imogen needs to rediscover her past to understand and make decisions about her current situation. The problem for her is that she doesn't know what part of her life is going to catch up with her, and how she will handle it when it does. I loved writing about her – she's a really complex character trying to do the right thing, but not sure if she's succeeding.

Turn the page for a sneak peek at
Sheila's next novel

The Missing Wife

Turn the page for a sneak peek at
Sheila's next novel

The
Missing
Wife

Chapter 1

Standing in the line of passengers boarding the intercity coach, Imogen started to panic. A cold sweat dampened the back of her white cotton blouse and she froze on the spot, wedged behind a tall man in a brightly coloured Madiba shirt and an impatient Parisian woman who'd been checking her watch every five minutes for the past half an hour. The woman made a disapproving sound, indicating that she should get a move on, but Imogen stayed where she was, on the bottom step of the coach, clutching the handrail, unable to move.

'*S'il vous plaît,*' said the woman through clenched teeth.

'I'm sorry.' Imogen moved to one side. 'Go ahead.'

The woman pushed her way past, followed by the remainder of the passengers, while Imogen remained at the doorway, unsure of whether or not to board.

'*Madame?*' The driver looked at her enquiringly.

'Yes,' she said hesitantly. 'Yes. I'm . . . I'm getting on now.'

But she could hear his words in her head.

What on earth d'you think you're doing? You can't manage on your own. You'll make a mess of it. You always do.

She shut him out. He was wrong. She wasn't going to make a mess of it. Because she had a Plan.

Don't make a complete fool of yourself. It was his voice again as her hand tightened on the handrail.

She wouldn't make a fool of herself if she stuck to the Plan. It was foolproof. Hopefully. And she'd already success-fully carried out the start of it. There was no need to doubt herself about the rest. Besides, she thought, it's too late to back out now.

It's never too late.

This time the words were her mother's, one of the many clichés she'd liked to use on a daily basis. But in this case, they were true. It wasn't too late. She could still walk away without too much collateral damage. Whatever problems that might arise from her actions could be fixed. She could find a way to explain them.

But going back and trying to make excuses wasn't why she was here now. It wasn't why she'd spent so long refining the Plan. Nevertheless, she had a choice. Go forward, or go back. She reminded herself that this was the chance she'd been waiting for. Her first opportunity to execute the Plan. How would she feel if she let it slip away?

She took a deep breath and began to climb the steps.

The coach was comfortable and air-conditioned, which was a pleasant relief after the unexpected humidity of the June day. The exhibition hall had been hot and crowded, and she'd spent a lot of time wishing she'd worn something lighter than the navy wool business suit Vince had told her was appropriate for her business trip to France. But whenever she'd broken out in a sweat that morning, she'd been unsure if it was because of the suit, or because she was worrying about what she was intending to do and the way she was going to do it.

She walked down the aisle of the coach. Having let so

many people board ahead of her, her choice of seat was limited. She slid into the first one available, beside a long-legged young man with earbuds in his ears who was busy scrolling through playlists on his phone. A student, Imogen decided, as she glanced at his stubbled cheeks, logoed T-shirt and ripped jeans. She felt a pang of nostalgia for her own student years, even though she wouldn't have considered them to have been typical. Unlike many of her peers, she hadn't wanted to travel or have assorted life experiences. She'd wanted to put down roots. Her own roots in her own place instead of somewhere decided for her by someone else. That had been very important to her. Unfortunately.

She gave the young man a brief smile, but he was far too busy with his phone to notice.

The driver put the coach into gear and it moved slowly away from the station.

A few minutes later, they turned towards the Boulevard Périphérique and Imogen's phone buzzed.

She counted to ten before she looked at the text.

Are you at the airport? she read.

On the way now, she replied.

How long?

She looked at the facades of the buildings around her as the coach driver waited for the lights to turn red. They were mainly office blocks of glass and steel. They could have been anywhere in the world.

Twenty minutes.

Text me when you arrive.

OK.

Love you.

She hesitated before sending her reply. *Love you too :)*

She saw a sign for the airport as they moved forward again. The coach gathered speed, then turned in the opposite direction. She exhaled slowly. The student beside her was still absorbed in his music. Imogen stared out of the window. When the coach passed an exit marked 'Disneyland', she sent another text.

At airport, it said. *Phone battery about to die. Talk later.* This time she didn't add a smiley face.

She picked up her handbag from beneath the seat in front of her and opened it. Then she slid her engagement and wedding rings from her finger and dropped them into the bag. After that, she took a hair clip from a small bundle in one of the side pockets and used it to pop out the SIM card holder on the phone. She took the card from the cradle and held it between her teeth while she closed the phone again. As she bit down hard on it, she realised that the student had begun to watch her.

'You'll damage it,' he said in French as he removed one of the buds from his ears.

'I know,' she said in the same language once she'd taken the card from her mouth.

She balanced it between her thumb and forefinger and began to squeeze. After a while, the SIM card started to bend. She kept the pressure on until it had doubled over and the tiny metallic bands had cracked. The student shrugged. Imogen sat back in her seat and stared straight ahead.

Vince Naughton always had a plan. He liked to have his day scheduled and he hated being taken by surprise. Years earlier, at one of those corporate think-ins and staff bonding days, which he thought were a total waste of time, a colleague had called him controlling. Irritated by her snap assessment, Vince had said that he wasn't controlling but he did like to be in control, a comment that resulted in a round of applause from the group and left his colleague looking embarrassed. A few months later, Vince had been promoted and she'd left the company, which made him feel vindicated. It was good to know how things were supposed to pan out, he thought. And good to ensure that they did.

Which was why, when he turned into the car park at the hotel in Cork, he was within ten minutes of the arrival time he'd set himself – the ten minutes was to allow for the unexpected. Vince believed in allowing for the unexpected. It was why he was one of the company's better associates. He thought of every eventuality. Very few things ever surprised him. He planned for the worst and hoped for the best. It had served him well all his life.

He parked the car, checked in at reception and went to his room. He'd specified a first-floor room if possible, and he was pleased that the conference organisers had met his request, although the room itself overlooked the car park instead of the river, which he would have preferred. Nevertheless, everything else was fine: the Wi-Fi worked, there were tea- and coffee-making facilities, and the TV was a modern flat-screen on the wall.

He sat on the bed and sent a text.

Arrived on time. Room OK. Text me when you're home.

Then he left the phone on the bed and went into the bathroom to have a shower.

According to the bus timetable, the journey would take more than eleven hours. There were, of course, infinitely quicker

469

ways to travel from Paris to the south-west of France than by road (although if she'd driven herself, Imogen knew she could easily have cut the time in half). A flight would have taken less than ninety minutes, but catching a flight meant having to give your name and credit card details, and she hadn't wanted to do that. The train would have been the best option of them all, given how superb the French rail system was, and would have had the added advantage of taking her exactly where she wanted to be. However, although she might have been able to buy a ticket without having to reserve it, she felt sure there were plenty of CCTV cameras throughout the marble concourse of the ultra-modern Montparnasse station, and she didn't want to be caught by any of them. She'd watched too many news reports with grainy images of unsuspecting people going about their daily business not to know that public places were hotbeds of CCTV surveillance. She realised that it was possible she'd been caught on camera buying the coach ticket too. But she didn't think so. Besides, nobody would have expected her to take a bus. That was why it was part of the Plan.

It began to rain as they arrived at their first stop, four hours into the journey. Imogen dodged the languid, heavy drops as she hurried into the service station and made her way to the ladies'. In the cubicle, she took the battery out of her phone and threw it into a red plastic bin. At their next stop, another four hours later, she disposed of the phone itself in a blue bin near the coach park. It was the first time in more than fifteen years that she hadn't had a mobile phone, and it was a strange sensation. Even though the phone had been useless without the SIM and then the battery, it had been a part of her. Now it was gone. She wanted to feel that everything it signified was gone too, but the truth was that she wasn't feeling anything at all. Other than apprehensive. Or maybe just scared.

When she got back on to the coach, the student was playing a game on his own mobile, his fingers tapping urgently at the screen. He looked up as Imogen settled herself in her seat and gave her a faint smile before turning back to the game.

She was pretty sure that she'd received more texts by now. *Are you home yet?*

Where are you?

And then perhaps the voice message.

'Haven't you charged your damn phone? Ring me.'

But she wouldn't be ringing. That was part of the Plan too. And because she'd destroyed her phone, she had to stick to it.

She held her hands out in front of her. They were shaking.

The student finished playing his game and took the buds from his ears. He turned to Imogen and asked if he could get by her so that he could take his rucksack from the rack. She stood up while he got his bag and rummaged around in it. Then he slid back into his seat and she sat down again. He lowered the plastic tray in front of him and put a bottle of water and a triple-decker sandwich wrapped in cling film on it. He had other food too – a KitKat, a chocolate muffin and a couple of bananas. He offered one of the bananas to Imogen.

'No thank you.' They continued to speak in French.

'Are you sure?' he asked. 'Maman packed all this for me. I like my food, but two bananas is one too many.'

'It's good of you to offer,' said Imogen. 'But I'm not hungry.'

471

'Fair enough.' He unwrapped the sandwich and took a large bite.

Imogen tried not to look at him. Without a phone or a magazine to distract her, it was hard to stare straight ahead.

'Do you mind me asking why you trashed your SIM card?' he asked when he'd finished the sandwich.

She hesitated before replying. 'I wanted to get away from it all.'

'You could've simply switched the phone off.'

'It's not the same.'

'A bit drastic nonetheless.' He grinned at her.

'But at least I know I can't be tempted by it,' she said.

He nodded and turned his attention to the muffin. It disappeared in two bites and he spoke again.

'Are you on holiday?' he asked.

'Um . . . sort of,' she said. 'I was working and now I have some time off.'

'Cool,' said the student. 'I've got summer work in a vineyard.'

'That'll be fun.' Imogen's plan hadn't included talking to anyone, because she hadn't anticipated casual conversation with random strangers. She wasn't used to it. Besides, she'd wanted to remain anonymous, forgettable. But it was an unexpectedly welcome distraction. Anyhow, the student was doing most of the talking. All she needed to do was nod a few times.

'What's your name?' he asked, during a pause.

'Imo . . . gen,' she mumbled.

'Nice to meet you, Jen,' he said, apparently unfazed by her hesitation over what was a simple question. 'I'm Henri.'

She didn't correct him.

He talked a lot. He was twenty years old and studying environmental sciences at Orléans University, and he was interested in winemaking and viniculture. The previous year he'd travelled to California to visit the vineyards there, which had been great, he said, but he was looking forward to Bayonne. Would she like to meet up for a coffee?

She couldn't remember the last time she'd smiled with genuine amusement, but she did now. Henri was at least ten years younger than her, but he was happily hitting on her. Which was sort of flattering, she supposed, if very French.

'I'm sorry,' she said. 'I won't be staying in Bayonne. I'm travelling further.'

'*Dommage*,' he said. 'It would have been nice to have coffee with you. But perhaps another time? Where are you from?'

'Provence.' She'd lived near Marseille when she was small.

'My family holidayed in Cannes once,' said Henri. 'But I don't remember very much of it.'

'It's a nice town,' Imogen said. 'Though very bling-bling.'

He laughed at the English words. And she smiled again.

It was midnight when they finally pulled into the terminus, near the train station in the Aquitaine city of Bayonne. It had stopped raining about an hour previously and the sky was completely clear. Imogen sat in her seat while everyone around her stood up. She'd felt herself relax talking to Henri, but suddenly her hands were shaking again. She'd been protected for the last eleven hours, cocooned from the rest of the world as the bus made its way through the country. Now she had to step outside and face it all once more. And she was having to do it on her own. There was nobody to organise her, to tell her what to do. Nobody to help with the Plan.

'Excuse me, Jen.' Henri, who'd fallen asleep a little while earlier, had been roused by the activity and was ready to get off.

'Yes. Sorry,' she said, standing up. 'Enjoy the vineyards.'

'Enjoy your break. If you come back to Bayonne, please call me.'

'No phone,' she reminded him.

'I'm at the Bernard Noble,' he said. 'Look me up.'

She knew she wouldn't.

She followed him off the bus and waved as he walked away, his rucksack on his back. She waited while the driver took the rest of the luggage from the storage area. Her silver-grey case was one of the last to be retrieved. She picked it up and looked around her. Beyond the car park, the surrounding buildings were typically French, their warm brick illuminated by street lights, wrought-iron balconies at their shuttered windows.

She'd memorised the location of the hostel where she hoped to stay, and so, after taking a moment to orientate herself, she crossed the road and walked down a narrow side street. At the corner, she could see the dark green canopy over the door, embossed with the name. She hesitated when she reached it. She'd never stayed in a hostel before. Not having done the student travel thing.

She pushed open the glass door, which was set into a brick surround. The interior of the building was clean and reno-vated, with a black and white tiled floor and exposed walls decorated with iron sculptures. A middle-aged woman was seated behind a small reception area, engrossed in a book. She didn't look up until Imogen stood in front of her and cleared her throat.

'Can I help you?'

'Um . . .'

You can't manage without me.

Imogen whirled around, convinced he was standing behind her. But there was no one there.

'*Mademoiselle?*' The concierge looked at her enquiringly.

You'll fail. You know you will.

'I . . . I'm looking for a room.'

She realised that she was waiting for the woman to ask her why she'd turned up so late at night. And why she was on her own instead of with him. And where she was planning to go. And what she planned to do. And . . .

'For how many nights?' The woman sounded bored.

'Just one.' Her voice was barely above a whisper. She cleared her throat and spoke a little louder as she repeated herself. 'Just one.'

The woman took an electronic key from the desk, coded it and handed it to her.

'*Premier étage, mademoiselle,*' she said.

Imogen wondered if it was fetching up at a hostel that had turned her from a *madame* to a *mademoiselle* again. She glanced at the bare finger on her left hand before starting up the stairs with her bag. She stopped outside the door of room 14. The card didn't work the first time.

You can't manage without me.

She dropped the key and it slithered along the corridor. It took her a while to pick it up because it kept sliding out of her grip. When she finally had it in her trembling fingers, she inserted it into the lock again the right way up. The light turned green and the door opened.

*   *   *

The room was better than she'd expected. The walls were painted pale cream, brightened by some framed floral prints. The single bed was surprisingly firm. There was a net curtain at the long window, which led out to a tiny balcony overlooking the street. The window also had a pair of green-painted shutters, which Imogen pulled closed. Apart from the bed, the only furniture was a tall, narrow wardrobe, with interior shelving. A full-length mirror was on the wall beside it. The en suite bathroom (the reason she'd picked the Hostel Auberge in the first place; whatever else, she wasn't going to share a bathroom!) boasted a shower, toilet and hand basin. Two dark green towels hung on the rail beneath the sink. Though nothing was luxurious, it was impeccably clean.

It was also empty. She realised that she'd half expected to see him there, waiting for her. She sat down abruptly on the edge of the bed, a wave of relief washing over her. Her breath was coming in short gasps. She put her head between her knees, terrified that she was going to faint.

'I am a strong, capable woman,' she muttered to herself. 'I can look after myself.'

But she wasn't sure she believed it.

If you'd like to find out what happens next,
pre-order

The
Missing
Wife

now and be one of the first to read it in
summer 2016.

www.headline.co.uk

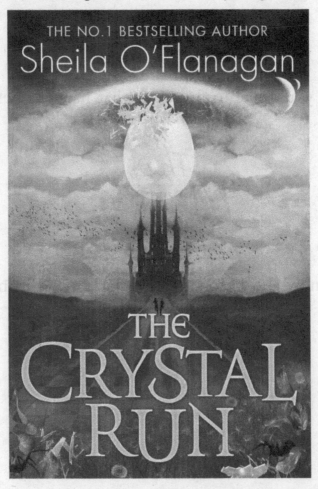

Have you read all of Sheila's irresistible novels?

IF YOU WERE ME

You're engaged to a great man. You're on a countdown to your wedding day. You stopped thinking about your first love a long time ago.

But what if one unexpected, forbidden kiss were to throw your life upside down?

Carlotta O'Keefe suddenly finds herself wondering if the girl she was would recognise the woman she has become.

She thought she was living a charmed life. But what if she's got it all wrong?

What if her past is meant to be her future?

THINGS WE NEVER SAY

A husband is afraid to say that selling the house his wife loves is the only option...

A son can't say how useful his ageing father's fortune will be when he's gone...

A woman hasn't said that even though they live thousands of miles apart, this man is always on her mind...

But if those things were said, the results might be surprising. As Abbey – and a whole family she knew nothing of – are about to find out in Sheila O'Flanagan's warm-hearted, thought-provoking and touching novel.

BETTER TOGETHER

Sheridan Gray has discovered a secret. . .
When journalist Sheridan loses her dream
job, she's distraught. She's forced to relocate
to the countryside. Her career is over. . .
until she discovers that her landlady holds
the key to a big story.

But the longer Sheridan stays in Nina's
home, and the closer she gets to a certain
handsome man in the town, the tougher
it is to expose their secrets. When it comes
to love or success, will Sheridan go with
her heart or her head?

ALL FOR YOU

**As TV's favourite weather forecaster,
Lainey is good at making predictions.**
But what she doesn't foresee is that her
own life is about to hit a stormy patch.
With a string of failed relationships
behind her, surely history isn't about to
repeat itself with her beloved Ken?

Uncovering some long-concealed
family secrets, Lainey begins to reassess
her life. Is the happy-ever-after she's
always dreamed of really what she wants
after all?

A SEASON TO REMEMBER

What if a secret from your past has come back to haunt you?
As Claire and Neil Archer open the doors to their luxurious Sugar Loaf Lodge for the festive season, it's with worries of their own.

But can they, along with their troubled guests, find the magic of Christmas – and a happy ending – within the walls of this beautiful hotel? Maybe Christmas really *is* the happiest time of the year!

STAND BY ME

Dominique Brady's life changed the day she met Brendan Delahaye.
He was a man with big dreams and she was the girl he wanted to take with him. Madly in love, they married, Brendan's business hit the big time and they became the most powerful couple in Ireland.

Then one day Brendan disappears without a trace and Dominique's world is shattered. Will Brendan ever return? And if he does, will Dominique stand by her man?

THE PERFECT MAN

Brit doesn't believe in love. One painful mistake was all it took.

So she's as surprised as anyone when her novel THE PERFECT MAN becomes a huge bestseller.

Heartbreak has never stopped her sister Mia from being a hopeless romantic. She can't be with the love of her life, but she's never stopped hoping.

They both have to let go of the past to stand a chance of being happy in the future. Could a Caribbean cruise be just what they need to open their hearts?

SOMEONE SPECIAL

Romy Kilkenny loves her life in Australia.

She has her dream job, a fun lifestyle, and best friend Keith who understands her better than anyone. But when a phone call summons her home at short notice, Romy's world is turned upside down.

Romy has never fitted in, and with Keith too far away to give comfort, she feels like more of an outsider than ever. What on earth has Romy let herself in for?

BAD BEHAVIOUR

Darcey and Nieve were best friends for life.

Until Nieve stole the heart of Aidan, the boy Darcey had fallen in love with.

For the next ten years Darcey has been haunted by the memory of her humiliation. And then the invitation comes: to the wedding of Aidan and Nieve, neither of whom she's seen since they left Ireland for life in the USA. Will Darcey be there? Will there be fireworks? And can the past be put to rest at last?

YOURS, FAITHFULLY

Two worlds are about to collide in the most shocking way...

Iona Brannock has always been impatient. She married her gorgeous husband just months after meeting him and they have lived happily ever since. Now all she needs is a baby and her life will be perfect.

Sally Harper has been blissfully married for almost twenty years. Her life is complete. But a surprise pregnancy is about to change everything...

CONNECTIONS

Romance is very much alive in the hot Caribbean nights...

There's Tara, who's arrived with the man she wants to marry only to find that a rejected lover is planning to get in the way; and Grainne, who's been sent with her husband by their children to celebrate their anniversary, and who thinks the time has come to move on.

Rudy's on an idyllic break with his young son which is set for an unexpected ending; and Isobel's ex-lover Nico might be staying just next door...

HOW WILL I KNOW?

It was love at first sight for Claire and Bill Hudson.

When baby Georgia came along, it was the icing on the cake. So when a tragic accident snatched Bill away, Claire felt like she'd lost everything – except Georgia.

Now Georgia's a teenager, though, and there's one thing Claire can't advise her on: dating. And so, purely to help her lovely young daughter in her journey through the teenage years, Claire sets out on some serial dating. And destiny is watching, again...

ANYONE BUT HIM

Andie and her sister Jin have never seen eye to eye.

Andie doesn't envy Jin her marriage to a wealthy businessman, while Jin can't believe Andie's happy with her man-free existence. But when their widowed mother comes back from a cruise with more than just a suntan, Andie and Jin are united in horror.

Who is this gorgeous young man who's swept their mother off her feet? What they really need now is a friend – but can they be friends with each other?

DESTINATIONS

A myriad lives captured…

Two eavesdropping train passengers learn more than they bargained for about their own love lives; an office-party fling has unforeseen consequences for a young woman and for a marriage; a suburban housewife is forced to face her past when her estranged mother makes contact; an adopted woman journeys to meet the woman who gave her up all those years ago, and finds that all is not what she imagined…

DREAMING OF A STRANGER

Dreams are not always what they seem...

When Jane O'Sullivan meets blue-eyed Rory McLoughlin, she knows that he is who she's been waiting for.

And when Jane walks up the aisle to marry Rory, she believes all her dreams have come true. What she doesn't know is that she's not going to get quite the happy ending she expects.

TOO GOOD TO BE TRUE

Carey Browne is in for the holiday of a lifetime...

When Carey Browne decides it's time for a holiday she flies into New York City – one of her favourite shopping destinations – knowing she'll have a good time. Within days she's met and married Ben Russell, and a week later they're heading back together to Dublin, where they both live, to share the happy news with family and friends. Except not everyone's thrilled.

Carey and Ben are about to discover whether they've found the kind of love that can survive a blast of reality...